Henri Lopes

THE LAUGHING CRY

an African Cock and Bull Story

translated by Gerald Moore

readers international

The title of this book in French is *Le Pleurer-Rire,* first published in Paris by Présence Africaine in 1982.

First published in English by Readers International Inc., New York and Readers International, London. Editorial inquiries to London office at 8 Strathray Gardens, London NW3 4NY England. US/Canadian inquiries to Subscriber Service Department, P.O. Box 959, Columbia Louisiana 71418-0959 USA.

Cover art and design by Jan Brychta
Typesetting by Grassroots Typeset, London NW6
Printed and Bound in Great Britain by Richard Clay Ltd.,
Bungay, Suffolk

ISBN 0-930523-32-6 Hardcover
ISBN 0-930523-33-4 Paperback

It's no use my crying, the laughter will always slip out somehow.

Beaumarchais

Whoever writes the history of his times must expect reproaches for all that he has said and all that he has not.

Voltaire, *Letter to Valentin Philippe de Rocheret,* 14 April 1772

The argument of the following pages draws all its force from the fact that the story is entirely true, since I have imagined it from beginning to end.

Boris Vian, *The Froth of Days*

BE WARNED

Our first impulse was to ban these pages, to have them shredded and burned at the foot of the Palace steps by the executioner of the High Court, for their impudent expressions and charges, so scandalous and injurious to the High Magistrature in general and that of Africa in particular. But fifteen years of experience have wisely turned us aside from such excesses. Banned books always sell, under the counter, better than good ones. And we hold files on authors who, just to make a reputation at little cost and get better sales for their goods, cynically seek the publicity conferred by the censor's decrees.

Our information services have, besides, supplied us with the names of many of them, whose secret dream is that one day they will hear the air hostesses at some African airport caressing the ears of disembarking passengers with their announcement that SUCH-AND-SUCH AFRICA, AFRICA EXPOSED, LONG LIVE THE AFRICANS...and his forthcoming work are forbidden throughout the territory.

Our second thought was to employ a more elegant and centuries-old procedure: to buy up all the copies from the publisher and burn them under cover of a bush fire. But, all things considered, that would merely be to enrich in record time a wretch who really deserves a dungeon, a few good lashes and oblivion.

Thus, at the hour when Africa, confronting her historic destiny, has need of heroes exalting our positive moral values and our ancestral cosmology; at the hour when you, our readers, demand a literature of diversion; our esteemed writers use their unbridled imaginations to paint Africa and the Africans in the blackest colours—but in a manner which has nothing to do with negritude.

If a few of them can be excused as the playthings of a vast plot orchestrated by obscure forces that seek to spread subversion to every corner of our dear continent and introduce foreign, destructive ideologies, there are certainly others (anarcho-decadent aesthetes) who have mastered the most primitive methods of mass psychology, and employ them in the most Machiavellian way to increase tenfold the profits of the poison they sell.*

While we expect from them spiritual nourishment, they unceasingly glut themselves with the basest material concerns.

But the people of Africa will know how to judge for themselves how these freethinkers squander the riches that the schools have generously showered on them, thanks to the sacrifices of their fathers and mothers in our countryside. We trust that they will know how to draw lessons from this and to deploy them in the elucidation of coming generations.

That is why, in conformity with our semi-secret Resolution No. 006/79, voted by a simple majority during our recent historic conference at Bobo Dioulasso, we shall no longer fall into their trap.

From now on, we shall allow publication and sale of all works.

In exchange, every book, every film, every record, every cassette that ought to be struck by our interdiction for the safeguard of our morals, will be preceded by an introduction; written, visual or oral; prepared or delivered by Us.

So, on the present occasion, for THE LAUGHING CRY.

Africa begs for clarity, and this book brings confusion. It misleads curious spirits, throughout some two hundred fifty pages, in the pursuit of false problems.

---

*Here, some would want to describe this plot as "imperialist", and a majority as "communist". The adjective "obscure" is thus a compromise chosen to preserve African unity.

No, all sane readers know that no President exists so flippant, burlesque and cruel as Daddy.

The heroic masses of Africa would not tolerate it, and the other peoples of the world, in the interests of justice and peace, would help them to overthrow him.

Daddy is the image of a black president such as the racist and nostalgic whites, still dreaming of a vanished colonialism, imagine him. They hope, by means of this gross example, both to demonstrate the incapacity of the blacks to govern themselves without barbarity, and to discourage all forms of cooperation between the developed world and ours, so as to let us founder in misery. The African writers who lend their hands to this game hope by doing so to hasten the fall of certain regimes, not seeing that they are really preparing a new bed for the colonialism of old, which will find it all the easier to reconquer us and recover its old privileges.

No, Daddy does not exist, cannot exist, in these days and on this continent. He is the fruit of a macabre imagination that is close to frenzy: a comic strip character!

We even suspect the author to be a white man who has had the chance to spend some time in Africa. An African worthy of the name would never dare to write such trash.

A true son of Africa would never describe his milieu and epoch with such detachment.

We are dealing with an unscrupulous forger, whose work is stitched together with threads... WHITE ONES, for sure.

Real Africans will know how to laugh, anyway, at the inauthenticity of these characters and situations.

Finally, thank God, this gutter style cannot seduce the amateur from good art. Yes, strictly speaking, this is how we talk in our streets, but not how one should write about it. THE LAUGHING CRY is an offence to good taste.

If by chance, nevertheless, some feeble and honest souls should allow themselves to be hypnotised by the sentimentality, the subjectivity, the malice and partisan spirit of the author, we know we can count upon the wisdom of our literary critics and the vigilance of our masses to raise a wave of counter-

propaganda that will obliterate, beneath a sea of sanity, this drop of anti-African poison.

So that Africa may live as herself, or die.

For the Secretary-General
and Assistant Secretary-General
in Charge of Written Works.
Anasthasie MOPEKISSA

Inter-African Association
of Francophone Censors*

---

*This association is an independent and non-governmental organization. It draws its resources from its own contributors, from gifts and from various legacies.

The Laughing Cry

Did she notice my moment of hesitation when entering the yard? Usually, when I come home at that hour, Elengui is still asleep and if I clumsily let the door of our bedroom squeak a bit, she just sighs, turns over and plunges back into her land of dreams.

That morning, prey to some strange agitation, she was prowling up and down the verandah.

Mam'hé! What's going on?

She shouted my name.

Some misfortune?

Her head against my breast, she was gasping heavily, as if just finishing a race.

Who the devil can have told her?

I let her pull me over to our small sitting room.

"What, what, what?"

The radio was bawling out some vile melody.

Oh, to be a soldier in the Marines...

Or some rubbish like that.

The wake was held in a little alley in Moundié: the Avenue Général-Marchand. I recall arriving at the place and beginning, as always on these occasions, by dropping a few coins in the collection bowl before scribbling in the book of condolences. The niece of the deceased was careering about the yard with a broom in her hands, driving off the clouds that threatened to chase away the friends who had come to honour the dead man. She forced a passage for herself between the mats scattered on the ground, which were bordered with sprawling women, wrapped up in their cloths. Their faces all fixed in a scowl, they were recovering the energies they had used up during the day. Some were accompanied by their babies, who sucked half-asleep, indifferent to the hubbub, the drums and the mosquitoes.

Young voices were singing the dirges to the rhythm of the drums and in a language other than mine—girls sitting on the floor in the small vestibule. Simply clad and with their feet bare, they each had a headscarf negligently tied. Whoever speaks one of our languages can understand them all, and I could easily have followed the songs of these nubile maidens. But a song always sounds better if we don't understand the words.

Farewell, my brother, farewell. Death has stiffened you like a stone, éhé, éhé, but we are with you here, for the journey. You lived among us and we spared you only a few rare moments, éhé, éhé. Each of us carries alone his own huge world, éhé, éhé. Today, in your death, who among the great of the earth is more venerated than you? Éhé, éhé, éhé...

As for the old women, they had their shoulders bare, with wrappers tied under the armpits, their hair and faces liberally powdered with dust. Relieving each other, they came and went untiringly, in groups of two or three, singing incantations to the ancestors above the grave rhythm of the drums, in the language of the tribe. The great piece of orange up there in the neon-blue gazed impassively at the movement of their slow convoy of dusty cotton.

A sacrificed frog, wrapped in a cellophane bag, had been nailed above the doorway. The spirits had been offered their due for holding back the rain.

I went to sit among the menfolk, in the midst of a group of friends. If you are not among friends, those we call friends in moments like these, the subject of conversation always changes immediately.

"Those Vietnamese, old boy,"said one of them, turning up his thumb. "The Americans can stuff their B52's."

From that point, someone else developed an argument too complicated for me to recall now. And a third contributed:

"No, in all of that, the one I like is Mao. Un-bel-iev-able! A genius! See how he controls that Cultural Revolution over there!"

"The Great Proletarian Cultural Revolution!"

"Yeah, you're right, the Great Proletarian Cultural Revolution... And the others don't understand a bit. They think it's just anarchy, whereas he's always there in the wings, pulling the strings, organising the smallest details, always gaining ground. As long as Africa still isn't capable of ..."

"Exactly. We must cut the umbilical cord."

"Really! Otherwise we ..."

"Just corrupted, totally" (wrinkling his lips with contempt).

"Agreed. But those Chinese are real workers. Here among us..."

It was old Tiya who had just cut in sharply. The intellectuals didn't even bother to answer him. They allowed themselves to share a smile. I found their disrespect wicked. But the old man was a match for them. He gave them another smile in return. A smile from another world, full of its own mystery.

The barrage of military music which, since dawn, had kept us company, was suddenly cut short. First came a torrent of static, then something like the call of a muezzin, then the radio thrust its speech into every hearth of a town suddenly turned to stone.

Day of anger, day of wrath, the Guinarou growled. The hour was critical, and the demagogic politics of Polépolé, which ... I could easily fall into parody; but you have all heard, or read, a thousand and one patched-up speeches sewn on the same pattern.

The tones of a schoolmaster, carefully distinguishing the short from the long *a* on the one hand; the short from the long *o* on the other hand; and, finally, the *i* from the *u*. I could even imitate the voice for you:

As a re-
sult the Na-tio-nal
Arm-ed Forces

com-posed of ...

Mam'hé, this is no time for jokes!

Someone crossed himself close beside me and saw the night fall at his feet. From now on we must be on our guard, salute, chin-up, half-turn. Quick march! Lef, rai; lef, rai; lef, rai; lef! Halt! Half-turn left! No, right.

Hell, as for me, I'd better get back to work.

"You want to get killed?"

"What should I say to the boss, then? I'm not one of your faint-hearted blacks, Elengui. Not one of those who take advantage of the lightest shower..."

"You want to get killed?"

"Kill *me?"* (I looked at her disdainfully). "What have their quarrels to do with me? Have I eaten any of Polépolé's money?"

"But those men in berets, Mam'hé!"

She clapped her hands thrice.

"Listen, Elengui, you just don't understand. What does my boss care about these local affairs? It's not Uncle Whitey's problem, this business."

To tell the truth, Elengui unsettled me. It's for the men to command, but we shouldn't ignore the presentiments of women. Delicious animals that they are, they can sniff trouble coming.

Bwakamabé? Colonel Bwakamabé Na Sakkadé? Yéhé! A son of my own tribe... And a whole clutch of officers with him. Known, unknown, known—all of them big shots from now on. And Yabaka among them.

So the youngsters went on with their international politics. My word, what a lot they knew about what goes on in the big world! I'm certain our journalists, Aziz Sonika included, have never known half as much.

And they spouted philosophy in terms much too complicated for me to follow, using lots of obscure words that all end in *-isms* or *-ists.* Real scholars, I'm telling you. They kept citing names that escape me now. They kept attacking France and the Uncles. They insulted General de Gaulle. There I don't agree with them, because Papa de Gaulle... But don't dream of speaking up, when you don't know the jargon.

Old Tiya, now, he knows. And he told them he didn't like it. And he spelled out all the things General de Gaulle had done for the country. And I was happy to hear the old fellow talking so. Really, he knew the arguments all right. But those intellectuals there, instead of respecting the age and wisdom of Tiya, and saying "thank you, Father," went on pressing the contrary. Ah! that school-learning of theirs. They claimed that de Gaulle was a pater...a pater-nalist, I think, or something else that sounded like that. And they went on arguing, arguing, arguing—but it was all very complicated. Too complicated to be expressed in Kibotama.

"You walk on the whiteman's tarred road. And the soles of your feet don't know the feel of our own mud."

One of them pulled a face, as if to say that the old man had made a remark in bad taste. But the others admitted he had a point.

"Yeah, you're right there, old man. But we were educated by the Uncles. It's good to know one's enemy."

"And France is our enemy?"

The intellectuals insisted that France was indeed our enemy, and that we were all alienated.

"Alienated? You want them to throw us all into an asylum, then? Go on!"

The young men protested.

"*Wo*! you certainly said 'alienated'. Yes, yes! Here are the witnesses."

The conversation was getting serious. Very serious. Among us, when someone is treated as mad, it's like naming his mother's privates. Fortunately, the young men kept cool and showed some sign of repentance. Then they explained again. And Tiya calmed down the other elders and sorted everything out. Only then did they calm down, because they had confidence in Tiya.

Now the conversation turned back to France. The young men pressed their point. France was not our friend. We were simply her neo-colony.

"But we're independent now. What more do you want? Anyway, you are the most alienated ones."

Anyway, you are the most alienated ones."

Then an intellectual explained that they were not responsible for that situation. It was the neo-colonial environment! Yes, the neo-colonial environment! Polépolé and his clique! The neo-colonial environment! The student added that when they made the revolution, they would break with France without a pang, but that it wasn't yet the revolution, even though Polépolé and his clique were always talking about it. The neo-colonial environment!

Old Tiya concluded by remarking that blacks were indeed blacks, and everyone burst out laughing like a forestful of monkeys. Not so loud as that: it was a wake, after all. But loud enough, anyway, for everyone to understand that, even there, one couldn't spend the whole night just pulling long faces like a Djassikini totem.

I left the wake towards midnight. The young intellectuals also left then, and I still remember, as if it were only yesterday, how they exchanged instructions while parting. No one was to phone the others at home that night. Then they all laughed. And I, who caught their words in passing, also laughed, for I was in the same position: we were all going to sleep somewhere, but none of us in the right bed! They were bandits, and so was I, all our hearts swelling with joy as much as with pride. As the elders say, to have only one woman is like having only one cord to your *kora*. And anyway, where's the sin? It's almost an obligation, if you've married your wife in church. As for me, I married Elengui according to native custom, bringing wine, whiskey, a machete and several cloths, besides satisfying the other demands of her blessed family, who obliged me to get a loan from the Development Bank. A loan it took months to repay.

Ah! Elengui! When I think of her nowadays, I always feel my heart melting. Her way of doing the thing ... I forget all about her wickedness. More possessive than a whole army of educated women, she ceased visiting her women friends right from the start of our marriage, just to deprive them of the excuse of visiting us. She even denied the house to her younger sisters and cousins, preferring always to go and visit them. Very beautiful "connections", too, those girls were! And when I said so to Elengui, she flew into a rage like a clap of thunder in a tornado. And I reminded her that, according to our custom, the wife's sisters are also little wives to her husband. Then she soared into a rage even fiercer than a tornado. Just joking? Very bad taste, sir! Well, what do you want? Modern women are no longer women. They fight against custom at the very time when our mothers are trying to hand on tradition, teaching them that a wife who wants to keep her man to herself is an egotist.

Just let death strike one of your brothers-in-law. Then you'll have to accept seeing your husband take up his widow. That's the law of the ancestors, which expresses our sense of solidarity. Elengui herself is always saying that an unguarded banana belongs to everyone. And she watches me more closely than a whole grove of bananas.

I always lightheartedly reassure her when the subject comes up, whilst continuing to do as I please; otherwise my friends would all mock me. A man who stays with just one woman is a weakling. Even the other women despise him. They tell everyone who cares to listen that that man there, oh well! he just isn't a man. And the disgrace spreads to the family.

On leaving the wake, therefore, I steered towards the compound of Soukali, a very grand lady. A member of high society. Her husband is really somebody—a customs inspector, if you please. A man who makes even more than the other officers, an extra quarter of his salary; then, bonuses for returned goods; bonuses for risks; commission on this and that; and other little privileges that belong to the job. Also, the right to live with the foreign aid workers in the Plateau Quarter; in the building called the Fifty Flats, where in any case I love to pass the night. Naturally, it's better than our house in Moundié. A very discreet place, what's more, in which to conduct secret affairs in perfect tranquility. Most of the inhabitants are Uncles working in technical assistance; people who, as one knows, are from an individualistic culture and don't much occupy themselves with the actions and proclivities of their neighbours. It's said they can live for many years in the same building without knowing each other, or even going to attend the wake for the man across the landing. Very different from the village, or even Moundié, where everyone lives, whether in the courtyard or on their own doorstep, with their eyes well fixed upon the compound next door. If Soukali lived in Moundié, Monsieur the Inspector would long ago have settled my hash.

I ought to have felt some qualms in going to caress someone else's wife. But if your crop is far from your house, isn't it natural for the birds to come and peck at it? And anyway, even when the Inspector is in town, it's just as if he were away. What an existence! He only lives to catch evaders or to write nasty reports. Going to bed soon after the chickens, he's up at dawn to work vigilantly for his country, and to swell his bank account. If he hears Soukali sigh too deeply, he may deign to give her another child; she's just a space in which to leave his signature. But that doesn't satisfy a woman. A woman needs someone to wear her out. Soukali confides in me that her man does the thing with the same haste as a cock among hens. Let him throw a tantrum if he wants, I tell you. But he'll just have to find a way of bearing with his lot. And with no scandal, either. For who would pay him back the dowry swallowed by her family? She "arranges" matters, therefore. Like everyone else, she adds, with a wink. Marriage is an institution for the profit of the family, the clan, the tribe; to avoid having problems with your people, in short. The sweets of love are for before marriage, or on the side. What's more, in our case, Monsieur the Inspector is always up hill and down dale, either scouring our frontiers in search of public receipts, or off on international conferences and other missions, all of them more important than the problems of the state. I must admit that, all things considered, I have the noble feeling of playing the Good Samaritan, in my role as stand-in. And Soukali, beautiful as the blue flame dancing on burning liquor, restores in me all the vigour of a newly circumcised boy.

If a beautiful woman isn't a thief, say the elders, then she's a sorceress. And so it was with Soukali. She only needed to hear the sound of a key in the lock of the front door, and she would immediately check if it was me by opening her own bedroom door a little. She didn't light up the sitting room, where I kept stumbling against the Inspector's furniture on my way to join her. Obviously, this was the darkness of precaution, the darkness of robbers in league. Even when bush-meat is well-prepared, it's never really tasty without a pinch of pepper. All precautions had been taken. Her little darlings had each drunk a harmless spoonful of Phenergan syrup.

"It's so useful, and not at all dangerous."

She would offer her antelope's muzzle just at the level of my lips and I loved to feel her naked body beneath the simply-rolled cylinder of her wrapper. She would murmur a few words in a childish voice, gay and carefree. I gently unwound the cloth from her body and my hand caressed the plains and hills that proclaimed her beauty and sang of her emotion. She closed her eyes, and her movements rapidly took on the jerky rhythm that led to her climax. Over her shoulder, I was looking at the Inspector, behind a square of glass on the bedside table, smiling at me with his conquering air, in his pilot's helmet and gold-laden uniform.

Losing balance, we would fall upon the bed. While I sat up to remove my remaining sock, she attended to certain last details: turning off the ceiling-light, putting a magazine on top of the bedside lamp, turning the Inspector's face to the wall, pulling a towel from the wardrobe ... Soukali, yé! Soukali, a whole ballet of flames trembling to the beat of a randy tom-tom. A current through the loins inspired us like two singers and we babbled through a litany of foolish, incomprehensible words. Indiscreetly, I demanded to know if she loved me. With closed eyes and rapt face, she confessed it, letting me guess by the light gulping of her throat that she was lapping up an invisible milk. That was her way of communicating: movements, caresses, sighs, cries, her eyes upturned; never those long phrases springing from the blue dream where water becomes the most potent of drinks. Love restored all her health. Her last sighs confessed as much. I was her element of life.

Then we came together. She showed me her whole array of poses, and we tried out those of the gladiator and the panther, then of M. Pascal's wheelbarrow, then riding the sea horse. Wonderful, wonderful, really. Bathed in the indescribable odour of our intimacies, rocked to the rhythm of the Inspector's air conditioner, we would be surprised suddenly into sleep, our arms and legs all entangled, as banally as on the covers of one of his detective novels.

All day the radio had kept up its battery of military music, interrupting it at regular intervals, without any additional comment, to rebroadcast that morning's communiqué, delivered in the tones of a pedantic schoolmaster. Twiddling the knobs, I managed to pick up everything, except what was happening now and what I wished to know. It was all about the preceding situation which, according to them, explained everything about the present event. The connection didn't seem that obvious to me, but politics and I... Radio France-International gave us the voice of Polépolé. A declaration from some overseas haven, describing the new leaders as "putschists". Having given a very stern account of them, he announced that, in order to avoid useless bloodshed among his people, he had chosen exile, trusting in God and the common people to restore one day soon an order more favourable to the labouring masses. So he was saying *au revoir* to us, rather than good-bye.

Elengui and I thanked him for his attitude. We didn't care for bloodshed. Because in these matters it is always we, the innocent, who have to shed it. But would the blacks really have brought out their spears and arrows if Polépolé had insisted on staying? Had he really governed in their interests? Who would have gone out to die for him?

Whether it's him or another up there, for us it's always the same. Yesterday, our miseries were all the fault of the whites, whom we must chase away in order to win happiness. Today, the Uncles have gone and misery is still with us. Who should we chase away now? Polépolé's guards didn't resist, that night.

I don't blame them or laugh at their plight. Can one push back into the ground a yam that has already hoisted its vine?

It didn't take long. From the next day onwards the radio began to broadcast messages of support from different branches of the armed forces and from the commanders of all the military districts. Then, a few days later, one of the eastern provinces declared its allegiance by announcing the appointment of a Patriotic Provincial Council of National Resurrection, which had immediately dismissed the Prefect, that "valet of the puppet Polépolé". Is it necessary to add that the province concerned was the birthplace of Colonel Bwakamabé? Certain ambassadors transmitted messages warmly welcoming the "Liberation". Those who held back, whose dignity wouldn't allow them to join the procession, were swiftly recalled. But soon every province in the country had sent messages of support to the new regime. The western province from which Polépolé hailed was not behindhand either.

Ah, now I remember something—at the wake, the youngsters were talking about the Yabaka affair. A captain much loved by his men. But dangerous. Dangerous. A wild fellow. Wanted to introduce political discussions in the barracks. Had refused to carry out the punishment meted out to one of his corporals. The Chief of Staff, who was then Polépolé, flew into a rage. Transfer. To the bush. To the eastern borders, among the gorillas and the pygmies. Yabaka had refused to submit. Polépolé had signed an order for his demotion. All Moundié was agreed that the captain had balls of steel between his thighs. And *wollé, wollé, woï, woï.* The barracks were full of mutterings, but continued with their duties, in order and discipline. A sudden hunting-call at sunset. The secret service and the security police had drawn up their charges in perfect accord: Yabaka was plotting and preparing a brutal coup. He was picked up at once, together with several officers of his tribe. On State Radio, not a word from Aziz Sonika, but radio grapevine gave all the details to Moundié. We were just waiting for the trial to begin.

Standing five feet seven inches, weighing a hundred and seventy pounds, he stalked proudly, his impassive face ringed with tight curls, which also circled his thick lips, proudly proclaiming their negritude, and his left breast embellished with an enormous, many-rayed silver star, itself surrounded by innumerable rows of ribbons in bright and glistening array.

When he took off his gold-encrusted cap and set it on his knee, posing for the official photograph, he held it caressingly with his left hand, and one perceived a half-bald head that gave a certain air of wisdom to his narrow forehead.

This, more or less, was the image of Bwakamabé Na Sakkadé presented that Saturday evening by the editor of *The Southern Cross,* the one and only weekly newspaper of the Republic.

His identity card stated, for the record, that he was born in 1914, the very day as well as the very year of France's entry into the war against Germany. Malicious tongues didn't want to admit this, and claimed that his date of birth was more like...without further precision. Anyway, who in his backward village (so these venomous tongues of Moundié added) knew the calendar of the Uncles in those days? There's no need to hide the fact. He'd lopped a few years off his true age, like us all. One had to get into school, or remain forever a savage. No, there was nothing to be ashamed of in that.

In primary school, it was reported, he had learned more quickly than his fellows and had distinguished himself in the eyes of the monitors by his exceptional qualities. He would have missed in those days the training and environment, insufficiently prized by the younger generation, which would have enabled him to get into one of the great French colleges. But he would never make a single spelling mistake in his dictations. He was always the quickest in mental arithmetic and the best at solving problems. For otherwise he would not have been admitted to the General Mangin Army School, and wouldn't have been President of the Republic today.

That is what we learned from Aziz Sonika's editorials in *The Southern Cross;* the same Aziz Sonika who had nourished the cult of Polépolé and had transfixed the enemies of the former

President, his pen steeped in hyena's bile, and his oaths full of spittle.

Colonel—sorry, General (the day following the coup, the Promotions Commission had nominated him General despite, it was said, his protestations) Bwakamabé Na Sakkadé was not one of those black officers who had climbed into the higher ranks only after the departure of the severe white regime. No, he had himself earned the progression of his stripes from his chest to his shoulders in close combat.

He had taken part in the Libyan campaign, the landings on the French Riviera, the victorious march to Paris, with the Uncles. He was one of the few survivors of that epoch, which had begun to mingle with the stuff of legend, and which the young despised or knew nothing of, in all the frivolity of their spoilt youth. He would indulge in reminiscence of these adventures when he was angry. Either because he had drunk deep (always Chivas), or because he could no longer listen to those junior officers, scented with the fine perfumes of St. Cyr, demanding a war against a neighbouring country for a mere yes or no. Then he would really shout, Daddy Bwakamabé Na Sakkadé. He shouted that they knew nothing of war, of hand-to-hand fighting, of butchery, these lily- (or, if you prefer, black-) livered boys! They couldn't imagine what it was to go for days without proper food, when all the same, one had to make forced marches over difficult terrain. They didn't know what it was to be shit-scared, passing the night a few yards from the enemy, not knowing whether the crack of a branch was friend, foe, beast, or just the wind. And, when you are fighting with your heart full of courage, excited by the noise of the guns and the smell of powder, your blood faithful to the ancients of Djabotama and, profiting from a sudden lull, you touch the shoulder of a comrade, only to discover that he is no more than a sack full of sand. Lifeless. Then you think harder than any master of philosophy. He himself had known all of that, Daddy Bwakamabé Na Sakkadé. He had known Bir-Hakeim. Yes, Bir-Hakeim, with General Koenig. When the Germans had them surrounded and called for their surrender, because their goose was really cooked. And Koenig just replied: "Shit!" (that's what is claimed by Daddy Bwakamabé Na Sakkadé, according to whom Cambronne did no more than reuse this celebrated word). And that night, along with the boys of the Legion, they broke the encirclement, fighting hand-to-hand, with bayonets fixed, blind with courage. God will always recognise his own ...

From all these battles, what's more, Bwakamabé Na Sakkadé still had a scar on his thigh. The explosion of a mortar shell. During the landing of the Second Infantry Battalion. And if he was really launched upon his reminiscences, he would show it to you, then quickly excuse himself for the gesture—but he had to hammer it home to these chocolate soldiers, who had never had their baptism of fire, and who thought themselves made of the stuff of heroes just because they'd been favourably noticed on manoeuvres, or even on parade!

As for him, he'd even fought in Indochina, against the Viets. He'd also fought in Morocco, and then in Algeria, against the *Fellaheen*.

After all that, it was only natural that he became an officer even in colonial times, no? The only one. None before him, none after him.

As an editor, Aziz Sonika had to interpret certain phases of this biography by adapting them to the political atmosphere of the times. Thus, Adjutant Bwakamabé Na Sakkadé was said to have rendered great services to the Vietminh patriots by giving them information and so aiding their many victories against the French colonial forces. Likewise, in Morocco, Lieutenant Bwakamabé Na Sakkadé had helped nationalist prisoners to escape. In Algeria, Captain Bwakamabé Na Sakkadé had always opposed torture and had kept casualties among the freedom-fighters to a minimum by collaborating with the FLN. He had done everything possible to spare the civilian population.

Aziz Sonika emphasised that the qualities of strength and courage that had made the new Head of State a worthy fighter didn't prevent his possessing unsuspected resources of intellectual finesse; resources which, according to Sonika, merited special mention in a former adjutant. These had led Captain

Bwakamabé Na Sakkadé to serve during the fifties in the headquarters of the French Chief of Staff in one of the federal capitals. Radio grapevine whispered that this had really been in the secret service section.

For Aziz Sonika, the General was also a model family man. Page 2 of *The Southern Cross* carried the identity photograph of the lovely Mireille Bwakamabé Na Sakkadé: slender, fine-limbed, with the flat belly of a virgin and the clear skin of a mulattress, which she owed to the use of certain soaps and pommades whose names must not be mentioned. When I saw this body, I quite forgot that this was the wife of the Head of State and I felt my pulse beating in my temples. A real mannequin, with a long neck and breasts like mangoes. At the time of the coup, she can't have been more than twenty. Up to that time, she'd been presiding only at ceremonies and on official journeys. For other occasions, one knew of at least five more sweet little "First Ladies". Two were of our country, though not of the Djabotama people. The others came from Mali, Guinea, Somalia, Sudan, Congo or Zaire where, as you know, there are enough beauties in the streets to take away your breath. If one adds to these a genuine mulattress, a Thai girl, one from Nice, a Swedish blonde and a Yugoslav (reported to be a singer or—according to the Uncles—a communist agent), one will understand why it was forbidden to show these political expenses in the Republic's budget, even under the formula proposed by a Minister of Finance, of truly mediocre imagination: "stables and parks of the presidential estate".

His progeny is vast and worthy of a real head of family who doesn't want gossip, but knows how to furnish the clan with proofs of his virility. Not to speak of children left behind in Indochina, North Africa and even France. He did just what the whites and the Senegalese troops did here, between bursts of gunfire.

The Southern Cross also noted that the new President was an extremely pious man, who went to Mass every Sunday, always taking Communion at Easter, Ascension Day, the Feast of the Assumption, Christmas and St. Silvester's Day. From that time onwards, he was to do likewise on every anniversary of his seizing power.

This is, more or less, how our press handled the event.

The Uncles' newspapers were practically silent. One magazine, however, did reproduce a map of the country and describe its contours, its natural resources and mineral deposits, before going on to give a brief account of recent historical developments. In conclusion, the journalist stated brusquely that he had just given an account of the events leading up to a change of regime, evidently not very democratic, but scarcely threatening either, so obvious was it that the new masters were not in the service of Moscow. *Le Monde,* I believe, had an editorial on military regimes and an article on page 3, under the headline "Africa", signed by a certain "Th.M.". He explained the coup d'état in ethnic terms and divided the country into three zones, with as many dominant tribes. Our history since independence, according to my recollection of his words, had been nothing but confrontations among these three groups, and the victory of Bwakamabé Na Sakkadé was no more than an episode in that struggle. The former chef of the *Relais,* an Uncle who had already returned to his own country, wrote to say that he was afraid for me and that he didn't clearly grasp what was going on here. He asked me to reassure him and explain everything. This was pretty difficult, because we, the common people, understood nothing of this episode in the war of the Great.

A nobody like me summoned to the Presidential Palace? My boss, hands on hips as usual, couldn't stop shaking his head over it.

"Tell me, little swine" (he was no racist, the boss, but it was a matter of habit; he said "little swine" with real affection, just as men whisper "slut" in the ears of a woman they are teasing), "tell me, little swine, how does it come about that you enjoy such a relationship? You've been hiding things from me."

I'm sure it would have turned many people's heads to know they were going to be received at the Presidential Palace in a few hours. But I just had cold feet. Great ones like that, higher than the highest, as we say in Moundié, are best kept at a distance. And I was the more afraid for another reason. The gendarmes who came to give the news didn't seem particularly friendly. Yes, okay, they clicked their heels and saluted when presenting themselves, and again when leaving, but are those not simply the mechanical movements of wound-up toys? And while the boss went on with his remarks, still leaving me in doubt whether they were truly admiring or simply sarcastic, I was asking myself what imprudence I had committed to justify such a summons? Politics and such I avoided like the plague. Express an opinion? I took care lest anything of the sort might slip out. A popular story running around Moundié served as my philosophy: two detainees in the prison at Bangoura introduced themselves as follows: "I'm in here for telling a political joke. And you? Oh, I'm in for having heard one and smiled."

To begin with, I haven't understood a thing about our politics since independence. A swamp full of crocodiles—no one who ventures there manages to stay honest. It's true that since the coup some people, however little they might know you, have ventured to give their opinion: some saying that Polépolé got what he deserved; others that things would go to the dogs. I just listened and shook my head, like a modest black boy seeking his education; and this wasn't just a tactic on my part, but the sincere expression of my nature.

"You're not going to present yourself in that outfit, anyway!" shouted the boss. "Run home and get yourself properly dressed."

Properly dressed? Yes, just like a corpse for its coffin.

"Well, at least you can use your connections with those gentlemen to tell them that the State always has drinks on the house here. If you can just put in the good word for me..."

Bwakamabé looked up from his papers and lifted the phone.

"Hullo! Send the Head of Security to me at once."

He dropped the phone again.

"Anybody wants to play stupid games, I'll sort him out."

Sentries crusty and irritable at having to leave the coolness of the shade, bodyguards enraged at being torn from their comic-books, arrogant and officious ushers, a waitingroom crammed with suitors, with smartly dressed women and men bearing briefcases—I was obliged, despite my summons, to surmount many obstacles and wait several hours before being admitted to the great man's office.

"Ah, it's you, *Maître*!"

"At last..."

"Is it true that you're the *maître d'hôtel* at the *Relais*?"

I nodded.

"Well, then! *maître d'hôtel*—that's too long for me! I'll just call you *Maître*. In any case, it sounds much better."

I explained stammeringly, that, in theory...

"Well, I'm the boss here now. I shall call anyone *Maître* or Doctor, just as I please. Anyone who doesn't like it can just step forward. Then he'll see! No, but really..."

He softened his tone.

"They tell me you're the best headwaiter."

I felt obliged to make a barely perceptible movement of my head.

"Yes, yes. That's what they say. Even the Uncles admit it."

I looked solicitously at the end of my tie and tugged at it clumsily.

"You are also the first, and at present the only one of our countrymen to rise so high in that profession."

"Not quite, Mr President."

I gave the names of all the other black headwaiters I knew. The General drew back sharply, frowned and stuck out his lips.

"What's that? Are you not a Libotama?"

"That's to say..."

"Aren't you the son of Pa-Louka and of Ma-Voukouti?"

I admitted it, smiling with amusement.

"So, it's as I thought. The country isn't so big. We all know each other."

And he launched into a long explanation to convince me that he knew well, not only my mother and father, but their parents also, knowing that some were from Libotama and the others from Kinassi, which isn't more than six miles away. He raised his eyebrows.

"So we are really compatriots, *Maître*."

I agreed once more. But understand me well and don't judge me too quickly. A fledgling like me couldn't put himself in such a solemn place and start giving lectures to a president. I could have explained to him that for me, so accustomed to look words up in the dictionary, even before the advent of Madame Berger, a compatriot was really...

"What's more, you'd better call me Daddy. That's the true politeness of our ancestors."

He glanced at his watch. A big gold bracelet, with hands and numbers also in gold.

"Good, let's get to the point. I asked you here, my dear cousin, to get your help. We military men are used to talking directly. I need a butler here who is properly qualified and in whom I can have full confidence."

Yéhé! I put my hand to my mouth.

"Your Excellency, do you want me to recommend a good one?"

"No need of that, boy. Decide for myself."(He lowered his voice.) "Otherwise, no point in being the Chief. From tomorrow, you are the butler of His Excellency President Bwakamabé Na Sakkadé."

And he let out a big, rough laugh, as if he had just played out a good farce.

I swallowed hard. I had no wish to lose my post at the hotel. A steady job like that...

"There are no more regular staff in the Palace. All those who were here before" (he waved his hand) "...I've shown the door! Just think! All flunkies of Polépolé" (grimace). "From today, I'll sign an order naming you an official of the Palace." (He winked at me and dropped his voice.) "No need for anxiety on that score."

"If Your Excellency..."

"Daddy! Not Excellency."

"—"

"Come now, no shyness. We aren't Uncles here! Blacks, Djabotama! No nonsense. Just authenticity."

"Daddy..."

"Bravo! You see?"

"Daddy, I'd be glad if you allowed me some time to consider."

"Bravo, bravo, my dear cousin. In the family one always thinks things over first. Think before speaking. Think before acting. That's excellent. But we soldiers are men of action. Not too much reflection. Have to jump to it! Have to make people feel the change. So I'll give you twenty-four hours."

Despite my emotion, I summoned up enough courage to make a fresh objection...

"Listen, *Maître*, you must understand that this is a political post. In my position, I must be surrounded by my own people and no one else."

"But, politics and such..."

"Right, right, right! I too dislike politics. The politicians have brought the country to the brink of ruin. But when I say a political post, I mean a post outside the ordinary. Don't joke with political posts, *Maître*. A butler is like a cabinet secretary or a doctor: absolutely must be one of us."

"Just let me think it over, all the same—"

"Think, think! But quickly."

"This politics..."

"With me, it won't be like before. With me, no blablabla. Action, action, action and always action. Everyone jump to it! Lef, rai; lef, rai; lef, rai! It's action that counts. It's by this means that the people, and the judgement of History, I believe the judgement of History"(he lifted a finger), "will measure us. My word for it—nothing to fear. There'll be political stability. No opposition. I, Bwakamabé Na Sakkadé, son of Ngakoro, son of Fouléma, son of Kiréwa, will never become an ex-President, like that coward Polépolé."

He paused a moment, breathlessly, as though fixed upon a vision seen only by himself. Then he glanced again at his watch, ignoring the piteous phrases I was babbling, and showed me firmly to the door, compelling me to pause at the threshold to answer the questions he posed about the health of my family, about...

"You must understand, *Maître*, I have to be sure of those who serve me food and drink."

While crossing the waitingroom, I caught the enraged glances of those I had left before my admission. Others had come to swell their number.

They had to wait a while longer, because the Director of Security was admitted immediately after me.

"These blacks, really, they're not serious."

"Just lip, lip—it's only in lip and palaver that we're strong."

"Too true, brother-o! Blackmen know not'in' but mout', mout'."

"Exactly, I tell you."

"Ye-e-es. They all cry 'Polépolé or death! Polépolé or death', then they let the boys in the berets take over without lifting a finger."

"They say there wasn't even a shot fired."

That's because the mercenaries lent a hand to the new masters, *dé*!"

"The messenries?"

"I tell you, brother."

"It's not possible."

"You! When you're told something, you never want to believe it. You say it's just rumours—radio grapevine. But you don't know that what radio grapevine says is true enough. Toads don't croak unless it's raining, *dé*."

"But those messenries, aren't they white? How come they weren't recognised right away, then? The difference of skin is too much-o!"

"Black mercenaries, then."

"Eh, eh? Black messenries?"

"Yes, my brother, Americans, Cubans who hate Castro, Guineans who don't like Sekou, Katangans and ... and, many others."

"When did they come, then?"

"The very night of the business, I tell you. The plane dropped them then came back for them in the morning, when it was sure the bananas were well boiled."

"But how'd you come to know all this, eh?"

"You, you doubt too much-o!"

Despite his profound respect for our metropolitan mother France, and his admiration for the civilisation of good wine, Daddy was never really at ease unless he could freely practise the customs of the village. So, in the courtyard of the Palace, he had built a round thatched hut within which to receive his cronies, as well as diplomats coming for official audiences. Captain Yabaka and the young intellectuals didn't appreciate this gesture and thought it smacked of indulgence. But I found it authentically Djabotama and, all things considered, no less dignified than St Louis delivering judgement under an oak tree. Besides which, it was thanks to this practice that I was able to overhear the discussion of many secret affairs of State which I am about to pass on to you. Discreet and silent, I stayed always within hearing range so as to be ready, at the first click of the fingers, to serve Daddy his Chivas.

He had this hut built immediately after coming to power and I remember in detail the first conversations I was privileged to overhear. The one, for example, with the rich Lebanese Monsieur Karam, who was later to sell the plans of the fabulous seventy-five billion franc palace that they are still constructing. On that occasion, Monsieur Karam was vaunting a project for the breeding of giant turkeys.

"I don't want to meddle with your internal problems, Mr President, but this Captain Yabaka looks to me like someone who wants to sabotage your policy of economic development. The money is there, the backers are ready. All it needs is a signature."

Daddy wondered whether the people of the country would like giant turkeys.

"What does it matter, Your Excellency? These are for export. A splendid source of foreign exchange! If you hesitate, Ghana, Uganda, Senegal and Peru are all interested. I diverted the project your way because I love this country. I am eager to help you."

Daddy was still dubious, but one heard in his tone that more and more he felt it made sense.

"Of course, Excellency..."

The Lebanese wanted to make quite sure that they understood each other.

"Naturally, Excellency, you will get your share."

I have no memory for figures, and I'm afraid of appearing to exaggerate by quoting any without checking, but it was certainly a matter of millions. Not just a few, but hundreds of them.

They summoned me to lubricate the agreement. Like all those of my calling, I simply pretended at first not to hear. Then, after three shouts of mounting impatience, I came running. Daddy stayed faithful to his Chivas, while Monsieur Karam wanted to try our palm wine. With a constipated air he insisted that it was a delicacy; that one could, perhaps, with His Excellency's blessing, find a company which would bottle or can it successfully; that this would be all the rage, both on the African and European markets.

"You like it? No problem. *Maître*! *Maître*! Give several litres to Monsieur Karam."

But I, having served them so often, knew these whites well. I pretended that there was no more wine; that the tapper hadn't passed by for the last two days. Mourning in his village.

I saw Daddy's eyes grow round immediately. If he had possessed those powers which fetish priests sometimes confer, that wine-tapper would have dropped dead there and then. But we must keep up appearances. No scandal in front of the whiteman, even if he isn't an Uncle. Only when he was among blacks again did Daddy begin roaring. Like the Guinarou. He insisted that the tapper should be brought immediately.

"But he's at a wake, in his village."

"Let someone go and bring him here, dead or alive."

Then I summoned up all my courage.

"Excuse me, Daddy, I beg you, don't punish that poor man. There was palm wine in the fridge all along."

"*Maître*...excuse me (he coughed), *Maître*, I don't quite understand. You say that ..."

I nodded my head with a sheepish expression.

"Well, what do you mean by that, *Maître*? Sabotage?"

I explained that I knew whites very well.

"But he's not a white. At least not a white-white. Just a Lebanese."

"He's still not a blackman."

He conceded this.

"By serving them so long I understand whites."

Anyway, the bottles in the fridge were not presentable as a gift. Taken away like that, without preparation, the wine could become sour, which could only damage our reputation in Paris.

At the end of this plea, Daddy called everyone around us and presented me with a big sweep of the hand.

"Behold a good citizen. That's how I'd like you all to be. Instead of always whining: 'Yes, Daddy, Bravo, Daddy, Bravo!' (He imitated a mewling marmot.) Here, at least, is someone who really loves me."

God is great, and good actions are always rewarded, even when we least expect it.

"In any case, just listen, you lot. I warn you once and for all. I'll have no pity for anyone who, through foolish flattery, leads me into error. Forewarned is forearmed!"

He questioned the Chief of Protocol.

"Is Monsieur Girard there? So why don't you admit him right away?"

Monsieur Girard entered, his arms encumbered with two flat suitcases, which he threw open in front of Daddy. One contained a whole array of spectacle lenses, the other a rich selection of frames. He presented a card with printed letters, which he wanted our chief to read aloud. Bwakamabé, having at first begun with good grace, suddenly flew into a rage.

"No, but what are you trying to do?"

Monsieur Girard opened his mouth to explain.

"I can read, I can. Primary School Certificate to prove it! I'm not an illiterate. What do you think?"

Monsieur Girard managed to slip in a phrase.

"A hundred times two eyes I have. To see my enemies coming, even at night."

And Daddy, who had jumped up, began trying on several frames. He chose the thickest and heaviest among them, in tortoiseshell. At every fresh trial, he looked at me, as if at a mirror.

"Excuse me, Mr President, I thought I understood that you wanted reading glasses."

"Well, you understood nothing."

"No problem about that, Mr President. I took the precaution of also bringing a choice of sunglasses."

A wary smile on his face, Daddy now lowered his voice.

"Always get things wrong, Monsieur Girard."

The oculist had the unhappy air of an innocent victim.

"Haven't you got a mirror?"

"But of course, Mr President."

Daddy admired himself. Each trial was made without a smile. Indeed, he even tried to put on a solemn expression. His choice tended always toward frames with thick arms. Each time, he consulted the Chief of Protocol. Finally, Daddy chose seven pair. And in a sharp tone, he demanded that they be ready by the evening.

"And with clear glass, you hear?"

In Moundié, everybody knew what that meant: windows.

With his face thus prepared, Daddy was presentable to his own taste for the official photograph and Isnard, the celebrated studio photographer of the Champs-Elysées, was there in the afternoon to prepare the decor down to the last detail.

The shots that one sees nowadays always show the Chief in white tie and tails. This was the recommendation of one of his French advisers who won his favour on the eve of one of his visits to France. But at the time I'm speaking of, he never wore that sort of formal dress. He put on his officer's uniform. Still, with the ribbon of the Grand Cross on his shoulder-sash, he fixed the camera with a disciplined eye, resting his right hand on three volumes of the Quillet Encyclopaedia (from A to Cot-es, a sharp eye could perceive) while grasping his cap with his left.

From then onwards, these eyes watched the whole country, under the sun's rays, under those of lightbulbs and kerosene lamps, as well as in the dark. Whenever we passed a public building, they gazed down on us. Whenever we entered shops or offices, we met their stare. Whenever we stuck on a stamp, they looked up at us. Whenever we got our wages or helped our relatives, they saw it all. Whenever we picked up a newspaper, there they were. Whenever we flicked through a book, they jumped out of the pages. Whenever my mother undressed, she took care to cover his photo with her scarf, a photo that she always kept near her bed beside her crucifix and her *gri-gri*.

In those days, no Uncle would allow a native to come close to him, still less to touch him. We knew it, and took care never to violate the custom. Niggers were dirty, and even when they washed, their smell could cling to a white skin across quite a distance. Madame Berger never hesitated to come right up to me, in order to teach me how to leaf through the files and correct my work. I must say that, every time, I did my best to draw back discreetly. But there always arrived the moment when, pinned against the wall, I was wedged in beyond hope of escape. I told myself that she had no right to play at this game, because she was far from ugly and knew it very well. Ah! with that skin the colour of banana-palm's heart, with that hair, blacker than my own face, rippling like a mare's mane and ending with that comma which curled back up her neck again. Ah! those eyes like the strained juice of a lemon. When she came to me like that, when I sniffed her subtle perfume, when I saw her legs moving across each other as if in a gesture of protection, then I felt paralysis seize all my limbs. I tried to think of something dull and neutral, but her full, up-turned lips, which seemed to be always sucking in some unseen nectar, made my feelings all the stronger. In all this, to be sure, there was nothing more than adolescent innocence. The Uncles seem seldom to think of those things. But, despite my catechism and the education of the reverend fathers, I was always prey to wayward ideas. Ah, but we blacks....

I won't describe the swearing-in ceremony for the supreme magistrate of our nation. Aziz Sonika, in his usual boot-licking style, reported every detail of the event as it unrolled at the former parliament building, in the presence of the foreign press corps. It was nothing but a faithful copy of similar ceremonies engaged in by whites, throughout which Bwakamabé Na Sakkadé played his role conscientiously, with a serious demeanour and evident relish. It's enough just to go through the special number of *The Southern Cross* and look closely at the photos. There you will see a Bwakamabé smiling at the angels, playing before the cameras a part of which he had doubtless dreamed since infancy. No, that sort of thing isn't very significant. I'd rather tell you about the night of his traditional investiture.

I can no longer recall the exact date, because the event obviously wasn't covered by the press, but with the help of a calendar of that year, and knowing moreover that it was in June, I could easily figure out the day, or rather the night, because it was the first one of the full moon.

The guests began to arrive discreetly at the Palace some hours after sunset, in screened trucks, specially hired for the occasion. The whole Djabotama tribe was there. When I say the whole tribe, it's a manner of speaking, for no politician has ever succeeded in solving all the problems posed by his tribe. He can only help a few of them, and satisfy even fewer. So it was that night. All the celebrants authorized to pass through the gates of the old Governor's Palace without visiting cards were among the best-known Djabotama: leading traders of Libotama origin; in all, some two or three hundred people, which is far below the number of our tribespeople living in the capital. But, needless to say, no members of any other tribe were invited.

In the half-light it was difficult to make out faces, for all the lamps in the presidential quarters had been extinguished. Only the moonlight and a few candles illuminated the moving shadows. It was easy enough, however, to discern the group of women, amongst whom Ma Mireille stood out, wrapped in a cloth that left her shoulders bare. This costume of a poor and simple villager conferred upon the manequin figure of our President's wife all the allure of those barefoot island maidens seen on the beaches in some American films much fancied by the youth of Moundié. Forgetting my position, I allowed myself to gaze searchingly at our princess. This lapse lasted only a few seconds. I felt myself transfixed by a steady glare from Ma Mireille, in which I read a recall to order that made me tremble. I had already noted how strong a physical repulsion I inspired in Ma Mireille. I must try to find out why. One day I must find some means to rehabilitate myself, because when the Chief's wife takes a dislike to you, the heavens can easily fall on your head.

I drew away from the group of women with the detached air favoured by the spies of Monsieur Gourdain, and went to check on my staff, to make sure everyone was at his post and everything prepared according to my instructions regarding drinks, snacks and the main feast. Just think, this was my first big reception! Daddy was going to judge me by it.

There were two other groups. One consisted of politicians and high officials of our tribe, the other of nobles and traditional priests, all in tribal dress and bearing the insignia of their offices. They surrounded, at a respectful distance, a throne covered with scarlet velvet, all embroidered with gold and silk, separated from the ground by a precious carpet imported from some Arab country or other, which I will leave some more cultured taste to identify. Here and there stood young men of our nobility, hiding the royal insignia beneath white cloths. Finally, circling this whole group, the mass of the tribal family was already dancing to the music of a traditional orchestra consisting of drums, gongs and bull-horns. The movements were still only preliminary stretching, like that of athletes warming up.

When Daddy appeared on the steps of the Palace, standing humbly in a loincloth, his feet bare, under a palanquin carried by four pages, a murmur ran through the crowd. The orchestra stopped and a most impressive silence fell on everyone.

The *griot,* shouting like a drugged mountebank and deliberately making himself hoarse, presented the new Chief of the Djabotama. He recited the fifteen generations of his predecessors. He recounted their feats of arms and their moral qualities. The orchestra began again, accompanied by the droning of grave voices and the wild ululations of the women, while Daddy advanced with a processional stride, preceded by the Chief of Protocol and the tireless *griot,* whom the Djabotama nobles covered with large bank notes as he passed by.

The cortege stopped before the throne. The *griot* intoned the famous *Pouéna Kanda,* a sad, slow melody that laments the weakening of the Djabotama whenever the throne is vacant, because the enemy has killed through treachery all the men capable of protecting them, as a father protects his son. The song thus recalls the qualities required in anyone claiming to be the father of the whole tribe. It was then that, in a completely different tone, one of the traditional priests announced that all disquiet should be chased from our hearts; that the Nation was saved, because the sun of the shadows, which that night diffused its pale yellow light, had transmitted to us the message of the ancestors: they had chosen Bwakamabé Na Sakkadé to lead all the Djabotama and impose their will upon all the other tribes of the new country, as defined by the Uncles.

The music changed its rhythm, becoming much more jerky, almost drowned by hurrahs from the men and *you-yous* from the women.

Then silence fell again, and the voice of the priest proclaimed the name of Bwakamabé Na Sakkadé three times, the crowd replying:

"We want him! We want him.! We want him!"

Daddy was led by the hand and placed before an altar covered with a leopard skin on which rested a drum and a lion's tail, both symbols of strength and all-powerful authority, together with a necklace of human teeth. These, as every Djabotama learned in his childhood, were the teeth of those who died in war against the Chief's predecessors. Daddy knelt in front of the altar, between the lines of fetish priests, to take the oath that bound him to all the duties of a Djabotama ruler.

When he rose again, the oldest of the priests took him by the shoulders, then leaning his brow against the Chief's as if to transfer its contents, declared:

"Boka litassa dounkounê!" This might be rendered as: "Receive the power of the ancestors." Understood, of course, as the power of the chieftains of the Djabotama. In truth, the word *litassa* contains more than the word *power*. It is at once the power of command, the intelligence to dominate others and the strength of a bull, or more, of a supernatural being. These are powers in which Uncles don't want to believe, and which place us beyond the reach of our enemies. Whoever has received *litassa* can communicate directly with the ancestors. He reads all consciences like the clear waters of a spring. No woman can

resist him. He can walk on the waves and fly over the peaks. He can resist the venom of serpents. Bullets change their course when his breast approaches them.

Daddy then received the raffia helmet that he sometimes wore during certain traditional ceremonies, but which usually rested in a shrine stuck in a corner of his bedroom. The young nobles unwound their white cloths and displayed the royal insignia: the lion's tail that must never leave his grasp; the *tounka*, a chain of iron with many pendants, which he doesn't wear on his chest like a Christian scapular, but on his back, as a woman bears her child. For a chief has nothing in common with the kings in the Uncles' history books. He is, before everything else, a father who must occupy himself with his subjects as if with his own sons. The President could no more separate himself from this chain than from his lion's tail. They also proffered him a bag, which symbolised the power to raise and receive tribute, and a bracelet whose meaning I never properly understood, but which he likewise always wore. Finally came the display of the royal bow and a quiver of arrows with golden points. Here the orchestra burst forth again, while the men shouted with joy and the women uttered the strident *you-yous*.

It was then that the oldest of the Djabotama nobles offered him a handful of earth. The nobles and the priests formed several lines in front of the Chief Bwakamabé Na Sakkadé and danced the *loukita,* which is in origin a war dance, as one sees clearly enough by the gestures. In the course of it, the nobles and priests passed one by one under the right foot of Bwakamabé Na Sakkadé, each time he raised it.

Then came an abrupt, syncopated rhythm accompanied by hand-claps. And we saw the newly installed chief advance at a dance-step towards Ma Mireille. The movements of his hips, arms, shoulders and torso announced that Ma Mireille was a beauty that the wind could not breathe upon without trembling, becoming troubled and losing its way, and that he, the Man, the Man of the Nation, was worthy of her. If you don't want to believe me, just see what I am capable of when the drums are beating and the xylophones are singing. See my body, my muscles, my limbs, my belly. Do you know, woman, in all the country, a dancer so supple, so agile and so strong? Come, come, my sister, you won't, no, you can't regret it. And Ma Mireille rose like an overpowered virgin. But when she began to dance, ayay'hé! It was enough to take your breath away. The elders are right to say that, to the same rhythm, each dances his own step, according to his nerves, his build, his heart, his belly, his head, and according to whether he's good, evil, a dreamer or a hypocrite. Ma Mireille's step was quite without equal. One would have thought she had practised daily for many hours, so precisely did her every movement reflect the wishes of the drummer. And I just gazed at this slender, fragile figure with her bare shoulders. And I told myself, before the parted legs of our First Lady, that if both Elengui and Soukali had each their own charms, Ma Mireille must have possessed others that would surely make you dizzy.

Ah! what a woman!

At that moment, Bwakamabé electrified her. He was like a great boar. Doubtless because of his rhythm and above all the power with which the priests had just invested him. Head back, eyes closed, legs opened as if in appeal, she was upright, in position... Just as in the *limbo* dance. And the Chief, from his loins, began to assert his virility. And the crowd shouted and rejoiced. And Bwakamabé Na Sakkadé continued, persevering, with the serious expression of a diligent student. And Ma Mireille's shoulders began to shake. And the crowd roared. And the movements of both dancers became ever more jerky. And the crowd went mad. Daddy suddenly unleashed several thrusts of his loins in the direction of Ma Mireille's belly, while she lifted her arms and showed her empty, rejoicing hands above the heads of the crowd and her body wriggled like a fish on a line. The crowd was delirious. I was blessing the skies for allowing all this only within the strict confines of a tribal assembly, with no prying white eyes. Even if it's only in the dance, a President and his lady are not supposed to do that in public. Papa de Gaulle must have danced some time in his life, but never like the common citizen. If the Uncles ever get to hear of this, they'll exploit it to say, yet again, that we are nothing but savages.

With their arms linked, Daddy and Ma Mireille made the rounds of their cheering people and then went to seat themselves on the scarlet thrones, fringed with gold and silk.

The rest of the reception was my affair, and that of my men. The moment arrived for the drinks and the feasting. We drank like at the end of a period of mourning, or at a marriage in Moundié or in the village. Without restraint. Joy and rejoicing. Some spirited away bottles of whiskey and ran to hide big chunks of mutton in the trucks that brought them and took them away. Towards two in the morning, Daddy and Ma Mireille disappeared. But we had been given orders to let people enjoy themselves till dawn. The nobles, politicians and high officials of the Djabotama didn't linger much after the departure of the Chief and his wife. But the mass of people wanted to profit from the party till dawn broke, and they did. If it was easy for the Presidential Guard to heave into the covered trucks all those whom drink had quitened and who lay about the courtyard as happily as on their own mats, it was another matter to convince the hard core that the party was really over.

In his bed, Daddy slept the sleep of a conquering hero, his conscience at ease. He had taken every precaution that God, the ancestors, the natural and supernatural forces would protect his mandate to the end. All his enemies would be crushed. Thus it had been determined.

Feeling some lack of confidence in myself, I have consulted a compatriot, the former Cabinet Secretary to Daddy, now living in exile.

Here is his reaction to the pages you have just read.

> My Dear *Maître*,
>
> The evening at the wake is depicted with striking accuracy, and whilst reading it I felt all my nostalgia aroused for the warmth of our native land. The words of Tiya, now recalled, take on a prophetic tone to which we

were insensitive at the time. But you are unjust in your portrayal of the young intellectuals.

In the light of later events, it's true that we were then excessive in our assessment of Polépolé and his politics. We certainly made a grave tactical error in accepting government posts under Bwakamabé. That's because we underestimated the fellow, believing that our self-confidence, our level of education, our experience of militant politics, would easily prevail over a peasant blockhead. But do these errors justify such a biting condemnation of our group as you seem to invite? It's unjust to reduce us to the level of raw terrorists, empty and voluble orators, or disciples of the dialectic of Thomas Diafoirus.

Consider that in scoffing too much at us in the name of some undigested truth you may be playing the enemy's game. If you want to be of service to the country, make haste to offer us a positive hero in your story.

As for the rest, I hesitate to pronounce an opinion. Whilst reading your work, I was constantly asking myself how to classify it. Sometimes you aspire to the precision of a historian or a sociologist; sometimes you resemble more the *griots* in whom some see only dream-peddlars and entertainers, and others a key to decoding the life of the village.

I'll continue, all the same.

Ah yes! the Country, the Country, the Country—but which Country?

Somewhere on this continent, for sure.

Choose for yourself, after a hundred calculations, or just follow your hunch, take a point on the equator, and steer either northward or southward, keeping your nose with the wind, and at a slightly oblique angle. Your craft then, after surviving air-pockets and overcoming tornadoes, will arrive, after a certain time, at a point from which you can just discern the capital of our country. Experienced travellers will tell you that this is the long way and that, to save time, it's a hundred times better to go first to Paris, London, Lisbon or Madrid, from which, after a night of dedicated dissipation, one can arrive at one's destination in a flight of a few hours. Surveyors and theorists may shrug their shoulders at this, but Africanists and Africans (not forgetting businessmen of all nationalities) will confirm that this is certainly the shortest way. But Bwakamabé, at his own whim, has added complexities to enter and exit the native land, making us feel how much the access to our paradise is a privilege one can't accord to the unworthy multitude, and that, after all, there's no reason for voyaging at random from a state where the people live perpetually in Nirvana.

Despite the intentions delicately and officially expressed by our Chamber of Commerce, the formalities of disembarkation are richly elaborated at the Hannibal-Ideloy Bwakamabé Na Sakadé Airport. Whether or not you are equipped with a visa that is perfectly in order—that's not the question—you must in all cases await patiently the laborious reading of every page of your passport, by policemen and officials in a constant bad humour. If your papers show evidence of a passage, even in transit, through one of the countries on the Index, then you will be invited to step into an office where a thousand preparations have been made to receive you. Photographed full-face and in profile, you will then have to fill out a special three-page questionnaire. So that the orderly record-keeper will not feel deprived of attention, the police of this particular branch are also obliged to search your pockets, your shoulderbags and your handbag. They are looking, it seems, for firearms, or for those newspapers, reviews, books or records that are, according to Monsieur Gourdain, far more dangerous than bombs. But if they find (or better still, if you offer) a bit of money, you will greatly shorten your delay here. There are still the health formalities to be undergone. Apart from the usual ones, you must show an absolutely clean slate. Nothing less than a bloodtest for syphilis and the taking of samples for the detection of gonorrhoea.

An elderly English lady, who was a consultant for the WHO,

a specialist in the fight against sexually transmitted diseases, was so enamoured of this practice that she never ceased speaking and writing in its praise on her return to Europe, claiming that in this field our country was the most progressive and the best-organised, and its head of state the most enlightened, in the Third World. The World Health Organisation, as one may imagine, didn't greatly appreciate this type of publicity and decided to dispense with the lady's services, censuring her moreover for having made a value judgement on a member country. Bwakamabé, by way of reprisal, called a conference, widely reported in the world press, at which he poured forth buckets of rhetoric and compared the Regional Director for Africa to a fish which I refuse to name here. Since then our delegation has regularly opposed the candidature of this distinguished man, who nevertheless continues to represent Africa with great dignity in the councils of the UN. As for the lady, she comes frequently to the country, personally invited by the President to every national celebration. She enjoys exemption from the medical examinations at Hannibal-Ideloy Bwakamabé Na Sakkadé Airport. But so filled is she with the honesty of all great models of sanctity, so much the enemy of all corrupt privilege, that she declares herself every time ready to undergo them, and even goes so far as to demand them. Evil tongues, which understand nothing of moral sentiments, claim that the elderly lady takes pleasure in the inspection. They say that she will allow no one to perform it except him whose delicate fingers know how to proceed from the first penetration. In that way, she experiences every time the same transports as on the first occasion.

All things considered, these formalities will take you, let us say, a certain time. The upshot will depend upon those on duty, their domestic problems, the contents of your baggage and, finally, the degree of your cooperation. For if it should happen that you lose patience and show it, your fate will vary according to whether you are a foreigner or a citizen of the country. In the former case, you will either be put on the first plane out or kept for some hours under close guard in the airport police post before being expelled; or even (if God so helps you) simply dismissed and followed everywhere you go, under strict prohibition of taking any photos during your stay. In the second case, everything imaginable and unimaginable may happen to you. But if you understand the art of slipping a few dollars discreetly into a palm, then you will discover a land bathed in perpetual sunshine.

I will say nothing about the glories which that sun can display, as if seen through a colour transparency. I will say nothing of the sounds, the smells, the rhythm of the women's hips as they walk with their headloads. The apostles of exoticism or of negritude, the transcriptions of the scholars, have already sufficiently described our villages and the markets of our cities. There is nothing more to be said. Unless by that genius whom the century still awaits, and who has only a few more years in which to present himself.

The city consists of two quarters: Moundié and the Plateau. Moundié is the African quarter of the colonial epoch, our Adjamé, our Treichville, our Poto-Poto, our Casbah or Medina. When the Uncles were in charge, we had no right to come out of it, except to go to work. If you look attentively at the map, you will see that the quarter is spread in the form of a Traveller's Palm. All the avenues converge on a central point, where a police post has stood ever since colonial times, which has long since become the Central Commissariat for the city.

In Moundié, all the main streets bear the names of the most prestigious tribes of the continent, along with those of our rivers, our districts and our divisions. There are two exceptions to this rule, however: the Avenue Charles de Gaulle and the former Avenue of France, now renamed Avenue Ma Mireille. There circulates, along with a little water in the street-fountains, a whole crowd of workers and idlers. Whatever their condition, they dance and sing, to relax, to seduce a girl, to forget, to weep for the dead at some wake.

There one seldom sees any cleaning services. Dirty waters drain as they please, whilst scraps and rubbish build mountains in the gutters, sometimes blocking up the channels, sometimes the roads. The dust of the dry season, the mud of the rains, the squadrons of ubiquitous mosquitoes and flies fight for living space in a cunning contest with humanity. There are smells here that act as landmarks at night for the children of the quarter. And I have spoken only of the centre of Moundié.

On its fringes, the last few years have seen the growth of Moundié-Vietnam, where all the latest arrivals from the bush pile up, paying rent to no one. They squat there while continuing, in some cases, to raise animals or plant gardens. "Built in the village, the same house might look less sad, and certainly cleaner," wrote one Uncle, only to be expelled by Daddy for trying to instruct him in urban development. Daddy's Minister of the Interior has found a most elegant expression to describe this zone: "the quarter of spontaneous growth".

To complete this description, it must be added that even in the centre of Moundié there exists an area more chic than the others. An area of solid houses, with tiles, running water, electricity, often a garage and television ariels. This is Moundié-loi-Cadre: the area once set aside for the élite emerging in colonial times, now inhabited by civil servants and small traders. Here lived the young compatriot Cabinet Secretary and all that crowd who considered themselves wiser than Tiya.

Between Moundié and the Plateau quarter flows the River Kunawa, which washes the banks and swallows the sewage of both worlds. A bridge joins them: it's called Hannibal-Ideloy Bwakamabé Na Sakkadé Bridge.

The Plateau is what we used to call the Uncles' quarter, in colonial days. Blacks never went there except in the daytime, to work. Nowadays its population is, on the whole, much the same, though more and more black officials and officers are beginning to move there. That's where Soukali and Monsieur the Inspector live.

The panorama from the terrace of Daddy's Palace never fails to move those privileged to view it, above all those of us who can compare it with colonial days. At that time, only "the building" displayed its six storeys above the low level of the other roofs. Nowadays, a clump (Aziz Sonika would say a forest) of new skyscrapers announces to the visitor that the capital is no longer a bush village. The farthest off of these buildings is the headquarters of the University. Nearer at hand rise the towers of banks, insurance companies, mining cartels and airlines. On all of these, Daddy has imposed a minimum height of seven storeys. (At first, the Uncles protested and complained that they couldn't rent the space, saying that if they couldn't build as they chose, they would leave the country. But their ambassador made them see that it was better to put up with Daddy's caprices than the *goulags* of a communist regime.) This creates in the air a festival of cement and glistening windows which makes the fortunes of architects, expresses those of the high-ups, and delights the cameras. Above all, affirms Aziz Sonika, it's a concrete image of Daddy's policy of development.

A little apart from these stands an immense tower of twenty stories. This is the Libotama Hotel, thrown up by a big international chain which came here to compete with us and break the monoply that we (I mean, my old hotel by the airport) had enjoyed since colonial days. Its entrance gives onto a vast esplanade, in the middle of which rises a statue of Bwakamabé, all in ivory and rising to a height of ... well, many feet, you know. Looking at it, one sees a Bwakamabé older and more careworn than in reality, with smooth, well-combed hair. He points towards the clouds and invites us to admire them.

Whenever it rains, I never tire of watching the slow dripping of rivulets over the polished surface, and I allow myself some doubtful thoughts about History and Immortality.

To support all this, and to ensure the comfort of traders, businessmen, officials, officers, ambassadors and technical assistants, a modern city has grown up, complete with office blocks, shops, hotels, cafés and residential areas. And this is Daddy's pride. Personally, I preferred our old capital. It was more modest, warmer-hearted, fresher to breathe in, and possessing, with its greenery and its trees, a human dimension that I no longer discern. But who understood that? Everyone urged that one mustn't be against progress in the country, and that the more one cut down the trees, those refuges of wild beasts, reptiles and mosquitoes, the better it would be. Before this spectacle of skyscraper and concrete, the citizen of Moundié declares: that Daddy, really, he works, and he deserves well from his country.

But I've said too much, and allowed myself too many indiscretions in my description. Some people might begin to think that it's in the capital of their own country that Bwakamabé Na Sakkadé lives, which is, of course, totally false and absurd.

To tell the truth, I must say the country concerned is not on any map. If you want to find it, it's in time that you must go searching.

So go on, turn the page!

After each swallow, the beer foamed for a moment on our lips. We had to lick it off. We tried hard to keep our backs straight. In the hall, French banners and paper lanterns swung in the powerful cross-breeze. All around us the Uncles, mouthing the oaths of sailors on shipboard, tried to catch the attention of the women by their monkey-tricks in imitation of Charlie Chaplin, while the champagne flowed in a thousand sparkling cataracts. From the beginning of the ball the orchestra, with condescending smiles, had dished out tangos, waltzes and other such steps. With our noses in our drinks, we amused ourselves watching the antics of these robots on a track, and the oldsters talking football.

A sophisticated West Indian shone out in the midst of this crowd, with the royal allure of a natural gentleman. We were all gazing at him, but he ignored us completely.

From the nearest table, over her husband's shoulder, I caught the sympathetic smiles of Madame Berger. She looked regretful whenever her gaze turned towards the dancefloor. The singer, grasping the mike with a dolorous expression, pronounced his vowels with a most curious accent, as he sang of sun, sand and muddy pools.

We were entitled to sit near the door. When the percussion began booming out the samba, one of us nevertheless got up to invite a woman to dance. A colleague from work. She glanced at her husband and regretted that she had sore feet.

The orchestra, now with straight faces, broke into a jazzy air. Ay, how we longed to move our limbs! The West Indian got up and gave a performance which brought down the house. Our own applause was more slack.

Taking advantage of the warmer atmosphere, the band gave a two-step. The dancers, singing words to the tune, broke away from their partners and made a ring around the floor, placing their hands on each others' shoulders. The shy ones were chivvied to join in, as the snake passed them. The rhythm reminded us of the méringué *and we joined the line. We moved forward, swinging our feet gaily. They improvised a series of movements—bowing, kissing on both cheeks, catching-the-star, bowing and curtseying again ... Strictly among themselves, of course. It was during these games that my hand rested a moment on Madame Berger's shoulder. We changed direction. Now we were two links in the chain. My hand tightened on her shoulder. She had her back to me and went on with her step. Encore after encore—nobody wanted to stop. A few people dropped their arms. The swinging band had managed to dissolve all the couples. Without a break, and amid a big roar of laughter, the band began a well-known Java. Madame Berger, firmly held my arms, began to turn around. With her breasts against my shirt, I led her in the movements of the kébé-kébé dancer. She pressed back against my hand, hard. Hard, hard, hard. I made her dizzy. Hard, my brother. I no longer saw the hall and she closed her eyes. We could almost have taken off. And the band delighted in playing ever faster.*

At the end, I had to help her back to her table.

As soon as the first notes of the next dance began, I saw her follow her husband.

At that time there were still civilian regimes on the continent. Every new republic capped with berets, helmets or képis made them tremble and sit up. In our country, with dread of the unknown gradually fading away, radio grapevine whispered that this was the Fascist regime prophesied by Polépolé when he was warning us against agitators. Then, insensibly, but quite quickly, people began to say that, all-in-all, life was much the same, just as God had made it for donkey's years now. The way one spent one's time—the shops, the schools, the factories, the offices, the hospitals—nothing much had changed. Everything had even kept the reassuring aspect of good old habit. No need to go on hoarding sugar and cooking oil, as one had begun to do at first reaction. One could go on baptising or burying the dead after the wake. The women were still fertile and, despite the smell of the maternity wards, still brought forth enchanting little creatures who were just as difficult to feed as ever, once weaned from the breast. Men continued to abuse fellows of other tribes, to go to Bangoura Prison for a yes or a no, to lose their jobs, to dance and to screw. Shops continued sticking on prices and officials going on overseas junkets. Life, in short. Was it more dangerous than before? No one seemed to think so. You had to read foreign newspapers to be troubled about our fate. They all insulted our new chief. They provided information we didn't have. Daddy decided to forbid the import of the Uncles' press to our national soil. Aziz Sonika supported this measure in *The Southern Cross,* where he explained that the presidential decree was healthy. He told us that all serious countries acted in this way, careful of the moral welfare of their children. We had to protect ourselves against the corruption of a West in the full fever of decadence. And anyway, what peasant in the bush was going to bewail the disappearance of trifles only a minority could afford? And Aziz Sonika called our intellectuals every kind of beast you can think of.

As for me, I arranged a means to get hold of this literature, which I devoured with the same relish that I had at one time bestowed on illustrated weeklies and at another on the publications of the Alliance Francaise. There I learnt that the *coup d'état* of General Bwakamabé had cost several hundred dead; that those democrats who refused to bow had been herded into concentration camps; that our liberties had been suppressed; that torture had become commonplace; that there was no news of our great writer Matapalé.

These articles were all very fine and proved that, even if we weren't afraid of what had befallen us, others were anxious on our behalf. But from where we stood, I repeat, reality seemed a good deal more banal. The guards of Polépolé and the forces that the foreign press saw as "lively and democratic" had soon let themselves be intimidated by the guns of the plotters. The democrats didn't acknowledge each other, and the prisons had been swollen above all with members of Polépolé's tribe. The camps? Why go to the trouble of creating institutions needing so much organisation? Lucifer's hell couldn't be worse than Bangoura Prison. Those who, like old Tiya, had experienced it at different times of our history, even claimed that it was more humane when run by the Uncles—something which I obviously can't believe. Of all those prisoners, the fate of only one seemed to trouble the Uncles: the writer Matapalé.

Of course, I too found his arrest unjust. He was a brave man, and unfortunate besides. Add to this that since my time at the Alliance Francaise I had developed a weakness for writers. But why did the papers weep only for Matapalé? All the unknowns whom Bwakamabé hurled into Bangoura were no less precious to their own folk. I've never understood why our leaders are always driven by a hunger to punish with imprisonment or death their defeated opponents, not to mention those who simply had the temerity to think "outside the ranks". The European papers knew of no one but Matapalé, whom they presented moreover as a writer of genius. There, they were certainly greatly exaggerating. *The Legends of Lake Eworowo* couldn't stand as witnesses against the severity of my judgement. They offer nothing of the marvellous or the fantastic, no real fire, and what magic there is, is displayed with great clumsiness. The *Grand Prix* of the French Union which he won proves nothing, if not that in those days other blacks wrote no better and that the Uncles stood astounded, as at a marvel, before even twenty pages written by a negro. The language is poor, in a style that borrows its effects, sometimes from that of administrative reports, sometimes from the swollen rhetoric of the age of Corneille. And I don't see any improvement in *Songs of the Baobab.* Those are certainly true alexandrines, but equally feeble, insipid, insignificant, tiring, overwhelming, soporofic, monotonous and grotesque, with all those piles of vocatives which are enough to make you sick. I couldn't finish them, even by pushing myself. No thrill, no life. I feel sorrier for the readers who have the courage to penetrate to the last verse than for the author, who had to arrange these posies of apprenticeship, like a schoolboy recopying his lines as a punishment.

All this campaign against the new regime seemed to have an effect on the other Heads of State, and Daddy found a certain difficulty in getting himself recognised by his peers. One of our high officials let slip during a conversation that it would be more prudent for the new Head of State to stay away from the next OAU meeting. The spies of Monsieur Gourdain got to hear of this and informed him, which sent him scurrying to the Chief.

Daddy's anger exploded as violently as a storm in the mango season. He had this enemy of the country (it was the Secretary General for Foreign Affairs) handcuffed and dragged before him, accompanied by the Minister.

"So, monsieur! It's you who don't want me to travel?"

"Mr President, ..."

"However, it doesn't surprise me. You Zukas have always despised the Djabotama. Do you really think it can go on like that, eh? Forgotten that there's now a Djabotama in command?"

The other man tried to babble a few words.

"You don't want me to meet the Emperor of Ethiopia?"

The Secretary General visibly had something to say, but he saw the futility of it.

"So, don't know what to reply? (Grimace) Your mother's cunt! Had your tongue cut out? Not nowadays. But dearly like to do it. Good enough at insulting me behind my back, but silent when face to face. Hypocrite! Pederast! Me, when I have something to tell someone, I spit it in his face, I do. Because I am a man, I am. A soldier. Not a Zuka." (Another contemptuous face) "Talk now, if you're a man."

The Secretary General opened his mouth.

"Stop it, now. Everything you're going to say is a lie. You Zukas know nothing else but lying."

He lifted his lion's tail over his head.

"Mr President, ..."

"No good spouting 'Mr President.' Agent of Polépolé, you. Know all your schemes. Yah! even you don't realise it, I know everything. Yah! no use making your little mischief there, like an innocent. Documents are there! You've been seen, and heard. I know that puppet of a Polépolé wants to come to the Summit to oppose me. And you, you don't want me to go to Addis Ababa to fight for myself. Your mother's cunt! Throw this bandit in prison and squeeze him a little for me."

He squeezed something in his hand and made a face. Two policemen seized the victim, while their leader, a sergeant or something of the kind, crashed his heels together and snapped his hand to the peak of his cap.

"At your command, General. We'll give him a good thrashing, as usual."

While all this group went off, Monsieur Gourdain silently approached Daddy.

"Punish him, Mr President, but, I beg, not the prison."

Daddy looked at him in amazement, then gave an exasperated grin and smacked his thigh with the lion's tail.

The morning after the ball, it was as if nothing had happened. Madame Berger did her work, I did mine. Not a word. Not a single allusion to the dance. Perhaps even an unusual coldness. As for me, I tried not to look at her skin the colour of a banana-palm's heart, her hair blacker than my face, rippling like a mare's mane and ending with that comma which curled it back up her neck again, those lemon-juice eyes.

I drew off whenever I sniffed her subtle perfume or when I saw her legs moving across each other as if in a gesture of protection. She mustn't discover my obsession. I buried in the deepest part of my being all the black in me.

The journey was prepared in feverish haste and Daddy, the General *emeritus*, attended to every detail.

A single order circulated among the staff of the Foreign Affairs Ministry: get recognition of Bwakamabé Na Sakkadé's regime, whatever the price. I saw him give instructions toward this end in the hut to Kijibo, the Minister of Foreign Affairs, sometime before the latter's departure for the city of the King of Kings, where he preceded us. Kijibo took pains to explain to the Chief the delicacy of his mission. Daddy shook his head repeatedly and called his orderly officer. After a short disappearance, the latter returned with an envelope, which Daddy proffered with a carefree air. I saw His Excellency Kijibo kneel down and kiss the hand of our Chief.

The nearer we drew to the date of departure, the more time the General spent on protocol and with his Cabinet. He lingered over the list of costumes. He made a list of all his decorations, planning his descent from the airplane in full parade dress, stars on shoulders and medals on chest. But Monsieur Gourdain intervened.

"If you'll excuse me, Mr President, I'm afraid it won't be...er...quite opportune to...Wouldn't it be better to make them forget...?"

Ya-a-ah, have to listen what this Uncle says. These people have experience of such matters. So he wouldn't wear the uniform of his new rank. Pity. But he possessed, apart from his dinner-jacket, as many different suits as there were days to pass in Ethiopia, plus more besides, by way of reserve.

"A president seen twice in the same suit isn't taken seriously. Don't joke with power."

"In Liberia, in Tubman's time, protocol demanded different-coloured costumes for various times of day. Light colours in the morning, grey in the afternoon, blue at early evening and black at night."

"It's not possible."

"I'm telling you, brother."

"Well, that's power, like I said. Don't joke with power. If you do, no one will respect you."

"In any case, what are twenty suits, for a president?"

The great Parisian tailor Serge de Ruyvère, of the Faubourg-Saint-Honoré, was flown over first class and accommodated at public expense, to work on the wardrobe in detail, and was able finally to produce a good two dozen of three-pieces, some Dakar-style costumes and innumerable shirts and ties, all bearing his famous monogram: SR.

Ma Mireille profited from the opportunity to order the latest creations from that year's collection. On the tailor's advice, she decided to include in her delegation the West Indian hairdresser Theodora, the same who has since become the world specialist in Afro styles, those plaits dressed in fine black cords over a close-shaven cranium, including the addition of false hairs and all those other ideas which have happily sounded the death-knell of the wig.

A certain newspaper, in revealing these facts, presented them as official secrets which it was the first to "scoop". Nothing could be more false. The movements of such personalities never pass unobserved. All this was done in broad daylight and every effort made to give it publicity. Not because somebody chanced to recognise them, but because our President so wished it.

Received by protocol in the presidential reception hall, Serge de Ruyvère and Theodora were interviewed by the press and their declarations widely broadcast, at the very time of the foreign paper's so-called revelation.

The former emphasised in his remarks the acute sense of elegance among Africans, which he associated with the flourishing of Black Art. Not *negro*. He didn't dare. And he affirmed that this was an aspect of our special genius to which particular attention must be paid. That, for his part, he was most willing to welcome trainees in his Parisian studios. No need to repeat that. Next day, some twenty tailors and various unemployed presented themselves at the Presidential Palace. Serge de Ruyvère firmly announced that he could not accept more than five. Daddy inserted one of his nephews, who was about twenty-two at the time and had just entered Class Five, after many failures and repeated years. He added three other Djabotamas and, on the advice of Monsieur Gourdain, one individual of another tribe.

The young compatriot Cabinet Secretary presented the itinerary for Daddy's voyage. He had to spend forty-eight hours in an East African country in order to make the connection; the only way in which he could arrive two days before the Summit. Unless he passed through Paris.

"They'd say that I went to get my orders from the Uncles."

So he chartered a special plane. The young compatriot Cabinet Secretary timidly suggested that the flight would be more convenient in the Commander-in-Chief's aircraft with its four strong, well-proven engines.

"Nothing for it but to hire a plane, look! Power is a serious matter. When one is looking for recognition by the OAU, one doesn't joke. One doesn't disembark from a scooter. Go and charter me a jet. Plenty of money here."

When the young Cabinet Secretary saw the estimate, he could think of nothing better than presenting it to the President.

"Well? I've already told you, for God's sake!"

The President rapped the table with his lion's tail.

"By the way, where's Yabaka just now?"

The reply came from the young compatriot Cabinet Secretary.

"All right, go and tell him to return right away. Must come with us to Addis. No question of leaving behind that..."

The message was sent on the spot. As soon as he got back to the capital, the captain asked to be received by the President. Serving Chivas and refreshments with an absent air, I managed to catch the gist of the conversation.

Yabaka made an issue of the concerns of the peasantry and the necessity he felt of remaining among them if one hoped to obtain, as already announced, some satisfactory results at the end of the coming agricultural campaign.

"You will continue on your return."

"Excellency, ..."

"Daddy."

"That's all right with me. But the farming calendar has its times and its demands which can't be deferred, Daddy."

"Everything can wait when the Chief commands it." Daddy reflected a moment. "Anyway, the technicians can carry on in your absence. Ministers shouldn't lose themselves in details."

But Yabaka loved to debate and I think Daddy was fed up. For him, a minister must instantly obey the Head of State, like a woman and children their husband or father. I know because I've often heard Daddy express his theories about power when he had occasion (which was often, for, as is well known, great men are ever alone) to lament the incompetence of his staff. As for Yabaka, he returned to the assault, demonstrating that in a country such as ours, and so on..., spouting the Uncles' tongue with the ease of a dancer wielding castanets. And Daddy was no fonder of this demonstration of his talents.

"Got to come just the same."

As soon as the captain left the Palace, Daddy confided in me, as I cleared the drinks table:

"His mother's cunt! This Yabaka, who does he think he is?"

Then he turned to the young compatriot Cabinet Secretary.

"Oh yes, my lad. I was forgetting. The treasurer must also be part of the mission. And you must tell him to bring all the cash with him."

And from the terrace he surveyed all the forests which covered the hills around the capital, with a roguish smile on his lips.

Soukali had informed me that Monsieur the Inspector was leaving for a mission on the other side of the world. For my part, I had told Elengui that Daddy was giving a reception and would keep me late that night. The children had drunk their Phenergan and were already dreaming about mountains of goodies. My foot had scarcely brushed the carpet of the Inspector's bedroom when I was seized by Soukali and we began to chew each others' mouths, ears, eyes, nipples, every inch of flesh, crooning like doves, closing and reopening our eyes, so full of recognition and invitation. With heavy eyelids, we rolled from side to side of the bed, jolting and grinding the mattress, checked only by those shrieks of surprise that make women more beautiful than ever and lend them an air of indulgence which makes the world look suddenly sweeter. Soukali unmasked her battery of positions and, having turned Monsieur the Inspector's portrait towards the wall, we tried out that of the tumbler and his assistant, of the willing captive, of the "slow Javanese" and of the Bengal Lancer, only to end with the comfortable dance of the missionary.

Her head sought the crook of my shoulder.

"You've neglected me all this time."

"What's all that? You know for yourself that it's not easy when your man's here."

"Yéhé! You're scared of him?"

I shrugged.

"What, then?"

"I don't like rows. Besides, if I did have them it wouldn't be good for you."

"Get on!"

She dragged out the *o*.

"Rows with high-ups like him are not a good idea, I'm telling you."

"What high-ups? Aren't you the *Maître* at the Chief's place, eh? Who'd be fool enough to attack an intimate of his? As for you, I just don't understand you. You could at least take advantage."

I put on an indulgent smile.

"But I myself know the real reason."

"What is it you know?"

"I know only for myself, *wo*!"

"I don't get you."

"You're scared, that's it."

"Scared of whom?"

"Of your Elengui-thing there. Yes, yes, yes. Anyway that woman has put *juju* on you. All Moundié knows it."

I shook my head to show her she was talking nonsense.

"My seer told me so. Anyway, he's more powerful than your *juju* man. If he wasn't, you'd have abandoned me long ago."

"I don't like discussing Elengui while my hands are playing truant. That would seem like deceiving her. Biting into another mango isn't betraying the mother of your children. One betrays her only when one bites her with one's tongue."

"Darling?"

"Eh? Cut it out. I don't like that word."

"Darling?"

As if she couldn't use my name! I'd like it better if she called me *Maître*.

"I want to get a job."

"A job?"

"Yes, I'm getting too bored, being a nanny to my children."

Soukali has got these white woman's ideas into her head. A job? As if the children, the household, the market, the kitchen and the wardrobe were not enough to occupy a woman's life. A job. When Monsieur the Inspector, with his salary, his extra quarter-salary, his expenses on this and his bonuses on that, makes enough money for himself, her, the children, the nephews, the parents and all the hangers-on of the clan. A job. All the women in the country are beginning to want to play the white woman like that. They want to have a bank account of their own, for themselves and their children, houses in their names... Aziz Sonika had denounced this trend in several editorials, but I hadn't really taken account of it until now.

"If you really love me, you'll help me."

Love. Love. A white woman's word, I'm telling you. Did our own mothers ever use words like that?

"What do you say, darling? You don't take enough interest in me, you know."

"And when I caress you and play about on the lawn there, I'm not taking an interest? What more do you want? Does Monsieur the Inspector know how to sort out your insides like I do? A chicken, yes. You said so yourself."

"If you wanted to, you could, you know. You've only to ask

the Chief and he'll give the orders."

Mam'hé. Poor me! I who thought that with you, at least, I could do the thing simply for its own sake. No strings attached.

But I couldn't resist. If I didn't quickly make love again, Soukali would pass to the attack, a smile on her lips, and make me her slave. Impossible to resist. After the missionary position, we tried that of the frolicsome convolvulus; of the slippery tench and the roach; of the life-raft, and of the mad horsewoman. After almost swooning, I promised her everything. Yes, I would talk to Daddy and he would arrange things.

An hour later, when I was pulling on my trousers, I began to ask myself how I could really broach this to the Chief. How could a nobody like myself succeed in convincing him?

That day, Daddy had summoned to the reception hall of the Palace the most celebrated diviner in the country, the same who had officiated on the night of his traditional investiture in the gardens. He also called his maternal uncle, some close members of the family and the Minister for Customary Affairs. I had to circulate about the group more frequently than usual, for the Chief was emptying his glass with unaccustomed rapidity.

This wouldn't do. This wouldn't do. Another gulp of Chivas. Pah! Weird dream, weird dream. He hadn't dared to shut his eyes since. Had made use of the occasion to check up on all the night watches and guard posts. Lots of 'em asleep. Had half-a-dozen of 'em shot since dawn. With immediate effect! No bureaucratic delays. Caught in the act, caught in the act! Hé! No joking with those things. We're not in a nursery school. No joking, either with security or with power. The others, straight to jail! Off you go! But this dream? No, this wouldn't do, this wouldn't do. The Head of Political Security, the very one who was advised by Monsieur Gourdain, had come to him with a gun in his hand and made him do "Hands-up!", just like in a cowboy film. Can you believe it? However, the man in question was one of the tribe. A real Djabotama.

Put at the head of Political Security for that very reason.

For his role in the overthrow of Polépolé also, of course. So, what then?

Daddy took another swig of Chivas.

I was in the corner of the room, silent and erect, with my friend the orderly officer. He, ready for any eventuality, had unscrewed the bottle top for me.

"Impossible. No, but..."

"Yes, it's possible."

"How, possible?"

"Just want to say...Listen well. That man is really a son of the tribe. A proper Djabotama. Even Libotama itself. Your childhood friend and schoolmate, besides."

"Even chased women with me."

"Your friend in everything you like. Your brother, in short."

Daddy nodded and took another gulp of Chivas.

"But there are some things that you youngsters don't know ..."

A story going back two generations. An ancestor of Daddy's had clashed with an ancestor of the Chief of Political Security, over a woman.

"Now, so it's like that, eh?"

At the time, the incident had been settled in a friendly way, according to custom. As for the dream, it was complicated. Mam'hé! Very complicated. Suddenly Daddy snapped his fingers. I came up to refill his glass.

"No, not you. Him."

The orderly officer came up at the double. Daddy whispered something in his ear. The latter shot off and came back with as many thick envelopes as there were visitors seated around Daddy.

The dream was a warning from protective forces. The ancestor of the Chief of Political Security had never really swallowed the way in which the quarrel had been settled. Like a toad stuck there, at the bottom of his throat. One had to be careful about his descendant. The spirit of his ancestor was sure to come some nights to the pillow of the Chief of Political Security and, my God, whisper to him, even against his will, sorcerer's ideas against the Father of National Resurrection. But no disquiet on that score. One was going (the country's most famous seer had opened his envelope and counted the bundles of paper printed with the Chief's effigy), one was going (the seer nodded his head), one would go and take care of the subversive spirit of this ancestor.

"But that won't be enough. I'll take care of the one who is already in the other world, you must take care of the one who is still in this world."

"And how! I'll sort him out for you, from today. His mother's cunt! I'll break him and I'll..."

"Calmly, calmly, my son. Calmly. Today, you are the Chief. The Daddy of us all..."

The General took a big swallow of Chivas.

"You are the Daddy of us all. One always holds back a little when aiming a blow at one's child. *Wollé, wollé?*"

"*Woï, woï!*"

"*Wollé, wollé?*"

"*Woï, woï!*"

A few hours later, the radio announced the first ministerial reshuffle since the coming to power of General Bwakamabé Na Sakkadé and the Patriotic Council of National Resurrection. The Chief of Political Security was, conspicuously, promoted to Minister of Culture, the Arts, Museums and Leisure, while Monsieur Gourdain had a new master in the person of Ma Mireille's same-mother-same-father brother, senior advisor on development and hitherto Counsellor at our London Embassy. There, he had covered himself with glory by the many messages sent directly to our Chief, thanks to which a communist plot was brought to light, organised by his hypocritical boss, Monsieur the Ambassador, in liaison with the sinister Polépolé.

The truth is that the successive directors of security were no more than front-men. The central and controlling figure, the real inspirer of perpetual repression, was that same Monsieur Gourdain to whom you have frequently, but always rapidly, alluded. As it is highly probable that he will still be in place beside Bwakamabé when your book appears, it is time to unveil to the public the career of this chief of all our torturers.

The only diploma he posseses, according to the *curriculum vitae* in his file, which I was able to consult at the time, is the Primary School Certificate. During the 'thirties, he was simply an obscure employee of the Credit Lyonnais at Nort-sur-Erdre, a little town in the west of France. An N.C.O. in the Fortress Infantry Regiment, and later in the Free Corps, he joined the colonial forces and served in Senegal during the 'forties. He commanded a parachute company in the Third Thai Battalion. He was among the defeated troops at Dien Bien Phu, where he was taken prisoner. Once liberated, he was admitted, by right, to the Senior Staff College in Paris, from which he emerged to fight in Algeria, where he held his first post in Intelligence. After auditing courses at the Security College in Paris (1959), he became adviser to the Madagascan Minister of the Interior (1960-61), served in the Comoro Islands (1962-63) and then in Fort-de-France, before being posted to our country. All this information, which I have been able to check with political colleagues, both French and African, proves abundantly that this sad character has a very low educational foundation, but has enjoyed a vast experience in repression, both colonial and neo-colonial.

His arrival was followed by that of a dozen bodyguards, all French citizens, charged with the physical protection of "the Marshal". In order to mute their presence and permit their use on trips abroad, they were recruited from among French West Indians. Their leader, on the other hand, was a white Frenchman (who was second-in-command to Monsieur Gourdain), and he passed officially as surgeon to the President.

Unlike other technical assistants, Monsieur Gourdain did not await the allocation of his villa by the housing committee before starting work. Right from the time when he was still living at the Libotama Hotel, he set about the reorganisation of the security services, selecting systematically all those people who spoke Kibotama, or who came from neighbouring areas, who were unemployed or had just been rejected by educational establishments. All this mob was to form the core of the secret police, hypocritically styled "The Presidential Documentation Service". Monsieur Gourdain also created an auxiliary corps, recruited by means of advertisements inviting the following groups to present themselves at the Central Police Station: all watchmen, all taxi-drivers, all café waiters, all the *maîtres d'hôtel* of those holding political office or high official rank. All those whose names or places of birth signalled the native region of Polépolé were dismissed out-of-hand. As for the "compatriots" of Bwakamabé, it was explained to them right away what duties they had now to perform, in addition to their official ones, and how much they would be paid. Finally, the other candidates were made to understand that, if they wanted to keep their present posts, it would be strictly in exchange for these minor services rendered.

At the same time, the streets of Moundié were suddenly flooded with young women equipped with scooters, nicknamed "the playgirls of Judas". Every minister was donated a brand-new telephone set, of the very latest type, free of any installation fee. These sets enabled the "Presidential Documentation Service", and even Bwakamabé himself, to tap at will all ministerial conversations.

At that time the capital already possessed several hotels, at least two of which were of international standard, each of them links of those well-known chains that have no need of publicity from my pen. One of these had also become renowned for its conference hall, in which many international meetings had been held, right from the days of Polépolé's rule. So all the facilities existed for welcoming the Heads of State of citrus-exporting countries, and the reception committee made its plans on a scale proportionate to this infrastructure, submitting an estimate which aroused the indignation of the Minister of Finance.

Daddy, who was asked to arbitrate, rejected the plans with disgust. Who did they take him for? O.K., the country was underdeveloped, even if he didn't much like the word.

But it wasn't the desert, nor yet the Sahel. Times were hard, admittedly, but a country which respects itself never exposes its buttocks, however poor it may be. Never. One musn't confuse modesty with vulgarity, or a sense of economy with misery, unless one wanted to spoil one's name, one's reputation, and that of all one's fellow citizens. All to the benefit of the opposition in exile and the Russians, who never lose an opportunity to encourage those bastards of the Fifth Column. No, no and no, it shouldn't go like this! At least, so long as he, Hannibal-Ideloy Bwakamabé Na Sakkadé, son of Ngakoro, son of Fouléma, son of Kiréwa, was here (he pointed impressively at the carpet with his thick forefinger). Even less so, when he had just been recognised by his peers of the OAU.

"'Sweet-Jesus!' as my company commander in Indochina used to say: 'You know how to win a fight, Hannibal. You know how to exploit victory!' We must immediately, im-med-i-at-ely, you hear? construct a complex of twenty-one villas, plus an international conference centre. More imposing even than the UN headquarters. So that posterity may talk about the Sun President!"

"But, respected President, recreator of the nation, we've only nine months left."

"And so? As if you hadn't been to China with me. Didn't you see over there monuments built in six months, eh? So, then. Why can't we do just as well? Bunch of natives, bunch of shit-carriers! What have the Chinese got over us, eh? After all they've only two arms, two legs, a head...and a prick. Like us. So-o-o, if you have a prick, nine months is enough for making a man. All the better for putting up a few buildings. Get on with it!"

"So, investment of human resources, eh?"

"Above all, no buggering around. Simple stuff. Instead of confiding the whole thing to one firm, it will be better to entrust it to a dozen of 'em."

"And the funds?" demanded the Minister of Finance, fingering an invisible wad.

"Funds? No problem. You always find them when you want to. It's the political will that really counts. If no one is willing to give you money, nothing for it but to print some. This is just the occasion to test the good will of those gentelmen who claim to be our friends. A developing country comes to them for aid. Concrete proposal this time! As for you (pointing at the Minister of Finance), don't just stand there with your arms folded like that. Time to fight *now*. Yes, fight! Flannel 'em. Everything depends on knowing how to present the problem to the Uncles. Go and fight!"

"A delicate matter, respected President. They handle these matters better at a summit meeting..."

And the country became a vast building site. What should we call this new complex? This was pondered from the beginning. Many proposals were advanced, but rejected one after another, some for being too pretentious, some for lack of originality, some for incompatibility with the line chosen for our national cultural identity. Finally unanimity was achieved and applauded in respect of two names: City of the First of April, for the whole complex; and Hannibal-Ideloy Bwakamabé Na Sakkadé Palace, for the conference hall.

Once the site was chosen and the plans accepted, the work rolled forward as if on wheels and because, as the Uncles say, you must build upon the rock. The blacks toiled, in a fever of emulation, like the yellow men, or the ants (or simply, like blacks), from the moment of sunrise to the first flutter of the fireflies; even during those hours when the air itself is like a rock and bellies sink into the calm of the sacred siesta. Work went on every day of the week; public holidays, Sundays (God alone knows whether the country will have to pay for this) and at night, under the arclights. On their own initiative, with an incomparable gesture of generosity, public servants sacrificed one day of office work, each ministry in turn, but excluding Sundays and public holidays. Aziz Sonika published and publicly declaimed a poem praising the glory of this innumerable host of pyramid-builders. The teachers at the high schools and colleges replaced their usual courses in practical work and physical education with these operations of "human investment". (Daddy raised his eyebrows at this, let it pass, but asked Monsieur Gourdain to keep a close check on it.) The primary school teachers led their pupils to sit beside the building sites, so as to give them lessons in practical morality, which began and ended with litanies of *wollé, wollé, woï, woï,* followed by the recitation of Sonika's poem. The Minister of National Orientation delivered a long and moving harangue on "the Model of the First of April", an example to inspire and concentrate much healthy emulation. Every day, delegations of workers flowed in hoards across the site and piled up around the works in progress: trade unions, Wolf Cubs, Scouts, Girl Guides, women's clubs, fishermen, benevolent societies, religious congregations, associations for feminine solidarity, the Great-Historic-Courageous-and-Intrepid Armed Forces, delegations from the provinces, ministers, artisans, cooperatives, the honourable wives of ministers (the mistresses, choked with jealousy, sought to ridicule this patriotic gesture by circulating scandalous stories, about which I express every reserve and which I refuse to report here) following the strong line taken by Ma Mireille, who intransigently chased away all the lesser "first ladies".

Since everyone had been invited to work "in the spirit of the First of April", the artists decided to popularize it in their own way. Painters and sculptors carried their easels, their adzes and engraving tools to the edge of the field of operations and there gave birth, amid trances and ecstasies, to thousands of canvases and statues, which all recounted and celebrated this modern epic of the nation. No day passed without a band playing for several hours in honour of the event. If each concert always began with "When Daddy came down to us from on high", they went on to compose great popular successes on "the model of the First of April". The young, always ready to exploit any situation to amuse themselves, spontaneously devised "the Dance of the Pyramids".

In his incessant war against bureaucracy, Daddy spent hours inspecting the works, never hesitating to put into effect any sudden inspiration, thus precipitating all kinds of last-minute changes which plunged the architects into high fever.

Thank God the "human investment" melted away imperceptibly, like a sweet on the tongue. Thank God! Because all this mob, who couldn't do a blasted thing with their hands, created every kind of obstacle to infuriate the workmen and overseers.

Once the work was finished, everyone unhesitatingly agreed to call it "the first miracle of the nation" and "the latest wonder of the world".

It was a jewel for its stonework, for the management of space and the style of decoration. Aziz concocted a piece of eloquence in which Daddy was compared to Pericles, and the City of the First of April to the latter's policy of promoting great public works.

*"...People of our country, you have every right to hold your heads high, for you have carried high the banner of our policy of national cultural identity, and have thus raised up, thanks to the dream of Bwakamabé, a work more solid and enduring than bronze..."**

He took issue with the prophets of doom who, mistrusting the creative capacity, innate genius and love of work of our people, had dismissed as unrealistic the time allowed for the project; who had claimed that the investment would not yield an economic return; who had dared to argue that the cost was beyond the means of the Treasury; who had maintained that it was bound to arouse the so-called anger of the masses, which had in fact been the chief beneficiaries, because of the many jobs involved.

---

*The young compatriot Cabinet Secretary, who knows his classics well, asserts that this "more solid and enduring than bronze" is a flagrant plagiarism from an author of Antiquity.

Yes, it had been a good thing. A coin lying in the road. Not only for the contractors. For certain ministers too, whose fortunes began with the bribes that came their way through this affair. But that's another story, which all Moundié can tell better than I, and of which the young compatriot Cabinet Secretary claimed to have proof of which he would make use, he said, when the right moment came.

The bauble was there, flamingly new, right on the summit of the hill, all ready for the opening session of the conference. The very evening before, Bwakamabé Na Sakkadé had passed in review and checked every last detail, from the dishes and the functioning of the TV sets to the presence of toilet paper and perfumed soap tablets in all the bathrooms. Not a single button was missing from a gaiter—everything was polished and gleaming for the parade. If there were blemishes, they came from elsewhere. From the guests, first of all. Nearly half the Heads of State expected were prevented from coming, in the very last days preceding the encounter, and had to send representatives; either in the shape of a vice-president, or a prime minister, or just a plain minister. Again, the weather: rain ruined the ceremonies of welcome and the opening itself; something which could easily have been avoided, God's Whorehouse! by generous payment to a top rainmaker.

"Their mother's cunt! Want to play it the European way. While we're in Africa, with all its mysteries. If I'm not there myself, to take care of everything!..."

Needless to add that once the conference was over, Daddy made another ministerial shake-up, in which the Minister for Protocol was the first to suffer. Actually, this was simply a regularisation, because he'd been thrown directly into the darkest cell in Bangoura as soon as the first rain began to fall.

"Natural? Hell no. An obvious act of sabotage."

Despite my lack of sympathy for Aziz Sonika, I've got to admit that the man is an artist endowed with a certain talent. No one knew better than he how to distract attention from these defects, which were, when all's said, no more than a few spots on a dark robe. Equally on the television and radio as in the printed media, he knew how to find the words and the tone appropriate to his affirmation that the people of the country, as much as the distinguished foreign visitors, were living through an historic event; that prosperity had reached new heights; that... And everybody asked nothing better than to believe him; the more so because the guests, "on treading the soil of this beautiful land", never failed, right from the airport, to breathe their satisfaction into the mikes of our journalists, without even bothering to glance at the streets and gutters of Moundié. But such is the courtesy of kings.

A presidential decree ordered four days of paid holiday, two before and two after the conference, to permit and give thanks for the general mobilization at the airport, along the course of the official cortege and all around the conference hall. A reward most certainly not unearned, because, despite the rain (consequent on not having summoned the rain-priests), the activists, dancers and spectators were numerous, everyone swarming in the hope of being mentioned in the attendance registers of party stewards. Only the big shops were deprived of this presidential generosity, for a further circular ordered them to keep their doors permanently open to the public, in order to avoid the disagreeable spectacle of a dead city, at the very time when we were living in the epic spirit of "the City of the First of April". The commercial world grumbled at first, but came to appreciate the gesture.

Greatly angered by the negligence/sabotage of the Minister for Protocol, Daddy felt it his duty to check all the details personally. Thus he came to modify the arrangements for the opening ceremony. No, he wouldn't welcome his peers, either at the bottom or the top of the steps of the new Congress Palace. No. At sunrise, troops of folk dancers and masqueraders to be all in place; several minutes later, arrival of activists and other guests to take their seats; same number of minutes later, seating completed for diplomatic corps; same number of minutes later, arrival of members of the government—seating completed; same number of minutes later, arrival of members of National Council of the Resurrection, to be greeted with a standing ovation;

fifteen minutes of musical interlude by the Thick-Lips Band and entertainment by the dance of the Shock-Troops of the Militants from District Seven of Moundié; arrival of representatives of absent heads of state (their mothers' cunts!), some applause, in proportion to the importance of their titles, gradually mounting to animated applause for the more significant; then, at five-minute intervals, the arrival of a head of state, ending with the most senior in actual attendance—loud applause and drum and bugles.

"Everyone will thus be in the hall for my arrival, and must rise as the Chief of Protocol announces my name and each of my titles. All of them, mind. All, you hear? Don't forget a single title, or else, watch out! And with no hesitation or stammering, either. Applause. Applause, I'm telling you. Take a note of it, or you might forget again. Ap-plau-se (he articulated the word, as if in a dream). Put it in black letters on the programs distributed to the guests. So everyone knows what he has to do, and no one has any excuse. Let's at least give our guests the impression that the country is well organised and loves its Leader! Sweet-Jesus!"

She would carry away the country, like a cloth wrapped closely around her. She would never forget the splash of the flametrees, the perfume of mangoes, the flesh of guavas, the sweet milk of soursops. Like a wound, the smiles of the men and the hearts of the women; like a troubling talisman, the vibrations of the drums, memories floating through and invading the rainy days.

I looked at Madame Berger as she opened her lips, the glass of champagne in her hand, her eyes reddened like the skies when the sun sets behind a bush fire.

There was clapping. She wept, twisting the ivory bracelet that our poverty of imagination had chosen for her parting gift.

Yes, we shall see each other again...

A woman must follow her husband according to...

For God who watches us all...

This sweaty awakening was to be expected. She had pursued me through the mystery of my night. Smiling, sitting cross-legged like a tailor, she talked to me in that voice which I have heard her use to comfort her child. A tangerine that slowly opens. A mother's voice. I was in the act of caressing her calves, moving up and down her legs with a soothing friction like a masseur. Blood flowed through me in all directions, stiffening my cock and swelling my heart. Breathless, I found myself sitting up in bed.

I would not sleep again. A storm was passing somewhere over the town.

Who can forget the entrance of Marshal Hannibal-Ideloy Bwakamabé Na Sakkadé, President of the Republic, Head of State, President of the Council of Ministers, President of the National Council of Resurrection, Recreating Father of the Nation, holder of many ministered portfolios to be included in his citation in hierarchical order, not a single one excluded, son of Ngakoro, son of Fouléma, son of Kiréwa, his breast many-coloured and shining with rows of decorations, to the sound of the famous "When Daddy came down to us from on high" played on the harmonium by the priest of St Dominique of the Plateau? I can still see him advancing, his face severe, like an actor fully steeped in his role, ignoring the familiar faces glimpsed in the throng, seated on a catafalque draped in velvet in the colours of the national flag and borne on the shoulders of four Uncles in the service of Monsieur Gourdain, while this last held an enormous state-umbrella over the head of our Chief. The applause burst out spontaneously. Spontaneously, I assure you. I saw it, saw it with my own eyes, I was there. Daddy is a dictator, right enough, but the people love to applaud him, as if they had need of him. However, the young compatriot Cabinet Secretary, former student of political science, never stops asserting that the people suffer under his tyranny; that they will one day awake, because they love revolution and the tradition of resistance to oppression; that the health of the nation resides in the people alone; that there is no such thing as a supreme saviour; that the little... Nevertheless, I assure you, at the cost of cutting off my finger, there are times when the people cheer Daddy with the same spontaneity as if he were King Pelé.

Applause and laughter, I swear, while the Chief blessed the room with his lion's tail, his face filled with a ravished smile. Applause and laughter, I tell you, which no one expected. There was certainly a moment of suspense when he was about to set foot on the ground, but it passed off well, which caused a doubling of the applause and of the most beautiful cries of *wollé, wollé, woï, woï.* Daddy, for his part, continued waving his lion's tail above his head, like a hand-bell gone crazy, then proceeded to hail each of his peers, replying to their congratulations and maintaining that it was nothing, it was nothing, really nothing. By the movement of his lips, his familiars were not sure whether he greeted them with "dear cousin" or buried them with thanks. A bit of hesitation; then, carried away by the African atmosphere, he accorded the same treatment to the representatives of all the absent heads of state.

Having completed all these embraces, Daddy signaled to the assembly, like the director of an orchestra, to be seated and silent. Immediately, a piece composed for the occasion was performed.

Union, unity, union
For the citrus-us-us-us,
Ehé, wollé, wollé, woï, woï,
For the citrus-growers.

The refrain kept repeating the name and date of the conference while each verse cited the name of a head of state, whether present or absent.* And applause was showered equally on all.

---

*While the names of the actual representatives of those absent heads of state could have been mentioned, it was judged prudent to spare them from possible tragic reverses on their return home, since standing-in for the chief can cost dearly on this continent.

Standing beneath his portrait, which was bigger than those of his peers, Daddy's face was highlighted by the flashbulbs of the press. Carefully distinguishing *é* from *è* and *ai,* on the one hand; *au* from *o* on the other; and finally, the *i* from the *u;* raising his head occasionally to scan the assembly, the General began to read the speech handed to him by his orderly.

He recited the titles of all the high personages present in the hall, ending with "Ladies and Gentlemen, dear Brothers". He seized the occasion of this event to express in the name of all our peoples, in the name of our principal institutions, and in his own name, all the pleasure which all those mentioned took in welcoming to our country, which he qualified as "great and beautiful", all these distinguished guests. And they applauded as if Mohammed Ali had just entered the ring. He wished them welcome and expressed the wish that their stay in our capital be as agreeable as possible, that their deliberations would be successful and would bear the stamp of African wisdom. (He finished the page and the orderly took it from behind him.) His welcome was equally addressed to the representatives of those organisations whose presence at this meeting, and the constant interest they took in our affairs, were so many eloquent witnesses to their solicitude for the welfare of our sub-region, rather than a simple manifestation of the necessary human solidarity before the grave and immense problems awaiting solution in the world today. He saw in their presence a mark of confidence in this enterprise and a token of success for the organisation. He recited yet again the titles of the heads of state, the Excellencies, the ladies and gentlemen, and affirmed that this meeting would take on a historic significance and a great importance on the economic and political planes, for this union consecrated a striking manifestation of the will of member states to work together and to pool their efforts so as to increase their efficacy in the struggle for the economic and social well-being of all their peoples.

I could go on for hours, imitating Daddy's style and those of his peers. Then you would conclude, and swear, that I had followed a course of instruction at the School for Heads of State.

In reality, I have no special merit in this direction. Every child in the country is as capable here as I myself. It's the result of the bath of sonority in which they grow up as soon as they leave the maternal breast.

In conclusion, Daddy asked all the fraternal delegations to excuse any shortcomings in their reception, which did not reflect any lack of will on our part to do things well, but a simple lack of means. He added immediately that in any case the brothers and (he smiled) the sisters of the country (he smiled again) would do everything possible to make their stay enjoyable.

This time the applause was as if an African team had just beaten Brazil at football. The Marshal, waving his inseparable lion's tail in the air, bellowed a series of hurrahs and rounded off with *wollé, wollé, woï, woï.* The hall rose and responded with a general ovation.

A few miles from the capital lies a mysterious lake, in the midst of which a little island, attributed to Mammywater, cast anchor centuries ago: Lake Lamartine, according to the maps issued by the Chamber of Commerce. The reader will easily recognise in this the consecration of a certain sickness of soul dating from a lost epoch. The Little Uncles gave it that name by way of mockery. But I don't mind admitting that the place attracts me and that I've gone to walk there more than once, first with Elengui, and then with Soukali, and several times alone, ignoring the sarcasms of the sophisticated. It is one of my Sunday promenades.

Daddy had the idea of developing the area. No advance preparations, a cargo plane simply arrived from Paris with its hold full of electricians to see to the lighting of the surroundings. A projector, like a powerful white sun, scrupulously cut out a piece from the black slab of the night. Everything was ready for the hour when Daddy, the great producer, could present his spectacle.

Everything began with a roll of drums, amplified by carefully disposed microphones and loudspeakers. A girl appeared, lifting a placard with the word *ANGOLA* written in phosphorescent letters.

Angola! A shout went up from every throat and, as if by habit, applause burst forth. The drum became more and more frenzied in its rhythm and shrill voices, almost nasal in tone, sang a ballad well-known around Libotama, about a young beauty loved by a crocodile. A group of young men and women began the dances. They mimed successively all the traditional labours of the countryside, season by season. The choreography was simple to follow and the hearts of the public quickened to it. I can still see Daddy bending to the ear of the guest on his left, then to the one on his right, and both of them nodding their heads at length in acquiescence. After the labours of the fields, the dancers broke into more syncopated steps, punctuated by strident whistles, and began to simulate, without disguise, scenes of joyful mass copulation. Cries of delight and cheers burst out behind the ranks of honoured guests, like a great flood suddenly set free. The chiefs in the front row, while carefully guarding their dignity, permitted themselves an indulgent smile addressed, I believe, as much to the performers as to the spontaneity of the crowd.

Suddenly, terror broke over the island. Canoes were landing a group of explorers in pith helmets who, armed with rifles and aided by Senegalese troops in red fezzes and puttees, began to kill and rob the population. The dance continued with an evocation of the forced labour system and the age of white domination. The Portuguese flag was hoisted to the top of the mast, while couples with their faces well plastered with cocoa-cream danced to the strains of *The Blue Danube,* accompanying their graceful circles with thrusts of the loins completely in our own style. Black servants waited on them, while "natives" in rags fought for the bones and crumbs carelessly tossed over their shoulders by the feasting colonialists. As the dance ended, the gentlemen accompanied their crinoline-clad ladies to their places, with the gestures of princes emerging from some Perrault fairy tale. Silence, silence. The call of a bird familiar to all inhabitants of the bush. And then, quite unexpectedly, real gunfire. Terror and panic among the Portuguese. And in me also. But we were quickly reassured. Everybody laughed. It was our army, which had landed on the islet with all its equipment and began manoeuvres as if on campaign. The dancing ceased, but the spectacle continued. Now we were watching a demonstration by the Great-Historic-Courageous-and-Intrepid Armed Forces of Daddy, showing off their technical prowess. They liberated Angola from Portuguese colonial domination, to the formal applause of the public. Looking carefully at the soldiers, one could distinguish among them some whose dress and headgear evoked the bearded Cubans. In the midst of this indescribable confusion, which could be appreciated only by specialists in the martial arts, the Portuguese flag was hauled down and that of the Angolan resistance slowly raised, below that of the OAU and above our own. When the gunfire died down, the spectators realised that this was the end of the show and applauded. Then the police band played our national anthem, resounded by the throats and chests of our countrymen present at this unforgettable display.

In recalling it, the Western press headed by *Gavroche Aujourd'hui,* ridiculed this manifestation, which nevertheless echoed profoundly in the hearts of all those who watched it. The visiting heads of state, when interviewed on the matter at the time of their departure, declared, in their various ways, that this was the didactic, militant and realist art that Africa needed; that it was a spectacle far preferable to the karate and gangster films, or the miles of pornography, invading our screens; that the African writers, whose poems were desperately penned in a charade of obscurity, and whose plays or novels revelled in a snivelling or subversive tone, would do better to absorb the spirit of this virile and moral epic; in other words, to take their inspiration from "the Model of Lake Lamartine"; that Marshal Bwakamabé Na Sakkadé, in short, was not only a great leader, but an artist and director of the first rank.

And *wollé, wollé, woï, woï!*

The man clad in the see-through white *bubu* was drinking-in the felicity of the blue evening, seated in one of the innumerable air-conditioned rooms of the Palace. The day had been quite full. Under the effect of the ice cubes, the Chivas—prepared by my own hand according to his taste—irradiated the glass with fine silvery drops. He had taken off his slippers and was wriggling his toes, lightly powdered after his evening shower. The sacred hour of television news filled the room. Thérèse Oualambio, dressed in a wrapper and a nobly elegant headtie, stumbled through the lines of one of the news agencies and distributed strained smiles to the anonymous spectators. Daddy took a slow sip of Chivas. He loved to see her like that, smiling in the glass window of the set. It was he who had put her there. She was his. Everybody knew it, even Ma Mireille.

Thérèse, relieved at having reached the last phrase, disappeared in a magical blink and one saw the Minister of Information, accompanied by a muted jazz theme, happily visiting the radio and television studios. I was standing in a corner of the room, silent and erect, with my friend the orderly.

A close-up of the Minister of Information.

"It's impossible!" (Daddy rapped the arm of his chair, hard.) "No, but..."

The Minister of Information beamed at the spectators.

"Your mother's cunt!"

Thérèse Oualambio's voice described the opening of a polio clinic by the Minister of Health. Daddy, suddenly on his feet, took a swig of Chivas.

"Their mothers' cunts!"

Then one saw the President of the Republic, smiling, affable and majestic, receiving the special envoy of one of his colleagues and dear African brothers. Daddy, who was striding towards a corner of the room, paused a moment to watch the sequence closely. As soon as it was over he resumed his rush towards the telephone corner.

"What the hell is this, for God's sake? Eh? ...Since when do ministers come before the Leader? ... Eh? Zero...Zero...Your mother's cunt! I said YOUR MOTHER'S CUNT. Got it? And what about the hierarchy? Eh? Fuck your excuses!"

I glided forward noiselessly to refill the glass of Chivas. Daddy, changing to another phone, talked to the Palace operator.

"Tell the Secretary General to call all the Council of Ministers...immediately! And jump to it!"

Some hours later, the radio told us of the third ministerial reshuffle since the seizure of power by General Bwakamabé Na Sakkadé and the Patriotic Council of National Resurrection.

What matter the price, I paid it. I knelt between the candles and opened my heart. I named the woman.

The diviner nodded his head and closed his eyes, with an understanding air.

I offered the snow white, immaculate cock. I was silent on the heart of the banana-palm. I spoke of her hair, blacker than my face, rippling like a mare's mane and ending with that comma which curled it back to her neck. I spoke of her lemon-juice eyes.

The diviner let the cock's blood spurt.

I was silent on the heart of the banana-palm. I spoke of the fire in my breast. I spoke of blood like the sea in the streets. I spoke of the dance and the obstacles. I spoke of the man. The ship on the water and the howl of the siren, lingering in my eardrums, never wanting to die.

The diviner threw his cowries. The diviner drew the sky in the sand and the world began to spin. The man of God gave out a devilish laugh. And I felt the force of it. I spoke of her hair, blacker than my face, rippling like a mare's mane, and which....

"Go, my son, go. She is coming."

I took my pen and my paper.

To recreate the meetings of the Council of Ministers a book cannot serve my purpose. A film would offer greater possibilities.

The members of the government were all required to attend before the Leader. Frisked at the door by an orderly, they had to give up their pistols, which were restored to them upon leaving. The Director of Protocol would check that all the ministers present in the capital had responded to the summons. Then an electric bell would sound: once, twice, thrice; then came the fierce reply. The Director of Protocol announced, in the voice of a herald, the arrival of "the President of the Republic, Head of State, Head of the Government..." and followed with a list of all the other titles and government posts held by Daddy.

The ministers stood up like good-mannered schoolboys in a classroom, while the media filmed the scene which, however, was repeated every time and never varied. Daddy could now make his entrance, lips wreathed in that benevolent smile that had been taught him by one of the technical aid workers who served as protocol adviser. He blessed everybody with his lion's tail. He shook hands with each of his colleagues, making a patient circuit of the table, but always in an anti-clockwise direction, as he had been warned by his diviner. Then he regained his place, where the Director of Protocol awaited him, offering him the chair with the highest back. Daddy arranged his arms like a Muslim at prayer and then sat down, followed by all the others.

Each minister then opened a thick attaché case lying before him. These were of a well-known brand, which I shall decline to publicise further here. A film-maker would have loved the scene because, shot from a certain angle, it was just an array of attaché case lids, listening to the proposals of the Chief.

I had the right to stay in the chamber, to serve refreshments, empty ashtrays and carry out messages the ministers scribbled to their staffs, as need arose.

I clearly remember the debate about democracy, introduced after a shower of leaflets fell on the town.

Captain Yabaka made a long confession of faith in favour of freedom of opinion. It was necessary to let every point of view in society find expression. The more one prevented the people's right to criticise and protest against their leaders, whether justly or otherwise, he asserted, the more one increased either the potentiality for violence, or the inertia of the masses, either of which rendered the task of government more difficult. He invited everyone present to harken to the voice of the people, that great sound that swelled above their collective march, and which heralded their labours, their productions, their creations, their joys and travails, their struggle to live or simply to survive. These were his exact words. A lyricism to strain the guts. See how I am moved by it even today, in my efforts to recreate for you the Captain's voice.

Someone immediately replied by extolling the virtues of the one-party system. It was the only realistic solution for the country. Democracy must be pursued, of course, but not by aping the whites. Authorizing several political parties would only encourage a realignment in antagonistic tribal blocs, and promote fratricidal conflict. No, not a single example could be quoted where this system had worked in Africa. It would never work. Africa was not Europe.

The next speaker stressed that the fight against underdevelopment imposed the need for a strong regime: "Don't be afraid of words, we must have a dictatorship: a dictatorship expressed in the interests of the people." And he cited, by way of examples, pell-mell, Nasser, the countries of the Far East, Stalin, Hitler and Mussolini.

At this point, I missed some of the discussion, because Daddy signaled to me and whispered something in my ear, sending me out to look for a file forgotten on his desk.

On entering his study, I had a brief moment of fright: a noise just behind me. A lovely young thing was waiting, yawning upon the sofa...

I re-entered at the moment in the debate when a young orator was stigmatising the blackman's complex about the judgements of the West. He slashed asunder the French paper *Gavroche Aujourd'hui,* which dared to caricature our presidents without having its journalists flung into prison. He demonstrated that to hold elections in our country, even under a single-list system, would simply create opportunities for disorder by power-hungry politicians.

Many nodding heads.

This was the last speaker.

During a long and heavy silence, the President shuffled his papers. Then, gravely, he scanned all round the table, his chin slightly lifted.

I looked at Yabaka. I thought I discerned, for only an instant, a desire to return to the charge, to add one forgotten point. No.

"No?"

Daddy then thanked everyone for the frankness of his contribution. The debate had been conducted "at a very high level" (unanimous nodding of heads). This showed the maturity attained by all of them in the exercise of power. Daddy continued by singing the praises of democracy and of elections. Then he mentioned, in vague terms, the ancient kingdoms and empires of Africa. He spoke of the wisdom of the ancestors. He spoke of our traditional societies, our pride in being Africans and the danger of letting ourselves be dissolved in the corrupt and individualistic morals of western countries. One must be realistic, and take into account the *specific* social and psychological structures which no western theory had studied, or at any rate, understood. It was all very nice to dream of elections. No doubt that would legalise the regime. But that would be to fall into the weakness of *legalism*. When what was needed was to show confidence in the direction taken, in those who had had the courage to save the nation when it was on the brink of the abyss into which Polépolé threatened to plunge it. Ever since Africa was Africa, the chief of the village, in our culture, had never been elected. To thirst nowadays for innovation in this domain was to be as uncustomary as asking a man to do the cooking or carry a calabash on his head. Notions of European pederasts! No. The chief, that was always the bravest, the wisest, the best orator, the man with the strongest fist. He imposed himself through the occult will of the dead, and everybody recognised him. Whoever dared question his authority was immediately called to public account and punished by the community, which crushed him like a cockroach. The vote was a hypocrisy of the white mentality.

In a sound family, there was no place for a child who wanted to command in place of his father. If he was a real member of the family, not a snake or a slave, he wouldn't be afraid to make his disagreement known. He would express it openly. What was all this nonsense about wanting to write on an anonymous paper, while hiding yourself in a booth? We musn't encourage that kind of *falsity.* Against the education of our ancestors, dead against it. Of what should he be afraid, a son like that? Of what, tell me, if what he said to his father was just? Eh? If he needed the protection of booths, it was because he knew quite well that what he had in the back of his head was some filth which would anger his poor old father; some nastiness of no importance. Because, after all, the country was one big family.

"*I, I am the father. And you, you are my children. All the citizens are my children. You must advise me with frankness, or if you want to spare me, for fear of my reactions, you must keep a respectful silence.*"

The truth was, he claimed, that the vote was "a huge bluff", a hypocrisy, an institution that favoured those whose reputation was already made (God knew how) and who talked well, which didn't prove anything, and certainly not their honesty. It wasn't the most forceful that the illiterate and irresponsible populace would chose. Irresponsible, there you are! That was the word he was searching for, that fitted. To abandon the choice of guides for the community to a chaotic mass, was to renounce that innate sense of responsibility that resides in the breasts of all those who feel themselves to be chiefs. He knew he had been chosen by the Eternal Will, and that it would be a sacrilege to put that in the balance with a population armed with votes. There could be *from thence forward* (as a result of reading this expression in the speeches prepared for him, he had naturally adopted it) no question of ceding power to a rabble bemused by Satan. Only the influence of divine inspiration could induce him to place his power in play, or to renounce it. Don't joke with power. He was ready to fight, to die and to kill to keep in his pious hands the power conferred on him by God. Yes, African societies, by tradition and historical necessity, needed to be well controlled and well directed. If not, gods of our ancestors, what would become of us? What would this country be like? And Bwakamabé replied to his own question, carried away by his peroration: *"A hash of different tendencies. And that isn't the way to govern. No. That's the way straight to anarchy, the bed warmed for the communists."*

He rose, eyes widened and full of fire, mastering his voice with difficulty.

"May God protect you all! Go in peace."

He blessed them with his lion's tail.

No one had the right to leave the chamber before him, and no minister before his senior in the order of protocol. Myself, last of all.

One minister was looking around him with an embarrassed air, an envelope in his hands. He wanted to get a signature from the Chief. I took the document and tried to enter Daddy's study. The door was firmly shut. I knocked, but my blows were futile, muffled by the padding.

The lovely young thing, no doubt!

...I have just met by chance the former President Polépolé. They talk about a leader of the opposition in exile; what I met was the mere shadow of an ex-leader, who seemed anxious to forget and to make forgotten that whole slice of his life which he had devoted to politics.

Arriving in France without a penny, he had been able to get help from a few reliable friends, some heads of state among them. In seven years of power, he had put nothing aside. Just a small house in our country, which he hadn't finished repaying to the Development Bank and which Bwakamabé had nationalised with a tremendous fuss, as though what was in question was the fortune of ex-King Farouk; to whom, in any case, Polépolé was compared by Aziz Sonika in editorials of a nonsensical and disproportionate rhetoric. A number of his former colleagues—heads of state, that is—maintained a discreet friendship with him. Some had even invited him for a private visit, but he didn't want to put anyone out.

Did he dream of recovering power?

Now teaching Oriental Languages, he had a comprehensive distrust of those who came to talk politics with him, suspecting them either of provocation or of flattery, neither of which he would have anything to do with. Although he was very concerned about the situation in the country, he was visibly unwilling to plunge again into a world the mere memory of which sickened him. But this silence of his, so unusual among defeated political animals, caused disquiet, and he was constantly plied with the most fantastic projects.

He met few people and kept both his address and telephone number secret; at first, to leave undisturbed the warmth of a family life which he had happily rediscovered; later, in order to devote himself totally and with all the necessary concentration to a research project which was related to our country, but of a purely scientific nature. The countries of Africa, from which he was physically separated, filled the pleasant atmosphere of his modest apartment through his books, his paintings, sculptures and artifacts created by our many craftsmen.

As for his real intimates, he had occasion to correct them, in a friendly manner, whenever they addressed him as "Mr President". Rather than that title, which he was trying to forget, he much preferred that of "Professor", in recognition of a *métier* whose nobility he was constantly praising and from which he had been too long removed.

When someone asked him why he had chosen Paris for his refuge, rather than some country closer to the political orientation he supported, he would smile with a quick, discreet shrug and pass to other matters, or else take his leave...

All his collaborators, bureaucrats. All his officials, bureaucrats. All the civilians, bureaucrats. Always shut up in their offices, curdling under the air conditioners, imagining that everything was going well in the land. It was to be wondered whether they didn't do it on purpose, these sons of bitches. The military men had to go out into the field, to take stock of things. Physical control, if you like. While those fellows there... In God's name, wallaya! he was alone. They had no understanding of power, that lot. But for him, the country would plunge into chaos. All of them incompetent, starting with the intellectuals. Theory, theory, all very well, yes. Especially with those acrobats of a foreign tongue: French long, long, long like so. But practice, but action? Zero, as round as my eye. Ah! what would become of the country without him, eh?

Action, it's my whole life. After the war (the Great War, against the Kraut) I could have retired into civilian life. With all my medals and my pension. Like lots of others. Become an old soldier for the rest of my life. Led a snug life in the capital, or in the colony. No. That's not the life for a Bwakamabé Na Sakkadé, son of Ngakoro, son of Fouléma, son of Kiréwa. Me, I preferred to re-enlist. Preferred action. Action.

Indochina...

Indochina? All I can say is that it's a marvellous country. In those days, at any rate. Now, with this American war, and then the communists, I can't say what's become of it. Not the same thing, you say. Must be a shitty place, now. But then, ah! a little paradise. A marvellous country for us French colonial soldiers. Sun always shining, sky always blue, like at home. Couldn't find anywhere better.

The whites and the yellows were strictly separated from one another. Almost like the whites and the blacks here, before independence. But over there, we had the right to be with the whites. Normal, no? Those yellow men, with their eyes like slits and their miaowing language, you can never tell what they're thinking. Hypocrites. Heartless people. Indifferent to suffering. And what's more, cunning with it. Not like us blacks. The yellows were in minor posts. No yellow allowed in white society. In government administration and in commerce, there wasn't a single one in a high position. The nickname for a Vietnamese, for example, was nhaqué *and he had no right to a high post in the administration, even if he had a doctorate. Whether he was qualified or not. That wasn't the question. He just couldn't get in. A* nhaqué *was a* nhaqué... *But we others, we colonials, we had a lovely war in Indochina.*

"Protocol, Protocol! You take all the precautions for me. This afternoon I'm going to visit the farm at Kaboula. No publicity. No journalists. Surprise visit. Just to see if those bastards are really working, as they claim in their reports. Shake up that whole civilian bureaucracy a bit, you see?"

In fact, my friend the orderly officer had already given me wind of the affair.

"But, above all, don't say a word yourself. Don't give me away"

"Hey! Who could I tell? You too, what do you take me for? Tell me, am I the treacherous type?"

"Ah, if you blab it out! That man doesn't joke. Anything like that and *pfft,* he'll chop off my head."

Everything had been arranged so that the Chief could make a secret assignation in a presidential villa on the outskirts of the capital. As for me, I took the chance to ask for my half-day off. If only I could lay hands on Soukali...

Daddy waved and moved his mouth in a way which conveys in our language that there's no problem.

But Ma Mireille cut in.

"No, I'm sorry. I shall need you, *Maître*."

The camel! The shrew! I could have squashed her, the little whore. Exactly what I suspected, what I had read in her look: that woman can't stand me. She's happy just to cross me, yes. And this Daddy who doesn't say a word. Ah! that one, in front of Ma Mireille... Just when I wanted to take the chance to go and see Soukali. A good moment like this isn't easy to come by. She informed me just last night that Monsieur the Inspector had left for some mission in the Americas.

"I'm expecting to receive some friends," Ma Mireille elaborated.

Pouting like a child denied a visit to the cinema, I began arranging things so that the President's lady and her friends wouldn't lack for anything to embellish their gossipy hen-party. Lemonade, beer (especially Gloria, our national beer), tea for some of the snobs, European fruit and cakes, embroidered cloths and napkins, silver dishes, flowers—nothing should be lacking. But in which room was Ma Mireille going to receive? Cécile, her lady-in-waiting, knew nothing of the matter.

It was siesta-time. In our country, waking someone from their siesta is like taking food from a famished dog. And if it's a Mrs President who's involved...Above all, as was evidently the case, when she can't stand the sight of you... It would be wiser to wait.

A moment later, Cécile came to tell me in a mocking tone that she, the slut, had been given leave for the whole afternoon.

"Madame is tired. She wants to be alone."

And the little miss tossed that to me between snatches of song.

What on earth does it all mean? Let that little whore go to hell! And I myself am not free? Really, that woman detests me.

And at the last moment, she rang for me.

Ma Mireille was stretched out in a long beige nightgown. A transparent bottle through which I saw the body of our mistress, with her two little well-formed mangoes. I was embarrassed and my heart began to beat like the tom-tom at a wake. It was as if I had spied my mother's nudity. And wasn't it a bit like that, after all? But I knew how to control myself. It wouldn't do if she guessed what was passing in my head. She would immediately have me put down as a sex maniac. And she hated me quite enough as it was. She was capable of saying that I wanted to rape her. And then, Daddy... Yé!

"Madame needs me?"

"Ah, it's you, *Maître.*"

A voice which seemed to reach out from a world of suffering.

"A glass of water with plenty of ice, please."

She moved her gown a little and it fell open, revealing a thigh and calf gleamingly naked. Not a swelling calf, nor a plumped-out thigh, but the long limb of an antelope, lean and fragile. Not the fragility of sickness, but of a flower one longs to caress.

"At once, Madame."

Mam'hé! I came out wringing my hands. What a whore, that woman in there!

When I returned, bearing the glass of water, I found the room a little darker than before, as if the curtains had been drawn. Ma Mireille had got between the covers. I saw the transparent nightgown thrown over a chair. Her arms and shoulders, which showed above the sheet, were naked. I proffered the glass. I could see those mangoes.

"Madame doesn't need me any more?"

The reader can easily hear my dry throat.

"Wait a while, *Maître.*"

This was whispered in a lazy tone.

"Wait ... Oh! my head... Am I feverish?"

Kibotama or French, both my languages collided.

"Feel my forehead, *Maître.*"

Not hot. She must have felt my hand tremble.

"Ah, my dear. My heart, my heart. Feel how my heart is racing."

I placed my hand there, where the President's lady wanted it. She hoisted herself slowly, like a wriggling snake, murmuring in a suppliant and plaintive voice.

"Yes, *Maître...* Yes."

I was terrified and didn't really know what was happening. And my pants were straining outwards. Ayay'hé! Suppose this woman were to die? A President's wife, dying in the presence of her chief "boy"...Yé! It would be the scaffold for me.

"No, *Maître,* not the doctor. I've no confidence in those people. Don't leave me, *Maître.* Don't leave me."

She grabbed me and pulled me towards her. And my pants were straining.

"Ah, *Maître,* I can't stand it any longer. I can't stand it. I need you. Come."

Having lost my balance, I had fallen on top of her, lying in a ridiculous position.

"Yes, *Maître,* yes."

Her voice pleaded.

"Yes, *Maître,* yes."

Yé! But who, who had dared to thrust me into bed with the President's wife? Between her fresh sheets?

"Yes, *Maître,* Yes. Oh! Oh! Oh!"

I feared I might have hurt her. Who then had dared to thrust me?...

"No, *Maître.* No, no, no."

Her eyes closed.

"Yes, *Maître.* Yes. A chief, *Maître.*"

Ma Mireille was ablaze, a real daughter of Moundié. So well educated, too!

"Oh, yes, *Maître.* Yes, yes."

I suddenly took the measure of my responsibilities. I had to rise to the height of what was expected of me.

"Ah, *Maître,* what are you doing? What are you doing? Ay! You're going to tear the heart out of me, *Maître.* You want to take it all? Eh? Eh? Is that it? Eh, *Maître?* But why? Oh, *Maître!*"

Too late. No wind could now hold the buffalo in all his strength. He was giving. He was giving, giving, giving.

One could no longer awaken in the mornings without finding the streets of the capital strewn with leaflets demanding elections and dressing Bwakamabé in the names of various birds, fishes or beasts of the savannah. At least, not if one rose early. For the services of Monsieur Gourdain, long before those of the street-sweepers, gleaned the tarmac roads of the Plateau as thoroughly as the muddy lanes of Moundié.

Other leaflets claimed to speak for the *avant-garde,* arguing that soldiers are not equipped to guide the state properly and would do better to return to barracks, leaving the way clear for the "vital forces truly representative of the toiling masses." Early-rising citizens found these appeals plastered all over the walls, insolently blotting out the most scintillating brands of toothpaste and the sexiest brassieres. They clung to the trunks of trees, to letterboxes and even to walls of public latrines.

Monsieur Gourdain threw into action his whole regular army, plus his auxiliaries. Working day and night, they finally managed to catch, in the very act, some young fellows with Afro hairdoes who, once thrown into jail, immediately confessed everything. How many they were (few); who was their leader (nobody could decide); where they printed their clandestine literature (the duplicating room of a school in the quarter). They were well beaten, threatened with the most exquisite tortures, and wasted no time in spilling the beans. The leaflets were only the first step. They claimed that in the second phase they would become urban guerrillas, that they counted on having the collaboration of certain cadres maintained by Russian and Chinese scholarships (in those days, Russia and China were lumped into the same bag) who were training in secret camps in Guinea, Congo-Brazzaville, Algeria and Tanzania. A serious matter, a very serious matter, this conspiracy of "the Gang of Twenty"! Just as well they had got wind of it. Thanks, incidentally, to one of Monsieur Gourdain's spies who had infiltrated their ranks.

As the enquiries continued, whereas we thought them closed, we were informed that, at bottom, all this was by agreement with Klein's mercenaries. The corporals of Monsieur Gourdain's army even managed to mix up Captain Yabaka's name in the affair. Something which the authorities never confirmed, while taking care not to deny it.

All the youths who sported Afros were rounded up. The zeal of Monsieur Gourdain's henchmen was not cooled until they had arrested a superb mulattress who called them all kinds of shit, in the Angela Davis mode. There were days under arrest, transfers to distant posts, reprimands written into the record, dismissals without pay and retirements.

They laid hands on a young professor of philosophy whose hairstyle resembled a Russian flat cap and who disturbed them even more by his lectures, in which he had declared that God did not exist, adding that *the thing* was just as important as mathematics and deserved a whole course of education to itself. He was a well-known character in the capital, and above all in Moundié, where the young called him Spinoza and their elders considered him a sympathetic eccentric, no more dangerous than the madmen who wandered naked through the city. But there were those who had marked him down for a long time and many complaints had been lodged against him in former days by the parents of foreign students. These had been shelved, since the authorities suspected in them a plot by the Uncles to ruin the first black philosopher in the country. Of course, when the political scandal broke, the Uncles declared that it was only to be expected, and that if their complaints against this vicious freemason had only been taken seriously, matters wouldn't have come to this pass. Spinoza defended himself like the devil, repeating everywhere that they wanted to submit him to a rerun of the trial of Socrates. The police informers reported his words deducing from them that the man was a "blockhead", a "fool", and that they'd have to lay hands on this fellow Socrates if they really wanted to get to the bottom of the affair.

"No, no", corrected Monsieur Gourdain, intelligently.

"Sly, the professor. Very sly. He acts the simpleton, but he knows plenty."

The young compatriot Cabinet Secretary approached Daddy about the business, but was advised by him not to meddle.

"Very complex affair, my boy, but I'll consider it, all the same, since it's you who's raised it with me."

The teachers at the Hannibal-Ideloy-Bwakamabé Na Sakkadé School got together to make representations to the higher authorities in favour of Spinoza. Whatever their countries of origin, most of the foreign teachers refused to get involved in a political matter. From temperate, foggy or continental Europe, as also from the New World, they reckoned that this was a palaver among blacks. Two exceptions showed among the Uncles, however: a long-haired professor and a white girl in jeans put their names down for the delegation which had to present itself before the gates of the Presidency.

We learnt from Aziz Sonika that on the night following the request for an audience, the two Europeans were chucked onto the first plane, and their black colleagues handcuffed and dragged to Police Headquarters. Our journalist wrote a long editorial, his pen filled with venom and roasting a whole kekab of the most choice insults in our rich vocabulary of political polemics. The girl in jeans was clearly a whore who sought to assuage her sexual desires through romantic gestures in very doubtful taste.

Aziz Sonika claimed to have proofs of her involvement with Spinoza and of plans for an orgy which the two scoundrels wanted to organise with their students, in the disgusting tradition of modern bacchanalia practised in those decadent societies from which the strumpet hailed and to which she had now returned. The hairy Frenchman, "a vulgar leftist drop-out from May '68", was accused of wanting to foment, in our "beautiful land", the uprising which had so dismally failed in his own. He and the black teachers were simply agents of Moscow and accomplices of mercenaries. The Russian ambassador protested and, in response to the snub received from our Minister for Foreign Affairs, withdrew all his aid workers. Aziz Sonika grabbed the microphone in the radio station to demonstrate that this was the very proof that Moscow was somehow involved in the whole affair.

The young compatriot Cabinet Secretary saw a gross provocation intended in these events and wanted to approach Daddy about it.

"The story isn't quite clear to me."

"But look, *Maître,* how can you stuff Moscow, the progressive African regimes and the mercenaries all into the same basket?"

"Who knows the father of a bitch's litter? Take care, my friend."

Once back in Paris, the hairy Frenchman and the girl in jeans made their statements. The left and ultra-left press made great play with them, while a big French evening paper published only a short extract buried on an inside page. A morning daily replied with an article which tried to demonstrate that independence had been too big a gift for them. The Rights of Man had fallen into peril.

In any event, none of this fine literature penetrated our way. In Moundié everyone assumed, when making his analysis, that the rest of the world had the same opinion as that supplied by our talented *griot* Aziz Sonika; that it was a sad business and that the best course, all things considered, was to resign oneself to it.

When I recall images of that time, I can't help remembering my mother asking me, uneasily, when we would see the last of that independence kerfuffle.

"Everything was much calmer, before."

It irritated me to hear that. As if we could stay for ever under the heel of the Uncles!

As for the young compatriot Cabinet Secretary, he had a head stronger than the rocks under a waterfall. Despite my prudent advice, he went to plead on behalf of his friends.

"If you were not a son of the clan, I would consider you just an exclamation mark. I've already told you that I will reflect on it. But you are really naive, my boy. These fellows there are not, believe me. Rum fellows. Rum fellows."

And Daddy repeated that, if there were many more such interventions, he would add the young compatriot Cabinet Secretary to his list of exclamation marks.

"And this Socrates who can't be found!"

Monsieur Bruno de la Roncière, the French Ambassador, requested an audience, which was accorded to him in the round hut. Serving the drinks and keeping close enough to watch for refills, I managed to catch the essentials of the conversation. The diplomat began by announcing that the F.A.C. had agreed to finance a bridge over the river which flows past the entrance to Libotama, the Marshal's native village, and had decided to grant a credit of a billion West African francs for some other project. The young compatriot Cabinet Secretary took note of this, Daddy shook his lion's tail from time to time.

"And where do we stand with my request for an increase of the French garrison here?"

"I'm coming to that, Mr President."

Daddy shook his head comprehensively and shut his eyes, giving another lash of his lion's tail.

Describing the debates in their National Assembly with one hand in the air, evoking the contest between two ministers with the other hand, demonstrating their political struggle with both arms in the air and practically with the same gestures as our children at an evening wake, the Uncle assembled bouquets with that beautiful language of theirs.

"Can I therefore assume that the thing is going well?"

The young compatriot Cabinet Secretary got ready to note the answer. Daddy chased the flies off his legs with big sweeps of the lion's tail.

"Don't make me say what I haven't said, Mr President," the diplomat resumed, a smile on his lips and his head slightly inclined, as when one is trying to seduce a woman. "The Elysée is following...uh!...is following the matter very closely."

"You must insist, insist with the Elysée. If they don't wake up, the Russians..."

"I will note your remarks, Mr President, and your message will be faithfully transmitted. But here and now I am authorised to assure you: France..."

"Your Excellency, you know that I'm a military man of blunt speech. Tell my brother the President Pierre Chevalier that I never believe promises. I need actions. I need those troops."

The ambassador took from his inside pocket a folded envelope and wrote on it solicitously. Daddy lowered his voice.

"It's extremely important."

His throat sounded tight and hoarse. I hastened up to refill the glasses.

"Hear me, now. No confidence in these natives, I haven't. Don't know how to fight. Not like me. Never made war. Me, I'm a former Free French soldier. Look at that!"

He jumped up and exposed the wound on his thigh, then excused himself.

"The soldiers of the Mother Country, they at least are..."

The ambassador was pinned, blushing, to his armchair.

"...the finest soldiers in the world!"

Monsieur Bruno de la Roncière thanked our President. He broached then the final point of his interview. After some humming and hawing, he observed that, in this atmosphere of subversion—which must be attributed to external forces seeking destabilization—his government wanted to express to Marshal Bwakamabé Na Sakkadé its sympathy and unwavering support.

"Better say that to the press here."

His Excellency made a gesture which indicated that this could be dispensed with.

"Definitely. Must declare it."

Monsieur de la Roncière coughed a bit and stirred in his armchair.

"Certainly, there isn't any problem about that... But I don't want to commit an indiscretion which could be damaging to you."

Daddy lifted his eyebrows, one higher than the other.

"Oh, yes?"

Monsieur de la Roncière coughed some more.

"You know how all this rash and extremist opposition always claims—quite wrongly, of course—that you do nothing without consulting us. They even go so far as to insinuate that you are..."

The ambassador coughed again.

"I'll employ their own disrespectful expression...our 'creature'."

Daddy rapped on the tightly-stuffed arm of his chair.

"It would seem sufficient, therefore, if I were to confirm our support officially, to make all these interpretations..."

The diplomat made a vague gesture. Daddy took his lion's tail and began to stroke his chin with it, as if with a badger's brush. At last, he nodded his head. Monsieur Bruno de la Roncière's remark was pertinent.

The young compatriot Cabinet Secretary was taking notes. The diplomat announced some measures against the long-haired professor in spectacles and the girl in jeans.

"Is that all?"

Monsieur the French Ambassador explained that they were in the middle of an election year and that...also...the unions...you understand. Daddy sighed. The diplomat continued that the project of a state visit by President Bwakamabé Na Sakkadé was viewed favourably, but that it was advisable to avoid drawing the attention of the French press to events in the country; that the French government had absolutely no desire to meddle in the internal politics of (here he spoke the name of our country), but that he suggested, simply *suggested* that the case of the professors be kept separate from that of the leaflet campaign proper; that the former could be released; that one hoped that, if the latter should be punished, it would not be at the cost of human lives; that anyway Monsieur Gourdain, with whom the ambassador had already discussed the matter, was well aware of these realities.

The young compatriot Cabinet Secretary was noting every word with the diligence of a student. Daddy rapped with frenzied insistence on the stuffed arms of his chair.

"Yes, if we could only lay hands on that Socrates!"

The audience having finished, I saw the young compatriot Cabinet Secretary conduct Monsieur Bruno de la Roncière onto the steps of the Palace, with great ceremony and solicitude.

Daddy, left on his own, watched the procession of the clouds, the colour of river water, advancing or halting overhead.

"*Maître,* some Chivas! And leave the bottle here."

In Algeria, against the Fellaheen, *I was already in command of a company. About a hundred and fifty well broken-in boys who dearly loved a scrap. Two sections of Senegalese riflemen (lots of Voltaics among them, really, as well as Dahomeans and Togolese), a section of local guides who knew the area well (brave fellows, loyal to France) and a section of French paratroopers (professionals in the martial arts). Ah! all of us good comrades. Real men. True men. No more races among us. All united in the same blood.*

We are the Africans
Who've come from afar.
We've come from the colonies
To defend our Mother's star.
Wives and friends we've left behind.
Papom papom papom papom pa-pom
Papom papom papom papom pa-pom...

The group of guides was particularly solid and united. When the Fellaheen *caught them, they didn't burden themselves. Tchiouf! no quarter. No prisoners. They loved me, those guides. One day, those young fellows came to see me and said: "Captain, we're coming with you the next time." I had already increased my reputation with the Operation Batna.*

At the beginning of September 19.. or 19.., no, it must have been 19.. . Yes, that's it. Same year when we captured Si Lacheraf, the great Fellah *of the Aurès Mountains. Already twelve years ago. God's name, whorehouse of shit, how time passes! Well, at the beginning of September 19.., they told me they had desperate need for shock-troops for the Aurès region.*

They said to me: "Bwakamabé, you have been proposed: if you want, you can go there." And I went. I took my paras and my guides. Goes without saying that I took the Senegalese riflemen (many of them Voltaics, Dahomeans and Togolese).

We are the Africans
Who've come from afar...
Papom papom papom papom

After resting several days at Lambèze, I got orders to go on and take Khenchela. On 15th September I moved to the attack.

Commandant de la Martinière, Pierre de la Martinière, who was my head of operations, then told me: "We're going to Khenchela. And from there onwards, Captain Bwakamabé, you will be in charge of operations." That's all ...

If anyone comes to touch us,
To touch us,
We will be there to die at his feet,
Yes, at his feet.

At Khenchela, in the Aurès, I began by making a circuit of the town. This was necessary, if only to show the Arabs that the French were there. During my training at Pau, I'd been told that French troops had a fantastic reputation among the Arabs.

Then I decided to go to the nearest farm house.

It was about thirty miles off. I had confirmed that there were Fellaheen *in the area. The so-called FLN. Revolutionaries, men dreaming of the liberation of their country, but socialists, too socialistic. They'd never have won if the French at home, intoxicated with communist propaganda, hadn't stabbed us in the back.*

When I arrived, I found the white settlers of the farms in a good position. They hadn't been disturbed, and they said to me: "There are plenty of rebels in the area, but the situation hasn't yet become dangerous for us." That's why I didn't evacuate them. Told them "O.K., if you feel secure, stay here."

Next day, I continued my advance. With my blacks, my Arab guides and my whites. I began Operation Tebessa... And I finished it successfully. In a few weeks...

The young compatriot Cabinet Secretary touched his brow and grimaced. Neither water, nor wine, nor herbal remedies could relieve his malady.

We were discussing the coming match. Voices floated out of the windows. Backing this club, abusing that one, and believing intrinsically in the vision of the diviners. Hands were clapped, gods were called to witness, someone gestured as if to cut his throat.

The young compatriot Cabinet Secretary touched his brow.

"Let me just get rid of this."

Yabaka smiled. The old man was thinking.

We turned to the subject of pretty girls. Those of the swaying wrappers, the dances and the flicking bandannas. We made mock fights, we measured boastful words. We remembered whole verses learned in the forest. The old man seized the torch from us and turned them into song. She was beautiful, yes indeed, don't you see? Whistles thrown at her all along her way, like confetti, my brother. Even an Uncle among them. All the profits he had made through dealing in ivory tusks. Two dead, so they say. One stabbed, the other through drink. A queen who drove men crazy. She gnawed at my breast, too. Ah! what a superb conquest she made of me! Nudges and giggles behind my back. Tiya went on with his poem, drunk with this breeze from the past.

But as for that one, the young compatriot Cabinet Secretary—neither water, nor wine, nor herbal remedies.

Like a fever in full flow: Zola, the Algerian war, Dreyfus, Sartre, names, names, names. Names from Asia, Latin America, Haïti, enough to burst the pages of a dictionary. And the prison too.

"Yes, a Ché in every heart. No scraping that out."

Yabaka, with his eyebrows crooked, was stroking his moustache.

"One more martyr doesn't change the course of things. The day of the hero hasn't come yet."

"At least, let's protest."

"Pouf! protest of despair... Against whom? The gods?"

The laugh of a malicious child.

"Listen, boy ..."

A hand on the shoulder of the young compatriot Cabinet Secretary.

"Boy, the air is infested with bugs which are spreading madness."

Laughter from the teeth and deep in the bellies.

How good it was at the old one's house. The glasses overflowed upon the table and his voice closed our eyelids. Hours of glory and hymns to bravery resounded from the walls. The chambers of our lips resurrected epics long buried. Mysterious names, jawbreaking in their scansion, flowed in endless waves along our guitars. It was back then, never mind the date, it was back then. We heard, shining with faith, machetes cutting into the thickets, biting into trunks as round as the earth, cutting...wanting to eat into the rock to hew from it warriors with gestures of fire. How many rivers and savannas, how many mountains and forests, how many precipices, how many dry seasons leapt over? How many buffaloes, elephants, lions and pythons put to flight? How many tortoises startled? How many grass-snakes, vipers, hyenas and scorpions crushed? How many moonless nights, when the hearts were paled by the gibbering of corpses? How many moons must the caravan continue? How many days, how many drinks, how many heavy crosses, to reach the goal? And you forget already. And you will forget again. It's a long march through the entrails of the earth. And the blacks always forget. And longing to take the road again, our backs to the sea. And to set off, barefoot, emptyhanded, a fly-swatter as your only shield, words in the drum, the word as talisman, like the promised lamb. And the blood in the sea, then? As if the sea could ever wash it away. As if everything could be invented anew.

How many crosses still on our shoulders for having insulted our mothers? How many stakes ahead for having too soon dropped the hands of our fathers? Thus passes away, like life itself, the grease of the palm snake, rotting. But in the decadence of time, let's still respect the vanished grandeur.

Tiya thundered as if on the day of resurrection.

If your teeth are respectable, it's thanks to good habits.

The young applauded, laughing with amazement.

And suddenly, the radio. News to make one rub one's eyes. As if the pleas of the young compatriot Cabinet Secretary had lodged in the soft flesh of that heart on high. So now, listen. The laws, in their quagmire, can they still...? Let me laugh... The air is infested with bugs.

The radio was precise. Only the professors. Let the others rot in what seems to be their natural hole.

And those others—Spinoza at their head—who refuse the hand offered by the Saviour?

"They asked for it."

In Moundié, everyone admired the courage of these youngsters, though still wondering whether it was wise to rouse the panther, when you've lost your gun.

I've read your last installment in one go. Remains to be seen whether it will have the same interest for those who've never lived in the country. You have told very effectively the story of "The Gang of Twenty", just as I recounted it that evening when we met at old Tiya's. But was it necessary to emphasise my support for those young victims? I did no more than my duty, and if everything like that has to be looked at in terms of calculation, I'm afraid those good actions I've had the chance to perform are far fewer than the times I've kept quiet, from fear, even if that tended to pass unnoticed in the ocean of silence in which we lived. However, it's necessary to know that there were other anonymous comrades who began at that time to work for the undermining of Bwakamabé's regime.

You alarm me with all those daring love scenes. In reading them, I couldn't hold back a mounting sense of disquiet. Without claiming to be any saint in my private life, I ask myself whether one has any right thus to confuse politics and porn, without risking that the one will spoil the other?

When you first broached to me your idea of writing these satirical and critical memoirs of a slice in the life of a dictator during the last part of our century, I encouraged you, and even offered my collaboration. It's a question for me, I repeat, of contributing to the struggle against that tyrant Bwakamabé. Now, by the way the manuscript is developing, as for instance in this latest installment, I fear that in yielding too much to intimate memories, you are mixing up genres and losing sight of the objective of all committed writing. And the African book coming from these times, and having any respect for itself, cannot choose but be committed...

Daddy was reading aloud, following the words with his finger and articulating each syllable with the care of a master giving dictation, bringing out as clearly as possible the difference between the *é,* the *è* and the *ai,* on the one hand; the *o* and the *au* on the other; and, finally, between the *i* and the *u.* Daddy was reading more than one report. Jeddah, the emirs, the oases, the harems, the oil, the royalties, the dollars, the dollars, the dollars...

His Excellency, our ambassador, had been able to watch that very morning, thanks to television, an event celebrated with great pomp, all organised by the Grand Chamberlain in one of the city squares. A hooded executioner, after reading a few verses from the Koran, had chopped off the hands of a string of robbers.

Discipline. Discipline. Civic spirit. We have lost that. People don't work any more. They steal. The black has reverted to his blackness. We must reintroduce the lash. At bottom, those were good times. In nineteen thirty-something (the year when Governor Marchetti replaced Governor Berthiaux), I entered the French Army, in the section called Militia. Second Class Rifleman. Stayed two years in that rank. We were well trained. That service in the French Army was extraordinarily encouraging to me. Could do sensational things, that I could never have attempted in an army commanded by blacks. In any case, there weren't any in those days. Learnt discipline. A soldier is nothing if he doesn't know how to obey. All men must learn how to obey. If not, no question of being able to lead. And it was precisely in the French Army that I learned how to obey. That's why today...

"Ko-ko-ko-ko."

"Come in!"

It was Za Hélene, Daddy's eldest sister.

Reality sometimes comes up with these coincidences. And the fate of whole peoples sometimes depends on them.

"Hannibal, Hannibal, it's me, your sister Za Hélène. Damned bandits! Show me that you are a chief. Show that you're a man. Show that you're my younger brother. The best of my brothers. The only brother same-father-same-mother. The son of Ngakoro, son of Fouléma, son of Kiréwa, all brave ancestors who never heard of an injury without making those who dared defy them swallow their own blood and shit. (A jet of spit on the floor.) Ayay'hé, ayay'hé (a clapping of the hands). Hannibal, it's me, your sister Za Hélène who's talking to you. Robbers...no doubt Djassikini (a curse on their mother's darkest parts!)—never could Djabotama do such a thing—came to our house. They burned that herb that brings sleep, then killed our dog (those sons of bitches). They plundered the whole house, all, all, all, all. These savages, these niggers (absolutely, a curse on their mothers' privates!) crept right into the room where we ourselves were sleeping. No, no, we heard nothing, because of that drug they burned which brings heavy sleep. Then they (a curse on their mother and their grandmother!), they shaved the pate of my husband. A Greek merchant! A white man! Shaved the head of a white, like a common prisoner... Gang of Savages, get off! And then they, they...in the name of the Father, the Son and the Holy Ghost, my God, forgive me for what I'm obliged to tell, they sprayed me with their milk; I, Za Hélène, sister of the whole country's Chief, daughter of Ngakoro, son of Fouléma, son of Kiréwa, who never heard of an injury, without making those who dared defy them swallow their own blood and shit.

Ayay'hé, who will repay us for our lost savings, ayay'hé! (The Chief patted her head and sent for the orderly officer, who returned with an attaché case full of envelopes.) Hannibal, my brother, we must be revenged. We must revenge. In the name of God (she cut her throat with her forefinger), if you don't punish these thieves, these dirty natives—all Djassikini—you'll lose your own authority. In the name of God. The people are disappointed. Really disappointed (a grimace). There are too many robbers. They say it, but they don't dare say it to you because you're the Chief, because the protocol even to come here is too complicated. They say that with a military leader, they were hoping that the rule of discipline would return, the rule of work, of peace, of tranquility, but now it is the contrary. They say they're fed up with it. And the whites, above all the Uncles, they say if it goes on like this, they want to go home, *wo*! They think highly of the countries of coffee, cocoa and oil. Paradises upon the continent, free of bandits, and most important of all, with guaranteed security of capital. *But now,* if they really go, what will become of the country? *But now,* if they stop investing, where will you draw your power from? Hannibal, my brother, this must stop. You must punish. Make examples."

"Their mother's cunt!" yelled the Chief. A yell like that of a giant from whom a live fingernail has been torn.

"Their mother's cunt!"

The same night, a radio announcement called all members of the government to an extraordinary meeting of the Council of Ministers.

A very brief one. The President explained what he wanted, while calling on the Minister of Justice and his Supreme Court to devise appropriate legal terms. Any person (citizen of the country or foreigner) who stole a bull, or just a piece of wool, or anything inferior, equivalent, intermediary or superior; furniture, building or ringing piece of metal, would have an ear cut off; in case of a second offence, the second ear would go; in case of a third, amputation of the right hand and in case of a fourth, public execution in the main square.

She has come. I knew it.

The power of the diviner, the power of my words.

That skin the colour of a banana-palm heart, that hair blacker than my face, rippling like a mare's mane and ending with that comma which curled it back to her neck again. My hand has stroked it, my tongue has licked it. Ah! Madame, do you feel how I speak of you? The lemon-juice eyes have slid under their lids. My head between your knees, you have let me play with my tongue. You were more beautiful than ever, Madame, your hands clutching at the lifebelt of my hair.

Why this rough awakening, enough to kill us both? I was still... No, Madame Berger won't be coming back.

Your smile like a waving handkerchief on the horizon.

On July 13th, the whole capital, civilian, military and diplomatic, was summoned at nine p.m. for a spectacle of "sound and light" in the marketplace. Daddy wanted to kill two birds with one stone: "Punish with maximum suffering" all the robbers and the "Gang of Twenty", with their accomplices—all in one go. The officials, as if in rank, were ranged along the stands, fascinated by the circle of white light. An orchestra opened with the popular *beguine*, "May Daddy Bwakamabé live for centuries and centuries."

Then Protocol announced the arrival of the Leader. He smiled and acknowledged with a nod of his head, with perfect presence, the well-managed ovation of the audience. A claque then shouted slogans of loyalty, followed by *wollé, wollé, woï, woï,* charging the atmosphere as at a football final. Marshal Bwakamabé Na Sakkadé extended a hand to command silence and discipline. Really, that man has power over the *labouring masses*—if the young compatriot Cabinet Secretary will permit me to use his jargon. How to explain it? For to listen to radio grapevine, there's no doubt that the masses still retain their critical faculties. We whose souls have been whitened in school can no longer comprehend the native psychology. Only the traditional priests possess the secret of Daddy's power of fascination. The young compatriot Cabinet Secretary calls him a dictator, but a dictator, let's admit it (even if it goes against the grain), who's *beloved* and apparently needed here.

Then the Chief spoke. He spoke without notes, as he loved to do. His assistants didn't trust it, and the professors and schoolmasters feared it. He recounted the history of "The Gang of Twenty". A gang of "Moscow's apprentices". He declared that if these puppets didn't like the country, they had only "to go and make themselves heard among the snows of the Red gulags". (The Russian Ambassador rose conspicuously and walked out.) The Chief repeated that we were in Africa and that in the real Africa of our ancestors, the chief of the village was the sole master. In that Africa, opposition was unknown. There was applause, and it was difficult to decide whether it came from the *labouring masses,* the national officials or the diplomatic corps. I believe that, yet again, under the effect of Daddy's secret *juju,* a general hypnosis compelled the whole crowd to clap their hands. The Chief promised that he was going to punish and make suffer, well-well-well, all these little gentlemen. Their mother's cunt! He described, in a tone of lamentation that aroused pity, the misdeeds of the robbers. Their drugs which induced sleep. The heads shaven. The male milk in the faces of honest and faithful wives. The diplomatic corps looked like pupils who try always to sit in the first row. Same attitude. Same attention. Some of them were writing notes on their knees. The crowd exulted in reply to the tone of a village orator. He assured them that such things had never been seen, but that, thanks to God, and above all thanks to Himself, inspired by God, this slide into decadence was going to stop. In the name of God, bilai! He described again the ordeal of his sister. The milk of bandits upon her face. He described what was done in the Persian Gulf. They didn't joke there. They cut off the hands of robbers. Gba!

Applying himself to distinguishing carefully the difference between the *é,* the *è* and the *ai,* on the one hand; the *o* and *au* on the other; and finally between the *i* and the *u,* he read through the ordinance of the Supreme Court. To his mind, the country should turn solely to amputation. Applause. The *juju,* I'm telling you. And Daddy plunged, without a backward glance, into a long story which was quite beside the point. Off the subject, as they would have said at the Saint Raymond of Penyafort College. But Daddy, whatever Aziz Sonika may say, was one of the dunces at school. He took vengeance now upon the good students and the professors. Natural, no?

We had to listen to an hour's discourse before he consented to reveal the evening's program to us.

At the rise of the curtain, the "Gang of Twenty" and their accomplices, with bare fists, were confronted by the same number of adversaries, but all with gloves! The best heavyweights of the National Boxing Club, reinforced by the toughest of the Chief's own gorillas. A boxer against a distributor of leaflets. And let there be knockouts! Thirty thousand francs per K.O.

Each of the prisoners was carried off on a stretcher. Like so many inert rubber dolls.

The high point of the evening, the robbers. All handcuffed. Confronting each of them, a soldier, helmetted to the eyebrows and armed with a wooden cudgel. Daddy had ordered severe punishment. That they be beaten "well-well". His instructions were precise: one soldier to each bandit...let everyone go through it...you can beat them to the point of death...even in military manoeuvres, some losses are expected, so...

Let no one look here for an account of this bloody circus stunt. How could one describe the scene of violence which followed, and grew ever more atrocious, with the devilish rhythm of an animated cartoon? I hid my face in my hands. But there were still the cries.

One of the Uncles' papers, under the title "Bloody Ballet at...", told the whole story. Their mother's cunt! Daddy summoned Monsieur Bruno de la Roncière, and our Minister of Justice was instructed to make a demand straight to the Paris lawcourts for an action against the paper, for "insulting a foreign head of state".

The event fell during International Book Day. I don't remember the exact year. What does it matter, anyway...

The Writers' Society of our country had organised for the occasion, in the Hannibal-Ideloy Bwakamabé Na Sakkadé Gymnasium, an exhibition of works by all our poets, novelists, dramatists, literary critics, philosophers, sociologists, psychologists, educationalists, linguists, historians, geographers and scientists of various disciplines. To encourage, or placate the egos of some impatient aspirants to the title of author, and in response to political pressures ranging from the discreet to the crude, the organising committee had finally admitted to the glass display cases certain typed and duplicated manuscripts and even some works published at the authors' own expense. Only the works of Matapalé were missing. Although Daddy had released him from prison, he remained the victim of censorship decrees.

The Marshal in person, "in spite of his many burdensome duties", came to honour the opening ceremony, in the course of which he was hailed unreservedly as "the new black Augustus, great friend of literature and the arts, protector of all creative spirits", by the president of the Writers' Society, who went on to suggest a whole series of measures to the benefit of those who assured the renown of our culture in Africa and thoughout the world. Loud applause, in which Daddy applauded himself. In his turn, the Minister of Culture, having thanked Daddy for attending this ceremony, "modest as it is", something which "abundantly proved, if proof were still needed, his interest in affairs of this kind", went on to compare the number of authors published under colonial rule, under the rule of the "sinister" Polépolé, and since the coming to power of the Patriotic Council of National Resurrection. The comparison, according to him, enabled one to declare irrefutably that our President was "a Maecenas and an indefatigable inspirer of our entire artistic production". Before Bwakamabé, few if any works worthy of interest. Since his coming, hundreds of them. This passage was loudly applauded, especially by Daddy.

But once the speeches were back in the pockets and the

opening ribbon had been cut, the Chief's face changed expression. A cloud suddenly obscured the sun of his pupils. The man within was absent, far away from the explanations furnished by the President of the Writers' Society in conducting him round the stands. His eyes desperately searched for a book seldom sighted anywhere.

He cut short his visit and didn't attend the customary cocktail party.

Before anyone could understand what had befallen and while attempts were still being made to construct explanations, a radio communiqué summoned an immediate meeting of the Council of Ministers.

A pile of books on the table before him, the Chief was already awaiting the members of the government at his place in the Council Chamber. The ministers arrived one by one and took their places in an oppressive silence. Members of the presidential entourage kept bringing more copies of the same book, laying them like bricks on Daddy's table.

When the Council was complete, the Marshal began the proceedings by assuming, with disquieting naturalness, the voice of the Guinarou.

"Can someone explain to me why not one..."

He nearly choked.

"...not one of my books was exhibited? Eh? Just explain that a bit."

The Minister of Culture, sweating at every pore, tried to provide a response, thought he had provided one.

"And these, then?"

Daddy pointed at the pile of books with his fat finger.

"All shit, this lot? Your mother's cunt!"

He hammered the table with his fist. And he talked, abused, talked, abused, showed his fist, insulted, talked, so that...(dragging out the *a*).

And so it was that this day saw yet another cabinet reshuffle. The portfolio of the Minister of Culture was taken on by the Marshal himself.

Daddy had decided that he was born precisely in 1923, the Year of the Pig, if one follows Chinese astrology, on the 5th of August, under the sign of the Lion and not just "somewhere about then". So every year on that day the Nation was entitled to a paid holiday, with many messages of congratulations and an editorial penned with special skill by Aziz Sonika, who compared Libotama to Bethlehem, the Chief's mother to Mary, and the Chief himself to Bonaparte on the Bridge at Arcoli, then to the Messiah, and finally to King Christophe. If the anniversary fell on a Sunday, a decree would announce the closure of factories, offices and shops on the following Monday. Generally, the Saviour took the occasion to amnesty some prisoners, so relieving Bangoura Prison, where they could no longer be properly fed, despite the high ratio of deaths, compared with the statistics for other prisons in the world. Or so I was informed by the young compatriot Cabinet Secretary, whose information about everything was extraordinary.

That particular year, Daddy decided to give a garden party. By virtue of my office, I was the principal organiser.

I should have listened to Elengui and paid more attention to the signs of nature.

The dry season had been abnormally long. For several weeks, we nervously awaited the coming of the mango rains. Many times the sky was covered with heavy slate-coloured lumps, the wind raised the reddish dust, but the sky, with agonising coquetry, simply refined our longing for the expected deluge. People kept asking who had tied-up the rains, then they would fall back, prostrate in the humid heat. The weather-watchers had a field day. The most informed argued that it was a manifestation of the southward march of the Sahalian drought. In Moundié, the elders affirmed that they had never in their lives seen such an infringement of the laws of the seasons. It was just not normal. Some recalled, with shaking heads, that in olden days the mango rains came, with the punctuality of the moon itself, to their annual rendezvous with the Fifteenth of July; but that, of course, since the Russians and the Americans—nowadays even the Chinese—let off more and ever bigger bombs and threw themselves into an insane contest in firing those objects, manned or otherwise, into the atmosphere, in defiance of God, everything was upside down and nothing could happen as before. My mother maintained that these anomalies were signs from the Eternal One, announcing the imminent arrival of the Antichrist. The destruction of God's handiwork had begun, and the end of time was approaching apace. Mother multiplied her prayers, burnt countless candles to Our Lady of Moundié, ruined herself with offering many sacrifices, all to be the better prepared for the great cataclysm. A rumour ran through Moundié: a hunter had accidentally (while blinded by a spirit) killed a sea-cow (a hunter truly of a neighbouring country that borders the sea, but originally from a tribe found here, and thus involving us in the crime). The soul of the Mammywater was now threatening punishment of the whole country. The days were exhausting and the hot, close nights brought only fitful sleep.

But when you love your profession, as I learned to do when waiting table at the *Relais,* you pay no attention to such fantasies. And I had prepared my garden party with the utmost love and attention to detail.

The night before the party, I slept like one of the possessed. On my back, on my left side, on my right, on my belly, I sought the cooler temperature at which a grateful body might sink into sleep. I must have slept and awoken, slept and awoken many times. Strange phantoms persisted in my dreams. Fitted with uncouth helmets, they kept pestering me with demands whose general sense I understood without grasping the details, or torturing me with policeman-like questions which I was unable to recall minutes later. There was a kaleidoscope of beloved faces, mingled with a lunar Polépolé, cynically affectionate, delighted to have entangled me in a snare whose nature I couldn't discern.

Elengui had prepared an excellent dish cooked in palm oil for me. A woman who has seen her monthly blood should not cook for her man. Taste of chicken. A woman who has seen her... You have eaten a crocodile. A woman who has seen... A skinny white dog whose fangs were fastened in my arm. One movement and he would tear my skin and nail my flesh. Get out of this dream. Get out. A woman who has seen... Get out. Get...

Covered in sweat, I went to open the window. But the mosquitoes. Ay!

Unknown beings were climbing in the window. I shan't sleep tonight. My sleep is hacked to bits. Weariness. I mustn't fall asleep completely, or else, or else I'll suffocate. Elengui, shake me. Shake me, *ko*. I know. Dreaming. I'll suffocate. Horsemen in turbans and faces of Djassikini masks running, crying, laughing. Kwa, kwa, kwa. Run. And my hand, so heavy, heavy. My hand in Elengui's. Elengui who was also running, who had stopped running, who wasn't running. Shake me, *ko*. Deep lapses of coma soften the will. Sleep unto death. Sleep unto death. While the conscience. Drowning. The plane is taking off. The pilot reassures us. The plane is taking off. Wheels over the water. Take off, for God's sake. The horsemen, the grinning mouth-holes of the Djassikini masks. Kwa, kwa, kwa. Quick. Kwa,kwa,kwa. Quicker. It will be too late. The pilot makes noises with his mouth, revs the engines. Wheels trailing in the water. Vroom, vroom, vroom. I too, with my mouth. Perhaps Maracaibo. Mayumba. Amazon. Lagoon. Lianas. More strongly. Vroom, vroom. We are sinking, all doors jammed. Cursed be my... A woman who... the crocodile. Maracaibo. The crocodiles. Mayumba. Musn't try to... Lagoon. All doors jammed. Don't joke, the gods. Never joke, those. Those gods there. Stifling. No. Wake me, *ko*. Elengui! Give up. Wisdom. Sleep, death. Sleep unto death. Ah! they don't joke. Not crazy, no. Cry. Too bad if wakes... Cry. Sleep-the-death.

And instantly, yéhé! I opened my eyes, panting, brimming with sweat. Elengui, in the position of a foetus, breath calm and regular, was indifferent to the world. Tomorrow, she'll say these dreams were no good. Bad signs. Must consult the diviner. Quick. And if I'm obstinate or too doubtful, she'll go herself, she will, step off to see the seer.

That Sunday of Daddy's birthday was as grey and indecisive as all those of that strange dry season which was endlessly dying. I put on my newest dinner-jacket, recently ordered by the Marshal from Serge de Ruyvère, the great Parisian tailor. Elengui herself refused to come to the party, observing, with all the contempt of Moundié at the corner of her lips, that to spend hours dressing up and doing your hair just to drink a glass standing up wasn't worth the candle. I had suggested that she keep company with the young compatriot Cabinet Secretary and his wife.

"If it's a question of being with others, I'm not interested. If I put on my wrapper tucked up in the *my-man's-up-to-it* style it's to have the pleasure of parading with you, no?" And then the diviner had warned her that she shouldn't even go out that Sunday. She was wondering whether my dreams...

The estate where the party was to be held was outside of town. I had repeatedy insisted to the driver that he make all the necessary arrangements to get us there, according to my plans and my wishes, long before the arrival of the first guest, and I kept on about this throughout our journey.

"O.K. *Maître.* I'll do airplane-on-the-ground."

And he put his accelerator flat to the floor.

Our way was blocked by an army truck hogging the road. My driver kept honking to get past, and was already unpacking his baggage of the most colourful and savoury insults learned in the jostling backstreets of Moundié and allowing himself a severe assessment of the value of our army, when the khaki-hued vehicle consented to pull a little to the right. When we had already begun to pull out, I noticed a second truck ahead of this one, then a third, then a fourth... Mam'hé. These must be the troops charged with maintaining security around the perimeter of the estate. A natural enough precaution, even if, to my mind, Daddy was exaggerating a little. What fool would dream of attempting anything in broad daylight?

It was a whole military convoy, rolling in the direction of the Country Palace. The soldiers must be late. With haggard faces and uncannily fixed eyes, they seemed as if rivetted to their weapons, in the most theatrical attitudes. Although they could see from the corners of their eyes the mineralogical emblem borne by all Palace vehicles, they totally ignored our car and the perilous attempts by the driver to get past them. Some even shook their fists or their weapons in our direction. The comrade driver and I pretended not to notice these provocative gestures.

Having finally got past, the driver gave them a clear sign of his feelings.

"Up all your arses!"

Despite this incident, I arrived in time to inspect my staff and supplies. Everything was ready.

The wave of early guests flowed slowly inward, whispering along the gravel paths. These arteries, formed like quarter-circles, crossed each other at right angles, in the midst of a huge patch of *paspalum,* rising from which was a regular pattern of shrubs cut into the shape of peg-tops. In the centre, and in two other places, fountains were throwing out their multiple filmy spray, rising from a juicy sherbet of crushed ice.

A little below stretched the ditch enclosing the elephants, and a line of cages, restlessly paced by excited apes, looking like giant, plush-covered toys; while others sprang from branch to branch above them like trapeze artists. Whenever Daddy displayed the garden to any important guest, he would comment on it as if he himself had created it; as if he were the landscape gardener and custodian of this bright display.

"In those beds, three hundred and thirty-six different types of flower."

He pointed with his lion's tail.

"Over there, Super-Stars, Kabuki, Criterion, Diorama, Baccara, Golden Arrow, Europeana, Moulin-Rouge, Scania, Golden Shower..."

Daddy had a memory bigger than a troop of elephants.

Despite his civilian dress, I recognised in my tour an officer displaying a blood-red handkerchief in his breast pocket. What awful taste! No owner of the *Relais* would ever permit one of his *maîtres d'hôtel* to wear that. That's the taste of a real bushman. Get off, you village oaf! Well, well, you'd think I was the Chief of Protocol!

The women were competing in their dresses, cloths and elaborate hair-styles piled in fine loops upon their perfumed heads. Another guest with a handkerchief! Then another. Must be the latest fashion. They spread from Paris to this country faster than an office messenger going from room to room in the same ministry. Ridiculous at first sight, they take on so fast that soon even the grandfathers adopt them. Perhaps I myself soon, just to prove how young I am, or to please Soukali...

The bodyguards within the garden were certainly placed most discreetly. More so than usual. The soldiers of the convoy we passed must have been deployed outside the grounds.

The familiar faces of the dignitaries and their wives were now all present. A number of Uncles too. Big traders, bankers and development officials, together with an impressive contingent of doctors and professors.

The buffets were laid according to my instructions. Turkeys in aspic, big salmon heightening the reflections of the silver platters in which they lay, mounds of *pâté de foie gras,* piles of prawns and lobsters, pyramids of cakes built as high as a boy and crowned with marzipan all encrusted with crystallised fruit. Bottles of choice vintages were being uncorked by the waiters, under the direction of white *maîtres* brought in especially for the occasion, but all under my authority. Golden wines in long-necked flasks, blood-red wines in bottles lightly coated with dust, pale whiskeys, champagne in heron's-beak goblets, cooling in basins full of ice. The bands, after their initial chords, played one after the other, offering conga rhythms, accompanied by lyrics in praise of the Chief, all sung with an obsessive intensity. These rhythms gave the illusion of immortal verses and some of the whites, feeling the fire of the percussion in the pits of their stomachs, sketched a few steps, in the attitude of waltzers.

Suddenly the ryhthm changed and everyone recognised the famous signature tune: "When Daddy came down from on high." All eyes turned in the same direction and a voice cried:

"The President Bwakamabé Na Sakkadé, *wollé, wollé?*"

"*Woï! woï!*"

Three times.

Daddy, preceded by his Head of Protocol, advanced triumphantly, with a seductive smile, acknowledging with his lion's tail the applause orchestrated by the Director of Protocol and taken up by the guests, running like a wave from one end of the garden to the other.

"Wollé, wollé?"

"*Woï, woï!*"

Attired all in white, from cap to mocassins, he came forward with Ma Mireille on his arm, also radiant as an actress, playing her role of princess with a natural brilliance. I heard one old Uncle compare her to Elizabeth Taylor. The men looked at her with scarcely-veiled admiration. She looked at me and I felt wounded afresh by her severe and angry expression, like a recall to order. Daddy murmured to her and she replied with a lovely smile in which one read an indescribable affection. It made me boil. Behind them came a clutch of people, including bodyguards, members of the presidential family and some of the best-known figures in the political life of the country. Daddy stopped to shake hands with an acquaintance, doubtless someone he knew before his accession to supreme power, and to whom he wanted to prove his simplicity. All the guests then began elbowing their way forward, so as to be able, each one... And when they reached their goal, they would present themselves to Madame and attempt to open a conversation, try to distinguish themselves or obtain the promise of an audience.

The young compatriot Cabinet Secretary was standing somewhat apart.

"Don't you want to eat something?"

He pulled a slight face, as if he were feeling sick.

"A drink?"

It was just at this moment, I think, that I heard a dry crackling sound repeatedly breaking the air.

"It must be the fireworks beginning," said someone nearby.

"Fireworks in broad daylight?"

"Another trick of Daddy's. A mock attack, no doubt. He's playing again the trick of Lake Lamartine."

Whistling sounds were slicing the air across our heads. Bursts of fire from machine guns followed one another, punctuated by loud explosions from heavy weapons which shook the ground. Ah! a bit beyond a joke, this. The smiles of those who had expected a farce were frozen and I looked in vain for any sign of encouragement around me.

"If this is a stunt, it's in very bad taste," remarked a European diplomat, sententiously.

The nervous stuttering of small-arms was increasing. Suddenly, a guest who was standing by a corner of the buffet fell forward into a plate of sandwiches, spraying it with his blood and sending it flying. Eh? Eh? Does this look like a joke? An elderly man, as if taken ill, sank abruptly onto the edge of the fountain, clutching his ankle and smiling horribly.

"Oh! but I'm wounded!"

At the same instant, I feel a warm liquid between my neck and the collar of my shirt. I put my finger there. It comes back red. Mam'hé! But these fellows are really playing the fool. Blood? God is great, it can't be mine! Well, my brother, the joke is over. I remember the convoy I had passed just before arriving at the party. In the name of God, bilai, it's a *coup d'état!* The beginning of a revolution. The intellectuals like the young compatriot Cabinet Secretary? But where has he vanished to? I don't see him. The forebodings of Elengui were well-founded. I should have listened to her. Oh, where can I run to?

Here we are, all caught up in this unexpected disaster. But it's as if I were alone. My throat is dry. An invisible hand squeezes all the guts in my belly. I'm sweating like a white man. Alone. I feel alone. No one now knows who is his neighbour. Vanished in the flick of an eyelid, vanished all those courtesies that had perfumed the reception a few minutes ago. The bullets are whizzing past and ricocheting against the walls, smashing windows and plasterwork. My brother, if you ever want to see Elengui again, you had better quit this open esplanade. In any case it's already empty. Here and there, corpses lie on the pavement, each in the midst of a growing pool of blood. I manage to reach the kitchens and begin to look for cover. They are crammed. But people are pressing towards the threshold, looking outwards, as if just taking shelter from a passing shower. In the rear kitchen, a group of servants, some in white jackets and others in chef hats and aprons, are kneeling and jabbering the prayers of I-don't-know-what-religion.

This room is lit by a sort of skylight in clear glass. One of the waiters goes to smash it. I take a quick look outside: bodies piled against the foot of the boundary wall. In the name of God, I have never seen the like. Mam'hé, mam'hé! Their skirts and trousers are all soaked with blood. Elengui, my dreams, ayay'hé! An official who is standing beside me—I know him well, he lives in my quarter—also takes a look through the skylight.

"Yes, yes, yes, there they are! They're coming! They're breaking in!"

At that moment, some ten, fifteen or twenty helmeted soldiers, all in camouflage jackets coloured like dry-season foliage, are rushing through the main entrance. All carry an armband coloured blood-red. Bent over their guns, they are firing ahead of them at random. By now, they must have reached the threshold of the Palace. While the bulk of the troop deploys itself in a swarm, two soldiers detach from the group and appear in the opening of the kitchen doorway.

"Hands up! Everybody out!"

They have the voices of maddened beasts.

I am one of the first out, pushed by the great wave of guests who rush in disorder towards the arcaded wall which closes the esplanade on the side of the hills. The *boys* and cooks being a bit slow in following us, one of the soldiers throws a grenade into the pack. Ay! I hear the explosion, but don't dare to look. The women, close to hysteria, utter cries which rise like bells.

One *boy,* his nerves on a razor-edge, throws himself on his knees.

"Not me, not me. I'm innocent. Not me, I beg-o. Pardon, chief, pardon, *wo*. I've got kids."

"Shut your mouth, you slavey! Filthy black shit! Some *boys* you are, fit for nothing better. At every meal, at every banquet, you steal something. Whole legs of lamb, into your bags. You're part of the system, so pay up!"

The soldiers make a half-turn. Some of them stop suddenly in front of a buffet still laden with barely-touched remnants of the feast. Their eyes are blood-shot.

"Bastards! You've been stufffing yourselves like hogs!"

The one who shouted now points his gun at us.

"Now you'll pay!"

Trembling like a malaria patient, he pulls the cloth towards him, overturns the trestles with blows of his rifle-butt, and sends the whole mass of food crashing to the ground, together with the flowers we had spent days and nights patiently arranging. He tramples on the lot, amidst a great shattering of plates and glasses. The soldiers fire and fire, emptying whole magazines, blind with rage. One old man is begging for mercy, trailing on the ground and hugging the legs of a soldier.

"I'm wounded in the thigh... I didn't want to come here... Spare me, my children..."

"You could have stayed at home!"

And without giving him time even to reopen his mouth, he beats him across the head with all his strength. The old man falls back, his skull split apart. The soldier wipes the butt of his gun. His eyes look like those of a *wee*-smoker.

Chased here and there by some thirty soldiers, the crowd, hands in the air, veers sometimes to the right, sometimes to the left, like a flock of frightened animals pursued by wild beasts. One man tries to talk with a soldier: he is shot down in a burst of bullets at point-blank range. Another, who has been ordered to raise both arms, tries to indicate that he cannot, because one arm has been amputated. He is mown down in his turn. Professor Lourd, going to the aid of a wounded man, is violently ordered to stop. He reaches toward his pocket, doubtless to pull out his doctor's card, and is promptly laid out on the ground by another burst of gunshots. Who, then, has given orders to kill even Uncles? My throat closes up again and my limbs are completely paralysed with fear.

Dragged along, shoved, caught up in the crowd, I find myself in my turn pushed against the arcaded wall facing the hills. Why not try to escape that way? The forest up there offers me all the branches of its trees. If I could just get there... I know every path. As a Boy Scout, I was the best in field-craft. But it's a nightmare from which I'll never awake.

A little way off, sacks of meat, lying shapeless and inert. We are surrounded. Animals caught in the hunters' net. Everything has been devised against us. Is this another nightmare? This time, there will be no awakening. No one can escape alive from this killing game. A song comes back to me from childhood.

Here comes the night,
Why didn't I stay at home
To cut wood?
Here comes the night...

And all this in broad daylight, without anyone lifting a finger to prevent it.

Only *wee*-smokers could act like this. They go on shooting blindly for no other reason than the sheer pleasure of killing: a man who wants to protect his wife; another who couldn't answer in the same dialect; one who was too well-dressed; one who looked too arrogant; another who looked too frightened. What frightful *juju*-man is pulling the strings of this mass frenzy?

Step by step, the soldiers approach us. The expression of these eyes grows still more strange.

"Get out, all of you, you maggots! Clear the place! Get out! You stink! You've grown fat enough on the sweat of the people. Go on, get out!"

They are pushing us, with their rifles crossed, towards the entrance gate. We pass the threshold, trampling on a dozen corpses. But nothing matters now. In a minute, it will be our turn. The last survivors on the ground will clutch at our knees.

Outside, the scenes of massacre are even worse. The few guards who dared to resist have been shot down and their bodies, black rubber dummies, are stretched out here, in the wildest poses, silent and amazed. Seeing them like that, without feeling any greater fright, gives me the sense of being ready to receive death without any more terror than those who had accepted it according to the ethic of their profession. Wherever I look, the flowerbeds, the lawns and the paths are jammed with corpses or with those dying in agony. A vision even more atrocious than my nightmares.

"Go on, go on, move, you bastards."

A line of military trucks is standing before us. The very same that I passed before getting to the party. Some are already filled with civilians, packed in like animals.

"Go on, you swine, get in!"

I have great difficulty in hoisting myself up on the vehicle. I can imagine the pitiful clumsiness of my gestures. So where is the great sportsman, champion of the 110-metre hurdle, the pride of Raymond of Penyafort College? What's become of that great dancer of the *beguine*, the *pachanga* and the high-life? Rifle-butts in the ribs accompany my fall. We are packed like a cargo of slaves for the Atlantic crossing. I recognise right against me the face of the Minister of Justice. He seems transported by thoughts of another world. They can't have recognised him, or else... We are so packed we can't breathe properly. What do they want with us? Where are they taking us? I have a terrible struggle in my anguish to control my nerves, which advise me to break out, to rebel, to make a last appeal to the mercy of the soldiers. To explain that I'm just a man of the people. A *boy.* A victim. At the mercy of Daddy's caprices. But what is this new strength? Yes, sure enough, I'm afraid to die. But at least try to be brave. Just try to seem so. The slightest foolish move on your part could bring on the death of our whole truck load.

"Name of God, keep your hands up, you there, or I'll run you through, bastard!"

Under the sway of my fatigue, I must, without realising it, have let my arms fall. I quickly raise them again. God, how heavy they are! Like when the schoolmaster used to make us hold them up crossed, while standing in the corner. Ah! Let them finish us off!

The soldiers who are playing with our fate have now formed up in two files, on either side of the trucks. I look attentively, as if through a zoom lense, at that young man there, just level with my eyes. He's pointing a gun at my breast. Like all the others, he's wearing a blood-red armband. Less than two yards separate us. We are nothing but strangers to each other. To kill me will demand nothing of him but a flick of the trigger finger.

I have no more place in his heart than his training-targets. But why, then, does he hate me? I feel his pupil roll towards me with such an intensity of malice that you'd think he joined in this operation simply in order to settle a score with me. Face of a very young man. Almost a boy. By the two scars forming an equal-sign beside his eyes, I know his tribe. Djassikini. His gaze is of an intolerable fixity. His pupils are dilated. A little foam flecks the corners of his mouth. His gestures are like bushgrass tossing in a tornado. The safety-catch of the gun is off and the bullet is doubtless in place. A mere nothing would bring it on. I had thought it was the smell of powder and blood which made these soldiers haggard. No, they had all been drugged. No doubt about it. *Wee.* So nothing will hold them back. Hallucinated creatures, whose leaders have told them to give no quarter...

"Don't look at me like that! Drop your eyes, or I'll shoot!"

When I peer through my lids again, the young soldier is still marking me like a footballer. And always that horrible fixed gaze. Another soldier is beside him. They chuckle. He looks at me again, with that mixture of moral outrage and brutality.

"You there, get down!"

"How can I get out of this...?"

"Eh, half-witted bastard, don't play dumb!"

"Stop there! Get back in the truck. You'll get the same as the others."

One of the survivors tells me that, in the jeep escorting us, they had taken care to load some shovels. I noticed nothing like that, but these men were capable of anything.

Getting back into the truck is, at this stage, a thousand times harder than balancing on a tightrope over a ravine. I will never do it. They are going to beat me. The dream. Elengui. Better accept my fate with dignity. If...if possible. They hit me. I have no more reaction. At last, a hand stretches from the truck and pulls me up. It drags me in on my belly. I feel what's left of my dinner-jacket splitting.

"Thanks. I owe you..."

"Shut up or I'll fire! And put your hands up!"

Ayay'hé! Let them shoot once and for all, and be done with

it. But the truck is shaking. I recognise the route. Curious eyes watch us pass and wonder at the meaning of this procession. I glimpse a waiter from the *Relais.* One of my old colleagues. With his arm, he makes me an interrogative sign, but I remain impassive. Any response, any sign on my part, would serve as pretext for the junky guarding us.

Now we are taking a road which I recognise as the one to Prytanée. Here we are, a few minutes later, right in front of the Lamy Military Training School. It's almost deserted.

"Everybody out! Get on with it!"

They push us towards the cells.

"Go on, take off ties, belts and shoes. The party's over, you fuckers."

The cells are too small and too few to hold all of us. A mouse runs across the room and disappears. With three other hostages, I am taken to an office and thrown inside without ceremony. A soldier wrenches out the telephone cord.

"And let no one think of farting about!"

The door slams behind us. The shutters are closed. I go up to the window and make out, between the louvres, a soldier armed to the teeth.

After a few moments, we dare to speak. What on earth is going on? Who's organising the coup? Why are we the victims?

"Silence in there!"

The supervision is even stricter than we thought. So we must be quiet. And with silence, we feel the return of all the anguish which had begun to lessen. Outside, the sentries are talking in low voices. Too low for us to catch anything. We glue our ears to the door. No good. The guards turn on a transistor radio. My neighbour whispers.

"I can repair the telephone. I used to work for that department."

Too risky. They can return at any moment, open the door and surprise us. I agree nonetheless to keep watch at the shutters. The man, having repaired the broken cord and pushed the bare ends into the contacts, seems satisfied with his work. He whispers something to another of us captives, who rises and drags a chair noisily across the floor. The repairman takes the chance to dial a number on the phone. Who is he talking to? His voice is very faint, but I can see by the movement of his lips that he isn't talking French. All this happens very quickly. In the twinkle of an eye.

"It's alright, my brothers. I've given the alarm. I've told them where we are. God willing, we'll be saved. Have courage, my friends."

Our guards are still there, the transistor blaring out military music. Played by whom?

A voice floats out of the plastic box. Impossible to recognise. The soldiers seem struck by it. They move out of our line of vision through the slats of the shutter. And the waiting game goes on and on. After several minutes, I risk saying something aloud. No reaction. Then one of the hostages replies to me. Then another. No reaction from outside. The guards must have run away. We proceed to a final test.

Loss of country, exile, all these memories and echoes which float from home never tempt me to seek out new friendships.

When solitude becomes too heavy, I offer myself an evening of punch and flashing lights at one of the hundred discos in N..., taking home with me, to finish off the night, some partner for slow-dancing.

No visiting cards. Thanks, sweetheart, a kiss of appreciation, this is for the taxi, this for you. To each his own road.

Whether the sky hangs taut in canvass-blue or unrolls like a huge straw mattress, for me, it's always yesterday. Whatever melody is brought by the Atlantic breezes, there's an irremediable moment of silence when my heart grows heavy and listens. My tongue returns inconsolably to caress the place where the tooth has been drawn.

Just one friend: Boubacar Diagne. Boubeu, to his cronies. A stranger, like me. Senegalese, blacker than a mixture of all the purest blacks there are. Not liked by the other black workers here. Every time he calls one of them to order, the fellow begins to mutter behind his back that, if "that Hausa" isn't happy, he can always go back to his own country.

But he's got a heart of gold, I tell you. That black hospitality which we always talk of but rarely practise. A leader, what's more. Attached to the management, sir! In charge of public relations for the hotel. The only black occupying such a high post in the establishment. Besides which, the Uncles (he calls them toubabs*) respect him like one of their own: you can see easily enough that he isn't a native of N...*

It's because he's lived among them. Something like ten years in Paris. He even married a Madame over there. I've seen a photo of their son. A fine-looking boy! café au lait, *with hair curling like woodshavings. But black, very black. Then one day he got fed up with it all, Boubeu. Home-sickness. For Africa, above all. And he packed everything in, with his big smile, glistening like ivory.*

"Get up, get up!"

I jump. Is this it? I decide to play dead.

I've been sleeping. How long? A thousand dreams have flickered across the screen of my eyelids, with the speed of an accelerating projector. My nerves are even more excited than if I had never dropped off.

"Go on, get up, boys!"

Courage, *Maître,* you must be a clear-eyed witness to the climax of your fatal tragedy. I get up, tottering. Far away, we hear the noise of irregular salvoes. The torn air trembles with them and our breasts re-echo with the sound. Is this the hard core defending its last positions? Who? Against whom? What is the objective of the mutineers? Avengers who want to rid the country of Daddy? When will they recognise that I was neither a tool nor an accomplice of that fellow? Poor worker just earning his bread.

All those who have served Daddy are other Daddies, or sons of jackals who need a Daddy in order to breathe. To be exterminated without a qualm. In a revolution, no time to try the victims. Good intentions and pure souls sink in the common shipwreck with determined oppressors. The blurrings of history... No omelettes without breaking eggs. The young intellectuals knew those laws by heart. I felt it clearly enough a while ago, in submitting to that Djassikini soldier. It would have been different, though, if we had met before, at a funeral or at old Tiya's place.

A ray of light shoots through my spirits. A crazy idea. Isn't this a progressive *coup d'état?* Yes, really progressive. The awakening of just revengers. Led by Captain Yabaka, inspired by the young compatriot Cabinet Secretary and those other kids...

The salvoes continue at irregular intervals, but growing closer. Summary executions? The young officer is not wearing a blood-red armband. His face is calm. What's more, I think I've seen him before. He even looks quite friendly. But how do we know who is here?

"Come on, boys, get into the Land Rover."

One of us breaks out.

"Enough of this. If you want to liquidate us, just kill us now. We're not budging from here. We've had enough."

"Yes, kill us like dogs. We're not going to lend ourselves to your show."

The young officer, whose face continues to bug me somehow, still preserves his tranquil smile. The soldiers accompanying him are likewise impenetrable.

"Don't worry, friends. We've licked the mutineers. We've come to take you back to your families."

"Prove it to us."

"How would you know that we were prisoners in this dump, if you weren't in league with that other lot?"

The young officer explains.

One of our number, satisfied, climbs into the Land Rover. A second follows him. Then another. I myself now do the same. But all our doubts are not vanquished. Men whose faces were abased just a moment ago now confront the army's representative and are filled with the rage of sweet liberty. The young officer tells them that Daddy is safe and sound, and that Captain Yabaka is obtaining the surrender of the last rebels. I don't understand anything. The others are still demanding more proofs.

"We'll soon see!"

Lifting his fist like someone in a propaganda poster, one activist suddenly discharges all his energy in a *karatéka* shout:

"Daddy Bwakamabé, *wollé, wollé?*"

"*Woï, woï!*" comes the unanimous reply from the young officer, his troops and most of that day's companions in captivity.

I stayed quiet. What was there to celebrate?

As we are travelling in the Land Rover, the people around me are singing, but I don't know the song or the words.

The crowd, big as on marketdays in Moundié, flows all around the Palace. Daddy, from a balcony, blesses them repeatedly with his lion's tail. Someone tells me he's just made a speech in Kibotama, in which he handed out a lot of abuse.

"*Wollé, wollé?*"

"*Woï, woï!*"

My mother comes running towards me and cries out. She falls into my arms, weeping. She calls on all the spirits who have given her back her son, and promises them mountains of sacrifices.

"How long will this palaver go on? How long?"

A neighbour shakes his head.

"The country is accursed. They told us the whites were bad. In chasing them away, we didn't kill a single one. But now, among ourselves, we kill more than in a royal hunt. Just let's understand one thing. The country is accursed."

"*Wollé, wollé?*"

"*Woï, woï!*"

For a whole week, I shall be unable to touch meat.

I have been informed that this passage recalls Monsieur Benoist-Meschin and, having looked up the reference, I admit I'm worried.

It's obvious that the writer's lawyers, not appreciating an artist's right to create a collage, and preferring to stick to the coldness of their Cartesian logic, want to make a fuss and are hastening to slate me with the infamous label of plagiarist. But my publishers shouldn't allow themselves to be impressed by such threats. Let everyone get a grip on themselves and reflect for a moment. They must try to emerge from a view of the universe which is too mean and archaic, and try to understand the view of it held in the Black World—a universe of new horizons, but also full of mystery. Let them interview a thousand Africans, chosen at random from the fifty or so states which form the mosaic of our continent, and they will all affirm that, truly, no, it's an episode of their own lives that I've recounted here.

No, gentlemen of the Tribunal, I have not imitated anyone, no.

I have done nothing—plunge my hand in boiling oil if you will—but relate one of my own adventures. If from there I have, along the way, like a griot *unable to resist imitating the voice of a renowned predecessor, borrowed certain words from another, that is a phenomenon both possible and well-known.*

The truth, gentlemen, lies neither to the left, nor to the right, nor yet in the centre. It's in the depths that you must seek it. Penetrate into the marvellous world of our mysteries.

Gaze at the masks, harken to the notes of the drum. They will teach you that in fact Monsieur Benoist-Meschin has had the same dream as ourselves, one afternoon of intense reality, and that it's by this that men of the same epoch come to recognise one another.

I detract nothing from Monsieur Benoist-Meschin. I offer him my homage.

Olélé, dear sirs, behold, with all reverence, my quotation marks, at once open and closed.

Like water in the shell of a leaky canoe, news of the fusillade at the Palace ran in currents along all the alleyways of Moundié.

Those mercenaries, my brothers, made the assault, in order to remind Daddy that it was they who had put him in power. No. Guerillas descending from the forests of the volcanoes had made a lightening attack to put Polépolé back in charge. Well, well! Someone had seen, yes (he lifted the palm of his hand to the sky) the body of that swine Bwakamabé, dragged by a rope behind a truck. No, he was only wounded, and entry to the hospital was denied to visitors. Go on, they're all talking rubbish: in the area populated by people from Libotama, they swept aside all these versions with a shrug of the shoulders. Once again, the fetish-priests and charms had proved their power. As soon as the enemy fired *pa!* one saw the bullets, *wé!* change direction on approaching the Chief and turn back, *pa, pa, pa,* killing the amazed enemy, *gba!* One putschist had succeeded in getting near Daddy and was about to stick a bayonet in his back when, *wo!* the Chief vanished, reappearing behind the assailant and levelling him, *m'mah!* with a close-combat throw. He wasn't only a great marshal, he was the elect of the gods. Seizing the attackers' arms, he had decimated the bandits.

"Daddy Bwakamabé Na Sakkadé, *wollé, wollé?*"

"Woï, woï!"

"Wollé, wollé?"

"Woï, woï!"

Elengui's heart swelled in recounting all this to me.

My mother had rushed to the house together with her sisters and, having confirmed my absence, tore off her scarf, pulled down her hair and ran out bare-breasted to weep for my misfortune. Elengui, mistress of her own feelings, though somewhat agitated, tried to calm her.

"Ah! we know well enough, well enough, you don't love our son! Your eyes are as dry as a hearthstone. But that isn't enough for you. You don't want us to weep for our boy. You don't want us to plead with the Fates. You're an accomplice in his death. You only live under this roof to get his money. Now, we shall see."

And the aunts barked at her still more fiercely.

Elengui chose to retire to her room.

My mother, informed by word of mouth, had met me at the Palace. When I returned home in her company, the aunts, who had already encamped themselves for the anticipated funeral festivities, uttered those cries that the Uncles call savage and began executing around me the steps which had derived from our village cults. Elengui tore me away from those weepers, pressed her belly to mine and her cheek to my breast, then broke into wordless sobbing. We stayed like that for several moments, pressed against each other, strong, strong, strong.

Friends and neighbours were already arriving. They wanted to know, they wanted to confirm, they wanted to hear, and seemed ready to hoist me among the Heroes of the Nation.

But I didn't want to talk.

I switched on the radio. I too wanted to understand.

I urge all officials of the state and the whole population to remain calm—

"Oh! but isn't that Yabaka's voice?"

"Isn't it the same one I know?"

"It certainly is. The voice of Captain Yabaka."

...President Hannibal-Ideloy Bwakamabé Na Sakkadé, Head of State, Commander-in-Chief of the Republican Armed Forces, holds the reins of power... I order all civil and military authorities to stay within the law, under the aegis of our Guide and Supreme Strategist ...

"So the Government has recaptured the State Radio."

Long live our Daddy Hannibal Ideloy-Bwakamabé Na Sakkadé, long live the Republic, long live the People!

"I don't know what to think, *wo*."

"Our radio is always playing military marches."

"So, where is Captain Yabaka speaking from?"

"From the relay station of Radio France. The one right on the summit of the mountain. The rebels didn't think of that."

And the military marches began again, broken at regular intervals with the Captain's communiqué.

Finally, the National Anthem. Then, that well-known voice which detached its syllables as if in dictation, applying itself hard to differentiate, on the one hand, the *é* from the *è* and the *ai;*

on the other hand, the *o* from *au;* and, finally, the *i* from the *u.*

Dear people, dear relatives, dear children, dear adoptive brothers from Europe.

In the course of the last few hours, our Beloved Country has nearly suffered one of the worst catastrophes in its history. Under the direction, in fact, of Colonel Haraka...

"That one! It's impossible!"

We put our hands to our mouths in amazement.

And the voice went on. The young recruits had been misled. They had been told that Daddy was in danger and that they must save him. They had been stuffed full of *wee.* They would have killed everyone. Fortunately, the *litassa* powers... It was enough for the Chief to look one of the bewitched well in the eye and *wah!* the *litassa* worked its effect.

The listeners were thoughtful, but silent. One careless word might reveal to the police, or even to oneself, that one had been involved in the plot.

Next day, *The Southern Cross* brought out a special number, with an orgy of pictures of the corpses in all kinds of attitudes. Those of the victims, to demonstrate the barbarity of the deluded troops; those of the plotters, to prove that our Leader had been stronger. It seems that one Uncle, a professor of ancient languages, had seen here an analogy with Homeric practice. The other Uncles merely shrugged their shoulders: "Their everlasting barbaric savagery, sure enough." In Moundié this special number was torn to pieces, with the snarling of scavengers ripping up bloody flesh.

It was, finally, the account of events given by Aziz Sonika which assured the survivors that they knew more than they had realised. The bewitched plotters had each worn a blood-red armband, to distinguish themselves and avoid killing one another in the confusion. Their accomplices had mingled with the guests, each wearing a blood-red handkerchief or tie. Here, at N..., I've discovered this old number of *The Southern Cross* in the National Library. I won't reproduce here the most significant passages, for fear of boring my readers (too patient already) with such long and numerous quotations. There's another reason, too. I haven't the heart to play the star in events which I wish I'd never experienced. As for Aziz Sonika, in this article he presented himself, if not as a hero, at least as a war correspondent afraid of nothing.

They announced the opening of an enquiry to look more deeply into the affair, but the press spoke of it no more. Everyone wanted to slake his thirst, however. Aziz Sonika's version, *pouah,* they spat on it. Radio grapevine had a more tasty one. It was fresh, it was pure. From it, they learned, little by little, that Colonel Haraka reproached Daddy for not being radical enough; for having too many civilians in his government; for depending more on his tribe than on the Army; for thus encouraging the influence of the Reds; for doing a Polépolé without Polépolé; for preparing a bed for the communists, who were only waiting for their chance to return; they did not, however, seek the life of Daddy; they had simply wanted to anticipate and prevent a plot which Captain Yabaka, agent of the KGB, was hatching against the Republic.

So said radio grapevine, depending upon agents of Monsieur Gourdain charged with interrogating Colonel Haraka's accomplices. His accomplices only. For Colonel Haraka had accumulated so many proofs against himself that his execution could take place before his trial. Not even a court-martial. That would be weakness, would do him too much honour. Wasn't he caught in the act? Well, then...

In the meantime, however, Colonel Haraka couldn't be found.

But the buzzing of radio grapevine was as persistent and troublesome as a horde of mosquitoes. Daddy got annoyed and sent for Aziz Sonika, who left with precise instructions for a series of editorials, in French and in each of the local languages. Colonel Haraka's accusations were a tissue of lies, designed to hide the truth. The rebels were nothing but agents of Moscow and also profited from the support of certain African countries which one declined to name, in order to preserve the unity of the OAU.

In the corridors, among the best informed circles and the diplomatic corps, it was whispered like a secret of Pulcinello that it was unquestionably a case of...

I, who understand nothing of politics, couldn't help thinking that the real culprits should be sought as much in the times as in the heads of men. But I had only to open my mouth for everyone to cry *wo!* and mock me.

In the meantime, Haraka was on the run.

Soukali was growing more and more sickly. She was fading in the repetition of the daily, wearying activities of domestic life. Like a plant which no longer sees the sun, her blood was becoming poisoned by forever breathing the dust of cleaning, the smells of cooking, of washing up and of garbage. She wanted to get out, to work, make her own money and spend it as she chose, on the needs of her family (quite distinct from her husband) and herself. Woman's idea. If she'd been my wife, what I call a wife, I'd have put her in her place long before this. Contrary to what I'd promised her in a moment of weakness, I hadn't dared speak about her to Daddy. With this Haraka affair, the Head of State had too many cares to pay attention to the requests of his fellow citizens. But Soukali had a head like a rock. Thanks to her own efforts, she had finally found a job. In the Bulgarian Embassy. Among the communists. After all, she was an educated woman, Soukali. She had her certificate in typing and shorthand, or something of that sort.

As this job also gave her charge of the switchboard, she took the opportunity to phone me several times a day, and demanded that I do the same.

First thing every day I had to wish her good morning, by telephone. She longed to hear my voice repeat that I had dreamed of her, that I had thought of her, that I loved her. If I had time to give more attention, I had to specify the details. If these weren't enough to satisfy her, she would cry that I was lying, that I never thought of her, that I wasn't even capable of dreaming about her, that I didn't love her. If I swore that I hadn't dreamed of anyone or anything, she complained even louder.

"See how you are? A brute. Like all blacks, yes."

When I heard her make such reflections, I began to wonder if, perhaps, Soukali had been fooling around with an Uncle. A stupid and gross suspicion, sure enough. But they are the only ones who accustom women to such puerilities. And Soukali was such a strumpet that she would have been quite capable of such a liaison, not to be unfaithful to me, but just to please herself. Oh! nobody can imagine the flashes which pass through the spirits of women who are too lively and who like to play just as they breathe.

"I'm always thinking of you. But you men, you just want to screw, screw, screw. As if I were a whore..."

I didn't like to hear her compare me with other men. It was true that she never let a month pass without giving me a present. A shirt, a pair of slippers, a necktie, handkerchiefs, underpants (she made fun of my old-fashioned boxers), a bottle of *eau de toilette.* And I, when I took them home, would explain to Elengui that in passing *Tissus K.M.* I hadn't been able to restrain myself. And Elengui said she loved a man with taste; that anyway these were objects too delicate to be offered as presents and that it was really better to buy them oneself. Soukali would, of course, have loved it if I also gave her dresses, shoes, bags, perfumes, even roses, as the Uncles do. The essential thing was that it shouldn't be money. If it were, she would hand it back.

"You take me for a prostitute?"

Sometimes I thought that Soukali went a bit far with her questions.

"Tell me (she would whisper) did you do *that* to her last night?"

"To whom?"

She always said "my rival" with a feeling of pride in her voice. As for Elengui, she'd have ripped off her hair, scratched out her eyes and, to me...she'd never said what she would do to me, but...

"Did what?"

Soukali laughed like a child.

"Listen, Soukali, we can't talk like this on the telephone."

"I want you to tell me."

If I said no, she would retort in a stern motherly tone that I was lying. If I remarked on the indiscretion of admitting it, she immediately wanted to know whether her "rival" was content with the missionary position or whether she had enjoyed the slit and the sleight, the kiss of the fawn, or the coco-buns; and at what time did all these take place? And she invariably discovered that at the same hour an invisible hand had plucked her from sleep and she had felt the need to awaken Monsieur the Inspector, who understood nothing of what was happening to him. And she'd clap her hands and explain everything in astrological terms. If it was Elengui who had made me "stand to" several nights running, Soukali wouldn't see the joke at all.

"No, but what's happening to you?"

It was my turn to laugh.

"No, it's no good. Who do you think you are?"

My smile froze on my lips. She took an exasperated tone.

"Anyway, I'm convinced you don't want to see me any more."

"I do, of course."

"No!"

"But you know very well that it isn't easy when Monsieur the Inspector is there."

"When a man loves a woman, he always finds a way."

"Yes, but..."

"In any case, if you don't arrange for us to get together, you'll just see."

Yéhé! this was not just a bit of hot air. With her temperament!

"But you know very well, my heart, that there's a structural problem."

"Look at that! Now you're talking like a bureaucrat."

Well, if I used a word like *structure,* it was just because we were talking on the telephone. And those instruments...

"Okay...okay, I shall come this evening, in order to reconnoitre the place."

"Well, well...just by chance!"

"I mean that...I mean..."

"Too late."

"Soukali!"

"Too late, I already have an engagement for tonight."

"An engagement with whom, may I ask?"

"With a girlfriend, dear sir, what do you think?"

"Soukali?"

"Listen, for once they're showing a good film and Monsieur the Inspector will let me go out with a girlfriend ..."

"At night?"

"At night, at night, why yes, what? At night. During which time I'll leave you to *take stock*. Go on, *take stock, take stock*. You can take even more time over it. We have all our lives in front of us."

"Soukali?"

"Yes."

"Soukali?"

"Yes, go on."

"Soukali, I'm saying, eh, I'm saying that next week everything will be arranged."

"If you think that I'm going to wait till next week! Next week, look I'm going to Switzerland with my husband."

"To Switz ..."

"Ye-es. He's going on a mission there and he's taking me along."

"Eh? eh? And the children?"

"The children? They'll stay here, of course."

The children will stay? But that's not good, Soukali. You hear? That's not good."

"Listen. It's tomorrow, or else, you just see!"

"See what?"

"You'll see."

Ah! that woman, really ...

Next day, after the missionary, she took a magazine from her handbag and we studied how to do the sword and the scales, the horn of Roland, and the Cheyenne in ambush.

Colonel Haraka still couldn't be found. Some claimed that he had escaped to the bush to organise the guerillas. Others, that he had crossed the frontier with the complicity of an embassy, the country of which varied according to the informant. Another group asserted, may their hands be plunged in boiling oil, that he was right here in the capital, benefiting from the protection of Captain Yabaka. This was the theory of those who were not convinced of the role played by the Captain during the day of red armbands and handkerchiefs. That man, hum, was involved in the plot, hum, even, even... Like a chameleon, he had changed his skin as soon as he smelled burning and, a real cynic, like all those of his tribe, he had trapped his own acolytes in order to shake off all suspicion. Whoever ventured to doubt such assertions would be told that it was useless to look for rationality in this affair: it was thoroughly African, in its motivations as well as its development. The country was small. We all knew one another, we sons of the soil. We mustn't let our confidence be deceived by appearances.

Daddy, in his public declarations, praised the loyalty and courage of Yabaka, but during his meetings with certain intimates he let fall that the Captain must be watched. Confided only to close circles, this secret didn't fail to reach Yabaka's ears; to break his morale, some asserted; to send up a trial balloon, maintained others.

Monsieur Gourdain was not sleeping, and gave the President many notes for signature, all addressed to the Minister of Finance, conjuring him to find the means, by all imaginable methods, to reward the brave bloodhounds who were seeking their prey by day and night. The walls of the capital and all other towns in the land were plastered with posters of an astonished-looking Haraka. The radio announced his description every quarter of an hour, in French and all our tribal languages. Monsieur Gourdain obtained from France a pack of Alsatian dogs, together with their keepers.

But the fugitive remained elusive.

The Ministry for Customary Affairs advised calling for the services of a diviner whose talents had enabled our national team, against all predictions, to beat Mouloudia of Algiers on their home ground.

"Why didn't you think of it before?"

Puckering his eyes, Daddy rapped on the table.

"But the service isn't free."

"Very well, the means will follow."

The Minister of Finance, on guard beside his telephone, asked himself for a moment which great man had already pronounced these historic words, then quickly concluded what he had to do, if he was not to appear like an accomplice not yet caught in the inquiry.

But another long week followed and the great priest, learned in things occult and supernatural, had not yet come up with anything conclusive. It was because this matter was more complicated than anyone was likely to suppose at first sight. It needed time and great concentration, because this brigand Haraka had taken pains to protect himself. And those Djassikini priests...they weren't easy to beat, not easy at all.

A *marabout* from Senegal wrote to offer his services. Apart from the expenses of his journey and accommodation, his estimate included a sum which could be negotiated when he arrived. Daddy hesitated for a whole day. And because the priest produced by Customary Affairs had still not come up with anything convincing, the Chief was suddenly inspired.

"Why don't we put all these rascals in competition?"

"*Wollé, wollé?*"

"*Woï, woï!*"

"Let's send delegations to those African countries most renowned for their great priests."

More than forty delegations set forth and each returned with its rare bird.

"Ah! you there, don't forget Europe either. Let someone look out for their best clairvoyants."

At the conference bringing together all these experts, there were fewer Europeans than Africans.

"At least this is one field where we don't cut a pitiable figure."

But the French press, when reporting these events, had words only for its own fellow citizen, Madame Saturne, while in truth, in this foreign climate, this sister of the Uncles remained pretty lack-lustre. In fact, she'd probably have expired from malaria, having failed to foresee the attack, but for the intervention of a Shogun priest. At the completion of the first day, the conference reached a dead end. As might have been expected, there were problems of communication between the participants, since simultaneous interpretation had been provided only between French and English, and many of the clairvoyants were unable to understand or express themselves in either of these idioms. The traditional priests all avowed a patriotic and profound devotion to their mother-tongues, something which aroused a sense of affliction and of pity among the European clairvoyants. But quite apart from these linguistic barriers, profound differences came to light between methods of approach to the problem. Explosions of anger and bitter altercations broke out, while some say that evil fates were thrown in the cowries. The old ones said they could never remember a week with so many storms: it's nuclear war, declared the elders. Daddy, who was anxious for the success of his conference, had to pacify the delegates by receiving them one by one, in the presence of Monsieur Gourdain, to smooth out their differences and look for a consensus.

According to some, the Colonel was wandering in the bush. For others, he had already crossed the frontier. A third group maintained that he had taken refuge in one of the embassies accredited to the country. A last group argued that he was still hiding in the capital. When the first group was asked in what bush, they indicated either that of the monkeys, or else that of the elephants, or among the mountains, or among the lakes. The second group was divided as to which neighbouring country was harbouring the coup-plotter. In making up his summary, Monsieur Gourdain stated that all seven of our neighbours had been cited. As for deciding which was the hypocritical embassy which...

The one who has ruined you will lament your fate with the greatest eagerness.

The rat gnawing the soles of your feet is the very one that lives under your bed.

"Hmm. So it's that Great White Power?"

The hand tends the wounded foot, but the foot doesn't tend the hand.

"The green and white flag?"

Plenty of caterpillars, little oil.

"Isn't that one trying to suggest the communists?"

Saying good morning is not yet a sign of friendship.

"So, it's those others, then!"

Before killing the hen, you should know your guest better. Tomorrow you will pay for your carelessness.

"No, it's the Great White Power on the other side."

It's the tasty herbs that kill the dwarf antelope.

"The green, yellow and red flag, then?"

The leopard who wants to attack makes no noise.

"Better go and look in the direction of those who sell yoghurts."

Distant relatives are much better than close family.

"Ha! with their English and their Swahili, if it's those Kiswahili there, those blacks there have never inspired my confidence."

The hand that threw the stone hides behind the back.

"The...no..."

Monsieur Gourdain raised his eyebrows. Daddy scratched his head with his lion's tail.

"And you who claim that he's in the town... It's not as big as all that. Give the name of the street, the number..."

At this point, the priests, *juju*-men and clairvoyants said that it was quite enough, in terms of precision, if they wanted to respect the dignity of their profession, and that, for the rest, it was for the police to do their own job.

Monsieur Gourdain gave them the look that he always cast when he wanted to stop someone dead.

"Their mother's cunt!" thundered Daddy.

As it was said in Kibotama, no one was offended.

Every night, the warders whipped the captured plotters with bull-gut whips, by way of matriculation, to commemorate their entry into a prison which smelt of sewers, or perhaps simply to accustom them to life there, or show the detainees how they had themselves been beaten in colonial times.

In Moundié, the man in the street said it was quite normal.

"Ye-es, my brother."

A wink of the eye.

"Beat them well-well, those bandits."

"Kick them in the usual way."

"They should have killed them on the spot, yes. *Whereas,* they're going to get trial-trial there. White nonsense all that, for sure. You've killed, you've wanted to kill, I kill you and then it's finished."

"Yes, yes, my brother. Those soldiers have, anyway, already dug their graves in the cemetery. They say they should just be left to get on with the job. They are longing to do a bit of shooting: just hanging around and not making war, their guns are gathering rust and that's no good. Really."

The foreign teachers living near the prison couldn't sleep a wink. The screams of the *blues* were shattering their eardrums. The professors went to broach the subject with the young compatriot Cabinet Secretary. They invoked human rights, and described such behaviour as scandalous in the mid-twentieth century; furthermore, they had already alerted Amnesty International.

In their presence, the young compatriot Cabinet Secretary prevaricated, but as soon as they'd gone he admitted that the white teachers were right and should be supported.

"We can't renounce democracy completely and treat terrorists so barbarously."

I nodded my head and deplored the fact that there were too few Christians in the world who appreciated the need for pardon. The young compatriot looked at me pityingly and asserted that, as for him, he was an atheist and a militant in the class struggle to create a new type of man. That's what the young compatriot explained to me, in confidence. To the foreigners he had said that things weren't so simple and that it was difficult to master human sentiments after the massacre at the garden party.

The long-haired young Uncles looked at him with mistrust.

He wasn't discouraged by that. He explained to them that our jailers hadn't studied philosophy, and that if they had one, they drew it from a life denied all schooling.

The young Uncles concluded by saying that something must be done.

It was in his car that the young compatriot recounted for me these days full of the dramas of conscience.

We stopped at Yabaka's place. The Captain and his wife were still at dinner. On the table were enamel casseroles decorated with coloured flowers and bottles of water preserving their original labels. Spellbound by the television, which was broadcasting a documentary about dolphins, they were sucking the bones of a much-loved local meat. The Captain invited us to take seats at the table.

His wife had already risen to fetch plates and napkins for us. But the young compatriot Cabinet Secretary wasn't hungry. He even pulled a face. Well, I wasn't going to eat alone, apart from which Elengui would play the tragic queen if I didn't eat her food on my return. On the other hand, we accepted, one a banana, the other a guava.

"What intelligence these beasts have!"

We had to follow the film. The young compatriot Cabinet Secretary would make his proposal later.

At the end of the documentary, the announcer hailed one of those serials in which Inspector Colombo performs his miracles. Yabaka stroked his moustache and looked at us.

"Well?"

Madame Yabaka got up with a resigned air and was swallowed by the corridor, having scuffed her slippers on the floor and slowly waggled her bottom, in a coordinated movement natural to our women.

When the young compatriot Cabinet Secretary found the right moment to open his mind to Captain Yabaka, I recognised, almost word for word, the arguments which the young foreigners had used in besieging him. But I pretended not to be listening. I was captivated by the exploits of Inspector Colombo.

"Say then, do you think if they'd been given a chance, they'd have had pity on you?"

The young compatriot Cabinet Secretary replied, with that appropriateness of which intellectuals hold the secret; something right on the mark which I have now forgotten.

"You are right. Once again. But neither you nor I can permit ourselves to make remarks."

"Who then? Daddy owes you his post."

"Well, yes."

He stroked his moustache again.

"Yes. But the tribal lobby has already had another go at the matter. I am in their sights. You and the young intellectuals too, for that matter. They would have been very happy if it had been us who attempted the coup."

"However..."

He hesitated once again.

"I don't understand why you haven't seized the chance to come in like the third robber."

He had said this in a tight voice. The Captain shrugged his shoulders.

"I don't like either improvisation or adventurism."

The young compatriot Cabinet Secretary then went back to his first subject. Couldn't one do anything to put a stop to these brutalities?

"Play Don Quixote? In the present witch-hunting atmosphere, we'd be accused of complicity. The game isn't worth the candle."

"But..."

The Captain smiled like a man of experience listening to the Young Turks.

"You're too sentimental. History itself is cruel."

"Even the revolution...?"

"Certainly, the revolution too."

I could sense in the voice of the young compatriot Cabinet Secretary a great effort to find the right tone, which would enable him to explain without seeming to preach. At the outbreak of any revolutionary movement, was there not an impulse of revolt, therefore of sentiment? He spoke of torture and of execution. He cited the names of certian Uncles, spoke of the Algerian War, Vietnam, Papa de Gaulle; in short, a whole series of arguments which I can't reproduce, but which seemed to me well reasoned.

Yabaka was frowning and stroking his moustache.

"Torture is obligatory. It exists even in revolutionary regimes. How can you force a bandit to talk, unless you make him suffer?"

The other did not hesitate in his reply.

"But are you not in danger of making an innocent man confess to God knows what, by putting him to the question?"

"The fish trap, my dear fellow, has to put up with the cold of the water."

I knew that Yabaka was the military man closest to the young intellectuals. They all dreamed (without quite knowing how to effect it) of one day replacing Bwakamabé. But on that evening I felt there was a great gulf between them. Tired and put out, the young compatriot Cabinet Secretary seemed to turn his interest back towards the television.

In the car, as we returned home together, he smoked nervously. He needed fresh air. He opened all the windows and drove fast, letting the air strike him with the rhythm of a stiff wind-whipped curtain. The streets were full of patrols, but he paid no heed. The car radio, after broadcasting an educational program, broke off to announce the news. An editorial—one of Aziz Sonika's calling cards—castigated the coup leaders. He appealed to the vigilance of all citizens. All the traitors had not as yet been rounded up. Many were still at large or were even concealed in our own ranks. We must make a systematic hunt around ourselves to seek out the Fifth Column. Everyone had the duty to denounce whoever seemed to him suspect. Better to arrest an innocent for questioning than allow a hundred bandits to go free.

Hard words closed the end of the communiqué like a trap.

When the young compatriot Cabinet Secretary dropped me at my place, I found Elengui sleeping on an armchair in the front room. She had waited up for me, feeling disturbed. She had, indeed, kept some good dishes for me. We ate quickly and went to the bedroom.

We lay down side by side, clasping hands. That night I felt her go off to sleep squeezing my hand harder and harder.

At this stage in the story there should have been another encounter with Ma Mireille, thanks to the mediation of Cécile, her lady-companion. I had even written it, but on rereading I began to tremble; not, let me specify, because of the imaginative talents of the author, but the creative riches which Ma Mireille displayed under the hands of her lover.

Thus, all things considered, I decided to avoid an unequal clash with the censor.

The Army was still on alert. The troops were fed up with it. Far from their families and devoured by mosquitoes, tired of eating the meagre official rations provided by Monsieur Gourdain, the soldiers grew fouler and fouler in their language and made the village populations feel the full weight of their importance. Despite orders that Colonel Haraka should be taken alive, they grumbled that he, *walai!* that one, if they once got their hands on him, he would pay for all the fatigue-duty and days in the blockhouse that he'd imposed on them while still in command.

The people, who had been horrified in the days following the massacre at the Palace, began to forget that nightmare and, irritated by the behaviour of the troops, began also to find this undiscoverable colonel amusing. Stories and underground songs cast mockery at the unsuccessful security forces.

Delegations from the frontier provinces asked to be received by the President: they complained of the tendency of those in uniform to make exactions and demand sexual rights over and beyond what was allowed by custom and decorum. The services of Monsieur Gourdain were then asked to investigate these complaints. Calumny, calumny, insisted their report. Soldiers were soldiers; that is to say, not saints. But the whole affair must be looked at more closely. Was it possible that these complaints were nourished by a certain complicity with the fugitive? Eh? Let's put on our spectacles, make use of magnifying glasses and look a little closer.

It happened that, in the meantime, an elegant lady, passing the frontier check-points by rail, attracted the gaze of some hardened and happy soldier. Wrapped in a superwax cloth in the latest fashionable colour, the passenger flaunted a headtie fastened in that manner which young women in Moundié call *my-man's-up-to-it,* and which evokes all the allure that Caribbean girls can bestow on their madras. The officer demanded her papers, sure of detecting some fault that could form the basis of a little bargaining—an hour of affection to purchase his indulgence. But the lovely was perfectly (I was going to say "in form", which might seem like a mischievous play on words), let's say then, within the law in all respects. But a man of the law, with a little skill and plenty of malice, can always find that little defect which comes in handy at the right moment. The comrade therefore invited the lady to descend and step into the office where he passed his days and—as the campbed could testify—his very lonely nights. Severe up to this moment, the officer began to smile.

"Ehé, mama, we can arrange something, no?"

The lovely, obstinately silent, put her hand into her bag and pulled out some dollars, which she offered at the tip of her fingers.

"No,no,no. Don't switch roles like that. It's not what I want, mama."

The woman tried to dominate her fears, while the other continued with his rallying.

"Aaah! You too, sweet-mama, don't be afraid, *ko*. I'm not at all wicked."

He got up, walked round the desk and came towards her. She retreated. He wanted to seize her by the waist. Quicker than he, she opened the door to escape. But already, cries were raised to give the alert. And that wretched skirt in which one couldn't run! In a few strides, the sentry caught her and threw her like a parcel back into the office, slamming the door behind her and abandoning her to their chief, with raucous guffaws by way of musical accompaniment.

"It's just us two, now, mama!"

Grabbed at one bound, she was drawn without ceremony towards the thirsty brute. Disordered and anxious struggles. A woman is never very strong, and a man's muscles would always end by making her yield, even when she tries to play the vixen. But one would have sworn that this one had practised something like judo or—that style! the films, sure enough—karate. Well, well, look at that, mama! But even in such a case, these harlots can't resist the proximity of a male in good health, his odour, his breath. Body rubbing body, the solitude, awaken and unleash the sea within the belly of a woman, renewing all the desire of childish games in the forest. The man is sure of his victory... But what on earth is that long cry? Didn't you hear that? It wasn't a woman's voice. It wasn't the cry of climax. Then, like a reproach, in a huge gulp:

"But...but you've pricked me, woman!"

The door opens and the woman rushes out, as if carried by a powerful gust of air. A guard shoots. One, two, perhaps three bursts. The woman stumbles, tries to get up, then, like a footballer brought down by a foul tackle, falls at full length. They say that she breathed a few moments longer and that her lips framed one imcomplete, incomprehensible phrase. This passed in a few instants, and it was the end. The wrapper fell off by itself ... No, my brothers, it was not a woman.

Colonel Haraka!

The news was announced in a cry of victory to the Palace. Haraka's last victim was declared a national hero. With an official funeral, graveside eulogies, decorations and posthumous promotion. A pension for the widow. Bursaries from the state for his children, both those at home and those begotten on other mats. His name was to be engraved on the street leading to the Staff Headquarters.

The women no longer called that style of headtie *my-man's-up-to-it,* but *Haraka's headdress.*

Now nothing further could prevent the trial. Behind closed doors, it went forward of itself. The conspirators could not help but plead guilty. But there were some who insisted that, poor things, they had been drawn into it without understanding what it was all about. Like good soldiers, they had merely obeyed the orders of their superiors. Yes, Mr. Court President. They had been told that the President, the Chief, creator of a new regime of popular liberties, was threatened by Captain Yabaka and other enemies, and that they must therefore come to his rescue, *whereas* (the Court President corrected this in the record to *whereat*)... Yes, yes, yes, a story memorised and oft-repeated. See above. But the braver among them admitted that they had wished to rid the nation of Bwakamabé, because he was doing "Polépolé without Polépolé"; because his position, civil and military, against the communists was not clear enough; because he had too many civilians around him. But all this was said behind closed doors and one had to take the trouble of listening to radio grapevine in the back streets of Moundié if one wanted to piece it all together. Officially, Aziz Sonika and all the press claimed that the conspirators had freely admitted that they'd been involved in a purely tribal plot to benefit the Djassikini *racists. The Southern Cross* filled several pages with photos of every conspirator, head shaven, eyes forlorn, face swollen, a slate hung around the neck with the name chalked on. Already the faces of dead men.

> Colonel Haraka's *coup d'état* was a tragic event of utmost importance in our country's history. Many "Africanists" who have made names for themselves in the European, and even the African press, have tried to implicate Captain Yabaka in the affair, and have gone so far as to assert that his defection from it took place at the last moment, when it had become clear that the attempt had miscarried. Pursuing their "logic", they also blamed Yabaka for the violence of the ensuing repression, claiming that

he wanted thus to eliminate any embarrassing witnesses to his machinations.

As you know, I was absent from the country during those sad days, being in Yaoundé to represent the government at an international conference.

However, my position in Bwakamabé's regime and my relations with Yabaka enable me to speak with authority about this matter. It is even possible that my absence from the country that day will confer on my analysis a distance and objectivity which are lacking in many other accounts.

It is true that about this time Yabaka had begun to question the whole basis of our tactics, whose objective was to remain within the state apparatus, the better to control it, penetrate all its parts, and gradually remove it from the effective control of Bwakamabé himself. Some of his private remarks even led one to believe that the Captain was considering resignation.

Haraka, for his part, was disappointed with the Marshal's policies. Being very closely tied to Western circles and certain business interests, he nourished a secret hope of installing a dictatorship in which the governing group would consist entirely of military men. In his view, this was the only way to restore the confidence of capitalist investors, to whom he seems to have made promises of better deals. On this point, I have seen documents which make it incontestable.

In a word, his orientation was not fundamentally different from Bwakamabé's. Neither of them thought of anything better than perpetuating the neo-colonial model. The only contrast was one of style, Bwakamabé's burlesque antics were irritating to Haraka. He affirmed that the Western powers would not involve themselves further unless assured that the country was firmly held by a "serious hand".

The trip to China had infuriated Haraka. A visceral anti-communist, ignorant and inattentive towards changes in the world, he had interpreted that visit as a change of political orientation which must instantly be halted. In order to execute his plot quickly, he organised the soldiers of his own tribe, playing skilfully on that primitive solidarity which is fundamental in our country, and which was all the more effective because of a tradition dating from colonial times that favoured army recruitment from among the Djassikini tribe.

All this goes to say that if it is permissible to affirm that Haraka was at this time as opposed to Bwakamabé as Yabaka was, it is equally apparent that their motives were not only different, but even irreconcilable.

I am convinced that, in any case, Yabaka would not have given his consent even if he had been consulted. The Captain was profoundly democratic. Democracy was not just a principle of action, but a real faith. I must admit that many of us had tried to convince him of the necessity for a "progressive" *coup d'etat,* so dejected were we by the feebleness and fragility of peaceful methods.

It is now more or less proved that Haraka had obtained asylum in the Ugandan Embassy. He had lived there more than a month, and it obviously was not the seers but those Djabotama among the embassy staff who blew the whistle. Monsieur Gourdain had systematically greased the palms of all domestic servants working in the embassies accredited to the country.

If we look at the way Bwakamabé employed his time, we shall note that he was in Kampala some days before the capture of Haraka. This was obviously in order to obtain the release of the fugitive.

In the memoirs which he has published in English, Dibéke, then one of Idi Amin Dada's ministers, refers to the meeting of the two dictators and to the problems which then arose.* The communiqué published at the end of their meeting spoke of a "perfect identity of views" and underlined "the strengthening of ties of cooperation" between our country and Uganda. It is now irrefutably established that three army trucks were stationed in front of the Ugandan Embassy at two in the morning, during the night following Bwakamabé's return from Kampala. On board were Captain Botalayé and Lieutenant Kwilikali, both of them

* *Dark Days in Uganda*, Wallgren Publishing House, London, 1974.

well-known henchmen of the Marshal, and both since dead in mysterious circumstances. They took Haraka, tied up like a crude parcel, outside the town. All the rest was simply a Machiavellian charade.

What then was the episode of the officer stabbed by Haraka, disguised as a woman? The officer was certainly assassinated, but by someone entirely different: a peasant who wanted to avenge the violation of his daughter and who had implacably refused to make any sordid deal over the affair.

Spontaneous demonstrations were now being organised. From the thousand alleys of Moundié people descended, in party mood, with palm branches in their hands, towards the Hannibal-Ideloy Bwakamabé Na Sakkadé Square, in the centre of the Plateau. Beating drums, playing xylophones, clapping hands, wiggling hips, holding each other's shoulders, greeting each other from one group to another in carnival style, *wollé, wollé, woï, woï,* the people waved their banners aloft.

From the height of his platform, the Chief, flanked by his close comrades-in-arms and other colleagues, looked down on the flock of black-woollen sheep at their feet, as if it were a job to be proud of. The ground trembled under the tramping steps of the dancers. It was said that the noise reached even the condemned prisoners in Bangoura Prison, breaking their hearts asunder. Agents took note of any absentees among the throng.

Yes, we had all voluntarily left our houses. What with the radio battering us ceaselessly with the same sermons, we'd had enough. We'd also had enough of our national team losing all its matches. And of those cinemas showing a monotonous string of karate films, alternating with stagecoaches and Indians. And of the discos which emptied themselves every night to the strains of the same hits. Soukali apart, even our mistresses had begun to seem insipid.

They had baited us with loud posters in the same colours as for a singing tour by Bob Marley. Covered vans armed with loudspeakers on their roofs had been tumbling us from our beds for over a week, with the same news. The foremen had supplied lists to their bosses of those who... The chairmen of the block committees had supplied lists to the area chiefs of those who ...

Not a single tribe was missing from the assembly. All the masqueraders were there, all the *bubus* brought out from the cupboards, everyone had come to offer, aided by a thousand waggles of the hips, the most succulent morsels of their folklore. Dance, dance, dance and *wollé, wollé, woï, woï.* One urchin applauded so loudly that he lost hold of the branch he was sitting on and fell into the crowd. The Party organiser and the Chief of Protocol were fuming. The ambulance whined, the place was cleared up and the dances resumed. And *wollé, wollé, woï, woï!* The Party organiser, still enraged, hurled imprecations which the wind softened as soon as they left the loudspeakers and scattered to the skies. What matter? The people didn't need to hear everything before taking part.

"Wollé, wollé?"

"Woï, woï!"

One of the top local singers had just imitated Miriam Makeba.

"Wollé, wollé?"

"Woï, woï!"

The Party organiser burst again into his happy-fury act.

"Wollé, wollé?"

"Woï, woï!"

And the country's best male singer was imitating Bob Marley. He rendered *No woman, no cry,* with the refrain *O koma loka!* which in Kibotama means *O catch the bird.*

And the Paracommandos. And the Party organiser. And the Nephews. And the Party organiser. And the Ma Mireille Drum Majorettes. And the Party organiser.

"Wollé, wollé?"

"Woï, woï!"

Everyone stood on tiptoe, made giraffe-necks and opened both eyes and mouth wide, in order to glimpse the Chief blessing the crowd with his lion's tail. And while the crowd responded with a great shout, hands in the air, Monsieur Gourdain's spies frisked our chests, our backs, our arms, our thighs and our calves, in case some fool should think of playing the Dallas trick.

Unable to bear the constraint of a text, the son of Ngakoro, son of Fouléma, son of Kirêwa, switched freely between Kibotama and the language of the Uncles. When he used the latter, he neglected the difference between the *é,* the *è* and the *ai,* on the one hand; the *o* and *au* on the other; and, finally, between the *i* and the *u.* And if it was the language of the ancients which billowed forth, he mixed with it various exotic-sounding words, many of which ended in *-ism* or in *-ist.*

The orator spoke first of our Great-Historic-Courageous-and-Intrepid Armed Forces. Then, he pointed his right forefinger at someone in the crowd. Then, he indicated some objective lying behind us. By and by, he lifted his left forefinger towards the sky. He shook his hand as if he were slapping someone, well-well. Ah! that hand, that finger. Indefatigable as if in the midst of a battlefield, conducting an attack at an infernal pace or reviving his troops when they were threatened with exhaustion.

The Chief went up to the row of big metal cornets which lined the front of the platform and performed great movements of his jaws, as if he would devour all these objects with ferocity. He spat Kibotama words upon the body of Haraka. He insulted a group of the dead man's friends whose title ended in *-ist.* He abused the Djassikini. He sang the praises of some other group whose title also ended in *-ist.* And he broke off to swallow a mouthful of water.

A drum beat nervously and reawakened the Party organiser, who conducted us again.

"Wollé, wollé?"

"Woï, woï!"

And then he spoke of the Fifth Column. He threatened it with that finger. He hurled anathemas at the meeting-point of the thighs of his adversaries' mothers. And he revealed to us that Monsieur Gourdain had unearthed proofs of the support—the UN Security Council should hear of it—yes, in a plot to kill us all, all, all. And he explained to us again the so-and-so-there, if that so-and-so-there, with all those words in *-ism* and *-ist* pellmell, which clashed together and sounded good to the ear. And he abused a bit more. And he declared that all the Djassikini were thieves and their wives whores.

And the organiser ordered us to join in the abuse.

When the chorus fell silent, it was Daddy baying in baritone.

"Cunts of their motheerrrsssss!"

And applauding himself. And we applauding him. And he announced that the country was a paradise where it was sweet to live under him.

"*Wollé, wollé?*"

"*Woï, woï!*"

And he blessed us with his lion's tail. And he insulted Polépolé. Those gentlemen whose names ended in *-ist!* Listen! Listen! Enough names of animals to populate a whole savanna. And he lectured us. And he explained life to us. The goodies. The baddies. The traitors. Punishment. Vengeance. He assured us, cutting his throat with his finger, that he himself was no tribalist, no racist, but that those Djassikini were nothing but filth. Just that. The Jews of the country. And those gentlemen whose name ended in *-ist.* Always those.

The more intelligent among us nodded with an understanding air. But the majority had difficulty in following these flights. We were watchful to applaud whenever the organiser, or Daddy himself, gave the signal; to laugh whenever we saw a grin cracking; to shout whenever the tone of voice rose or the finger was waved quickly. Occasionally, ayayay! we made a blunder, but we were always quick to repair it. As for the babies, well-wrapped on their mothers' backs, they kept on sleeping as if they didn't give a damn for this palaver.

Daddy's inexhaustible finger continued its energetic dance: it protested, it denounced, it exhorted, it battled, it revolted, it ordered, it announced, in a word (and still more, in a thousand) it judged. And everything became clear to us. At least, to the elite. For the humble ones of Moundié, the voice of the Chief remained unfathomable.

A whole hour, in the attitudes and accents of a belligerent drunkard. And then once more the carnival of the militant masses. Many hours. And *wollé, wollé, woï, woï.* It was truly a great meeting. Our heads were turned. The Djassikini, treading with discretion, crept off with unhappy smiles on their lips to shut themselves in their houses before nightfall.

An enormous meeting. Five, ten thousand people? Fifty thousand, said the close companions-in-arms. A hundred thousand, affirmed Aziz Sonika's editorial.

"*Maître,* a Chivas! And a double, if you please."

"When?"

Soukali shouted into the mouthpiece.

"When?"

I wasn't sure if I understood her.

"Don't play the Mongolian."

Actually, she said the *Mongol*. "If you go on like this, you'll see."

"I'll see what?"

"Just go on and you'll see."

"Yéhé! But Soukali, you too, just listen to me, *ko*."

"I'm fed up."

"But how is that? Monsieur the Inspector is there at this very moment."

"And what of it? Are you scared?"

"Me, scared?"

"Yes, you are."

"Soukali... "

"You're scared."

"But, where?"

"Where? Where? In the street, of course."

I smiled, confusedly.

"Of course, you wait for me to find the place. One would think that you were tired of seeing me."

"Soukali..."

"Oh, yes. If I didn't force you, you'd go at least two weeks without seeing me."

"Soukali, don't talk like that!"

"I *will.*"

"O.K., O.K. I'll look for a place."

"I've already found one."

She dictated to me an exact address in Moundié.

"Good. About ten o'clock tonight. Is that all right?"

"Weeee! Listen to the man-o! So you too think the thing can only be done at night?"

"No..."

"When, then? Eh?"

"No, but in the daytime there's..."

"Stories! Stories!"

"Soukali!"

"If you were your own boss, even the emperor of the country, you'd still be frightened of Elengui."

"Don't talk about Elengui! It's not right. In the daytime..."

"Listen, you get your act together, or it's never again."

Trailing clouds of the anti-Djassikini storm continued to trouble the skies. Both radio and television kept broadcasting, blow-by-blow and many times a day, accounts of the "historic" meeting. For three weeks consecutively, these replaced the usual educational and variety programs.

Then fell a shower of messages. The Number One Federal District of the capital announced that "in these sad and decisive hours, marked by new criminal attempts from enemies of the Nation, and from puppetism, behold before you, Daddy, our respected and beloved leader, sons of the whole country mobilized into a single man to wash off the shame and the stain with which the unworthy Djassikini have disfigured it."

Other provinces and districts followed. Messages tumbled from the teleprinters like grasshoppers in the sun at change of season, all of them crafted upon the same model. Once again, the subversion of the gentlemen ending in *-ist* had shown its true colours, by unleashing a new phase in the permanent plot organised against our country ever since independence. But once again the vigilance and genial power of Daddy, Supreme Strategist, Creator of the New Regime of Popular Liberties, had unmasked and disembowelled the conspiracy. In this latest attempt, the enemy had made use of racism as an instrument, as a tactical means of demobilization, corruption, and recruitment to its ranks of all those who lent their ears to racial arguments. The plotters had thus attracted those individuals who thought that the welfare of the country couldn't be achieved without the protection of foreign powers and could be effected only by the satisfaction of their selfish needs, while the masses lived in a vast concentration camp; people who did not realize that rights were not bestowed by birth, but were earned by duty; people who could not lift their consciences to the same level as their education; people, that is, who "had eyes not to see and ears not to hear". Faced with this situation, the signatories wanted to express their extreme indignation. They had been deluded by those civic elders or members of the Great-Historic-Courageous-and-Intrepid Armed Forces whom they had innocently mistaken for sincere citizens, willing to put their knowledge, their expertise and their "expert-ease" at the service of our beloved Daddy, Father of National Resurrection, Creator of the New Regime of Popular Liberties, to whom they owed everything, while by contrast these traitors were nothing but ..."

There followed a string of animal names, each dressed in an appropriate adjective. They condemned and would always condemn without reserve those who would employ racism and force, for whatever purpose it might be. Consequently, they were firmly resolved to participate actively and effectively in the campaign of spiritual disintoxication and moral rearmament which must now restore health to all those who had been affected by the poison of racism spread by these scoundrels, thirsty for power and avid for wealth. They asserted that his personal example, that of Daddy, Creator of the Regime of

Popular Liberties, had taught them to place themselves above all irrational considerations such as racism, tribalism, regionalism, etc.

In conclusion, they all demanded the most exemplary punishment. "*Wollé, wollé, woï, woï*" and "an eye for an eye, a tooth for a tooth" were the signatures most employed. Elengui, clapping her hands and then carrying one to her mouth, observed that the country was growing more and more astonishing. Even those incapable of writing the simplest letter had suddenly become masters in the art of composing political resolutions.

A great Djassikini regional chief swore on his honour to fight side-by-side with Daddy against racism, from whatever source, even if from his own circle. Another Djassikini, personnel manager of a well-known colonial firm, wrote:

"I want to declare solemnly to you my availability to remain totally and permanently in the vanguard of the fight against racism, for the triumph of our resurrectional cause... Your pointing out the faults of certain sons of my tribe comforts me, for more than one reason, above all when it constitutes a rehabilitation. You have, O Supreme Leader, opened my eyes and brought me to the light. Before this, I associated only with members of my tribe. From now on, I swear, I will mingle *systematically* with those of other tribes, the better to understand them and improve myself."

So you say! observed Elengui. At the time reserved for the Kissikini programs, a physics professor of that tribe declared: "*Mana foléma, mana toukaré lowisso natina*", which could be translated as "We shall all fight resolutely against racism."A Djassikini permanent secretary in one of the ministries joined the chorus, then a joint director of the river-port, then a provincial engineer. Aziz Sonika opened an article in *The Southern Cross* with the headline DJASSIKINI LEADERS CONDEMN RACISM, which contained the phrase: "Our desire is to join the same train as our brothers of the other national tribes." "*Wollé, wollé, woï, woï,* for the campaign to re-educate the misled Djassikini." "To be rehabilitated means, for a Djassikini, to abandon separatism." "We must rise above our defects and re-establish ourselves in the breast of the Nation, wiping off the stain which has been put upon us by some of our false brothers." "Every Djassikini leader must join battle against those who have soiled our dignity." "Victory belongs to the camp of the Resurrection, not to that of racism." "We must not live for life's sake, but live to serve always in the cause of Resurrection."

It was this last phrase, chosen by Daddy, which the Party militants inscribed in letters of gold upon all the banners which they strung between the trees or the telegraph-poles along all the main streets of the capital. Our best known band composed a high-life whose refrain was true to the banners and whose verses, the rosary beads from other professions of faith.

Such was the ambiance in which the mutineers were shot and many Djassikini incarcerated in Bangoura Prison or deported to remote jails in the bush.

The Party Youth insisted that henceforth the papers for all examinations or national competitions must bear the name of the applicant's tribe. Next day, Daddy decreed it.

Several more Djassikini were executed and it was decided that they should no longer enjoy scholarships, nor enrol in the diplomatic service or the army.

After reading the preceding pages, the young compatriot ex-Cabinet Secretary is stupefied by my ability to reproduce, almost word for word, the texts of the messages, but he accuses me of depicting the Djassikini people as cowards.

On the first point, I will come clean. In reality, I have been content to copy the messages from a propaganda journal of our continent which I have before me. It comes from a country which borders on our own.

As for the second, it's enough to ask in reply whether we should continue to live on myths, or whether our weaknesses don't also deserve the truth, something which certainly doesn't imply any spite on my part towards the Djassikini.

It was an ordinary house in the elite quarter, a few streets inside Moundié. The house of an unmarried friend who had made her arrangements not to return home that night until very late.

I lifted all the flowerpots on the verandah—no key! Had I understood properly? I pushed the handle of the door. She was already there. She pulled me towards her and the ceiling spun.

"Wretch, couldn't you give me the news sooner?"

I said nothing, contenting myself with stroking her, like an opium-eater in his den. I heard her whisper.

I told her I loved the flimsy panties and the brassiere she was wearing.

"It was my husband who bought them when he was on a trip to Europe. Now, you talk ..."

To keep her quiet, I began Castor and Pollux, the thread in the reel, the embrace of the silkworm, the two slopes of the hill, the bow of the double-bass, and the carp and the gudgeon ...

We supped full of our own odours. But the silence never lasted long. God! What a babbler! A torrent.

"Look at that! Now you are going to look at the time!"

"I have to. Your friend will be back soon, no?"

"You're afraid above all to be caught in bed *flagrante delicktus,* I know."

I looked at her again, her belly lying on mine, half-rising, passing her hands over my face and brushing off some invisible dust.

"Big-head!"

"Big-head?"

"Yes, sir."

"Don't get you."

"Don't play the Mongol."

I thought she was becoming really touching. But no, this was no longer a joke.

"You're always in such a rush. One would think you see me only as a duty. As for me, I organise my whole life around us. You... "

She was right. But did I do it on purpose? When things took this turn, I threw myself into everything she was dreaming of:

the choice morsel of the cake, the wave and the censer, the wind in the gardenias, the salute to the moon, the arrow in the bull's-eye, the long tour of the Tropics, the missionary, of course. Everything, in short.

Yéhé! You'll begin to think I'm boasting, but I assure you that then it was really "life-and-a-half", as I've seen it called in a book somewhere, long since.

I haven't described all Daddy's travels. But, even if I've been content to describe only a few, the Chief loved movement. State visits or working tours, journeys of friendship, sudden oscillations in the service of his "good neighbour" policy, international conferences of this organisation or that, regional summits, national festivities of brotherly or comradely countries, and, frequently, private vacations in France or Switzerland. No opportunity to see a country was ever passed up. My friend the young compatriot Cabinet Secretary, devoting himself to a mischievous calculation, was able to prove that the President passed an average of less than fifteen days a month in the country. According to radio grapevine, he was always careful on these journeys to carry with him all the cash in the Public Treasury, so as to paralyze anyone who might toy with the idea of playing the trick he had played on Polépolé. These were doubtless only stories, which were given a certain plausibility by Daddy's style, but which I am in no position to confirm. The spirit of objectivity, on the other hand, obliges me to record that Daddy took his journeys very seriously. How often have I not heard him complain:

"Nobody wants to understand me! We are in the age of Concorde and of personal diplomacy. Anyone would think I travel the world for the sake of tourism. Whereas, all this travelling exhausts me, it breaks my back... I'm no longer the right age for it... If it wasn't for the prestige of the country..."

And his gaze seemed to lose itself in rich, secret, Eden-like horizons of which he was deprived by public affairs and the spirit of sacrifice.

"Not to mention that I risk my life every time."

"Your precious life."

"Thank you, my boy, thank you, thank you, thank you. May God bless you."

And he brandished his lion's tail above his obliging colleague's head.

"Whenever one embarks in those machines..."

And he plunged into long and knowing digressions.

The people of Moundié had their own vision of this politics of travel. When Daddy was in the capital, they loved to make fun of it.

"Eh! my brother, have you heard the latest? Daddy is on an official visit to our country!"

I went with him on a tour through the Libotama Province.

A week beforehand, the specialists in Monsieur Gourdain's service, reinforced by a diviner, had left to reconnoitre. They sounded opinions, inspected the rooms in the houses where the Chief was to stay, distributed handfuls of notes stamped with his effigy, made lists of the most appetizing virgins and drove off all evil spirits, in a thousand senses of the term. Suddenly, more agents of the Fifth Column were unmasked than one would have dreamed existed. The greatest haul was made among rivals, creditors and certain leaders high up in the hierarchy of the Party of National Resurrection. Once the initial moment of astonishment was past, everyone set his memory to work; shaking it a bit; even giving it a few knocks to make up for false contacts, when it wasn't quick enough off the mark; pointedly remembering such a gesture, such a remark, such a look, bizarre enough certainly, but to which one hadn't paid much attention at the time. Certain consciences, somewhat hesitant in the midst of this general movement, were, after a brief agitation, pacified quickly enough by one means or another. When all was accomplished, reports were sped to the capital announcing that the mission was completed, the way prepared, and that the Grand Priest could now advance into the jungle. These were the exact words employed in the coded messages. I've been told as much by the young compatriot Cabinet Secretary.

At Libotama, the Prefect, clad in the white uniform of a colonial administrator, was awaiting us on a landing strip camouflaged by a green carpet of grass, calf-high. He was flanked by his Sub-Prefect and by a Deputy for the region, a crow in his black jacket set off by a red-spotted necktie. The ceremony was much like that for a visiting president in the capital: bouquets of flowers, handclaps, reviewing the guard of honour...

"Gre-a-t G-o-d!" thundered Daddy. "What's the meaning of this?"

Smiles froze on lips. The entourage and the regional officials began asking themselves if this was a joke, or the beginnings of Chiefly fury.

"What does it mean?"

His eyes were balls charged with lightning. Always the Guinarou.

"Gourdain!"

The man addressed stuck out his chest and tossed up his chin, showing off his Adam's apple to advantage.

"Gourdain, seize this man!"

He pointed his lion's tail at the Prefect's chest.

"Gre-a-t G-o-d! Are there no more prisoners in Libotama?"

He didn't catch the word that oozed from the Medusa-struck visage of the Prefect.

"Can't reply, eh? Blockhead, get out! No more prisoners?"

"Y-yes, Mr President."

"All right, call them all out at once. You hear? And a machete apiece. This evening..." He looked them right in the eye and shook his head at the sky. "...I don't want a single blade of grass on this airfield. Good God! As for that one..."

He pointed his tail straight at the Prefect.

"Let him join the others. I want them to bring all the cut grass to him and make him eat it, you hear? Let them stuff him but good!"

"At your command, Mr President!"

"And keep me informed."

Daddy turned towards the crowd of Libotamas and blessed them with the lion's tail.

"Wollé, wollé?"

"Woï, woï!"

"Wollé, wollé?"

"Woï, woï!"

"You there!"

The Sub-Prefect, squinting blackly, watched the lion's tail advance dangerously, like a spear, towards his nose.

"Take command!"

The President and his close companions-in-arms mounted into the few Land Rovers possessed by the Prefecture. The entourage jumped sportively into a truck and followed the cortege in a hooting onslaught. At the entrance to the Prefecture, the whole convoy halted. The President descended from his vehicle. The traditional chiefs came to kneel before him. One by one, they offered the handfuls of earth they were carrying, then passed under his right foot, which he lifted slightly at each passage. He acknowledged their homage by blessing them with his lion's tail, thus indicating his acceptance of them under his protection and the offer of his aid and counsel. The drums sounded and the dancers wheeled around the Chief of chiefs, whom the crowd watched as he climbed into a sort of sedan chair, draped in the colours of the national flag. And the whole procession, blazing with songs and dances, advanced towards the main square—the Hannibal-Ideloy Bwakamabé Na Sakkadé Square. A ballet, coloured with the thousand choreographic riches of the land, intoxicated the senses. Officials and schoolchildren lining the route waved placards and banners, accompanying this warm tumult with movements of their feet or their torsoes. Daddy read all the inscriptions, rich in their philosophy and singular in their originality: "Long Live the Supreme Strategist"; and a thousand others of the same ilk, not forgetting a vigorous denunciation of the Fifth Column, insults against Haraka and against the gentlemen ending in *-ist.*

From the height of his chair, with a debonair smile on his lips, Daddy blessed all these woolly heads with his lion's tail. Joyous gunfire crackled in the air. The cortege halted again before the Prefect's residence. Before allowing the President to enter, a man dressed as a traditional warrior knelt before him and offered him a kola nut. By the way in which Daddy broke it, the crowd recognised a son of Libotama.

"Wollé, wollé?"

"Woï, woï!"

"Wollé, wollé?"

"Woï, woï!"

Excited by the cries of the crowd, the warrior began to dance jerkily around the Chief, shaking his head ceaselessly as he moved. Daddy looked on for a moment with interest and visible sympathy. Then, suddenly, carried away by the power of the rhythm, he joined in the final steps of the warrior's dance. Despite his Quai d'Orsay suit, he rediscovered the cadence of communal festivities in the days of his youth. The crowd, entranced, swallowed up the Chief with its applause and raised a long clamour.

With the movements of one possessed, but still under the penetrating orders of the drum, the warrior cut the throats of a white and then a black cock, spurting the blood onto the steps of the Residence. Daddy mounted them, taking care that his feet should tread through the scarlet stains.

The Prefect's family had evacuated the huge house, inherited from the Commandants of the colonial era, leaving it to the sole disposition of their great guest. The only people admitted to the reception room were the close companions-in-arms and the Acting Prefect. A young college girl recruited for the occasion, curtseyed before Daddy.

"Ek...(she cleared her throat)...Excellency, what shall I bring you?"

"Chivas!"

The girl, more and more ill at ease, stooped towards the President.

"'Scuse...'scuse me, I didn't quite understand, Mr President."

Paternally, the Chief took her by the shoulders and scrutinised her like a connoisseur while the entourage struggled with its embarrassment, but managed to display relaxed smiles.

"Excuse us, Excellency," intervened the Sub-Prefect, now

acting for his senior, "the other fellow didn't think of that. If it had been myself..."

"We have brought it along ourselves," the Chief of Protocol intervened. "Just a question of getting it from the plane, if you will permit..."

"Yes. Good. Just plain whiskey, then. That Johnny Walker...with ice."

Feeling the look of her beloved President fastened on her, the young girl moved off clumsily, her forehead pearled with sweat. Not daring to move her eyes, she nevertheless felt the Chief's powerful glance pierce her neck and insinuate itself around her shoulder. The Sub-Prefect approached her.

"Well, is there some ice?"

His voice was irritated.

"Some...some pieces, yes."

Relieved, he returned to his place near the great guest, who was at that moment launching into a long, scientific explanation: he really loved whiskey, Daddy. Like all military men, strong drink made him feel good. No better medicine. He held out his now empty glass for a refill. All serious doctors would confirm this.

"And then, if alcohol kills slowly..."

He smiled and completed the quip.

The whole group burst out laughing, with the sound of a sackful of palm-fruit tumbling down a staircase. Except Monsieur Gourdain. Daddy continued his lecture: this Chivas contained a certain product, what was it called, now? Ah! He looked towards his doctor, who raised his eyebrows in silent embarrassment. *In any case,* resumed Daddy, the name of the product had been given him by Professor Bouvier of the Medical Faculty at Montpelier, and it was a product in Chivas which permitted concentration of the vital faculties and cleaned out the kidneys. Yes, yes, there were even theses on this subject. The young girl brought the pale, tobacco-coloured liquid.

"That's a shot for a footslogger!"

The Acting Prefect launched, no, fired, or rather *discharged* a lightning bolt at the unhappy girl. More and more awkwardly, she came back to double the dose.

"It's like palm-wine," observed a member of the delegation, turning the discussion back to Chivas. "Doctor Malvoisier, who spent nearly ten years in Libotama, has proved that it contains certain vitamins."

"Oh, yes?"

"I assure you. Even, that it never makes you drunk. It sometimes turns the head, but it isn't truly...(he made a face) drunkeness, not that."

"Really? Really? I never knew."

"I'm telling you. It's good for the health."

"We must do some research into it."

Daddy pointed towards the young compatriot Cabinet Secretary.

"It's for you, the intellectuals, to discover all these things for us."

"Ah!" (A toss of the head backwards) "But our intellectuals here only want to play politics."

"True enough."

"All full of ambition."

"You said it. As if those Pasteurs and those Einsteins of theirs wanted to spend their time politicking!"

Daddy shook his lion's tail several times with a concentrated air.

"Good. Very good reply. Very good, my boy."

"However, those are wise men. Real wise men. There you are, then! They let their elders do the governing."

"As for themselves, they stay in their laboratories. You won't ever find one of *them* trying to give lessons in politics."

"Everyone to his own work, eh?"

"But here, our intellectuals only know how to stir up opposition, or else stay back in France."

"And among all those *-ist* fellows, to top it all."

"Oh yes, fooling with *-ist* in Paris. In the Pigalle district. But they're afraid to go to the *-ist* countries, those clowns."

"Ah, let them be. But you're right."

And glasses met mouths, and second shots were poured and

voices raised, and one laughed and was proud of oneself.

Like a man freshly clad in mourning, I no longer hunger for the atmosphere of dance balls, where not long ago I would discover life's sweetest pleasures. It was only to satisfy Boubeu that I let him take me last night to the Hibiscus, *a fashionable discotheque beside the sea.*

The bandy-legged company, three girls and five men, presaged an extremely boring evening. I only danced once. The politeness of a cavalier towards the plainest one, who never stopped beating the rhythm with her head or her feet, while her husband, an industrial tax official, developed some learned theory or other to Boubeu.

From the terrace where we were sitting, I looked down critically at the grotesque movements of the dancers, enclosed in that aquarium, shot through with beams of light flashing in time to the syrupy tones of the music. The ideas of our mediocre philosopher afflicted me and pushed me deeper into silence.

After each piece, the dancers came in small clusters, happy or romantic, to take their seats or enjoy the breeze on the terrace. Without retraint, my gaze followed a white woman in clinging white slacks. Her clothes highlighted the curves of her figure which, despite hips a little too emphatic, I found seductive. Her breast rose and fell slowly, like that of a sportswoman after exercise. One would have thought she wanted to fill her nostrils and her whole body with each draught of the sea air, with each patch of sky, with each element of the night.

In the half-light, the face looked familiar to me, without my being able to put a name to it. Some picture in a magazine? The curves of some celebrity whose identity escaped me? Or else the realization of some strange dream? I no longer heard the analyses of the executive, nor the small-talk of the table.

The D.J. had put on a "slow" that was all the rage. Fernando, *I think it was. A melody that twisted itself around your body. She began moving her shoulders, like a chilly bird fluffing out its wings. Turning quickly, as if coming to a decision after a pause for concentration, she came towards our group. She was making for us, for me, I knew it, I felt it. No, she ignored me. I saw her stoop and without warning, kiss the startled Boubeu on the neck. Her flattered friend laughed, recognised her in a sweep of his arms to the skies and, with great warmth, put his arm round her waist and abandoned the official in order to plunge onto the dance floor with her.*

I quickly swallowed my whiskey, lit a cigarette and made my way, coughing, to the bar to settle our bill discreetly. Boubeu and the unknown woman whose face was gnawing at my memory were dancing on the spot, in the middle of the floor, eyes closed, in a posture of intimate affection which stirred in me an absurd resentment. I ordered a second round for the company and settled the whole bill at once.

At the end of the dance, Boubeu presented her to us, with the gestures of a milord. *I didn't get her name clearly. When we shook hands, I thought I felt a hesitant squeeze, but she scarcely looked at me, while smiling already towards my neighbour. She rejoined her friends, who must have been inside awaiting her.*

I made an exhibition of myself to a rock number from the 'fifties with one of the girls from our table, glancing from the corner of my eye to see whether the woman in the white slacks was paying me any attention.

When we were leaving the Hibiscus, *I saw her dancing with a tall man whose hair curled over his neck. With her cheek against his chest, she was clasping that neck with her arms.*

Boubeu and the rest wanted to end the evening at La Maquina Loca.

"There are fewer toubabs *in that place and the music's better."*

I knew I would sleep badly, but I nevertheless insisted on taking leave of them. They uttered the protesting cries of a group in party mood, reinforcing their polite wish for my company, but I resolutely entered a taxi cruising in front of the club.

"I must talk to you."
Boubeu gave me an affectionate tap on the shoulder.

Everything was ready for the meeting in Hannibal-Ideloy Bwakamabé Na Sakkadé Square. First came the obligatory *wollé, wollé, woï, woï,* like welcoming bouquets of flowers. Then the provincial Chief of Protocol announced that the Acting Prefect would open the proceedings by giving "a great toast to the happy arrival". And told him to do so. An unconscious copy of the welcomes given by Daddy when receiving one of his peers on an official visit. Everyone clapped and the Scouts sang, conducted by a chorus master who bent forwards and designed arabesques with his fingertips:

Go,
Scout of France
With your staff in your hand...

When Daddy rose, the drums rolled and the *wollé, wollé, woï, woï* were even more prolonged and slower to die than before. He blessed the crowd with his lion's tail. And he talked. He said thanks, thanks, thanks, really great thanks. And he gave the opening formula for a tale and the crowd happily capped it with the reply. And he repeated it and the crowd responded. And he repeated it once more, on a more piercing note than the first two times, and the crowd replied more strongly. But that didn't satisfy him. And he asked if he should talk. And the crowd said yes. And he asked if he should reveal all and the excited crowd replied that he must. And he asked if he should get to the very bottom of things and the rapturous crowd cried that he must get to the very bottom. It was then that he claimed the joy of a father in rediscovering his children and the crowd interrupted him; singing and clapping:

Daddy has come back to us, wéwé,
The famine must end...
Daddy has come back to us, wéwé,
The famine must end...

He cried thanks, thanks, thanks, really great thanks. He announced again the joy of a father rediscovering his children. He reclaimed and reaffirmed his roots. He said he had forgotten nothing, that he would never break the vows made on the night of his circumcision. And he made promises. His Minister of Finance frowned heavily. What matter! He announced, just the same, a new road, a new school, a college, a high school, a hospital to replace that old dispensary which was more like a latrine. Water, electricity, telephones, television, a modern stadium, a hotel, a factory, jobs...and he just couldn't go on. His words were drowned in one great joyous sound. Drums, dances, ululations, hoarse shouts, wild cries...the organizer managed to restore a semblance of order with barrages of *wollé, wollé, woï, woï.* The Chief was conducted back to his seat and the gifts began to pour in: delegations from different parts of the Prefecture and its Sub-Prefectures presented, some, the tusks of elephants; some, freshly killed game; some, poultry or sheep with plumes or fleeces of the sacred colour; some, eggs; some, brilliantly coloured fruit; some, objects of symbolic value. Each time, Daddy stretched out his hands to receive the gifts, but Protocol snatched them in an instant and handed them to Monsieur Gourdain's henchmen for an examination which probed their length, breadth, and above all their depth, before whisking them off somewhere. The Chief of Protocol took careful note of the name of each delegation. Next day, any missing areas were called to account and required to explain their absence. The liberated schoolboys recited some complimentary verses and were quickly forgotten in the onrush of a group completely carried away by a well-known traditional dance. The women all advanced from one quarter, their breasts bare and their hips embellished only with a cord of vegetable fibres; the men faced them. At regular intervals, the two lines approached each other at a dance step, every dancer seeking to win over and attach a partner from the opposite rank. It was a long business, in which the sought-after girl generally didn't allow herself to be convinced by the initial contortions. For a while, she put on the airs of a timid virgin, eyelids lowered and head held askance, playing hard-to-get. But see that other woman, breast extended and head at a conquering angle, who announces her self-possession right down her spine and into the wriggling of her loins. *Wallai!* At last, both ranks, with a common accord, threw themselves into a demonic rhythm, borne up by the drums; movements of love-making in the freest and most energetic styles imaginable, with a richness and variety of postures expressing the imagination of each couple. The crowd, tenderly recognizing these evocations of the supreme pleasure, as much as those of intimate foreplay, felt something slip free in its breast and congratulated the actors with unrestrained shouts and hurrahs of applause, a thousand times warmer than those which had acknowledged the speeches a while before.

I saw Daddy stoop to the ear of the Acting Prefect and point out a young dancer with firm breasts. The high regional official responded with intelligent movements of his head.

Another speech was needed to end the ceremony. This was the business of the most senior host, the Deputy of the region. Filled with the importance of this honour, he came solemnly forward, instantly recognizable among everyone by his black jacket and long tie covered in red spots.

"The ceremony is concluded."

The crowd applauded, just like a bunch of kids greeting the recreation bell with a thousand cries. And while he was still orchestrating the last exchanges of *wollé, wollé, woï, woï,* a group came forward to unfold a certain situation to the President. He listened at first with an attentive expression, nodding his head repeatedly with an approving air, then suddenly exploded into the healthy laugh of a soldier on the spree.

"No joking? That's not bad, then!"

Daddy, looking towards the most senior minister present, crooked his finger, as if pulling a trigger.

"You there, just listen to this. Go and tell him, now."

The minister just managed a faint smile.

"Did you hear that?"

And Daddy became serious again, all of a sudden.

"Now then, no sentimentality. Let him be taken to the doctor, so that he can be brought round. And immediately after that, second course. He must eat all of it. That little cunt must learn. Nothing for it but the methods of Indochina and North Africa. You'll see. It's excellent."

Down there, the punished Prefect could no longer swallow the smallest sprig from the airstrip.

What finally happened to him? Radio grapevine reported that he had finally succeeded in swallowing all the prescribed grasses, had fallen sick thereby for several weeks, but survived. I would have doubted this had I not met the disgraced official later, many years later, in Moundié. But, even though I didn't dare question him about it, I have some suspicion of trickery on his part, or on that of his "executioners".

I'm certain I saw arriving at Daddy's residence that evening, first the girl who served him drinks at our arrival, and later one of the dancers. I underline this detail only to demonstrate the high amatory performance of Daddy, not with any other motive. How would I dare? Up to a certain rank, all the members of the delegation had the pleasure of discovering under their mosquito nets, at the end of the day, a gift that was living, young, hot and firm, and which it would have been maladroit, nay insulting, to refuse. I have myself profited from this custom many times. This is a legacy from our ancient traditions which, moreover, the most intelligent of the Uncles have urged us to preserve scrupulously, to protect ourselves from the alienating and isolating influences of the modern world. My grandfather, who was of high rank among the Djabotama—hence the possessor of many wives—never missed an opportunity to gratify a guest in this manner, for the sweetening of his stay.

Next day, there was a big meeting in the college. The tables were arranged in a U: the President at the base, the four deputies of the region beside him, the ministers a little further off, to the right of the Acting Prefect. After a brief introduction by the last-named, the doyen of the Djabotama parliamentarians (the one of the black jacket and spotted tie) spoke on behalf of everybody. He held his paper in one hand, while brandishing the forefinger of the other.

"Your Excellency!"

The poignant silence of the villages fell.

"*By the present intervention, oh! how much a message from us, it is my humble duty to relate succintly to you all our sufferings which require an appropriate response, for many wait with abnegation, due to the aberrant tendencies which impede the free passage of our products and our writings towards Your Excellency in particular and to all those surrounding you in general.*"

And the old one continued studiously, like a peasant indifferent to cruel mockery, a long speech larded with classic past tenses, subjunctives and allusions to the Pantheon of Ancient Greece.

Apart from myself, no one was really listening.

He was loudly applauded. *Pwa, pwa, pwa. Pwa, pwa, pwa.*

He stopped and folded up his paper. One might say that his nervous hands crumpled it. Looking from the nodding President to the silent hall, he threw his fist in the air and bellowed.

"*Wollé, Wollé?*"

"*Woï, woï!*" replied the hall.

"*Wollé, wollé?*"

"*Woï, woï!*"

The Deputy resumed his seat amid the applause of a satisfied audience. Another man now rose, breast adorned with a diagonal scarf in the Party colours. Another elected leader, no doubt. But a murmur ran through the hall, now blossoming into smiles. As the man approached, I read an inscription on his scarf. He came to a halt just in front of Daddy, to whom the Acting Prefect slipped a piece of paper.

The newcomer presented himself:

"Jim Ngwalessa, called Misadventure, C.E.O., elected by the business leaders and money-lenders of the Libotama community."

The crowd broke into peals of laughter and loud applause. My neighbour whispered to me that this was a former orderly of the administration, since retired, and now running the most popular bar-*cum*-shop in the Prefecture. Daddy, who had just finished mouthing through the Acting Prefect's note, smiled rapidly. I managed to decipher the inscription on the scarf. It was the exact title with which Jim Ngwalessa had just introduced himself.

"Speak Kibotama, *ko*."

The room was suddenly like a punctured tube. It struggled to restrain its impulse to laugh, but finished by letting it out, little by little. The man continued in the same vein.

"Leave off that foreign tongue, *dé*. Speak Kibotama now, *ko*."

"Kibotama, Kibotama! What sort of incitement is that, eh? You think you're the only one who knows how to knock that lingo with his tongue?"

"Ah, talk Kibotama, you too!"

"Okay. Shit! Just listen."

And bending his right arm with a theatrical flourish, he began in perfect alexandrines:

O combien de marins, combien de capitaines
Qui sont partis joyeux pour des courses lointaines,
Dans ce morne horizon...

And suddenly, like a kite which has decided to fly, he was off, reciting the famous verses of Hugo amid a reverent silence:

...de vieux parents, qui n'avaient plus qu'un rêve,
Sont morts en attendant tous les jours sur la grève
Ceux qui ne sont jamais revenus!

The crowd broke out in respectful and sincere applause. Jim was at attention in front of Daddy. He made a little Japanese-style leap, then returned to his place, his neck filled with pride, like a player who has just hit the mark. Just before sitting down, he paused, gazed at the representatives of Libotama and hurled at them:

"Your mother's cunt!"

The laugh that greeted him confirmed that there was no ill-will towards the old man.

There were several more orators to make their contributions, beginning with "as you have so justly remarked", or some such phrase, and who strove to impress upon Daddy that they, at least, had well understood the Chief's lecture, but that it would be a struggle to get it across to their fellow-citizens.

Daddy replied to all of them in one go, emphasising that he was pleased with this family discussion; that he loved the frankness of it; that it was not good to harbour evil thoughts deep in the heart; that by bringing them into the open one created the occasion for clearing up any misunderstandings; that he had not been insensible of his brothers in the bush; but that problems shouldn't be posed in terms of regions and that he, Daddy, was the father of all regions and all tribes, so... And he began to take issue with the Honourable Deputy. He shook him a bit with his words, certainly, but with discretion for, as the elders say, when one beats one's own child one softens the blows. And he went on to a fresh enumeration of all the promises he had made at the previous day's meeting. He was clapped all over again. I was not following at this point. I kept looking back towards Jim.

Daddy's conclusion was a recapitulation of his promises, during which the Minister of Finance kept nursing his chin, careful to ignore any looks in his direction.

"At the beginning it was action! An end to unkept promises. A promise is a debt! I'm not a blabbermouth, you see. In truth, I say to you that you can make the comparison between Polépolé and me, and you will regret nothing. My ministers will return here only to lay the first stones, and I for the inaugurations."

Unforgettable departure from Libotama. It was by road. Same festivities as at our arrival. They accompanied us as far as the ferry over the river which meanders along the borders of the Prefecture. The line of Land Rovers embarked upon the raft by means of heavy steel ramps, while the villagers on the Libotama bank sang songs and danced in a way to stir the most intimate chords of the Chief's heart. First he sketched the steps of the dance in response to the farewell, then he spoke to the orderly officer in a tight voice.

"Lieutenant, give me a bundle."

Opening the attaché case that he always carried, the lieutenant offered, in a clumsy manner meant to pass for discretion, a bundle of banknotes in glazed paper. Daddy, with big, nervous and dramatic gestures, tore off the elastic band and began to throw into the wind, in the manner of a seedsower, copies of his effigy which spun like propellers before settling on the surface of the river. Immediately, the children began to plunge into the water, quite forgetting the power of the spirits that normally inhabit it. Then the adults. Everyone swam with desperate strokes towards the sodden notes. In the spouts of water, one could make out the wild movements of one person and another tearing feverishly at this manna fallen from the skies. There were, no doubt, quite a few punches exchanged. Daddy began laughing and went on throwing notes into the wind and the water. How many of them were recovered intact, how many torn, how many carried away by the swirling river? Daddy laughed, laughed in fits, laughed and laughed again.

Daddy, like the Guinarou, was standing in his place hurling oaths at the sky, shaking the furniture, the windows and the mirrors. As frightful as the Guinarou, really. I had a problem even to keep the tray steady on my hand.

"Just look at that!"

Chin up, eyelids beating like the wings of a butterfly.

"Just read all this filth...those white swine!"

The office was carpeted with newspapers.

"Afraid that I'll become a communist! Because I talk about national resurrection and pay homage to our Chinese comrades. Always that racism of theirs. Although Papa de Gaulle himself used to talk about national independence. As if what I saw over there does not deserve any praise. And they begin to insult me. Like a nobody! Like a barbarian! Barbarians themselves, no? Just read this. *Gavroche Aujourd'hui"* (grimace of disgust). "Look at this cartoon. Have I got the head of a startled monkey, eh?"

He unfolded another.

"And this one calls me 'the black king'. Is that not racism? Their mother's cunt!"

As for me, I wanted to read everything, peacefully.

"And this one, just look at it. Look! It claims, it actually has the nerve to claim, that I pay for my trips with foreign aid—his mother's cunt!—with the aid pennies, instead of paying off our debts. Do you get that? Get it? And if *The Southern Cross* would dare to slight their President Pierre Chevalier, you'd soon enough see that miserable ambassador of theirs running to demand an audience and explanations."

"Even apologies."

It was the Minister of Foreign Affairs. He had entered the room without being announced. He was always bursting in on the President without any precaution or scruple. Daddy nodded.

"All right, get Aziz Sonika, right away!"

The smile of a malicious child.

"Our ambassador in Paris had better beat the table, too."

This was again the Minister of Foreign Affairs.

"Orders already given" (careless quip over the shoulder).

"Already carried out, respected President."

"Yes"(grumbling tone), "but those bandits only receive my ambassador with some petty official of their Quai d'Orsay. My am-bas-sa-dor" (punctuated with movements of his finger). "Do you hear? But do you really hear?"

The eyelids continued to flutter like butterflies.

"The whites are the whites. They always treat us like tramps. Just wait." (He stuck out his chin.) "They think I don't know them because I'm black. *Whereas,* I myself am a French citizen. I know their mentality, yessir. They'll just see."

He jumped up and began walking, still nodding his head.

"Can't let it pass just like that. Let them see who is Bwakamabé Na Sakkadé, son of Ngakoro, son of Fouléma, son of Kiréwa. Bandits! *Things!*"

His finger pointed at the notebook of the young compatriot Cabinet Secretary.

"Take a note. Inform the Minister of Propaganda that I'm going to make an important statement which must be broadcast in the mid-day bulletin. Bunch of swine, fuck off!"

He began pacing up and down with hands on hips, puffing his chest, like an athlete after a race. The young compatriot

Cabinet Secretary jumped up in his turn.

"Respected Daddy, have you got any instructions to give me for the wording..."

"No, no. Already done that myself. I must read a note that corresponds with the rhythm of my breath. No long phrases today, no big French. No Moliere, if it's really Moliere that I'm going to send them. Niggers' balls in the language of de Sévigné. Yessir. They'll see... Take away all this rubbish."

I hastened to help the young compatriot to gather up all the French papers.

What a tirade! Especially against the *Gavroche Aujourd'hui*. He abused it, all right, but in a manner...to make one put one's hand to one's mouth. I used to show it to Elengui, who opened her mouth and then hid it behind her hand. Mam'hé!

I must admit that, even if the Uncles have a different mentality from us, a mentality often difficult to understand, I admire the way their leaders allow themselves to be satirized in the papers... In our country, for a lot less...

A long afternoon. Boubeu hasn't come. There was, however, some question of an aperitif with the woman in white of the Hibiscus. *Strange how her face troubles me. Neither beautiful nor ugly, but with a power of penetration. Beauty of intelligence, beauty of character. Fierce like lightning. A piercing face. But whose, then? In another life?*

Tiya lived in the rue des Sénoufos. It was nearly a century since the Uncles had grouped there the locals recruited to lend their muscles and sweat to the first big public works in the town, notably the bridge which separates Moundié from the Plateau, now known as Hannibal-Ideloy Bwakamabé Na Sakkadé Bridge. Another gift, from the same people. But of which less is said. Blood. For the cocoa road. But that's another story altogether.

Apart from its brick structure and tiled roof, the old one's house had the least original form one could imagine. The plan was the sister, almost the twin of those of Moundié: a fence of badly fitted planks, a dusty courtyard with no garden, with a hazardous well at the back end and the rusty carcass of some ancient car. A brimming quarter, where music, good humour, carefree spirits, elegance, gentleness, pulsate everywhere, heating up the surrounding atmosphere. A rich coral island of the South Pacific, prosperous and without cares, where natives of both sexes, naked in their breathtaking beauty, instruct the traveller in search of sunshine in the pleasures of salt water, sand, flowers, dance and love. Nothing is missing from the picture, Hawaiian guitar, white teeth and beer massage tired nerves and stupefied hearts. No more sickness. Though an adventurous Uncle or two will die of syphilis.

For anyone circulating in the streets of Moundié, it is difficult, even with the aid of a telescope and a smoked lens, to detect a cloud on the faces of our townspeople. Pitched in a horizon of muddy skies, they live their lives with the naive lightheartedness of a child playing hopscotch. The spirit of a lively drunkeness? A subtle and delirious drug which nibbles in secret at the viscera and the nervous system? Daddy could as well survive and continue to legislate for centuries and centuries, so long as he didn't interfere with this happy carnival.

Tiya bathed in it in self-defence. He received us in a room with bare walls, covered with marks that a simple coat of whitewash could remove. I can still see the floor of raw cement coloured like cooked cassava and almost empty—a few wooden armchairs with rush seats and no cushions, a cupboard with faded varnish, superannuated relics of his time of glory. Always people. Old comrades, former electors, youngsters, a relative from the village, or simply a friend, tied by bonds that grew of themselves and couldn't be explained to the curious.

"Well, is that you?"

He would take off the iron-framed glasses which pinched the tip of his nose and put down a newspaper or some yellowing book. Moundié claimed that the old man made discoveries in ancient Latin texts that no one else could read. An amusing piece of magic.

"Why so long, tell me?"

Sometimes he would add: "What will you drink?"

He'd smile, rummage in the bottom of his pocket and end by sending some member of the household to buy some cold bottles at the nearby bar.

He teased the young compatriot Cabinet Secretary.

"So you want to revert to barbarism?"

His eyes sparkled as if he'd just seen a good comedy.

"That's the complex. The complex with regard to the Uncles. Afraid to wrestle with them on the same ground, we go back in search of another—or invent it—on which we are sure of not meeting them. But all that just leads to mediocrity. No good running away from the Uncles. When we chased them away, we were in effect fleeing them. And we still flee them, the better to stew in the juice of our own slippers. Believe me" (his eyes were fastened on a distant spot and his head wagging with conviction), "believe me, there is a way of keeping the Uncles, not as masters, but as competitors. A competitor, not an enemy. All the rest is just claptrap. An intellectual of your stamp shouldn't be taken in by all that blackman stuff. You, at least, have studied Latin, no?"

They came back with the bottles, well-frosted. Above the old cupboard, in a glass frame, dressed like a European of before the war, complete with butterfly collar and centre-parting, the young Tiya, neck stiffly erect, looked down on us with a conquering air.

"But tell me, my boy, what are you doing in that set-up?"

"Not *in* the set-up, actually, you know. Alongside of it. Just an official who lends his services."

"But too close" (he shook his head and pulled a face).

"Too close. In danger of getting assimilated. And anyway, those sort of posts are often just antechambers."

Who could say no to appointments suddenly announced on the radio, and keep his head on his shoulders? For my part, I absolved the young compatriot Cabinet Secretary.

"Can you, at least, tell him the truth?"

The young compatriot lifted his eyebrows vaguely.

"But what does it matter?" (Tiya shrugged his shoulders.) "Is it as if he could, I don't say comprehend, but simply follow your argument?"

The old man took a swig and motioned us to do the same.

"That man there has never studied Latin. A common soldier...if he was even a real Saint Cyrian, from the elite. Go on, you'd have done better to stay where you were before. You were doing more for Africa in practising your profession, yes. Nowadays, you know, all the noise you make is not advancing Africa's banner one bit" (he shook his head). "It's only in the world of work and study..."

He stopped, as if he had just seen something in the room.

"...and research, too. That's something concrete. Your political affairs there, are just an opportunity for loudmouths, nothing more. Storms in a teacup."

"Do you think I should resign?"

By common accord, they abandoned the subject. Smiles and mischievous glances. We asked after his health. He was just back from a cure in France. Vichy or Vittel, or some place like that. Brief replies. A great personage who fears to lose dignity in prattling too much about his petty ailments. Projects? To go and live in his village, in the bush. A vision of agricultural development. But the banks didn't understand it. And anyway, life in the city was too expensive. He quoted some prices and teased the young compatriot Cabinet Secretary.

"But, am I in power? I just draw up and send memos. That's all. Do they even consult me?"

"And your Yabaka there? It seems he's your post-horse? The progressive corporal! Bonaparte!"

Annoyed, the young compatriot Cabinet Secretary *closed his face,* to translate word-for-word the Kibotama phrase.

"Bonaparte!" (Tiya chuckled loudly.) "Let me tell you something. He doesn't understand anything of that kind. I heard him one time on television. He hasn't studied Latin any more than the other. A robber chieftain, him too. Knows how to seize power, sure. But as for exercising it..."

He stayed open-mouthed, admiring some beautiful vision,

invisible to us, which was right there before him. He sat down again and burst out laughing.

"You aren't in power?" (Another guffaw, then abruptly serious.) "Believe me, my boy, if one day the canoe should overturn, you couldn't explain that. All those people you see, out there, today they think only of dancing. A good rumba, jerk, *kavacha*, and all the rest of it. As for the older people, they are ready to do anything for you, especially when they see you in a car, with a tie, just like a white. They are even proud of you. But they are like dogs. Domestic animals, who are gentle and well-trained, just so long as the master isn't wounded. But the day when he sheds just a single drop of blood..."

"Listen, old man. let's make peace. I didn't come here to talk politics."

From the neighbouring house, the sound of a transistor invaded us. The signature tune for the news bulletin. Then the voice of Aziz Sonika. The national anthem.

"Eh? eh? It looks as though that fellow is going to speak."

The old man got up to switch on his own radio.

"What more has he got to say?"

It was indeed the voice which knew how to distinguish between the *é*, the *è* and the *ai*, on the one hand; the *o* and the *au,* on the other; and finally, the *i* and the *u*.

Agence France-Presse, open your ears as wide as rabbits, because otherwise you'll have the ears of an elephant.

For a long time to come, Moundié would quote that phrase whenever, all fires damped down, the inner walls whispered about the Chief's buffooneries.

If only you were lodged in a wall, here in our country, to blurt out your habitual lies and distortions. Just know that the day is coming when you will be chased from every corner of the earth.

Agence France-Presse, organ of lies, open you ears as wide as rabbits, or you'll have the ears of an elephant of our land, to continue lying tranquilly, saying that you find yourself in such a friendly country, when we know it's false...

We looked at each other, with wrinkled brows. Daddy seemed

to have jumped a passage. But in other broadcasts of the message, as well as in Aziz Sonika's *Southern Cross,* the phrase was certainly understood and read out as given above.

You are not far away, you are here with us. I declare that we were ready to cooperate with you; that instead of repeating all that balderdash, we proposed that you copy purely and simply the communiqués given out by our own press agency. But, you didn't want that. You have preferred, like an obstinate child, to defy the Father of the Resurrection and of our National Identity. You have remained deaf up till today because you have found the easy solution of camouflaging yourself in a wall of the embassy, right here in our beautiful modern capital, to lie all the better. Too bad for you, too bad! One day the hour will strike, and that will be the hour for the destruction of certain nests of lies.

Africa is still Africa...

Rolling of drums, like an approaching thunder storm.

...and no one can change it, or transform it, however hard they lie.

People of my country, my dear brothers, a working session has been held under my Pre...under my high and august Presidency, yesterday, 28th September, within the walls of my Palace.

Here followed a list of certain ministers and secretaries of state, whose names are lost (there were so many changes), but of whom one was charged with "expenditure from the Treasury", another with "control of State expenditure", a third with car parks and a last with "the presidential press".

The Order of the Day was essentially concerned with the debts of the Postal and Telecommunications Department, and their credits among different financial organisations. On my instructions, arrangements must be made for reciprocal payments...

Daddy had lied to the young compatriot Cabinet Secretary. What followed was no longer niggers' balls in the language of de Sévigné. A specialist must have prepared this part, which dealt with explanations of the postal debt. Very complicated explanations, anyway, only comprehensible to initiates in the arts of finance and accountancy.

Over and above the usual care to distinguish between the *é,* the *è* and the *ai;* the *o* and the *au;* or the *i* and the *u;* the whole speech was spiced with rhetorical flourishes and with resounding attacks on the Uncles.

Also, I count absolutely on the suppoort of all the employees of Postal and Telecommunications to enable me to correct this worrying situation, which throws discredit upon our nation, most of all in its relations with France, our mother country.

I saw Tiya put his hand to his mouth and close his eyes, his face afflicted as if seized by a sudden agony.

As for Agence France-Presse, which has reported a load of rubbish on the subject, yes, I say rubbish, let them just wait a bit. They will see,

Wollé, wollé?

Woï, woï!

Wollé, wollé?

Woï, woï!

Tiya, his face very serious, shook his head and jumped up to take a few paces in the room.

"I told you that man had never studied Latin."

The flames of the campaign of Cultural Resurrection progressed with a devastating vigour, violence, energy and imagination. Every time a spark was struck, it sprang into an idea, was reshaped in an editorial, expanded and unfurled in the shouts of the militants, who proved their courage and reconstructed the country by throwing into the sacred and purifying fire all those who, whether adversaries or faint-hearts, got in their way. There was singing, marching in step, smashing things with the tranquil faith of all great iconoclasts. And every morning the inspired tribunes erected platforms in the streets and squares, without asking for payment. Short-sighted souls who wanted to ignore the wind of history and pursue their own little paths towards contentment were astonished by the blasts of the cyclone. Thus it was with the Portuguese trader who had the bad taste to present himself several times at the counter of the Treasury with a bill owed by the Presidential Palace. An editorial from Aziz Sonika let him understand that, in support of the struggle of our Angolan, Mozambiquan and Guinean brothers, all Lusitanian traders had just forty-eight hours to pack their bags. The young layabouts of Moundié spontaneously lent a hand with this operation, and most of the stores were taken by assault, so that soon they suggested nothing but the carcasses left in the wake of an army of famished rats. I must say that nobody in the country was fond of the Portuguese traders. Whites who were worth no more than the poor blacks of Moundié, but were more wicked (more dishonest, yes) than they, when it came to making money and enriching themselves. It might have been different if they respent the money in spreading benefit around themselves. But no, they preferred to live poorly and pile up bundles of dirty notes in their cellars. Ah, real White-Beans, that lot! Misers, I'm telling you! It was more convenient to supply oneself from them, but we hated them. However, my day was spoiled when I saw their wives tearfully hugging their children at the airport, while their menfolk sold off their cars to arrogant sons of the land, for the price of a bicycle.

"They have sucked us dry enough already!"

Chuckles.

"And anyway, this will teach them for making the Angolan blacks suffer."

Foolish as I am, I didn't know how to reply to such arguments, but I was sick at heart. No doubt a result of my catechism classes...

Another day, a few weeks later, all Moundié awoke in stupefaction. The quarter of the Dioula traders had been encircled by the army. Any man wearing a *bubu* or a *fez* was stuffed into the military trucks along with his family and a small bundle. A joint operation by the Ministries of Health, Religious Affairs and the Interior. All types of Senegalese, Malians, Mauritanians, Hausas, Dahomeans and Togolese, with their *bubus* and their kola nuts, spreading gonorrhoea, syphilis and other diseases through the population, not counting the nastiness of their marabouts, with their bizarre beads and charms.

There were many of them and not enough airplanes. Stuck for several days and nights in the Hannibal-Ideloy Bwakamabé Na Sakkadé Stadium, some of the older ones never woke again.

Ohoho! Not many. Two. Two people, what is that? In any operation of that sort, one is entitled to expect certain losses, as on manoeuvres...

I can still see their sad faces, and the proud carriage of their elders.

Their houses and shops, like those of the Portuguese, were systematically looted by the young vagrants of Moundié.

The people shouted *wollé, wollé, woï, woï* at this manifestation of the politics of national liberation. The young compatriot Cabinet Secretary shrugged his shoulders and claimed that all this was only a smokescreen to hide the policy of neo-colonialism, while the real profiteers, the imperialist Uncles, were not threatened.

But the truth was that, despite a nice declaration in which Daddy called them adopted citizens and invoked the international conventions on residency, the Uncles began to be troubled by nightmares.

Residency conventions, residency conventions, fine! But what about this sudden infatuation with China...where was that leading to? Whether one liked it or not, it was flirting with a state which had nationalised the economy, suppressed private property, chased away the missionaries and held its women in common. A communist state, to be blunt. By citing its example for every yes or no, as Daddy delighted in doing, didn't one risk being borne along by the infernal logic, much stronger than all this folkloric razmattaz? Wasn't there already talk of the coming of Chinese *experts?* Experts, experts, all well and good. But experts in what? In what, if not for the installation of Red regimes for the Blacks? The Yellowmen, all those orientals, you know how they are. Secretive, very secretive, cunning. No way you can have confidence in them. Tricksters, yes. And especially face-to-face with our good blacks. Naive and stupid as they are. Don't want to distrust anyone, want to accept everything, and when they wake up it'll be too late. Kissed right to the slit. Colonised. And for real, this time. They'll begin to miss our colonisation, snug as it was. But it'll be too late. Us, well, you only have to get on with us. Especially if it's only a question of Daddy. Not a bad fucker, the Marshal. A bit brutal at times. Y-e-es. But that's natural, no, when one's been educated in the barracks? And anyway, *they* need someone like Daddy. If they didn't have him, we'd have to invent one for them. What do you want? *They* understand nothing but the lash. Not nice to say so, but it's the truth. Can't say it out loud, sure. But between ourselves, between four walls, at the bridge house. What's more, so far as superficialities are concerned, Daddy makes a cock-up. But, at bottom, that doesn't matter. No, sir. Knows how to command. Didn't serve for nothing in Indochina, Morocco, Tunisia, Algeria. All those medals on his chest, that's something. At least those he won before being President. He's always been on our side. If the home front hadn't stabbed us in the back, he wouldn't have given way to that snobbism of independence, a man like him. They even say he's kept his French citizenship. In short, a man you can rely on. Maoism? Bof! just a fashion that comes and goes, like all fashions.

But his entourage...(hands raised just above the head). Ah! his entourage... Above all, that Yabaka fellow! Dangerous! dangerous, dangerous, dangerous. A footslogger who takes himself for an intellectual. A notorious anti-white. It's he who deceived Daddy. It's he who dragged him to China... Getting him to hope that the Yellowmen would refill the Treasury. They must have learned better since, anyway. Also, it's he who composed the speech launching their bitch of an operation of Cultural Resurrection.

The tension was too high. Above all, too long. They had pulled too long at the rope: the nerves were giving way. And behold, one fine morning, all our Uncles all in the streets of the capital, brandishing placards and banners, crying incomprehensible orders in three separated syllables and singing war songs from the front line.

LONG LIVE DADDY, SUPPORT DADDY, THE ADOPTED CITIZENS ARE DETERMINED TO SUPPORT THEIR GUIDE UNTIL FINAL VICTORY.

No one was expecting it. The "radars" of Monsieur Gourdain's police had smelled nothing of it, nothing. And everybody helpless, there, with their arms hanging. The Uncles, it's the Uncles. What should one do when it's those people who are demonstrating? One can't, after all... Whatever happens, there's no question of calling out the army just like that, without precaution. Must consult Daddy first. And the hooters of their cars—Pa-pa, pi-pi-pi, pa-pa, pi-pi-pi, pa-pa, pi-pi-pi. They were marching towards the Palace.

It's we the Africans
Who come from afar
We come from the colonies
To defend the country.

A song for departure to the battlefield. Right to the Palace. There, a delegation demanded to be received by the Chief. The Republican Guard and Protocol scratched their heads. Radiant with good humour, the Chief agreed and embraced his "dear brothers". Laughter, hugs and champagne. Taking advantage of a calm moment, they pulled out a paper. Their complaints. Daddy received them like a list of compliments. He made a speech thanking them, reassuring them, but above all thanking them all. More champagne. Photos, there, like that! Another one, please. With those lovely ladies. There, that's it!

Aziz Sonika conceived out of this an editorial on the global prestige of Daddy, from the lands where the sun rises to the seas where the great star sets, not forgetting his fraternal homage to those brave adopted citizens who were our Uncles, who had, that very day, organised a carnival to celebrate their Patron Saint.

"Really, I can't do it."

"Just look at this man! For some time now, that baton of his has been like a weed."

"Easy to say. It's easier to have an open mouth than a stiff arm."

"You crude man!"

Elengui had exhausted all the skill of her hands and her lips. A housewife wanting to demonstrate the quality of her drinks couldn't have done more. Morbid hunger and debility. The attractions of her figure, her odour and her art of sending electric currents through my body didn't get to me. For a moment, I tried to play the game. They say the will can achieve anything.

"Too much work, too much."

"Go on, stop that nonsense. It isn't the work."

"Eh?"

"Yes, yes, yes."

"What are you imagining now? It's the work. You don't know what a dog's life that man leads us."

"No, it's not the work, that I know."

Elengui shook her head.

"No, the fatigue of work doesn't eat up the force necessary for *that.*"

"No, but listen to me, my heart, *ko.*"

I passed from irritation to sweetness, using the thousand skills and rare talents of an actor to try to convince and pacify her. No question of admitting the truth. These were sins at which even God the Father will smile on the day of judgement.

The evening before my day off, I was called to the telephone. The voice refused to identify itself. But by the singing cadence, peculiar to the Djabotama, I quickly recognised Ma Mireille. I didn't even have time to feel astonishment. The voice gave me instructions in an energetic tone which was close to menace. Where and when I must present myself next day. No discussion. Just like that. If not...if not, look my friend, it was a chieftainess speaking.

All afternoon, I was like a fire constantly fanned. I burned all over, provoking gasps of complaint and appreciation. Ma Mireille died many times. How many? What's it to you? I'm not the sort of man to commit such indiscretions just to make myself look good. What's more, the party over, it was impossible for me to be good for anything. A boxer getting up from a k.o. To the winner, spoils and a half.

I could well understand Elengui's agitation. A healthy woman can't leave her land fallow for long. Above all when she refuses to let it be pecked at by the birds and vampires which lust after it day and night with famished eyes.

Yes, I could have done like other men in our society. Not give a damn about what she might imagine, for better or worse, and live according to my own desires. Hadn't her mother ever told her that a man is never reserved for one woman alone, as a woman is, on the contrary, for her man? That's a man's existence. It's for her to be the magician and have the skill to wring him dry. But this attitude of our men isn't at all charitable. We shouldn't make the women suffer. It's inhumane. It would be better, in justice, to practise the same fidelity as the wives. But that isn't very human either. God has said that we shouldn't inflict suffering on our neighbour. That's why we take on the role of mutual dissembling over these sweet sins. It's a matter of not failing in respect towards the mistress of the hearth. Our society has, for centuries, rested on these important principles of our traditional education, although it was evident that Elengui, like many other modern women, would never have accepted the role of the deceived wife in the quarter.

Often, when I had a chance to think calmly of such things, I wondered why men had need to invent such a thing as jealousy. It wasn't God, but the Devil, who put this into our hearts. But we know also that the best men, unless pathologically unstable, are not able to respect the vow of fidelity which the Uncles have obliged us to take, before the mayors and the reverend fathers. Which isn't to say that in the course of these transgressions, they cease to love their wives. But no! And when I consider my secret activities, those with Soukali as much as with Ma Mireille, I come to the conclusion that it would be barbarous to punish us for them, and mischievous even to blame us. A reactionary attitude, to use the vocabulary of the Polépolé epoch. That which makes these two wives, like many other respectable mothers, so worthy and thoroughly honest, can't be very wicked. Or even, not so at all. Who would dare to claim that the world will begin its decadence the day when all the wives on earth decide to take lovers? That could even be a day of the brightest sunshine and the rejection of mourning! Instead of going to battle against injustice, hatred of others, violence, all of which plague the world we live in, our lazy hands prefer to stone the adulterous woman, when Christ has already told us to desist. Women who want to keep all the allure of young girls, ah!...if I wasn't afraid of the censor's thunderbolts, what an appeal would I throw to you!

Elengui threw back the sheets and turned her back on me. Her deep sigh resounded through my being. Of what was she thinking? Of whom? I descended alone into the well of sleep, as I used to do after a good Thursday football match, in the days when I was still studying at the Raymond de Penyafort College.

Next morning, a sensation at the level of my thighs awoke me. Elengui, armed with a big pair of scissors, was about to operate on that portion of my anatomy. I jumped.

"Hé! hé! what's going on? What are you doing?"

"Keep still, wait."

"But what is it?"

"Wooooh! What a fearful fellow, this one!"

"Yes, I'm afraid, I'm afraid. Is that okay with you?"

"Wooooh! All right, cut it yourself."

"Cut, cut...but cut what, eh?"

"The hair, of course."

My breath returned and I closed my eyes.

"If it's only that...but...what for?"

"Because your flabbiness down there, for so many days, isn't normal."

"All that work, I tell you. That Daddy, really!"

"No, it's not the work, it's something else."

"But no, dearest heart. But no. What ideas are you getting in your head? Anyway, if you really want..."

I lowered my voice, smiled and tried to caress her.

"...this morning, I'm..."

She pushed me off.

"No, no, no. Not this morning, I'm in a hurry."

"In a hurry? For what?"

"I have a rendezvous."

"A rendezvous? Who with? For what?"

She turned her head away.

"Elengui! Look at me. Who with?"

She went on avoiding my eyes.

"Elengui!"

I grabbed her and shook her like a branch full of fruit. But the higher my voice went, the more she shut herself in and escaped me. My blood took another course and I wanted to slap her. I assure you I would have given her a good beating if she hadn't finally admitted, in a sigh of a voice, little above a whisper.

"To the diviner."

I let go of her, laughing.

"Laugh. Laugh away, if you like. You're too fond of your doubts. You don't know that things like that are serious, eh? Anyway, it's not normal that a man usually so passionate as you, suddenly can't do the thing again. I'm certain that someone, from pure jealousy, has put *juju* on you. We must find out where it comes from and how to fight it."

And for her consultation she needed some of my hairs. If it was only that...I could breathe again. I smiled and shook my head, as if in disagreement. Taking the scissors gaily, I operated on myself and offered her with a triumphant gesture all that the diviner could possibly need for his analysis.

While going to the Palace, I whistled forcefully the latest hit by Prince Nico M'Barga. I made a detour to pass the Moundié market, in order to buy a few strips of a bark well known in the country. I put it in reserve, swearing to have it always in my pocket. How the devil had I come to forget this remedy, known to even the youngest bucks before tackling their first woman?

Every time that both Elengui and Ma Mireille wanted to exploit me, I had only to chew this medicine for a few hours and I could present myself to Elengui, fresh and eager, ready to put up any performance, any exploit, to beat any record with all the friskiness of a young sprig of twenty. Why on earth hadn't I thought of it sooner?

Many messages arrived from Arab countries. All congratulated Daddy for his break with Israel, and some for his conversion to Islam. Aziz Sonika wrote many editorials asserting that we had a head of state respected throughout the world, and that what was once called a country lost in the African jungle had become one of the most prestigious nations on earth, envied and coveted by those turbulent agitators whose names ended in *-ist*. These homilies in the published press were reproduced by their author on radio and television, for he refused to entrust their reading to a simple and common speaker. No one, apart from himself, would be able to add that touch of tone which only an experienced actor can command. According to radio grapevine, Aziz Sonika was afraid that some people would attribute these pieces of oratory to whoever lent them his voice. Also, despite his rank (for he had climbed many grades since that morning of 1st April when Bwakamabé Na Sakkadé had ousted Polépolé), he didn't hesitate to perform in person on the radio.

But the money so much hoped for from Mecca and other capitals of the Faith and of the Petrodollar still kept delaying its date of arrival. And accordingly the "months" worked by officials stretched out like Bazooka chewing-gum, attaining lengths of forty-five, fifty and even sixty days. A Saudi delegation came to make an inventory of the more promising projects and left with a list for further study. A Libyan mission, ready for action, followed on its heels. They announced a rigorous program of development, at the end of which a mosque had been completed, only two years behind schedule. But it must be admitted now that the promise was kept and that anyone can now see this listed monument, in front of which our tourists love to be photographed or filmed.

But liquid capital, none. And the safes of the Public Treasury were drying up. The officials and their families had to make do with one meal a day. Many of them made no complaint, or rather, they took care not to be overheard even by their own walls. Most of them survived this season of lean cattle thanks to a villa leased to an ambassador, or their taxis, their "moonlighting", their drinks business, all of which activities were listed in the tax registers under the name of a mother, an aunt or a grandmother; in short, all these people whom Moundié labelled *the highest of the high,* as well as those just below them, managed to make ends meet through their private businesses. The lot of *the lowest of the low* on the other hand, was as bleak as that of La Fontaine's grasshopper. Though even these, it must be admitted, were kept out of the reach of famine by the traditions of solidarity, lauded by the policy of Cultural Resurrection and aided by the fear of *metaphysical* reprisals. Everyone had a relative, at least, who owned a rented villa, some taxis, an outside business or a bar, in the name of a mother, an aunt or a grandmother, and profited thereby. "The product of primitive solidarity," observed the young compatriot Cabinet Secretary.

But Daddy, that wily political animal, was not ignorant of any of these facts, which were fed to him by reports from Monsieur Gourdain's cohorts. He issued a secret decree, laying down an order of priority for the payment of salaries. Before he signed it, the young compatriot Cabinet Secretary tried to convince him to send for the Paymaster General and give him verbal instructions, to avoid any..?

"No, no, no. I must have a record. Like that, if anyone should try to amuse himself tomorrow by disobeying me, I'll strike, *gba!* With blacks, must have a record. They are full of bad faith. When they are punished, instead of recognising their fault and begging pardon, no, they run complaining to their tribe that, *wo!* they are victims of injustice.

Looking for a compromise, the young compatriot Cabinet Secretary would have suggested a confidential circular, of limited distribution, but Daddy would have none of it. That's how Aziz Sonika was induced to read over the radio a decree laying down the following order of payment for all civil servants:

1st. President of the Republic, Head of State, President of the Patriotic Council of National Resurrection, President of the Council of Ministers, President of the Supreme Council of the Magistrature, Minister of many departments, intellectual author of the policy of national cultural resurrection

2nd. Officers of the Great-Historic-Courageous-and-Intrepid Armed Forces

3rd. The N.C.O.'s and other ranks of the Great-Historic-Courageous-and-Intrepid Armed Forces

4th. The Police

5th. The Gendarmerie

6th. The Ministers and Secretaries of State, in hierarchical order of their dates of appointment

7th. Ambassadors and other representatives overseas

8th. Overseas students

9th. Junior officials

10th. Officials of Category A

11th. Secretaries-General, Directors-General and other heads of service

12th. Bursary holders

13th. The etceteras

What a field day for the *Gavroche Aujourd'hui!* Nothing more was necessary than for the famous Parisian satirical paper to publish under the headline "The walls of idiocy have been surpassed", a photocopy of the original decree, seasoning it with a few comments very similar to those which radio grapevine, in its eternal anonymity, was broadcasting in the alleys of Moundié. Several columns were dedicated to the pilgrimage of Abd-el-Mahjid, "an innocent Balthazaar with empty hands, to Mecca and adjoining areas".

The issue was seized.

"Their mother's cunt, their mother's cunt! I'll make a *charcuterie* out of them if I ever get hold of them, these fuckers!"

Our Keeper of the Seals replied next day by announcing that

he was deposing before the Tribunals of Paris a complaint against the *Gavroche Aujourd'hui* for insulting a head of state. The lawyer chosen by the state, despite the handsome fee proposed, was hesitant, arguing that the offence was strange to him. Daddy prevailed by affirming loud and clear that he too was a French citizen; that he had spilled some of his blood for the Liberation, then the ultramarine glory of the *Tricouleur;* that no one could strip him of that citizenship and that he voted at every election in France, scrupulously, against the Left and adventurers of all types. He even made a gesture as though exposing the wound in his thigh.

The French Ambassador asked for an audience and was received in the presence of the young compatriot Cabinet Secretary.

I don't know what passed between our Chief and the representative of the Elysée, but in the same measure as the Marshal Bwakamabé appeared nervous and on hot coals beforehand, so he seemed afterwards full of the joys of living.

When I entered the Chief's office, in response to his bell immediately after the audience, Daddy was rubbing his hands; then, seizing the young compatriot Cabinet Secretary by the shoulders, he looked straight into the other's eyes.

"My son, this is a great day. Let's water it a little. Come on."

The Chief's voice was muffled. Surrounded by the bevy of bodyguards and orderly officers, I followed him into the corridor which led to the private quarters of the Palace. Daddy said not a word, and the young compatriot Cabinet Secretary didn't dare break the silence. Bwakamabé, visibly moved and withdrawn into a profound meditation, began pacing the long red carpet, sometimes looking down towards it and sometimes up, towards something before him. From the terrace, where they were now installed, one could see a fine white mist still clinging to the mountain, which stood all covered in its thick green fleece.

"*Maître,* bring a champagne for my son here."

I saw the young compatriot Cabinet Secretary consulting his watch.

"Ah, our young people have no military service to toughen them up. We soldiers can never be afraid of alcohol. From eight a.m. onwards, we're always ready to welcome it surefooted. The *take-off,* as a Martiniquan friend of mine used to call it in Indochina."

He turned towards me.

"Go along, *Maître,* a champagne for Monsieur the Cabinet Secretary. For me, Chivas, as always."

He looked at the sun, whose splendour announced another fine day.

"What a beautiful morning! If you can't take the champagne, you must anyway help to 'wash' such a victory. Come on, you can go and rest later. We've deserved well of the country, my boy. Even more. Ah yes, then! We've certainly deserved it. It's your master who tells you so. Now, a little private life, if you please."

He chuckled.

The sunshine was lighting up the beauties of nature like a colour film. Daddy sank into a new armchair and seemed to want to fill his lungs and his whole being with the spectacle.

After the first swig of his tobacco-coloured liquid came the moment of confidences. He spoke of a trip to Paris. Ah! *Maître.* This was the crowning achievement of his career. Up to now, he hadn't stayed in the French capital in his capacity as President, except for so-called private visits and some working ones. He had waited a long time for this official visit. To be received in France! In Paris! Like the Queen of England. This was incomparably more important than any reception in Senegal, Ivory Coast, Zaïre, Morocco, Germany or China, or even the United States. No, it wasn't the same thing at all. That must be understood. He had lived in France. Had practised his profession there. Could have stayed on there. No problem. Yessir. He had some cronies in the army. Well, look, let him just find a means of asking them to form a guard of honour with some of his old comrades-in-arms. He could send them a list. Hadn't forgotten their names. He picked up the telephone. Ah! bravo, despite the leave given him just now, the young compatriot Cabinet Secretary was still in his office.

"...Call Bruno de la Roncière. Yes, yes. No. You'll receive him yourself. Explain to him that I'm keen on..."

Great God, let them just see, those people, how he had succeeded, a nigger like him. Name of God, name of God! He took a swallow of Chivas and gave me his empty glass. Mouth open, he began breathing the air in great gulps, then smiled and shook his head. Gr-e-a-t God, he had some chums too among the ordinary people of the towns and the provinces. Ah! those, he knew them well. Look, whatever had become of Louisette, a salesgirl at La Samaritaine, whom he'd met at a dance, one Sunday afternoon at Maubert-Mutualité? A splendid girl. Not an equal to her for the waltz or the Argentine tango. It was that year when the *raspa* was all the rage. Lived with her parents near Les Halles: rue Rambuteau. Fine people. Not a bit stuck-up. Above all, not racists. Would have willingly parted with their daughter. I can still see them, reading their *France-Soir,* playing the horses, listening to "The Duraton Family" every evening on Radio Luxembourg and, every Sunday, "The Granary of Montmartre". Ah! if destiny had been... When they see him on television, on the steps of the Elysée Palace, addressing the journalists like Senghor or Houphouët, speaking from the tip of his lips, great God! They just won't be able to believe their eyes, they'll ask themselves if it isn't a fairytale. They won't be able to get over it. He, Hannibal (he didn't call himself Ideloy in those days, and they found his family name too complicated), President of the Republic! Can't be true. Not possible, by God. Well, *he* didn't waste his time, the old bastard. They'll be proud to have known him. Something to talk about in the café next day. It's certain to be photographed by *Paris-Match* and—whatever *Gavroche Aujourd'hui* may say—*France-Soir* is sure to make a feature of it. Important, that, very important. Isn't it the journals which sell *in* the country that make the real propaganda? Much more than the monkey-tricks of Aziz Sonika. It'll be good. Good for propaganda back home. True, there's no issue of *The Southern Cross* that doesn't carry a photo of Daddy's torso, but *Paris-Match,* that's something else. Something-or-other of the psychological there. (Have I already told you that he pronounced it "pisychological"?) Yes, something that gives still more force and brilliance to his renown.

"Yes, *Maître,* after that I can blow my horn, whistle and die, with the spirit at peace. Yes!"

I only understood half of this.

"And now, a little bit of private life, if you please."

One foot on the ground, my scooter firmly in my hands, I had my eyes fastened that morning on the traffic cop who, like an orchestra conductor, was beating his rhythm at the junction of the Kennedy and Jean-Mermoz avenues. I was watching for the signal that would permit me to take off like an arrow.

"Maître!"

The voice was coming from my left.

"Maître, maître!"

It was Cécile, Ma Mireille's lady companion, in a car stopped just beside me.

"Maître."

She went on in a whisper, switching to Kibotama.

"Instead of going to the Palais, you must follow me...*Maître,* it's very, very important. Too much-o! Follow me, and don't ask questions."

She took Kennedy Avenue, then Independence Boulevard, as far as the edge of town. There we took the direction of the airport; then, after a short distance, turned right towards Soweto, the quarter of prefabricated villas constructed by South Africa. By a sign, she told me to bring my scooter into the yard. She, usually so gay, had a preoccupied and troubled air, barely containing the agitation visible in her smallest gesture.

"There! Sit down and listen."

Ma Mireille had called her that morning, at five o'clock. Daddy had not calmed down since the previous evening. In the grip of his rage he had broken numerous plates and vases. His doctor, profiting from a moment of clarity, had been obliged to give him a dose of valium. And if I hadn't been arrested during the night, it was owing to all the feminine guile and the pleas of Ma Mireille. Throwing all her resources into the battle, she had sent one of her intimates to her diviner who, right from Moundié, had "tied" the Guinarou. The unhappy woman, nevertheless, before the valium and the diviner's magnetism had taken effect, had suffered many violent blows of the Chief's lion's tail.

"All this for me?"

"For you."

So someone must have betrayed us. I had a feeling they would. And it was fatal. I had repeatedly told Ma Mireille that we didn't take sufficient precautions during our encounters. Thank God I hadn't been stabbed in bed *flagrante delicktus,* as Soukali used to say.

Monsieur Gourdain had come soon after dinner to inform the President of his definite conclusions. I had been followed for weeks and my telephone conversations had been tapped.

For Monsieur Gourdain there wasn't the slightest doubt. I was the link in a vast plot ending in *-ist,* which was being hatched with the Russians.

"Okay, good. This is something quite different."

Moscow, to keep its hand hidden, played its whole game through the medium of the Bulgarian Embassy, whose agent I was.

"But..."

Monsieur Gourdain had first given this information to the Chief a month ago, and had asked that nothing should be said yet. He just wanted time to confirm everything. Now, he had swept away all his earlier hesitations. A telephone conversation, sometimes three (they had even recorded five in a single morning), every day with the Bulgarian Embassy, was a little too much.

I smiled.

"Ye-es..."

Difficult to deny it. The recordings were there, all on tape. My contact was a woman whose identity had not yet been determined and with whom I always spoke in a coded language. Ma Mireille herself was ulcerated about it and would gladly have strangled me.

Monsieur Gourdain was of the view that things should be left to develop, in such a way as to bring out all the contours of the conspiracy; then, and only then, clack, throw a huge net over all this trash. If he had told Daddy about my involvement, it was only to follow up on his first intimation, and above all to ensure that I was the object of a strict and detailed surveillance, all the stricter because I was so close to the Chief. The most dangerous element was, myself. I, the *Maître.* The most advanced element of the whole plot. The spy inserted into the heart of the institution. An agent of the Fifth Column! There! Exactly. An agent of the Fifth Column as it had been defined in his speech of 27th July. (Cf. p.35 of Vol III of the *Complete Works* of Bwakamabé Na Sakkadé.) At any moment, I might receive the order to act. For example, by slipping poison into Daddy's Chivas. Actually, Monsieur Gourdain didn't really believe in this mode of action, because...but no possibility should be ignored. It would be stupid to let oneself be surprised. The chief danger resided in the coded conversations, because no one was yet in a position to determine the moment when the fatal order would be given.

Great God! Daddy, foaming like the Guinarou, had wanted to hear from me himself. Immediately.

Monsieur Gourdain advised against it. It would be wrong to sound the alarm and give the conspirators a chance to escape.

No. Too much. It was too much. He couldn't believe his ears. Couldn't put up with it a moment longer. He was a bottle of clear glass, himself. Transparent. Couldn't play the hypocrite. To feel constantly at his side a fart like me, and say nothing? Make smiles and sweet faces, and my-brother-this, my- brother-that, and such like rubbish...no, it wasn't possible. Too bad for the tactics. Let them go and pick up this *Maître* creature, right now. This very night.

Monsieur Gourdain tried one last time to calm the Chief (although it was the report of this silly bastard which had infuriated him!). Then, it was Ma Mireille's turn. She used more convincing arguments (Cécile didn't tell me what they were), but succeeded only in winning a slight concession.

If I hadn't been alerted by Cécile, the worse for me. They were waiting for me at the gates of the Palace.

"But, anyway, there's nothing to fear. I'm innocent."

"Innocent? And those tapes?"

"I'm coming to that. An unfortunate *quid pro quo.*"

"A what?"

I explained to Cécile.

"Yes, agreed, but Ma Mireille says that, with that man there, what counts is not the truth, but *his* truth."

She stopped only a moment and then said, as if in a dream, "...and Yabaka, do you think he's guilty, Yabaka?"

Then she pulled herself together.

"In any event, Ma Mireille doesn't want to see you falling into the clutches of Bwakamabé."

"But I'm not a coward. I must confront the situation. By staying hidden, I only make my case worse. Anyway, how long could I stay like this, in this little capital where everyone knows each other and meets each other every moment, as soon as he steps outdoors? To end up like Haraka? Not for me!"

Ma Mireille had her plan in mind, to get me out of the country immediately.

"What? Me? To run away..."

The risks were too great. There was no other choice.

"To go away? Just like that, without even embracing Elengui? Without pressing my mother to my bosom? Go away with empty hands?"

Ma Mireille had thought of that and taken care of everything. The smallest details would be settled that evening or, at the latest, by the following morning. Didn't she have a brother who was Director of Security and another who was director-general of a bank? Besides, Cécile had to go to report on the first part of her mission and take care herself of the other preparations.

A few days before these events, we had learned of the death of Tiya. Over there in Paris, where he had been sent for emergency treatment. Useless, after all. But could anyone have known that? Cancer of the pancreas. Polépolé had been seen coming to salute the body, when it was embarked at Roissy Airport. Moundié had immediately reacted like a village at the death of one of its sons. The same grief, the same sincere pity. Daddy, informed by Monsieur Gourdain's reports, had decided that the State should undertake the costs of bringing home the body, as well as those of the wake and of the burial ceremony.

The coffin had arrived on the Wednesday flight. The one that arrives at four in the morning. A deliberate choice, according to Moundié. Bwakamabé had sent one of his Djabotama familiars expressly to Paris to help the family with the formalities of repatriation. In reality, to organise things in such a way as to avoid a welcoming demonstration. So, four o'clock in the morning. We were there. Two balls of white light, gliding towards the runway like parachutes ending their flight, suddenly cut their way through the darkness of the dying night. We were there, despite everything. More than a hundred of us, to receive the sad burden in our arms and to cover with our eloquent silence, as if with a protective shawl, the sobs, groans and cries of the family. From the airport to Moundié we accompanied the corpse in a slow procession of cars, trucks, scooters and pedestrians. A special route, lined by the police. Chosen so as to follow the least frequented streets. And the cortege grew, nevertheless, swelled by the curious who had been awakened by the noise of our footsteps under their windows. The more visionary murmured, in their dialects, that they were reliving the days when they marched in support of the Old One, in the times when one still had the right to choose him as a candidate, among many.

The night of the wake, the compound of the house was too small to hold us all. They had to put chairs and benches in the street, even blocking the entry to neighbouring houses. As was customary, drums and dances from his tribe. But others came from the native region of his wife. And people from other ethnic groups also, as if to the call of an inexplicable festival. Spontaneous collections were organised towards the expenses of electricity and coffee. A thousand anonymous men, some sitting, some standing. A thousand women singing or sleeping side by side on the mats. A whole community which wanted to participate, like a gift from its bare hands, in the Mass that lasted all night. And the old man's wife, Melanie, his companion, like a bewildered fly blundering against the panes that enclosed her despairing footsteps. Weariness and lack of sleep were not enough to hold her to the ground. She got up from time to time, threw a distracted glance over the crowd, moved from one group to another, showing us her empty hands, while she kept up a long recitative of lamentation. Napoleon, Napoleon, in an affectionate tone. Napoleon, Napoleon, Napoleon. She called him, like a child still fragile to her. Napoleon, Napoleon, Napoleon. She recalled his strong heart, his courage, Napoleon, Napoleon, Napoleon. You have left me too soon, ho! Napoleon, Nap...

There also, accepted like an older sister in the entourage of Melanie, was Philomene, known as Philo the Great, mother of Tiya's oldest children. Silent, as befitted the dignity of her position, she intervened nevertheless to help with the organisation: watching the coffee, welcoming such a member of the family or such an old companion of the deceased.

All his old comrades were present. The veterans of the struggle against the whip, companions in his electoral campaigns and in detention. One would have thought that the entire generation of forgotten militants had suddenly, without a sound and responding to a signal heard in secret, come out of its hiding and was assembled that evening, chest out, full of a youth renewed. All of them. Names, faces, once known, then forgotten, suddenly back on astonished lips. Those of the cells of organised resistance; those who suffered in prison; those whose loyalty was never found wanting; but also those who grew estranged from him, who had pursued the struggle in a different party, sometimes opposed to him. All were there, as if to celebrate a better age. Yesterday, tomorrow?...

The young intellectuals were not missing either. They were no more willing to miss the occasion than the others. Not so bad, after all, these young fellows. As always, they talked and talked and talked. Like everyone else, by the way. The wake is not the burial. Doesn't one come there to soften the family's grief and one's own distress? They were already choosing the place of Tiya in the history of the country, when the time came to write freely of it. For that time would come. The Old Man was already theirs. A pioneer. Isolated, misunderstood, but one of them. They recognised that his struggle had been harder, had called for greater courage, had been fundamental. A pioneer. Hadn't he been one of the first to speak of socialism?

And his dignified attitude in the face of Polépolé, in the face of...you say it, now. They too wanted to repeat "Napoleon, Napoleon".

Napoleon?

That night I stayed at the wake till dawn. Elengui, as well as Soukali, was there, discreet and well hidden among the mass of women, all wrapped up in their cloths upon the mats. And anyway, that night, I wouldn't have had the heart to...Tiya, that was someone! Something inexpressible. An epoch, our own epoch too, a part of ourselves that had vanished. Like our own youth disappearing in the rainy season. I, who have no taste for politics, felt I had participated in a slice of our history, despite myself, but without effort.

A giant tree had crashed in the forest, and all the beasts had fallen silent.

Tomorrow (but who could really know? No one believed any longer in opening the tabernacles and lifting the veils), would I not be questioned about Tiya, the fighter? I had been one of his contemporaries, one of his intimates, one of those for whom his door was always open, without formality.

And what did I really know of him? But for hearing Melanie just now, I would never have known that he was called Napoleon. An admired historical figure, or a name given him by Melanie, just like that? Because it corresponded with her imagery, the idea she had formed of her man battling for the freedom of his country. Or even because it was the only name, that evening, which came to mind?

The following afternoon, just before the removal of the body, preceded by Monsieur Gourdain and his prying sleuths, Bwakamabé came to bow before the remains of Tiya. The silent crowd drew back to let him pass. He seemed inhibited, timid and gauche. No doubt, because no one had applauded him. Just for once, the crowd could dispense with that.

In his uniform of a serving officer, he stood stiffly at attention, just beside the catafalque, and carried his hand, with a brusque gesture, to the peak of his cap. Standing there immobile, for several seconds, perhaps a minute, or even two. Immobile and serious, as if he were teaching someone how to give a military salute. Tiya didn't even glance at him. Impassive, eyes irredeemably closed. Bwakamabé, with an angry gesture, let his hand fall from his peak and slap against his thigh; then he retreated to the solitude of his Palace, leaving Tiya to be borne in the hearts of the anonymous multitude.

The carpenters approached the coffin, and the blows of their hammers resounded in our hearts.

The separation had begun. The funeral procession formed up for the march to the edge of the city. A long convoy. Longer than the procession for 15th August. No meeting, no marriage, no funeral in the country had ever called together so many woolly heads.

There was a pause at the edge of the town. One by one, groups came forward to deposit, some a wreath, some a bouquet, on the big wooden coffin. The cries of Ma Melanie became heart-rending, insupportable. There was no funeral elegy. Philo the Great, whose shoulders never ceased shaking, also cried out, along a line joining her belly to the skies. No benediction either. Old Tiya was an atheist. A freemason, according to some.

Nevertheless, we sang a canticle. The curves of the melody and the innocence of the words warmed our hearts. This was just what we needed to offer the Old Man, a present of naked adolescent beauty, in a last gesture of pity. Equally, to forgive him his atheism. So that our God, our gods, would pardon him. But look, he wasn't an atheist of Satan's. Our good God the Father doubtless has his own. The way they describe Him to us. He's too intelligent not to understand that sort of unbelief. I'm sure he has opened his arms to Tiya. One doesn't make a present to Satan of such a soul as that.

It's only a brief farewell,
My brothers,
It's only a...

The procession had divided into two groups. The larger stayed behind, singing and praying, then quickly dispersed. The other consisted of some trucks and Land Rovers. One of them was full of political militants of his generation—other Tiyas.

Ma Melanie cried out still louder, as if she had some devil shaking her from within.

That evening, amid the general announcements and just before the sports news, the radio stated that Monsieur François Tiya, retired teacher, who had died in Paris "after a long illness", had been buried.

The authorities claimed that, at the moment of dispersal, agitators had wanted to sing the hymn of Tiya's party. Immediately, they had been overwhelmed and arrested by Monsieur Gourdain's agents, mingling with the crowd. In Moundié, it was also reported that all the officials absent from their posts on the afternoon of the funeral had been rewarded with a dismissal without their month's pay.

That's how the Old Man left us, exactly. For the rest, you have so exploited my confidences that I have little to add to your account of the meeting between the French ambassador and Bwakamabé.

The meeting began in a stormy atmosphere. This one had summoned that one to express his displeasure at the articles of *Gavroche Aujourd'hui*. Crazy with rage, he did so while tearing diplomatic language to shreds, treating Monsieur Bruno de la Roncière exactly like a colonial master abusing his "boy". I myself felt a shame and humiliation such as I've never felt before or since.

Taking advantage of a brief pause, the Frenchman invoked the freedom of the press as experienced in his country, and besought "the Marshal" not to confuse the calumnies of an independent review with the respectful sentiments of the French Government towards him.

Bwakamabé broke out again, in the most brutal and vulgar language, going so far as to say that President Pierre Chevalier was really a poor fish, with no real power, if he couldn't even establish his right to punish journalists who insulted friendly heads of state, and that France was setting a bad example in respect to her *political children* in Africa.

In his book *In the Service of the Quai,* Bruno de la Roncière devotes less than a page to this interview and presents himself in the dominant role, which certainly doesn't conform with the truth...

The day was long in Soweto. I'd have needed a breast as broad as the earth to support the oppressive mixture of anguish and spleen that fumed within me. Even today, I could describe the smallest details of Cécile's sitting room. But I was also closely attentive to the noises in the street. Every car slowing down, every voice approaching, every telephone ringing made my heart sink. A day endless as the sand waves in the sea of the Sahara. I wanted to read. Some old numbers of *Jours de France,* of *Bingo,* a missal, *Evenings in the Cottages,* I think. *Love's Secretary,* a *Kama Sutra* in a fine edition, the *Complete Works* of Kim Il Sung; those of Daddy were also there.

Cécile came in very late. After midnight. She gave me, with a mother's conjurations, an air ticket, a passport in the name of Wapelu, some health certificates, an exit permit prepared by the security services, and a large khaki-coloured envelope. Inside were five packets of ten thousand francs each, bearing Daddy's effigy. I said to myself that the world was changing, if it was now the women who sent money. There was also a note from Ma Mireille, scribbled in the maladroit hand of a child. I folded it carefully and slipped it into my shirt pocket. While Cécile moved busily from one room to another, I counted the money. I'd never had so much in my hands before.

"Here."

Cécile threw me a pair of pyjamas.

"You'll be better in there for sleeping. Otherwise you'll get all cramped up."

A man's pyjamas, the little hussy!

"You can undress in the bathroom. Go through here and take the first door on your right."

There was plenty of time for all that. And anyway, I was fine as I was. Even at home, I never wore pyjamas.

"The light's just outside the door. On the left. Wait, I'll get you a clean towel."

At last, I obeyed her. From politeness, or lack of initiative.

Well-showered and wearing the nightclothes, I really did feel a brief sensation of physical comfort. I plunged into the wide arms of a chair in the sitting room and unfolded Ma Mireille's letter to study it properly.

"You aren't going to stay there all night? Come on, you must get some sleep."

I told her I wouldn't be long in dropping off.

"But you aren't going to sleep in there!"

I didn't understand.

"Too many mosquitoes there."

"Oh, poof! A few mosquitoes aren't going to kill me."

"Ts, ts, ts, come and sleep in here, you'll be much better off. There's a fan. That always chases away the mosquitoes."

Did she have two bedrooms, then?

A nice little square bed, without feet, which seemed to rest directly on a maize-patterned carpet.

"But, Cécile..."

"Cécile what?"

"But this is your bed, no?"

"So, then? Does it scare you? Don't be afraid, no bedbugs in it."

"I just mean that..."

So after all, I was the one whose ideas were misplaced. Cécile was a sister, no? Ma Mireille's most reliable friend. For me, a kid sister. It was obvious that she was abreast of everything. She wouldn't be the one to betray us. She just wanted to fulfill her mission to the last, completely, without a hitch and forgetting nothing. And then, why can't a man and a woman sleep side by side without immediately...? Cécile was my sister.

She fell asleep right away, ignoring me completely. I felt her through the rhythm of her breathing. As for me, I kept tossing and turning, my thoughts in a whirl. What an incredible story to fall on my head. Me, a conspirator! What an imagination these policemen have! They must have listened to all the telephone conversations between Soukali and me since she joined the Bulgarian Embassy. I knew quite well that one should never trust those machines. Just think, an embassy ending in *-ist,* too... The phone is sure to be tapped, twenty-four hours a day. I had a feeling it would all end like this. But Soukali laughed at my fears. I had to ring her up, talk to her, show my interest in her. Well, you've seen already. What a woman! A real torrent. She'd even have liked me to write songs for her. Not because she wanted to hear them interpreted by one of our bands. No. Just songs for her. To be read and sung only between our four eyes. Are there two women on earth like Soukali? After all, she was quite right. Love shouldn't be confined to the level of the mat. It's above all a matter for the guitar. Didn't I sleep in the same bed with Elengui, without automatically doing *that,* every night? Nevertheless, I love her too, Elengui. There, I mustn't forget. I can't go away just like this. I'll scribble her a word tomorrow, to explain this fuck-up to her. Must also leave her something. More than one check. Yes, I had my checkbook with me. Cécile could give her the whole thing. A sister, Cécile. A real one. Not *sister* in the aggressive sense of the word. A real sister, on whom one could count in moments of difficulty. Must also write a word to Soukali. They say you only love once. But I must be peculiar. I have loved, and I still love, Elengui and Soukali with an equal ardour. And if there are some nuances in my feelings for one or the other, it isn't a matter of quantity. Only of quality. For

Elengui, a profound and intense tenderness; for Soukali, fire, music and perfume. Ma Mireille? Not the same thing. Let's say, a certain hankering after forbidden fruit, plus the dizzying pleasure of being valued more highly than one of the great ones of this world.

Cécile stirred. She turned on her side, in the posture of a runner lifting one knee. She brushed against me. I put a hand on her shoulder to protect her. She was a sister. She cuddled up with a groan. She pressed against me with a little shudder. I squeezed her harder. My little sister. Our limbs, our fingers, interlaced each other in a multiple, complex way difficult to describe. Like the thousands of threads that advance and knot into each other to weave a magic web. Cécile, my sister. The hands, the fingers, the nails. Then the mouths. The hair. The tongues, like the wings of little red sparrows. Without even the murmuring of a single word. In the reassuring darkness. Cécile, my sister. What youth in her breasts and thighs! Really something to sing about! At what moment, the plunge into the well? Without any shock, like a movement in a smooth and well-rehearsed dance. At what moment, the step into the saddle? And those thighs trotting, trotting, trotting. Cécile, my sister. Cécile, éhé! Cécile! Cécile! Yééé. No, no. Oh! Yes!

"What have we...?"

She squeezed my hand, then muttered some incomprehensible endearment. I put my hand on her head and pressed her to me.

"Yes...you understand, yes?"

"Ma Mireille told me to take very good care of you. That you should lack nothing, right up to the moment you step on the plane."

"Are you going...to give her details of the way in which you looked after me?"

A barely perceptible shrug.

Cécile accompanied me to the airport and performed all the formalities for me. Thanks to a special card, she was entitled to go right to the end of the gangway. We kissed each other on the cheeks. With affection.

"Good-bye, my sister."

"Good-bye, *Maître.*"

Hard to leave one's country!

Nevertheless, as soon as the plane took off, a joyful excitement, something bizarre, uncontrollable, invaded me.

"Champagne, miss."

The air hostess didn't even notice my agitation.

. . .

I will spare my readers the long pages of rhetoric in which my young compatriot ex-Cabinet Secretary, in the name of revolutionary modesty, takes issue with exotico-pornographic writing. Some will certainly miss these pieces of eloquence, in which the pen of a gifted polemicist demolishes with implacable dialectic the depraved tendencies of a decadent bourgeoisie, which insists on contaminating a virginal Africa by the systematic export of its dissolute values. But I couldn't publish them without adding my own reflections upon these edifying lessons in morality. To his venerable and learned ethic and to my own banalities and platitudes, each in turn ridiculous in their conviction of revealing new truths, I have preferred the forgotten voice of the good Diderot.

To begin with, dear reader, these are not fables, but history, and I feel no more guilty, perhaps less, when I recount the fooleries of Jacques, than Seutonius did when he transmitted to us the debaucheries of Tiberius. However, you read Seutonius and make no reproach against him. Why do you not frown upon Catullus, or Martial, or Horace, or Petronius, or La Fontaine and countless others? Why do you not say to the Stoic Seneca: "What need have we of the antics of your slave with his concave mirrors?" Why have you confined your indulgence only to the dead? If you will reflect a little on this bias, you will perceive that it is born of a vicious principle. If you are innocent, you will not read me; if you are corrupted, you will read me without ill effect. And then, if what I have said does not satisfy you, open Jean-Baptiste Rousseau's preface and you will find my apology there. Who among you dares blame

Voltaire for writing The Maid? *None. So you have two scales for the actions of men? "But," you say,* "The Maid *of Voltaire is a masterpiece!"—Too bad, because then one will only read it the more—"And your* Jacques *is only an insipid rhapsody of events, some real and some imaginary, written without grace and arranged without order"—All the better, my* Jacques *will be the less read for it. Whichever way you turn, you are in the wrong. If my book is good, it will give you pleasure; if it is bad, it will not do any harm. No book is more innocent than a bad book. I amuse myself by writing under borrowed names the follies that you commit; your follies make me laugh; my writing puts you in a rage. Reader, it's for you to speak frankly, but I find that the more wicked of us two is not myself. How happy I would be if it were as easy to protect myself from your baseness, as it is for you to avoid the boredom or danger of my work! Villainous hypocrites, leave me in peace. F..k like unsaddled asses; but allow me to say "f..k"; I pass the action to you, just pass me the word. You pronounce boldly enough "kill", "steal", "betray", but the other word you dare to speak only between your teeth! Is it that the less you exhale of these so-called impurities in speech, the more of them remain in your thoughts? And that you have performed the genital action, so natural, so necessary and so correct, so as to exclude the sign of it from your conversation, or to imagine that your mouth, your eyes or your ears would be soiled by it? It is fine that the expressions the least in use, the least written, the best killed, should be the best known and the most generally understood; just as that one is; also the word* futuo *is no less familiar than the word bread; no age is ignorant of it, no idiom is deprived of it. It has a thousand synonyms in all the languages, it expresses itself in all without being expressed, without voice, without form, and the sex which does it most is that which keeps most silent about it. I can still hear you, you cry out: "Fie, cynic! Fie, impudent man! Fie, sophist!" Have courage, go on insulting at your will an estimable author whom you have constantly in your hands, and of whom I am only here the translator. The license of his style is almost a guarantee of the purity of his morals; it is Montaigne:* "Lasciva est nobis pagina, vita proba."

(Diderot, Jacques the Fatalist and his Master, *Paris, 1773 or 1774 or 1775)*

The French Government's reception must have been close to that accorded to the Queen of England, even if the microscopes of doctors in protocol could discover any nuances between them. Nuances of detail only, affirmed our ambassador in Paris, with a disdainful gesture and connoisseur's tone.

Before his departure from our country to that of the Uncles, Daddy wanted to sulk because, in the end (had that la Roncière fellow really done his job?) the French Government had held firm and refused the extradition or imprisonment of students or other opponents in exile. They had confined themselves to picking up the most active (those whom Daddy called "the ringleaders") according to a list furnished by Monsieur Gourdain, and to offering them a compulsory vacation in Corsica. Daddy had treated this action as an affront and threatened to delay his visit. Our ambassador had quickly sent a telex announcing that everything was ready for his reception and giving a description of the program which would make even the most obdurate colonial officer salivate. In the name of compromise, and on the wise, pressing advice of Ma Mireille and his chief diviner, Daddy finally agreed to go.

A certain rabble and several organised fringe groups (with whom I suspected the young compatriot Cabinet Secretary to be in contact) published protest articles and communiqués touching on democracy, human rights, and denouncing collusion, both characteristic and shameful, between the bourgeois power of Pierre Chevalier and the "Ubu of the Tropics".

The composition of the delegation posed certain problems, especially in the matter of the presidential household. Ma Mireille insisted upon being the only wife in his entourage. His concubines would hear nothing of that. Many of them already saw themselves posing for photographs in front of the Eiffel

Tower, at the doors of Dior, or chatting with Tino Rossi or Claude François.

"Who does she think she is, eh? If she were able to satisfy him, would he still need to come and find us?"

And to clench the point, they would spit at you some jibes as pertinent as they were gross. Daddy tried to settle the palaver by a judgement of Solomon: only Ma Mireille would appear at the chief ceremonies, in the role of the official First Lady of the country. The concubines, for their part, would be listed as ladies-in-waiting.

"Can't be done, can't be done. I have my own ladies-in-waiting, chosen by myself. I don't want them mixed up with those..."

"No, Ma Mireille. I won't allow it. Take back that word. My girls are not harlots. They are honest women. As honest as you are."

"What?" A cry from the heart. "You compare me with them?"

And Ma Mireille refused to withdraw what she had said. A long discussion was needed, at the end of which it was Daddy who had to lower his voice and display all the patience of a schoolmaster.

In the end, he proposed listing the concubines among "members of the presidential family". Ma Mireille called up her reserves. Appeal had to be made to her family, then to a tribal court judge who was the best-informed about Djabotama customs and the most prestigious in Moundié, to call her to reason by referring to many examples of our tribal law. Was she not the Chief's wife? Well, then... Who could take on such responsibilities without additional support, contenting himself like the Uncles, the hypocritical Uncles, with a single wife? And whoever had several wives must he not be scrupulous in dividing everything into strictly equal portions? Well, then...

Thank God, even the most impassioned palavers in our society always end in a happy solution. A Super DC8, called The Capital, took the whole delegation for this marvellous journey. But Ma Mireille, still deeply affronted, contemplated and secretly prepared her revenge, accomplishing it in a rendezvous with your humble servant, in the middle of the afternoon, in a suite of the George V Hotel.

At Orly, the French Minister of Cooperation was standing at the foot of the gangway, as announced by Monsieur Bruno de la Roncière. To tell the truth, the Marshal had hoped to the last moment that his fellow-President would welcome him at the airport, as he himself took trouble to do when one of his peers landed in our country. The French Chief of Protocol interpreted in a flash the unhappiness in our Chief's face and found the right tone to murmur in his ear that the official visit didn't really begin until the steps of the Elysée: the traffic jams, you understand...

But this little cloud was a mere drop of wine in the river. As he reached the V.I.P. lounge, Daddy had the satisfaction of seeing the journalists, with their Nagras in a bandolier, cameras at the shoulder, and with microphones extended on long metal arms, begging for a declaration, a few words from him. From him! His face flashed alive. He had to think of Louisette's family in the rue Rambuteau. He shifted from one foot to the other, like a child holding back a piss. They wanted to know what were his impressions on treading the soil of France (a very great emotion...he felt at home); what was the meaning of this visit (the strengthening of cooperation with a chosen partner); what he thought of French policy in the field of cooperation (very, very satisfactory, disinterested and effective, even though insufficient, if France wanted to help Africa to develop itself and above all, if she didn't want to see herself supplanted by another partner...just as the French people had freely chosen their President of the Republic—Pierre Chevalier, his dear brother, for whom he wished the support of all right-thinking French citizens—his country had freely chosen France as a special partner and he trusted she would not disappoint the millions of hopes placed in her...); what were the big economic projects being discussed (the ministers and technicians would see to all that); what he thought of the present evolution of Africa (the so-called progressive countries mess up the whole place and tip the continent towards the Soviet bloc... France must therefore help her overseas friends to counter this danger); what did he think of world developments (the menace ending in *-ist* was the most serious). No question was put aside by the Chief, and the journalists continued to press him. The interview soon turned, in the opinion of the young compatriot Cabinet Secretary, into a press conference and would have developed into a meeting, but for the reaction of the French Chief of Protocol, preoccupied (too preoccupied, according to Daddy) to stick to the program as planned, minute by minute. Daddy left the journalists with much bowing and cries of "Thanks, thanks, thanks, my dear cousins."

A star, a star, he was a star in the country of the Uncles: he'd quite forgotten the absence of his peer at Orly. Quite forgotten.

At his emergence from the audience chamber, he was met by a double line of Africans in *bubus* and cloths, yelling *wollé, wollé, woï, woï* with the same conviction as at home—something which the Uncles found primitive, contemptuous as they were of our cultural identity. I recognised among them some Djabotama students and some officials on prolonged stays, most unpopular with the young compatriot Cabinet Secretary. He claimed that these fellows, on the verge of retirement, came in truth to acquire a certain prestige by their European studies. I also noted a squad of security police, all armed and dressed in black, beside a bus with barred windows. Later we were told that they had just rounded up and removed, in similar buses, any students who seemed too nervous. Djassikini, for sure. Although all this passed off quietly enough, and without our even noticing it, my young compatriot Cabinet Secretary muttered to himself that it was the beginning of the fascistisation of France. Losing my calm (and the reader will have appreciated my calm through all the preceding pages), I retorted to Monsieur Intellectual that we Africans are not serious, and especially not they, the intellectuals. By what right could we, who lived on our knees at home, swallowing all the shit from Daddy's backside without a single cry or protest, sometimes even aiding the Guinarou in his work (follow my look)—by what right did we pose as critics of the Uncles' democracy? And I doubted even that the day when those intellectuals, with all their dialectical apparatus... But the young compatriot Cabinet Secretary dug me in the ribs and whispered in Kibotama that the driver was listening, and that it didn't look good for us to quarrel like this, in the presence of an Uncle, and in his language, too.

Along the route, the outriders opened our way with acrobatic skill, risking their lives a hundred times over, sliding with their cycles almost horizontally, with all the elegance and agility of star dancers, through a dense mass of cars and trucks, forcing them to pull off, with a bad grace, however resistant they were to the sirens of the cortege. One could even imagine that they wanted us to fuck off. Ah, these Uncles! So disrespectful towards the great. As if it were not clear enough that an official cortege was passing! They seemed to be fed up to the teeth. Really, our country over there is not so backward as people think. At least in the matter of order, it's far ahead of the Uncles. One would be amused at so much hullaballoo at home, where it's treated with such nonchalance. With the tones of an apostle vulgarizing the rich thoughts of a leader to his disciples, the Minister for Customary Affairs explained to us, on our arrival at the hotel, that we'd had under our eyes a living example of the decadence of Western morals, resulting from a too pronounced cult of individualism. Such was the irremediable fate of civilizations which, abandoning the sacred, demystified all values and had nothing left on which to base themselves. Live, my brothers, the policy of cultural resurrection! And *wollé, wollé, woï, woï*!

The orderly officers and gorillas selected by Daddy for this journey didn't want to be outdone by the outriders and freely added their number to the gapers, hoisting their torsoes through car windows and glaring distrustfully at the balconies in search of some criminal sniper. Alas...!

We sped through the Place de l'Etoile. As for me, I'd had the chance to enjoy it at leisure on earlier visits. But the little darlings of Daddy...they were like schoolgirls excited by a holiday jaunt. Our Chief of Protocol was irritated, shrugging shoulders and complaining of the impression they were giving (false, surely) that we are all yokels, savages who had never seen anything. Afterwards, both *Gavroche Aujourd'hui* and radio grapevine spread an anecdote about this event. Daddy wanted to ask the driver to stop, so that he could bow before the flame of the Unknown Soldier, but the Minister for Foreign Affairs managed to convince him that the convoy should proceed, because this ceremony had been provided for later in the program. Honestly, I don't know how much of this is true. I was in another vehicle at the time. But such a gesture would suit well with Daddy's character. He loves grand gestures that rise from the heart and strike the imagination of the crowd. But (how many times were we not told by Brother Anthony in his lessons at St. Raymond de Penyafort!) France is the country of moderation, not that of grandiose popular emotions.

On the other hand, the young compatriot Cabinet Secretary told me definitely that Daddy had insisted on the program including a march right along the Champs-Elysées to the Arc de Triomphe, but the French security officials had been fearful of provoking Parisian opinion by such a display.

At the end of the famous avenue, the cortege slowed down, and the cars were surrounded by mounted Republican Guards, who escorted us to the residence of the French President. Our host and the very charming Madame Chevalier were awaiting us on the threshold, and it was at this point, as already pronounced, that the official visit really began.

First an exchange of speeches. Welcome on the one part, including a eulogy for a country whose history was common with that of France and whose President was a tried and true friend of the French people, tied to them by many bonds, beginning with that incomparable common instrument of thought: language. Thanks and joy on the other part, with Daddy applying himself even more than usual to differentiate clearly the *é* from the *è;* the *o* from the *au;* and the *i* from the *u.* By the approving nods of the French authorities, one noted their satisfaction in tasting the correctness of his accent. They had something to be proud of in the education they had given. Colonialism, contrary to fashionable notions, had other things than crimes on its conscience. The Chief expressed himself as custom demanded in all the speeches delivered in such circumstances, not omitting to celebrate the secular bonds, the communality of the linguistic instrument, the eternal glory of France, land of liberty and the rights of man, which she had so generously exported to the African continent, hitherto sunk in barbarism. No one knows what passed between the two men in the subsequent *tête à tête* that took place just before Daddy's departure for the Hotel Crillon, which was to be his refuge during the visit.

The details of the whole affair were given in *Paris-Match* for the following week.

An agreeable visit, perfectly organised and crowned with a joint communiqué, strictly along the lines of diplomatic tradition.

"Come on, Edwige, no good refusing. Take this one, it'll be much easier."

She continued protesting a moment, tried once more and, rather shamefaced, ended by accepting the spoonful offered by Boubeu.

I was giving myself a big treat, quite at my ease, eating the tiebdjeun *with my fingers.*

The girl in white from the Hibiscus *had been seated at my left, and I kept asking myself where I had seen her before.*

The table was small and once already our knees had involuntarily brushed together. She paid no attention to my aplogies, which were those of a clumsy schoolboy.

Edwige complimented the host on his cuisine, and the movement of her lips in pronouncing "it's delicious" stirred in me a troublesome desire.

That hair, those lips, that voice, where then, my God, had I already encountered them?

Our knees touched again.

Boubeu, master of the situation, discoursed brilliantly about Senegalese dishes, cloths, bubus*, music, the* téranga*, the* diom *and other guttural words as difficult for my Djabotama tongue as for those of the other guests. It was a real course in civilization. Edwige, deeply interested, posed a thousand questions, seeking clarification, and the inexhaustible Boubeu, who had got up to brush away the flies with his sky-blue toga, was rich in replies that set even himself dreaming.*

I was licking my fingers, so as to lose nothing of the perfume of the tiebdjeun.

Edwige, having sat down again, pulled some cigarettes from her handbag. Black tobacco. She offered me one. I set a cigarette to my lips, licking my fingers again in the process. She rummaged in her bag without succeeding in finding either her matches or her lighter. I took one of the candles that Boubeu, as a man of taste, had placed on the table.

"Here, a cigarette lighted from a candle always tastes better."

Once again, our knees touched, the hand that held the candle trembled, and her eyes lifted towards the tip of the cigarette, towards the flame, and finally, met my own. She inhaled deeply, deeply, deeply, with a great thrust of her bosom. When she puffed out the smoke, I felt that her senses were satisfied.

Boubeu offered her a basket of fruit. With a hand on her stomach, she refused, a smile on her lips and her eyes shut. We all moved over to participate in the ceremony of drinking mint tea, seated upon the carpet. I tried not to let my gaze dwell on Edwige's calves, as she sat with her legs crossed under her.

She was leaving next day. That was the occasion for Boubeu's dinner party. She had spoken about her stay here in N..., about all that she had learned here, of her friends and the briefness of her visit... I discovered in this woman, who strove to display a masculine energy in all the traits of her character, the accents of an emotion that altered her voice. She stopped, leaned forward and sat up again, offering me my cup of tea between two fingers. She fixed me with her glance for an instant. I felt myself sinking. The eyes of an instructress who dominated me. Where had I seen them before?

Boubeu clapped his hands. When I saw him, upright and

majestic in his toga of a great Wolof lord, ready to inflict a speech on us, I felt a bad taste rise into my mouth. I didn't dare look at anyone. In fact, it was short, simple and moving. Edwige blew her nose and discreetly dried her eyes. One would have thought the eyes of... No, absurd.

Boubeu presented her, in the name of us all, with a cloth, two statuettes and some ivory bracelets.

Edwige replied in the same tone as Boubeu, but adding a little touch of love. Despite her emotion, she expressed herself easily, like someone accustomed to this sort of occasion.

I ought to have left the party. My duties began early the following day. But I was as if nailed to the carpet. Each cup of tea sweetened my tongue more than the last. And then this unusual and inexplicable fear of solitude which was haunting me.

Boubeu switched on his hi-fi system at a volume fit to wake all the neighbours, and everyone began to "shake" in a real party spirit. Shoulders, hips and heads swung to the rhythm of electric guitars and Latin American percussion. The girls devised movements as delicate as Chinese dolls. The men burst into improvisations like artistes. Edwige, the only white woman present, kicked off her shoes and let herself be taken by one partner after another, swinging her hips uninhibitedly in a puppet-like rhythm, a gauche imitation of our own. I sat aside, smoking cigarette after cigarette.

At two o'clock, I finally found the will to get up.

Edwige looked at her watch and exclaimed with horror that she hadn't packed her bags.

How did we find ourselves together on the doorstep and how did she come to propose giving me a lift in her Mehari? All along the cliff-road the sea wind pressed her skirt against her thighs.

"Come on, let's take a drink at my place."

With a serious air, she hesitated a moment, then descended without a word from her fibre-glass jeep.

We took a glass of strong liqueur.

There were no clumsy gestures, no coarseness, none of the

habitual comedy. She had breasts like God's thunder. And what freedom! At first, I was very self-conscious. Just think of that. But she soon put me at my ease. Her dance had the same sweep as her breasts. She swallowed me up in her fresh waters. We rubbed our skins against each other in the warmest of frictions. When her surprised throat gave out notes of deliverance in a tone close to solemn complaint, I couldn't hold back the cry of an angry child on the brink of tears. She hugged me maternally in her arms, sweet as vanilla.

This morning, I met Boubeu.

"I'm just just back from the airport. I took Madame Berger... She's really sweet on you, you know."

Then his big laugh, shining like sugar cane. He gave me a tap on the shoulder.

"Pity. But, you never know. Perhaps she'll come back, no?"

Daddy was presiding in his office, as usual, surrounded by a whole battery of telephones, buttons, panels, intercoms, levers, winking lights, loudspeakers, TV screens linked to spying cameras; not to mention, for those with eyes to see, a thousand concealed microphones. When I entered the room, he was speaking into two mouthpieces at once. He had scarcely laid these down when another phone rang, and I heard him reply in what he hoped was a softer voice:

"Oh, it's you? Good, I'll call you back in a quarter of an hour."

Ma Mireille? I must say, to be accurate, that during this interview, just as during many others, the telephone would interrupt us and I would hear, with small variations which I now forget, the same phrase:

"Oh, it's you? Good, I'll call you back in a quarter of an hour."

For the first time, I noticed the spots on his forehead.

Then he began moaning, as usual. The people didn't appreciate, any more than his colleagues, their good fortune in having such a leader. If Polépolé had stayed in power another month, the country would have plunged into the abyss. And he, modest Messiah as he was, had saved the situation. He hadn't hesitated a second to answer the call of the Eternal. The cadres, above all those accursed intellectuals whose mouths were filled with the titles of their diplomas or of their famous colleges, must understand this, once and for all. No one was willing to collaborate with him. All of them thought only of enjoying power, as if that power were theirs alone.

Those spots on his brow were intriguing me.

"*Maître,* if only you knew how the incessant pressure of the tribe and the incompetence of those under me prevent me from making this country what I really want it to be..."

And he began tenderly caressing the good old days, when he was still just a simple officer respected by everybody, without these wagon loads of shit to bear. He often felt tempted to chuck it all and let them sort if out for themselves, yes—do what Nasser had twice done...

"But what restrains me is that I don't see anyone capable of carrying on this task and being accepted by the people. Even if I forgot that" (he raised his finger in front of his nose), "the people would remind me. Just like Papa de Gaulle. I know it." (He opened his eyes with a wide, fixed stare.) "And even if the people wished, in a moment of folly, that I should go, God would recall me to do my duty. Every night, He repeats to me: 'Hannibal-Ideloy, my son, if you give up, you're a coward!'"

He showed me some extracts from the press, collected by his staff.

"Just take a look at this."

In an interview offered to some European daily, Captain Yabaka had attacked American imperialism, described sometimes, as need arose, as "global policing". The journalist went on to ask him to assess the value of American aid in the development of African agriculture. He had brazenly replied that all gifts from the U.S. were suspect to any honest and conscientious African, considering that this super-power was devastating the countryside of Vietnam and Cambodia by its bombardments and sustaining, against the wishes of the people *in general* and of the peasant masses *in particular,* the dictatorships of puppet regimes condemned by history.

"Who does he think he is, this fellow, to go giving interviews? Only one person can speak in the name of the Nation, in any well-organised country: the Chief." He rapped his chest with his fingers. "Anyway, all this, you know, is only to prepare public opinion. Got something at the back of his mind... Can't teach an old monkey new tricks."

He tapped his head.

"But I know the truth of it. The American ambassador has had precise information from the C.I.A. That gentleman there is an agent of the *-ists.* I've put Monsieur Gourdain on his trail. (A wink.) Wherever he goes, my eye will be there. Everything he says will be taped by us."

Chuckles.

"Wanted to tell you, because every time I talk to you about that fellow, you don't want to believe me."

I read the headline over a client's shoulder: SEVEN MEMBERS OF TELEMA TERRORIST GROUP ARRESTED HERE. *I had a moment's shock which nobody could have noticed. A buzzing in my head. I made a huge effort to control myself and set down the order I was carrying, as if nothing had happened. I returned discreetly behind the client, who was busy reading his paper. Yes, it really said:* ARRESTED HERE...*But the client then turned the page.*

I invented some excuse to retire for a moment and went to buy the paper in the hotel kiosk.

It was really true: on page 3, headed "From Overseas", at the top of three columns devoted to Africa: SEVEN MEMBERS OF TELEMA TERRORIST GROUP ARRESTED HERE.

A despatch from *The Voice of National Resurrection,* picked up in Yaoundé, Dakar and Abidjan, announced the arrest in the capital, on Monday 10th and Tuesday 11th July, of seven people suspected of belonging to the Parisian terrorist movement A.F.P. They were: Victor Bondou, aged 21; Pierre Dendissa, Gratien Embobelo and Ibrahima Fadiga (the last having both Ivorian nationality and that of our country), all aged 22; Pascal

Bowaboya and Mademoiselle Malaïka Yabaka, both 23, and a Monsieur Etienne Mwanga.

These arrests had been made thanks to certain informants, following a sweep carried out several days earlier in the capital. The seven militants had been arrested in the Moundié quarter.

The declaration by *The Voice of National Resurrection* confirms certain rumours which we have already reported in earlier editions, according to which, firstly, President Bwakamabé Na Sakkadé has escaped an assassination attempt and, secondly, the arsenal of the National Armed Forces has been attacked.

Our earlier report provoked, at the time, a violent reaction from the state authorities. After the seizure of our edition of 27th June, the country's ambassador in Paris sent us a communiqué in which he described our information as "gratuitous and fantastic allegations, inspired by the hatred and jealousy of totalitarian regimes." He added that the information obtained by *Le Monde* was "shot through with contradictions and untruths designed to discredit the regime of our respected President, Bwakamabé Na Sakkadé." According to the ambassador,then, the situation in the country "had never been so flourishing, because Marshal Bwakamabé had established a mini-Eden where it was a joy to live."

Today it seems that the regime of Marshal Bwakamabé Na Sakkadé, of which the French Section of Amnesty International has often reported violations of human rights, is experiencing greater and greater internal difficulties. The people arrested in the capital are not the real leaders of the terrorist organization. Former labourers, nurses and medical orderlies, they seem nevertheless to have played a technical role in the infra-structure of the armed group, especially in the collection of information.

They took part in some petty acts of intimidation and scattered terrorist actions, such as burning of cars and anonymous telephone threats. Only one of the seven, Mademoiselle Malaïka Yabaka, will be accused of a specific offence: the burning down of a bar in the Plateau quarter, the *Milk Pot*, in May of this year, leading to the death of a French aid worker.

A curfew has been imposed over the whole country, from 8 p.m. to dawn.

A presidential decree has set up a special High Court, charged with bringing to justice all attempts against the security of the State. Composed entirely of military officers whose identity has not been revealed, its sentences will not be subject to appeal.

(*Interim Report*)

The girl in question, Malaïka Yabaka, was really and truly the sister of Captain Yabaka. I remembered meeting her at her brother's place. She studied at the Felix-Eboué Technical College, I believe. I was struck by her Marpessa Dawn-like countenance. I can see now her strong chin and her coiffure of fine, long strands adorned with cowries.

I reread the article several times, then cut it out to keep it, to what end I don't know.

An opposition declaring itself at home? An armed opposition, working as commandos? As life went on, I had finally convinced myself that the heroes would never more emerge from the legends and epics where earlier epochs had definitively enclosed them.

I looked attentively at each of the names. All the tribes were represented, including the Djabotama.

And among them, a woman!

I was furious to know more.

No minutes. Once again, the agenda had been given on the spot. From my usual post of observation, with frequent journeys to carry coffee and refreshments (Chivas for the Chief), I studied the grave and venerable faces of the two supreme bodies which controlled our destinies. That day, many were in fear of a ministerial reshuffle, which would discharge upon their heads the rage excited by the loss of a file belonging to Monsieur Gourdain's services. I must point out here that, contrary to what strangers to our country might believe, the Guinarou's rages were no more benign than the loss of a ministerial post. The latter cost you some revenue (though one usually took care while in office to prepare against the future) and a certain fame, while the former touched your honour. It was no inconsequent joke—in any case for us Djabotama—to hear insults poured upon the secret part of your mother. In theory, a fit reply could be made only with a dagger. But no one dared attempt that against Daddy. And if everyone managed to swallow his anger like vomit, he didn't fail to have troubled dreams over it for many months to come.

Daddy swept into the room according to the usual protocol, his face clouded like one who passes most of the night toiling and reflecting over the well-being of the people, while the rest of the country sleeps, dances or makes love.

"Yesterday, I received your colleague, the Minister of Finance. Our Treasury is broke. The coffers are empty. The fruits of my journey to the Uncles' land can't be collected immediately. The groundnut planted today doesn't spring up tomorrow. We too must wait to harvest what we have planted." He made a vague gesture. "But conscious as I am of the duties of my post, the interview with your colleague hasn't failed to disturb me and keep me awake at night. I've even had to ask my doctor for sleeping pills. *Whereas* before this, I had already been thinking, thinking, thinking until..." He dragged out the last syllable. "Finally I retired to the Palace chapel and to God Almighty." He changed his tone. "My children, I must tell you, God exists and is very great. Truly, God is great. I felt how my besieged heart took on new vigour. Gba, gba, gba, gba, gba; little by little. Gba, gba, gba, gba, gba. An inner voice urged me not to let myself be defeated; it reminded me that a soldier must never lose courage; that the Eternal One can never abandon me, but that I must be able to read the signs; that the whites who came to see me last week were His envoys and that I must think carefully over their proposals; that it was only I who could save the country."

Daddy stopped a moment. The faces of the ministers and the members of the Council for National Resurrection showed both interest and confusion. They had been called very early in the day for this meeting.

"Yes, I received several days ago some envoys from South Africa."

In this ballet of comings-and-goings for audience at the Palace, where I often discovered things that should have been hidden from me, I had discerned nothing on this occasion.

"They came to see me in the game reserve at Fana. Made some interesting propositions. Ready to make us a grant of several millions of dollars and finance with very-low-interest loans all the economic projects we present to them. But the grant is in ready cash." He fingered some invisible object. "It was to them that the words of the Eternal One referred."

In the ensuing silence, I noted a barely perceptible shaking of the head by the Minister for Customary Affairs.

"...decided therefore to send a mission led by one of you to Pretoria next week, to carry a reply to their secret emissaries."

He looked closely at the effect produced.

"This is to inform you, my children."

Another silence, while he arranged the papers lying before him.

"However, if anyone among you would like to receive further information, I am ready."

Another silence.

"Anyway," his hands shuffled the papers, "they aren't so terrible as all that, those people. They behave. No sign of segregation, of that so-called segregation and all that stuff."

One minister (I forget who), in a movement of mingled timidity and courage, raised his finger.

"There can be no question, obviously, of re-examining the decision taken by our respected Chief: I refer to Daddy. I will say more: I support also the presentation, the rich and clear presentation, which has just been made to us by Daddy. We are talking here of a maturely considered decision, of the decision of a responsible leader whom every one of us here must support. My question, then, my question is just to ask whether these propositions carried some conditions along with them. Once again, to make myself well understood, I don't ask this question to oppose in any way the decision taken, but just to inform myself, you know."

"So as to lose no time, I'll reply right away. No conditions concerning our internal policies. No interference in our affairs, no South African base on our territory. They ask only that, by way of reciprocity, we say nothing about their internal affairs, that we leave them to take care of their problems as they wish. Natural enough, no? The principles of the O.A.U. itself. And here I must say that I was astonished at the open-mindedness of the

South African envoys. They agree..." (he coughed) "...they agree that *apartheid* must disappear in the end. But they want to advance step-by-step, so as not to shake things up, not to play the game of the gentlemen ending in *-ist,* and not to frighten the white population, who are, themselves..." (he raised a finger) "...Africans. We must understand them, after all. Thus, at bottom, they are in agreement with us—and that's the essential thing—as for the manner of getting there..." (he gestured vaguely) "...they ask only that we leave the management of their affairs to them."

The Minister of Foreign Affairs and the first speaker were plunged in a profound meditation, moving their heads slowly to-and-fro.

Another speaker launched into an appeal to realism and gave a brief sketch of the world situation to justify the remark that, all things considered, nations were guided in their policies by care for their own interests. He cited America, he cited Russia, he cited other examples and concluded that we must operate in the same fashion; that one couldn't build a country just on principles; that the people must be fed, and consequently we must make a league with the devil himself, if our interests dictate it.

Many heads nodded in agreement.

Yabaka asked for permission to speak. There was a silence even deeper than that for the previous interventions. The currents of two furious rivers met and clashed head-on in my bowels. It was as if I was forced to watch open-eyed a balancing feat in which the artiste ran the most frightful risks and where his life was more endangered than that of an antelope surrounded by wild beasts. I swallowed painfully and tried to stop sweating.

But the captain's tone was calm, like that of a mother addressing her son. He began by saying that he had followed with great attention the presentation made by Daddy, and that he also understood the necessity of placing the interests of the people above all other considerations. The people fed on meat, cassava or millet, not on ideals. He expected palpable results from our policies. But he permitted himself to remark that Daddy had acquired a wide fame and had raised himself to the level of the great pan-African leaders by the commitments he had undertaken during the Consultative Conference of Citrus-Exporting Countries. We must weigh the consequences of an eventual diplomatic link with South Africa. The Chief's peers must still have their heads filled with the heroic, edifying and militant images of the spectacle presented on Lake Lamartine. What confusion our abrupt change of line must spread among the peoples of Africa! Should we not fear the risk of diplomatic isolation, which would defeat all the brilliant efforts made by Daddy in recent years to make our country respected and appreciated in the outside world? He would submit to the decision of the majority, but hoped that everyone would reflect calmly upon the matter.

While Daddy, in profound concentration, shook his head several times, the Minister for Customary Affairs asked to speak.

"Respected Daddy, for my part I think this discussion has gone on too long. We blacks are too fond of blablabla. It's good, but (he made a face) it's too much. Above all, with this high French; big, big, big it is; we deceive the people too much. This diplomacy is fine, it's complicated, but believe me, the people of Moundié there understand nothing of your palavers. What they want is something to eat, a job to do, the chance to send their children to school and not be eaten any more by mosquitoes." If cooperation with South Africa would help us to realise this program, he was in favour of collaborating with her. He suddenly changed tone. Having started with a deceptive calm, he was bellowing. "Respected President, by day all the world is your friend. The whole world cries: Bwakamabé, *wollé, wollé, woï, woï!* The whole world declares itself ready to cut its own throat to confirm your power. That's by day. But at night, the best-tamed animals are transformed, with the help of I know not what *juju*, into birds of prey. At night—if the people in this room are afraid to speak of it, I will do so—at night, *coups d'état* are prepared by the very ones sitting around you. You imagine they are your friends, your brothers, your children. They are not. No. They do not love you. All these people here..." (his finger slowly turning the whole table) "...I'm speaking of." He shook his head several times. "No, my President. They do not love you. All of us here know ourselves. No one can tell us stories or perform miracles. We know ourselves. That is the truth, repected President." He paused, as if he had finished. "That is the truth." Another pause. "Ah, yes!" He opened his eyes wide. "And then, what eh? Daddy has told us that it was God himself" (he crossed his breast) "who whispered these things to him. Well then, are we going to go against the will of God? No, we know ourselves." Many heads nodded in agreement. "It's like that!" He shouted this last phrase. "By what right can we set ourselves against the will of God? Let's just support Daddy, finish!"

Another orator demonstrated the uselessness of debate. The Chief's communication must be considered simply as information which was not open to discussion, and that there was only one more thing to be considered, the choice of the delegation that would go down there. He added, looking only at Daddy:

"If, then, certain ministers are of another opinion, let them have the courage to submit their resignations. Let them go ahead and do it! Has any harm come to anyone who thought differently from us, in this country? Eh? Let them resign, it would be more honest... There, that's all I want to say for my part, ho."

In his concluding remarks, Daddy thanked the Council for having spoken frankly to help him in taking his decision. He wanted to add that the majority shown during the debate gave him entire satisfaction and that he understood the fears expressed by some present. But it was all a matter of confidence. He was certain of that. His move was in the direction of the interests of the oppressed masses in South Africa, because it was the same process as that which had led the black Americans to seize their civil rights. Was it not the presence of black diplomats in New York and Washington which rendered American segregration intolerable? It had been a proof for white racists as much as for the oppressed blacks, a proof of what the black man could do. In South Africa, the presence of our delegation in the hotels and other places forbidden to blacks would have a more revolutionary impact, and would, in any event, be more effective than the armed subversion sponsored by the countries ending in *-ist*. In adjourning the meeting, he asked for time to consider the composition of the delegation.

"*Wollé, wollé?*"

"*Woï, woï!*"

Last night I managed to pick up "The Voice of National Resurrection". The reception was appalling. Countless winds and storms swept across the announcer's voice, making his words as difficult to decipher as an erased and scribbled manuscript. The wind carried off and returned the voice in a most aggravating rhythm.

They were just announcing the names of those accused of belonging to the Téléma commandos. Among them, some syllables that sounded like Soukali.

I'm always a sloppy listener, but this time I sat up very late to catch the last broadcast of the news bulletin. The reception was clearer. No possible doubt. There weren't in the whole country two Mesdames Soukali Djamboriyessas.

This morning I rushed out to buy up all the papers. Nothing about the situation in our country. One paper just mentioned in a few lines, under the headline "Around the World", that the French Section of Amnesty International had launched a world-wide campaign against the arrest of twenty-five people by the security forces on 16th July. The human rights organization considered that their detention was arbitrary and their lives were in danger.

It was at Geneva, I think. The date doesn't matter, it happened so often. Every year, for a yes or a no. The chronological details, as you'll see, don't change the meaning of the event in any way.

The famous Edward G. Tupman, author of the best-selling *Sixty Days with the Vietcong,* presented himself to the protocol office. He wanted to interview Daddy and, as usual, the Chief of Protocol demanded a list of proposed questions as a preliminary step.

"So that Mr President can prepare himself."

In reality, so that a member of his staff could immediately set about drafting replies for submission to the Chief. Shortly, Daddy agreed and the list was given back to the journalist; shortly, too, the President had his replies by heart and would regurgitate them, in a remarkably intelligent interpretation, during the interview. It happened that, at the end of a summit of heads of state (at Niamey, if I remember rightly), one journalist had the affrontery to add an impromptu question. Daddy sulkily refused to reply and made a terrible stink about it.

E.G.Tupman began with a brief preamble explaining the spirit of his interview. He was preparing a book on the private lives of certain illustrious figures of the last part of the century. The President of the United States, the Belgian Prime Minister, Prince Norodom Sihanouk, Tito, the Shah of Iran, Brigitte Bardot, Picasso, Elizabeth Taylor, Mohammed Ali and Madame Trudeau had already accorded him the favour of their precious time, and he had fixed rendezvous with the King of Jordan, Presidents Bourguiba, Idi Amin Dada, Houphouët-Boigny, Kenneth Kaunda, Siaka Stevens, and Senghor, plus the King of Morocco and Emperor Bokassa. Daddy, thoughtful and approving, nodded his head at each phrase and opened his eyes with ever greater interest at every mention of a celebrated name.

"To begin with, respected President (the protocol office had well taught him that), could you tell me what are your *violons d'Ingres?*"

With a wrinkled brow, he considered the ceiling for a moment.

"No, not the violin. Never. I prefer the more modern instruments. As for mentioning all of them..."

E.G. Tupman coughed, just to get rid of the frog in his throat.

"I would like, eh, I would like...just to know what are your pastimes. How you fill in those moments of leisure you are occasionally blessed with."

"My moments of leisure? Do I ever have any? With (he motioned with his chin towards his ministers) these idle natives?"

And he plunged into a long complaint about the solitude of those who govern. No, he had no time to think of anything but the future of his people and that of humanity. A long discourse on his conception of power, about the forces dividing the world, non-alignment—a discourse interrupted by laments like those of women crushed by fate and demanding justice from the heavens.

"If you will allow me, respected President..."

No. He'd have to wait. Mustn't interrupt, above all. If he did, the thread of thought would be lost. There was still African politics to discuss. With a little bit of seriousness, the Africans could put right in just a few weeks, not more, a few weeks, the matter of the Portuguese colonies, as well as that of the occupied Arab lands. Israel, too, was not nearly so frightening as she was painted. He had made a trip there himself. Knew all their military secrets. Let him just have the use of two divisions of paracommandos, and then just see what you will see. Better than all this blather and all this fuss with tons of useless resolutions; let him just have those two divisions. Just two. Presenting his index and middle fingers. Even one. Yes, just one. The index finger. As long as they were commanded by a real fighter, with real tennis balls between his thighs. Just see. Ah, but, really...he was a military man, he was.

"Very interesting, very interesting. But...it's in your private life that I'm interested, respected President. At least, in the book I'm writing at present."

"A chief, sir, at least when placing himself in the forefront of African cultural resurrection, a chief has no private life. No private life apart from his official life." (He smiled.) "Otherwise, one would sink lamentably into Western individualism." (He laughed.) "His subjects, sorry, his citizens are his children, to a chief. Hence he is at their disposal twenty-four hours in every twenty-four."

"Could you tell me, Mister-er-respected President, if, for

example, you like reading?''

''Reading?'' (He raised arms to the ceiling and lit up a big smile of satisfaction.) ''Reading! I do nothing else.'' (Amiable grin.) ''Come for a while to my country and I'll show you my library. More than ten thousand works. Yes. Three quarters of 'em bound in lizardskin or snake.''

''What kinds of books do you especially like?''

''What kinds?''

''Yes, I mean, do you like...''

''No need, no need, I understand. What kind? Well, dictionaries, encyclopedias. Every time I see an advertisement for one, I issue orders. You must come and see that for yourself, in our country. I'm inviting you... You there, trying to swallow flies, take note that Mr... Mr...''

''Tupman, sir, Edward G. Tupman.''

''...that Mr (inaudible mumble) is my guest. Tell the Minister of Finance to pay his fare. First-class ticket, too. See... You'll see. A fine collection. Not another like it in Africa.''

''Really, Monsieur... Sorry! Respected President, I am really confused...''

''Get on, get on, no need to say thanks. In Africa, between friends, one never, never says thanks. All right, let's continue.''

''What is your speed in reading?''

''A lot.''

''Yes, but...''

''A lot, I say.''

''One, two books a week?''

''At least one a day.''

A pause.

''What kind of books do you especially like?''

''Encylopedias, I've already told you.''

''Yes, but do you like to read for entertainment? Novels? Novels of manners? Thrillers? Works of history?''

''Everything.''

''You must have a preference...''

''Everything (big gesture), I read everything.''

''History books.''

"History books."

"Concerning which period?"

"Ah!" (he relaxed in the chair and spoke as if sunk in a reverie) "...what I love is books about Papa...about General de Gaulle, I mean. And then, about Napoleon. Ah! what a man!"

The American then began an assessment of various biographies of Napoleon, whose names I don't remember. Daddy played the connoisseur, bluffed a bit, corrected himself, contradicted himself, but on the whole seemed to emerge with full honours by giving crisp yes'es and no's. As for Hitler, I have the feeling that Edward G. Tupman didn't quite succeed in grasping Daddy's reasons for admiring him. He wondered whether this was just a lapse of some kind. Especially as he was dealing with an old soldier, a former "Companion of the Liberation". Daddy smiled calmly. Soldiers are like sportsmen. War once over, they don't bear ill feelings. They don't hesitate to shake hands. The sporting spirit, if you like. Something which is getting lost nowadays. Yes, alas! Enough to make one despair. Happily, there had been some leaders of his own mettle to save a humanity in full decomposition, threatening every day to throw itself, all withered, into the maw of some totalitarian dictator! Happily, the military saviours were watching over it! Perhaps everything would go better when the day came that Africa was governed exclusively by military men. That day couldn't be far off, anyway. One had only to see the wind of history. Civilian regimes were living under sentence of death. But Hitler...? Hitler was the great German. A man who worked for his country, yes! (He puffed noisily.) Since then, just look. Nothing, nothing, nothing. Germany had never reached the same heights... Yes, economically, perhaps. The reign of traders, of grocers, of book-keepers. O.K. But politically, militarily, a dwarf. A dwarf... What's more, with those others next door who had degenerated into communism... (Grimace) Hitler? That man worked for his country. A *giant* (using the English word for emphasis). The autobahns, that was him. And what organization! What discipline! The feeling for parades! No equal since. Except Mao and Kim Il Sung. And then, all those battles he won. That's something. But for Stalin, Daddy was sure he would have won the war. Ah, Stalin! He too was an ace. Hats off to him (he lifted his thumb). "A chief, what I call a chief. No joking, that man."

"You would have liked Hitler to win the war?"

Daddy took time to reflect a moment.

"O.K., I'll tell you."

With one hand he blocked the mike. With the finger of the other, he pointed at E.G.Tupman, laughing.

"Don't record this."

E.G.Tupman pushed a button on his recorder.

"That Hitler, if he had won the war himself, would have brought happiness. Would have advanced European civilization a step further. Easy to understand why. Just as the Romans civilized the Gauls, just as European conquest benefited Africa, a German victory would have brought well-being to Europe. Absolutely sure of it. These are the laws of history." He raised his eyebrows and presented the palms of his hands. "That man there really worked for his country."

"Thank you, respected President." He coughed. "Thank you. If I could move on... What are your other hobbies?"

The reels of the recorder resumed their slow rotation.

"Your cup of tea, if you prefer."

"Don't follow you."

"What are your other activities, in your private life?"

"Ah! I see what you're driving at. For me, private life is just that."

"You love children?"

"And how! I've got seventeen of 'em. Who can say more?"

A ravished smile.

"And when I say seventeen, I mention only those I know about. Must include, to be comprehensive, those I left behind in Indochina and North Africa (then, dreamily, after a moment of reflection)...whom I am forever seeking out...to face up to my responsibilities."

"Tell me exactly how you spend your time with children."

"Children, yes, sure...but what has most importance for me, in the end, is my *private life.*"

E.G.Tupman nodded slightly and brought the big metal saucer of the microphone closer to Daddy's indefatigable lips.

"If anyone wanted to take away my private life, I'd rather be killed."

He smiled, then suddenly assumed the air of one staking a claim.

"Just try to understand what the life of a head of state is: cares, endless problems, meetings, signatures, signatures, signatures, people who play the fool, bastards, criminals who want to bump you off...just for love of power." He lowered his voice. "Because, once in power, they would do no better than you. In short, nothing but nightmares, nothing but mountains and mountains of shit."

E.G.Tupman looked rapidly at him, as if taking careful note of something which he had suddenly become aware of.

"Against all that, it's only one's private life which enables one to carry on. Private life is like a good shower after a long march in the sun."

And Daddy began to describe his private life. Ma Mireille was the centre of it, but didn't suffice him. No, no, no. That's why he kept a select group of women in guarded residences around the town. Yes, yes, the stories peddled by radio grapevine were true enough. These *petites mamams* were for his private life. Nothing to be ashamed of. Even that Louis XIV of theirs, the queen wasn't enough for him either. All those kings needed private lives. Mesdames de Maintenon, madams of the moment, what. And Daddy, warming to his theme, described his frolics and his exploits with a wealth of often spicy detail. Daddy, I assure you, was a blade in amorous performances, definitely a cut above the average.

I didn't usually read the papers. Politics and I, well, I've already explained that many times in these pages... But since these events, which shook the whole country, I began nevertheless to buy a bundle of papers every day with which one could make a complete press review. I didn't read them, really.

I leafed through the pages with the feverish haste of a student consulting the exam results. I was well aware of wasting my time and money, but it had become an obsession. The destiny of the country held me by the guts, like a mother rivetted to the news of her son at the front. And all these papers, which recorded every cough by a French deputy, were silent about events exploding like grenades in our homeland.

Last Monday, one of the leading magazines of the African continent, edited in Paris, devoted two whole pages to Bwakamabé. An article written by a journalist who knew nothing about the matter: a paragraph recalling the existence of the Téléma group, followed by a long retrospective piece on the history of the country and a biography of the general in power. That's all.

The young compatriot ex-Cabinet Secretary was here in N... a few days ago. He was heading for a country which borders on ours and, from there, was returning straight to Paris. Through the fog of military jargon, I gathered that he was in touch with "those in the interior", and that the moment was "historic" and "decisive".

Yes, he confirmed, Soukali had certainly been arrested. She had sheltered two members of the Téléma network. She had been denounced by her cook.

But he knew nothing more. "Brave girl," he said, simply. I had the impression that I was irritating him with all my fears and my questions about her fate. He saw history on a level quite above individuals. He assured me that "the process was now irreversible". What's more, he claimed, the Uncles were beginning to go home in panic. There was a vast transfer of funds towards Europe, and Daddy had had his family evacuated to Geneva...

There was no official announcement, nor any press release. The radio continued to make a great noise about the audiences and other activities of Bwakamabé; the messages he had received from his foreign peers; the ones he had sent them in return; the departures and arrivals of ministers; traffic accidents; tittle-tattle about the upper crust and their families; football matches and boxing. They added to these a bit of overseas news, well picked-over on the sortingboard of the censors. For anyone who went regularly and seriously to work, took conscientious care of his family, paid the customary visits to his friends, listened to our radio and read the gazettes issued by Aziz Sonika, it seemed that life was pursuing its normal course, like a well-designed and regularly serviced machine. The majority of citizens welcomed this purring rhythm, and only certain lamentable fools called in their prayers for a good drought, a hurricane or an earthquake big enough to make the rest of the world look up our country on the map. Somewhere north or south of the equator, I seem to remember. Probably in Africa, but not necessarily. Why not in some other continent of the earth, of our dreams or of our nightmares? To be looked for, as I've already said, more in the times and in ourselves than in the maps of geographers.

The first to spread the news was doubtless radio grapevine of Moundié, closely followed by the whisperings of the diplomatic corps. The press agency of a neighbouring country finally revealed the information while making use of countless conditionals. Reuters situated the source as "well-informed" and noted that observers had remarked for more than a month the absence of Captain Yabaka from all official ceremonies, as well as that of the Chief of Staff of the Great-Historic-Courageous-and-Intrepid Armed Forces, Colonel Kaputula.

To all such speculations, which were highly characteristic of the scandalous spirit that infects the Western capitalist press, members of the government responded with an icy silence, and their calm upset these indiscreet tongues. The embassies affirmed that there is never smoke without fire, and the common folk, that if the pot is boiling, it's because wood's been added to the blaze. Moundié observed, besides, that however much people of the same sect put up a common front,the blood of the palm-snake can still be seen beneath its skin. Was it mere chance or fancy that suddenly the members of the Council of National Resurrection and of the government, and the senior civil servants—in a word, all the cream of our society—began avoiding the ambassadors and refusing invitations to dinners or surprise parties to which, in ordinary times, they flocked with God knows what alacrity?

I responded with a shrug to the first rumblings of radio grapevine about all this. When mouths approach ears, it's always to hiss the same couplet. Elengui criticised my incredulity. Giving up the use of my forename, she baptised me Doubting Thomas. She finally shook my serenity the day when she told me that, at the weekly meetings of her mutual aid society, many women had lamented the arrest of their husbands and appealed to the community for help in the difficult times now facing their households.

My young compatriot Cabinet Secretary was, like everyone else, getting wind of all these rumours, but without being in possession of the details. When he tried to get the high-ups to speak about them, he stumbled upon the rule of silence and was given, he assured me, the impression of having uttered some indecency.

But we didn't lose hope. The thirst for knowledge is such... Offering drinks right and left; paying numerous visits; asking questions everywhere, morning, noon and night, especially in security circles and beer parlours; I finally saw tongues beginning to loosen, and soon received confirmation of what Moundié had known from the very day of the event. Yes, a plot had indeed been rooted out. The leaders were those suspected all along. The police files had been pointing to them for ages and ages but, as always in these cases, the bosses hadn't wanted to take this information seriously. A *highest of the high* has an innate tendency to think that another *highest of the high* is incapable of conceiving a crime or an act of treachery. If, from the start, they had treated this information with less aristocratic disdain, one could long ago have arrested Captain Yabaka and Colonel Kaputula. Anyway, all's well that ends well. This time they had bagged the same game and it wouldn't escape. Twenty or so civilians and soldiers had been *neutralized.* (At this word, the mothers of Moundié crossed themselves.) Some caught red-handed, others denounced while still posing with airs of Saint Nitoche and stiff with pride. There you are. But hush! we musn't talk about it. Secret. Don't repeat it to anybody, because the job isn't finished yet. The net must be thrown many more times. Shsh, shsh, shsh, don't arouse the suspicions of the remaining accomplices (there were many of them, many-many) and enable them to flee.

"So, it's like that?"

"Go on with you! As if those accomplices were half-wits. You think they don't listen to radio grapevine themselves?"

Instructions had been sent to the police and the populations of the frontier districts to make denunciations and arrests, and even to massacre without ceremony all those who made any attempt to escape. In this atmosphere of general witch-hunting, it wouldn't do to quarrel over a woman with anyone close to the services of Monsieur Gourdain. Everything was an excuse for an arrest and no one would waste his time over humanitarian scruples, just for the benefit of European opinion which, anyway, had no right to play the moralist, with all the deaths that they approved of, and with which they were sowing Asia and Latin America. And then, did we need the opinion of Europe to be able to distinguish right from wrong? Hadn't we reached the age of reason? What was independence for, then? Go on, let everybody sweep his own doorstep now.

The infiltration of Cuban, Russian, East German or generally *-ist* guerrillas was announced and trembled at. Radio grapevine underlined that the Great-Historic-Courageous-and-Intrepid Armed Forces were afraid above all, sorry, were preoccupied by the presence of...go on, were afraid above all of a certain Tché (or was it Chez?), or something like that: a man with hair like a white woman, who was believed dead, but whom they had never succeeded in killing (he had some anti-bullet *juju*), or whom they had thoroughly shot, all right, but who regularly returned (something even more dreadful) from the dead. Like Jesus himself, eh. What's more, they resembled each other, with that hair down to their shoulders. This Tché, or Chez, was more dangerous than a herd of buffaloes.

It was long afterwards that I managed to get the facts more or less straight.

The young compatriot Cabinet Secretary knew less about it than everybody else. No doubt his political opponents didn't want to believe him on this matter. They couldn't imagine that, being so close to God, he wasn't in on the secret. The truth was quite otherwise, however. I would add that this was equally the lot of many other members of the government, as well as many members of the Council of National Resurrection. This was because Bwakamabé kept two entourages: on the one side, his official colleagues; on the other, a staff of occultists, bound one and all by the cement of traditional ties. To the first, he confided tasks; to the second, his plans and secrets. And only the latter participated in the conception, elaboration and realization of great decisions. The young compatriot Cabinet Secretary didn't belong to this club.

The reader need not lament the loss of the various chapters originally planned here. One dealt with a famous audience given by Daddy to a delegation of Bretons, to whom he promised aid in their struggle for independence against French colonialism. Another described how all the footballers of the Mortier Club in Moundié were imprisoned, on Bwakamabé's orders, at the end of a meeting in which he had accused them of losing their match against Hafia of Conakry through lack of ideological firmness. The other chapters were simply tobacco from the same pipe.

I have suppressed them all, because I no longer have the heart to copy out my drafts of these opéra bouffe *adventures.*

News from the country makes my blood run cold.

A few lines in the French press announcing the execution of sixteen "terrorists and accomplices" of the Téléma group. But no names are cited. Not one.

I caught "The Voice of National Resurrection" with great difficulty. Still the same swarms of locusts and the wind carrying off the voice of the announcer.

Aziz Sonika was making himself hoarse with insults against the victims and praises for the country in "the century of Daddy, when it is so good to be alive, were it not for the terrorist dogs funded by certain great white totalitarian powers."

Impossible to sleep after that.

Among the guests at the hotel, I met a compatriot, a childhood friend. Same quarter of Moundié and same class at Saint Raymond de Penyafort. He was on a mission here, attending an UNCTAD conference on the North-South dialogue.

Still simple in manner, despite his high post, he gave me the whole of yesterday evening. A chopped-up conversation, jumping from news of common friends to recent developments, sometimes accompanied by analyses, interrogations, disquiet about the fate of the country. There were also many pauses. Silences. Afraid that his words might bounce all the way down there, to the Palace? Rather, the need to weigh for a moment the full burden of some anecdote he had just recounted.

It was, above all, news of my own people that possessed me. Elengui, Soukali, and Ma Mireille too. My relatives? None of them had the appetite for running risks. Furthermore, being all Djabotama, they were fearful of the prospects of a non-Djabotama running the country. To be fair, let's just say that they had sense to keep well away from the sackful of Gabon vipers which politics consists of. But nowadays, in our country, politics no longer waits for you to come to it. A wild beast that bursts blindly into the village, in all the rage of despair... Who, in these circumstances, can still find his philosophy in peacefully mending his nets?

Elengui was behaving, it seemed, like a woman of great dignity. Monsieur the Inspector had abandoned Soukali. They had given him the simple choice, his post or that "whore-who-sleeps-with-terrorists". The Inspector had no qualms in making a public declaration of his repudiation, disgustingly similar to those made by some Djassikini at the time of the Fifth Column scare. Although she said nothing of it, one knew through her lawyer that my beloved had suffered a thousand tortures during her detention. These trials had not changed her character. She remained more than ever sunshine, flowers, and a playful water fountain. It had been decided that she should be put to death, together with Malaïka Yabaka. It had been so decreed, and Daddy didn't want to hear anything of the appeals for clemency which were directed to him. Once again it was Ma Mireille who had thrown all her weight into the scales. No one doubted that this was considerable. The First Lady would not tolerate the killing of women. Radio grapevine murmured that Bwakamabé had even threatened his wife, but Ma Mireille had not yielded. Far from being impressed, she had double-locked herself in her room, launching a hunger strike and a withdrawal of conjugal rights. She had been helped by the support of her family and of her diviners. Daddy, deeply distressed, had wept upon his knees for an end of the hostilities.

Soukali and Malaïka were freed, but exiled to "their villages of origin". Poor Soukali! She was born in Moundié. Did she know a single person down there, in her clan's village?

Were they able to show their appreciation to Ma Mireille? No matter. The times were such that gestures of this kind had become superfluous; one had to understand, and be understood, on a level quite above these conventions. The country was embarked upon a season of clandestinity, where everyone learned without a primer the grammar of silence and valued its healthy effects. Perhaps they understood each other all the better because they were women. As superior to us men as are our mothers. They show us the way to a new life.

Even Ma Mireille...

I gazed far ahead of me, at a mirage which must have attracted the smiles of the angels.

The traveller from our country tapped me on the shoulder. He wanted me to take him to some nightclub in N... With that damned curfew, it had been an age since he'd been able to shake a leg.

The Captain had been arrested in the middle of the night and dragged to the Palace. Tied up like cassava, he had been thrown at Daddy's feet.

"So, you stink-hound! You want to play at filthy games, do you?"

But the Captain had resolved to be silent.

"Nothing to say? You won't reply?" He slapped his face with his lion's tail. "Go on, read us a bit of that declaration you wanted to make to the people. Read it, by God!" He struck him again. "Monkey's ass! Dog, go on! Yes, a dog. That's it. when you shove a dog's snout in his own shit, he can no longer deny ownership." A blow of the lion's tail on his head. "Go on, admit it, good gr-i-e-e-f!"

The Captain met Daddy's glare.

"Look at that! Unable to defend himself. What more proof do you want? Silence means confession, old boy."

"Untie me."

"What?"

"Untie me."

"What?"

Daddy bent his ear with his hand, like a *griot* who wants to hear his own voice on the tape, and suddenly expressed himself softly, in a playful tone.

"What's that? Will you repeat it? I can't hear you properly."

The Captain was silent.

"You don't like that, eh? So what of it? Go and claim the Rights of Man, too, while you're about it. That's it: the right to overthrow me, to kill me." He cried out and struck again at the Captain's head. "Your mother's cunt!"

The kick in the kidneys made the Captain tremble and close his eyes, restraining with an effort the cry that almost escaped him.

"Son of a bitch, go on! Just try now to make your *coup d'état.* What are you waiting for, eh? Good gr-i-e-e-f! After all I've done for you. You forget that it was Daddy Bwakamabé who took you from a dungeon and made you a minister. You forget... But for me, Polépolé would have cut your throat." He gestured with his finger. "No recognition." He made a face. "Foul Djatékoué, get out! Monkey's ass! Native! Savage! You think yourself stronger because you've been to Saint-Cyr. Like that bastard Kaputula. Poor idiots, yes, poor idiots!" He yelled: "It's me who made Kaputula Chief of Staff, you hear? Stronger than me, Bwakamabé? I, son of Ngakoro, son of Fouléma, son of Kiréwa. Just because you've made a little trip to Saint-Cyr! Stuff your Saint-Cyr, I say! Made war, I have. With real men. With balls beneath their backsides. Not traitors like you. Not afraid of war, not me. Nor of your Tché, or Chez, or whatever. Go on, talk now!"

In the face of the Captain, stretched out on the ground, they say there was still a look of scorn.

"Power! That's what you want. Say it!" A twitch. "As if you were capable of governing." He began shouting again. "Since when has a Djatékoué been fit to command? Eh? Savage! Son of a slave! It's my Palace that you want, eh? To make you proud. To sleep in my bed. Kiss my wife." Suddenly foaming like an epileptic, Bwakamabé began giving a flurry of blows with his lion's tail and unleashed a battery of kicks. "That's why you gave me these spots." He pointed at his face. "Never!" He raved like an angry dog. "You'll never have her, never...you hear me? No one, no one will ever climb on top of...," he seemed to be weeping, "...of Ma Mireille. Not even when I'm dead."

Ma Mireille had in fact told me that he often threatened her (especially when news had just came of yet another African leader overthrown somewhere or other) that he would take care to kill her, if ever the gods should reserve such a fate for him.

"Go on, you there. Open his mouth for me." He lowered his voice a little. "Foul snout of a traitor. Villainous gullet of a Djatékoué bastard! Go on, open it for me!" A yell from the soldiers. "Ah! the pig! You bite, do you? You bite?..."

A rain of blows fell on the Captain. They were aimed at his head, hammering and hammering at it till he became immobile. By the time they stopped, he must have lost consciousness.

"Open it now, I tell you...yes, like that...wait a bit."

And Bwakamabé pissed copiously into the mouth of the victim. The jet of yellow liquid fell noisily, like a nauseating beer. All the military men watched this scene without a word. With his bladder relieved, the Marshal said while rebuttoning himself:

"Come on, get rid of this filthy thing... That's how we treat the defeated after a battle, we Djabotama."

He patrolled his aides with a conquering glance.

"He has to pay for his treason with his skin now, you hear?"

He went to examine his face in one of the Palace mirrors. The spots were still there, like little purple anthills.

In another part of the Palace, several of the presidential guard were reanimating the Captain with great pails of water, just so as to begin beating him again with canes and rulers, exactly as they had been taught during the colonial epoch. And gba, gba, gba, as blacks yesterday thrashed their fellow blacks. Yesterday, they took their orders from the white man. But today...?

"Pardon us, Captain, sir, pardon us. Just yell out a little, otherwise he'll have *us* beaten. He'll be thinking that we're just stroking you. And then..."

Gba, gba, gba. But not a sound came from the Captain's mouth. His head fell sideways, onto a shoulder. They pushed it up and it promptly fell onto the other one.

Transferred to the police headquarters, the Captain was placed in the hands of a unit formed by Monsieur Gourdain and known as the Bazooka Commando. Men trained for their work much as one trains an acrobat or a boxer. Men who live in another universe and recognise ours only as a spectacle. Men carefully nourished, comfortably lodged, with no anxieties about their wages. Men capable of deeds that surpass normal imagination. Men with a crab for a heart, who could kill without blinking a member of their own tribe, or their mothers and fathers, just like that. Simply for the sake of obeying their superiors, so that society can be preserved in the good order they love. Specialists. Simply by the cries uttered, they could tell you what stage an interrogation had reached. They recognised the chumps who had received two punches in the guts by their way of speaking, of protesting, of maintaining their innocence. He who had tasted the cudgel on his brains had another kind of cry, which had nothing in common with those who had encountered electricity. They knew that those who had been suspended for two hours by the wrists and ankles (the Mount Cameroon, as they called it) had another voice again. After a ducking, there was yet a different voice. After...

The chief of the Bazooka Commando tried at first to get at the Captain through his feelings. He must make their job easier. Yes, true, the unit wasn't composed of saints, but they hated to show everything they were capable of. So he had to help them, be understanding, have pity on these policemen who practised their skills just so as to save their wives and children from starvation. Come on, Captain, the confession has already been prepared. Well-adapted. Typed up and everything. In it, the Captain acknowledged having wanted to overturn the State's institutions with the aid of a foreign power, from whom he had requested the services of mercenaries, one of them being this Tché or Chez. To make sure of success, he had also gone to a fetish priest, to whom he had given wads of dollars—sorry, roubles!—even though it was the unusual aspect of the notes which had attracted attention. He had brought to him, by way of moonlight sacrifice in a cemetary, a white lamb less than seven months old. Plus a photo of Daddy. There, at least, they had proof. And they showed a picture of the Chief pierced by a hundred needlepoints. And those incurable pustules had immediately popped out on his face. Exactly in the position of the holes in the photo... Could there be any better proof?

Yabaka had made many contacts with the younger officers, thanks to the complicity of Colonel Kaputula. He had dealt with the Russian ambassador over the introduction of *-ist* guerrillas, charged with supporting their coup. Yes, yes, yes, they had proofs: taped conversations, a film—but they could no longer be found. Even proof that the leader of the guerrillas was to be the Cuban Tché, or was it Chez? Anyway, what was the point of resisting? The long list at the end of the prepared confession was that of the accomplices whom the Captain agreed to denounce. He had only to sign. Fault admitted was fault half-pardoned. It would be taken into account when sentence was passed.

But the Captain shook his head.

"No? You won't do it? You prefer to play tough?"

The Captain spat at them a formula that touched upon the Emir Abd-el-Kader and Jesus on the cross.

"Be careful, monsieur, be careful! You're not making a film on the martyrdom of Saint Stephen, my boy. If you imagine that putting someone to death will disturb us, better get rid of the idea. Forget it. The truth is, we'd be very happy to kill you. We've been itching to do it for ages. We're not going to give you your death, but simply offer it to you. But not right away—that would be too easy. We want to hear you cry a bit first, you fool. Yes, yell a bit, first of all. Well-well-well."

The Captain persisted still more firmly in his calm and dignified silence. The chief of the Bazooka Commando resumed, in a quiet voice.

"Listen, if you sign without obliging us to bring out the Grand Slam, we'll put it in your report and he'll leave you your life, that Daddy... Eh? what do you say?"

"Life saved, have you thought of that? Even imprisonment is better than death. Sooner or later, the day will come for your amnesty and you'll rejoin your people. While death..." He raised his eyebrows and made a movement of his head and lips. "Go on, be reasonable, all your family need you. Especially your children. Because your wife, if you die, O.K., she'll cry a bit, sure... Even though she won't be obliged to, because there won't be a wake for a shit like you. Good, let's even admit that she wears mourning. Supposing she's courageous enough, because to wear mourning for a traitor..." He wrung his fingers and whistled. "But soon enough, and even before taking off the mourning, she won't be able to restrain herself, poor dear. The thing will be itching too much."

He guffawed richly, then lowered his voice, as though explaining a lesson.

"...she'll need a good thick meat injection to calm her down. Natural, no? If you were in her place, you'd do the same, no? The way you're made, you bastard, you can't go two days without getting your rocks off. That's life! Come on, Captain, think it over. Give us a hand."

Yabaka remained walled in his silence. Though seated, he looked down as if from a height at the man standing before him.

He passed a whole night upright, arms raised and hands stuck against the wall, watched over by shifts of soldiers with their weapons ready. At the slightest movement, at the least hint of relaxation, blows rained upon him. Then it was the regime of suspension, the Mount Cameroon, relieved only by loss of consciousness.

Next day, he was presented with people he didn't know, or only by sight, but every one of whom "swore" that the Captain had come to them to propose that they get ready for action. Passers-by who recited by heart with a grotesque pleasure a quickly learned lesson, accidentally changing a phrase here and there, or stumbling over a word strange to their everyday speech.

The security boys saw in this charade the most irrefutable and crushing evidence, which they piled up so as to outflank the blabbermouths of those Amnesty International cunts, who wouldn't fail to come whimpering here soon.

Only one witness digressed from his tale: the diviner, according to whom the Captain had brought to him a white lamb to be buried alive and a photo of the Chief. (They showed it to him, all pierced with the point of a knitting needle.)

The following night, they forced a bottle up his anus, commenting with obscene sarcasms, then they filled his mouth with water embittered with a soapy liquid. Frequent swoons helped the Captain to preserve his silence. But, that night, they had great difficulty in bringing him back to his senses. They had to call in a male nurse, one of those Djabotama militants who were used to render such services to the police.

But man, even if a hero, has his limits. It was in coming out of one of his comas, while he was still reeling in the swamps of delirium, that they succeeded in tearing a signature out of him. When, little by little, he managed to understand what he had done, he tried to retract it. But Daddy had the confession in his hands.

Since leaving the country, I have stopped dreaming. Even less do I dream of blue hours and skies. My nights are invaded by a host surging up from the vaults of the earth. Harpies with streaming hair, devils in tights with incandescent cloaks, Djassikini masks, zombies, fetuses with ancient faces tickle me, spin me this way and that, beat me, torture me. When I wake up, one or more faces from this museum of horrors is still watching me, silent and still, forcing me to cry out and lift myself, amazed and sweat-soaked, into a sitting position, struggling to awaken properly. My companions for the night hear my shouts and, seized with fear, flee my room at the first glimmer of dawn. Doctors, pills and diviners alike have been unable to subdue these spirits and bring them to heel like dogs.

Now, this last night, Soukali came to me, long and slender, in a park on the borders of a lake which resembled the gardens of Daddy's Geneva villa. By the appeal of her eyes and her smile, she drew me away from the fête to show me the mountaintops green with pines. Lifting her head towards my neck, she tried to kiss me. Her head was tied in a madras scarf like Marianne on the money. She was dressed in jeans and a T-shirt whose slogan I was unable to decipher. Her movements, like those of a young startled animal, disturbed the rhythm of my breathing and blew up the embers of desire. Soukali was promising me a confidence, a secret. I saw it in her eyes. A smile promised me yesterday. She squeezed my hand and pointed towards the blue heights. That smile again. I wanted to squeeze her breasts. Ah! too brusquely. I awoke, frustrated as a spectator at the cinema when the film breaks.

My beauty of the night will not return.

Yabaka was only a mango fallen in the first rains. Since then, other storms have struck even the soundest of our plants.

Drums are beating to summon the secret societies. Everyone will wear his mask and dip his arrow in poison. Our wives, with heavy eyelids, are already handing us our weapons. They have greased and loaded them for us. The young girls don't even take that trouble. Who, then, has taught them how to manage these commands? They show us, for example, the pathways where the grass has begun to grow again.

I am no hero, but, come what may, I am a man, and circumsized.

A pressure of the hand, a smile, a beating heart, are more powerful than the call of a banner.

It is time to go.

She smiled, scattering like a water-spirit these nightly monsters.

The hour has come to leave forever these memories, to mingle with the grasses of the bush.

Soukali, I am coming to you.

Three days after the confession, Daddy felt that the inquiries were dragging on too long. They must be finished with. Examinations, examinations and more examinations—all these legal niceties were fine enough, but the facts were there, established and fixed. It was a case of being caught in the act, quite ordinary. As for the laws (the Uncles' laws, colonial laws, some of them at least a century old), they were certainly venerable enough, but the policy of National Cultural Resurrection mustn't become a dead letter. This was the time, now or never, to apply it. As if our ancestors didn't know how to deal with affairs of this kind! One had simply to chuck away all this tissue of precaution, only invented to protect criminals. Let them just hand over to him all these coup-making bastards and he'd show that bunch of legalistic oafs (who didn't know how to revenge their Chief with dignity) how to deal with the lot of 'em. From time immemorial, loyal subjects themselves had carried out the sentences against traitors of this stamp, and accounted for them only after the act. Society worked better in those days. One couldn't joke with power. No child's-play, with cries of "Truce! I'm not playing any more!", nor a sex party either, where everyone stroked each other like women or pederasts. Ah! but all that... Anyway, what could be more inhuman than to let a man rot in prison when he was convinced of his crime and knew himself that the society had to finish him off? All these delays led to the day when one had to chop off his head in cold blood, and by then the criminal no longer knew what was happening to him, my friend. It was just a poor bastard one was polishing off. Enough of this legalistic nonsense. Daddy didn't want anyone wasting his time over it. Enough dawdling. Go on, go on, and make a good job of it. A decent execution, while the criminal was still bathed in the heat of his own offence. Got it? Dismissed!

And, commmented the Minister of Customary Affairs, a statement or opinion of the president, in a modern and well-organised state, is a decree.

At that time, there were still no African lawyers in the country. They were all Uncles. Yabaka and his companions chose some who excused themselves. Not that they were afraid of never getting their fees. They were not so miserly, or so odious. But they didn't want to get mixed up in the internal politics of an independent country. And it seemed they had been reminded of this, just in case they forgot. To save appearances, Daddy nominated two Djabotama court clerks to act as lawyers.

The meeting of the Tribunal took place at night. Scarcely a few hours after the nomination of the lawyers. Everything was done behind closed doors, so effectively that very little leaked out. One knew only that those appointed to defend had complained that they had very little time to study the dossiers of their clients. The President of the Tribunal replied drily that this was a Court of Exception and that no interruptions would be tolerated. The tone of this rebuke and the atmosphere in the courtroom didn't invite dialogue. In Moundié, the names of the judges were quoted, but it was difficult to accept these rumours without reserve, because it was known that the members of the court met with their faces hooded. One thing, however, seemed certain: many of the accused got cold feet and appealed to the mercy of the judges, protesting their love for Daddy and putting all the blame on Yabaka. He, pleading not guilty, exposed all these inconsistencies as if in a seminar.

They introduced some witnesses, fabricated for the ocassion.

The same ones as in the torture chamber, like a certain Lieutenant Talaba, whose evidence was the only one published, for obvious reasons, in the local press. He went right back to the fusillade at the garden party and claimed that at the time the Captain seemed to him to be the organiser of the massacre and that, feeling the wind turn in his favour, he had decided to play the saviour and get all his accomplices executed.

Yabaka and a dozen of his companions were shot at dawn, immediately after the trial. The lawyers had gone to get some sleep and had, theoretically, an appointment with Bwakamabé at eight in the morning, still hoping for an opportunity to present their pleas for mercy. When they presented themselves at the Palace gates, the protocol office informed them that the President of the Republic was sleeping and mustn't be disturbed. They were given an appointment for that afternoon.

But since five o'clock that morning, the bodies of Yabaka and his comrades had been lying in a common grave. This detail is often accompanied by a wry smile on the part of those recounting it.

Many stories are told of the last hours of the Captain. I will confine myself here to two versions, those most frequently circulated by radio grapevine.

According to the first, Bwakamabé attended the execution in person, and insisted upon being accompanied by all the members of the Council of National Resurrection and all the ministers. They began by killing a first batch, while the Captain and five of his comrades, without blindfolds, were obliged to watch the spectacle of what awaited them. Then it was their turn. Bwakamabé, with a machine-pistol, joined the ranks of the firing squad, all of them Djabotama.

The Captain was tied to a post in the form of a cross, with arms outstretched, his eyes exposed. The orders were to kill with single shots.

At the first command, they must shoot to one side, very close but without hitting him.

A pause.

At the second command, aim at the bottom of his legs.

A pause.

At the third command, aim for his thighs.

Another pause.

At the fourth command, shoot at his arms.

Pause.

At the fifth command, fire at will. Aim at his vital parts, to box him up well. The head, the chest, the belly.The soldiers, stuffed to the gills with *wee,* emptied their magazines with great delight.

"Cease fire, han! Ground arms, han!"

Having confirmed that his orders had been properly executed, General Bwakamabé, at the Captain's side, drew his Colt and gave him the *coup de grâce* with a theatrical flourish. He pulled a mirror from his pocket. The spots were still sprouting all over his face. Many members of the Council of National Resurrection and of the government couldn't endure the violence of the spectacle and swooned away. They were victims of the next reshuffle, which took place that very evening. This last point is easy to verify.

So much for the first version.

According to the second, Yabaka's fellow victims were shot to death at the first salvo. As for the Captain, he raised himself three times. Not a drop of blood on his body. The bullets only buffeted him, at worst throwing him to the ground. Three times, he got to his feet, saying:

"Didn't I warn you, you Libotama? Ah, you are filthy. Filthy. Too filthy to have the strength to kill me. Never, you hear me, never will you be able to guide the people of this land. As for me, I am innocent. I can't even feel hatred for you. You are too foul."

The mist of the dry season was only just rising.

Drops of sweat ran through Daddy's hair, over his brow and his cheeks. The men of the firing-squad trembled like the string of a bow just released. Bwakamabé hurled a torrent of incomprehensible oaths at them.

The Captain had, after each of the first two salvoes, risen silently to his feet. After the third he began to laugh. A weird and icy laugh, as if the curse of the gods had suddenly electrified his reason.

"Ehéééé!"

A long, mocking ehéééé, difficult to describe. A long, mocking ehéééé, with his head on one side and his hand at his mouth.

"Ehéééé! You are really feeble... Go on, now. I give you permission...you can shoot...I authorise you to kill me...go on. But I shall haunt you over and over in your dreams."

He opened his arms wide and gazed towards the heavens.

"When you are sleeping, I will come to watch at the head of your bed..."

It happened in a little valley, where the children of the neighbouring village amused themselves, when the air was still, by listening to the echo of their cries, thrown into space like stones ricocheting upon water.

But this dawn, the echo didn't send back the last salvo of the squad, as if the spirits of the nearby forests had swallowed it up.

The echo contented itself with repeating:

"I shall come to you again and again in your dreams."

Two, three, many times. More and more faintly, but in a piercing tone.

Daddy took a mirror from his pocket and examined his face.

Several new spots had puckered.

These are the two versions of the death of Captain Yabaka and his companions.

Stangers who come to Moundié and want to hear them from actual witnesses, or from the mouths of the *griots,* don't insist too much. This play is performed only to closed houses.

No lawyer. No forensic witness. Bands of madwomen had ravished the senses of the soldiers in the platoon of death. Quite recently, these men could be seen running through the streets of the Plateau, their pricks in the wind, giggling and forever repeating, "...come to you again and again...your dreams of swine..."

Daddy had them all shut up in an asylum. No, you won't hear

these two versions. Perhaps you will recognise the tune, but the words will remain a mystery to you. Unless an interpreter kindly consents to translate the last phrase.

A man can root out a mango tree, or even a plantation of mangoes, but never the species.

It is a story told only in scrupulously closed venues, or on certain evenings of a wake where those gathered in mourning are quite homogeneous. It's like those songs of which no one knows the composer, but which everyone learns without a false note, from generation to generation, from century to century. Soundiata Keïta, Almamy Touré, Chaka, Bouéta Bongo, Mabiala Maganga, Roland at Roncevalles, the Emir Abd-el-Kader...and others, many others.

Daddy goes several times a year to have his spots treated by a Swiss specialist of world-wide reputation. There, they virtually disappear. Two days after his return home, they come out again.

It's a question of blood.

WHEN SOUKALI CLIMBS THROUGH THE WINDOW OF THE NOVEL OR (IF YOU WILL) REALITY

Bandit,

Learn not to forget your briefcase at the homes of the women whom you permit yourself to pester with your favours in the absence of their husbands. My darling, I have read every word from beginning to end, some passages several times.

Conspirator!

With your absent-minded air, at once irritating and enticing, I should have suspected that you were stewing up a fine dish for us.

But will you dare to publish, as it stands, this intimate vision of all the comedy we perform every day, without being aware of it? You, you are there with us at the party, not as a dancer, but as a spy.

Despite a few transpositions, your friends will have no difficulty in recognising every one of the actors under their masks. Daddy is obviously the celebrated prefect of a certain province, which was inhabited for three years by a young heart specialist, then fresh from university in Europe, to whom I now entrust the care of my health. I easily recognise him, even if he defends himself by taking the precaution (while remaining grossly obvious) of shuffling the cards, borrowing a trait here and there from one of his relatives, not maître d'hôtel *at the* Relais Aériens, *but bouncer at a fashionable nightclub.*

The traitor hands me over to the public exactly as I innocently offer myself to his expert hands in the examining room, from which, however (hasn't he promised as much in the Hippocratic Oath), no secret should filter out.

I will tear your face!

Just imagine Adolphe discovering that he is "Monsieur the Inspector"!

I just hope my students don't recognize Soukali.

The presentation you make of her moves me deeply and utterly confuses me. I fear falling into the sin of Narcissism in confessing how attractive I find her. I would have preferred, however, that she stayed as at the beginning of the story, that young coquette, fluttering and full of life, with whom even a woman would fall in love. The metamorphosis in the last pages is not to my taste. Isn't there here some echo of the Latin American scene (Régis Debray throwback), which has nothing to do with the Africa of today?

And besides...

If the names of people and places sound strange to our ears, even though you leave here and there in the text the words of an imaginary dialect of your own invention, the most myopic of moles would recognize "the country".

There is scarcely as much difference between your story and our lives as between a Van Gogh, a Cézanne or a Modigliani and a photograph of the original model. But the magic and teaching power of art, isn't it less to resemble reality than to lend to reality the colours of the painter's heart? If that is your aim, your bleeding vision is certainly more acceptable than the prissy and edifying images demanded by the young compatriot Cabinet Secretary.

A good likeness of "Elengui". After all, you adore her and I love you the better for it.

But who are "Ma Mireille" and "Cécile"? Before or at the same time as me?

Who? When? Reply at once, if you don't want me to phone you every night and come landing in flames on your runway...

Be warned!

Signed: Soukali
in vinegar.

It's only my care for democracy, which the reader, unless blind, will have perceived throughout the preceding hundreds of pages, that obliges me to publish here Soukali's insidious and malicious intervention.

But I can't leave her letter without a reply.

In fact, I have borrowed nothing from reality, nor yet invented anything.

Here I end the telling of a rosary of dreams and nightmares that have followed one another with the cadence of a chronicle and from which I cannot be free until the last word is written.

NOTE ON THE TRANSLATOR: Gerald Moore read English at Cambridge University and taught for many years in Africa. He was at the School of African and Asian Studies at Sussex University from 1966 to 1977. His books include *The Chosen Tongue* (1969), *Wole Soyinka* (1978) and *Twelve African Writers* (1980). He has published translations of Mongo Beti and Tchicaya U Tam'si. He co-edited *The Penguin Book of Modern African Poetry* (1984). He now lives in Italy with his wife and son.